THE TEXAN'S
REWARD

THE TEXAN'S REWARD

JODI THOMAS

BERKLEY BOOKS, NEW YORK

THE BERKLEY PUBLISHING GROUP
Published by the Penguin Group
Penguin Group (USA) Inc.
375 Hudson Street, New York, New York 10014, USA
Penguin Group (Canada), 90 Eglinton Avenue East, Suite 700, Toronto, Ontario M4P 2Y3, Canada (a division of Pearson Penguin Canada Inc.)
Penguin Books Ltd., 80 Strand, London WC2R 0RL, England
Penguin Group Ireland, 25 St. Stephen's Green, Dublin 2, Ireland (a division of Penguin Books Ltd.)
Penguin Group (Australia), 250 Camberwell Road, Camberwell, Victoria 3124, Australia (a division of Pearson Australia Group Pty. Ltd.)
Penguin Books India Pvt. Ltd., 11 Community Centre, Panchsheel Park, New Delhi—110 017, India
Penguin Group (NZ), Cnr. Airborne and Rosedale Roads, Albany, Auckland 1310, New Zealand (a division of Pearson New Zealand Ltd.)
Penguin Books (South Africa) (Pty.) Ltd., 24 Sturdee Avenue, Rosebank, Johannesburg 2196, South Africa

Penguin Books Ltd., Registered Offices: 80 Strand, London WC2R 0RL, England

This is a work of fiction. Names, characters, places, and incidents either are the product of the author's imagination or are used fictitiously, and any resemblance to actual persons, living or dead, business establishments, events, or locales is entirely coincidental.

THE TEXAN'S REWARD

A Berkley Book / published by arrangement with the author

ISBN: 0-7394-5986-4

BERKLEY®
Berkley Books are published by The Berkley Publishing Group,
a division of Penguin Group (USA) Inc.,
375 Hudson Street, New York, New York 10014.
BERKLEY is a registered trademark of Penguin Group (USA) Inc.
The "B" design is a trademark belonging to Penguin Group (USA) Inc.

PRINTED IN THE UNITED STATES OF AMERICA

CHAPTER 1

JACOB DALTON BRACED HIS BROAD SHOULDERS AGAINST THE BLAST
of wind howling through Lone River Canyon and urged his horse forward. Dusty, a stallion he had trained from a colt, knew the shortcut
across the canyon as well as he did, but unlike Jacob, the horse didn't
seem to share his urgency to brave the treacherous path in order to get
home a day earlier.

Jacob knew he needed to concentrate while crossing Lone River after dark, but he couldn't clear his mind of the words he'd seen on a
telegram four days ago. He read it only once, but once had been
enough. He'd hardly stopped to eat or sleep since.

When he checked in at the Texas Ranger office in El Paso to pick
up his mail, he hadn't even opened the message from the sheriff in
Clarendon until he walked across the street, ordered a whiskey, and relaxed into a chair by the window. Jacob had no relatives and, due to
his occupation, few friends. Most correspondence he received came
under the heading of business. But he opened Sheriff Parker Smith's
note first, knowing the old man cared about the same people Jacob did,
and he hoped for news among the sheriff's correspondence.

He'd expected Sheriff Parker's usual report: *All quiet. Nell still recovering.* But Jacob ripped the envelope in haste, just in case Nell had
taken a turn for the worse. If so, he'd ask for leave and catch the next
train east, whether she liked him worrying about her or not.

But the news had left him no time to wait a day for the train. He'd departed without finishing his drink.

Dusty's front hooves slid over an icy rock, jarring Jacob back to the present. He leaned forward, shifting his weight, working with the animal with practiced ease. One wrong step could land them both at the bottom of the canyon with little chance of being found before spring.

Jacob forced his attention to the slow progress, but he couldn't rid his thoughts of the hundred images of the kid he'd called Two Bits until she came home from school all grown up and decided her name was Nell. She'd been the orneriest brat ever picked up out of the gutter. Mean, foulmouthed, stubborn.

An old madam who owned a house near the tracks in Clarendon took her in, claiming Two Bits was the daughter of one of her girls. Two Bits said her mother willed her to Fat Alice, and the old soiled dove took her responsibility to heart. She saw that Nell was fed and cared for until she was old enough to go back East to a fine school that wouldn't have let Fat Alice on the grounds.

Jacob remembered the first time he saw the kid. He'd been seventeen, a month into being a Texas Ranger, when she appeared one morning, following him around like a lost puppy, all big brown eyes and skinny legs. She didn't look more than eight, but she stood proud when she told him she had dreams. She planned to be the highest-paid lady of the evening in Texas when she grew up. He swore he'd marry her first and make an honest woman out of her.

Jacob laughed, remembering how she'd called him every name she could think of for trying to interfere with her dreams and yelled that she'd charge him double when he came begging to her bed.

From that day on, he'd been cursed with the need to watch over her. He smiled. She'd been nothing but trouble for almost a dozen years. He'd washed her mouth out with soap so many times that first year, he thought his hands would chap and bleed long before she stopped swearing. Every time Fat Alice tried to make her behave, Two Bits ran away, and the next thing he knew, Jacob would get a telegram asking him to come back to Clarendon to straighten out the hellion.

When he'd been twice her height, he'd managed to get his bluff in on her. But as she grew, it didn't take long for her to wrap him around her finger. She thought he was her own private guardian. When Nell was in trouble, she'd call him and, like an idiot, he came running, if for no other reason than that she needed him. He'd always managed to keep her out of serious trouble.

Except the last time. She'd been hurt bad, maybe even crippled for life, in an ambush. She held onto his hand through those first days of pain, depending on him, needing him. Then as soon as she'd recovered enough to hire a nurse, she'd told him she never wanted to see him again.

Jacob had spent three days drunk and angry, trying to figure out why. They'd been in each other's lives for years, fighting, caring. Now suddenly she wanted no part of him. Maybe she'd seen the pain in his eyes when he watched her try to move. Maybe he reminded her of happier days and lost dreams. The more he'd argued that she needed him, the more she'd insisted he leave.

Dusty reached the far wall of the canyon, and Jacob relaxed. He'd be within sight of Clarendon by dawn. And he'd better be on time.

Sheriff Parker's telegram echoed through his thoughts. *"Two Bits plans to buy herself a husband."* Fat Alice had left her enough money to do just that.

"Like hell," he mumbled to himself. He had to get home in time to stop her. No sorry, money-hungry, worthless excuse for a man was going to take advantage of her while she was down.

If he missed the wedding, Jacob decided, he'd be making her a widow before nightfall.

CHAPTER 2

NELL LEANED BACK IN HER CHAIR AND WATCHED A WELL-DRESSED man in his late twenties climb from the best horse the livery in town loaned. He was taller than most, a few inches under six feet, she'd guess. His jaw square. His carriage proud. His dark hair had been cut short. Everything about him seemed to be in place. Fat Alice, Nell's adopted guardian, would have said he looked like a man who had generations of breeding flowing through his blood.

"This one just might do, Miss Nell." Mary Ruth, her nurse, leaned over the back of Nell's wheelchair. "Nice- looking man, I'd say, and cleaner than most who come to call." Mary Ruth's eyebrow lifted almost to her salt-and-pepper gray hair as she emphasized her point. "In Number Twelve we might just have husband material. At least his clothes look tailor-made, which is more than I could say about the past eleven men who've come to call."

"I don't care about the cut of his clothes," Nell said more to herself than anyone. "I hate him already." She watched the stranger move down the long path toward her front door below. Hadn't Mary Ruth seen the way he climbed from the horse? Like a man who hadn't ridden in a long while. Couldn't the nurse see how he walked, slow and careful as though fearing he might step in something on the way to her door that he might have to wipe off? "I could probably outride him, even crippled up." She lifted the curtain slightly. "And thin. He seems walking bones inside that suit."

Mary Ruth, as usual, paid no notice to Nell's grumbling. She rushed to tidy the room. The nurse had been with Nell for three months, and she'd organized everything upstairs a hundred times. She would have liked to work on the downstairs, but that was Gypsy, the house-keeper's, territory. Mary Ruth considered herself so far above Gypsy's station that she only talked to the old woman through Nell.

At first Nell had found it interesting being the interpreter between the second floor and the first, but she'd long ago tired of the game. As she'd tired of everything within the walls of her home, her prison. The porch was as far as her wheelchair would allow her to roam.

She looked down from the window once more. The man walking toward her front door had shoulders that weren't wide enough. His smile seemed forced. She didn't trust a man who smiled with so many teeth showing. What did he have to grin about anyway? He must be on hard times if he was knocking at her door.

Dropping the lace curtain, she decided to cut the man some slack. "Who knows? He might be the one." Nell tried to smile at Mary Ruth, who hoped for Nell with every visitor who knocked.

Nell shrugged, "He doesn't look all that bad. A little thin." At least she could think positive until he proved her wrong. He'd been smart enough to pick a good horse to rent. "I'll get dressed before going down. I don't want to meet what might be my future husband in a robe and gown."

The nurse let out a long breath as she headed for the closet. "I've only been with you a few months, Miss Nell, but one thing I've learned is that you're particular. When you told the sheriff to post a notice for a husband, I thought you'd lost your mind. I was sure that within a week you'd be swindled out of all that woman named Fat Alice left you."

Nell only half listened as she carefully stood long enough to pull a dress over her head. Six months ago the dress would have fit her curves; now it hung like a hand-me-down.

Mary Ruth tied the band of the dress, then moved the wheelchair back in place. A few weeks back, Nell couldn't have stood for so long. She wasn't sure if she was getting better or simply getting used to the pain. To take her mind off it, Nell planned what she'd say to this, her twelfth caller. She'd grown used to Mary Ruth's chatter and knew she wouldn't have to respond. The woman rarely had anything important to say. In the months since the accident, Nell had adjusted to never being allowed to be alone. First, there had been her three mothering friends, hovering around her out of concern and maybe a little out of guilt. The bullet that crippled Nell had been meant for one of them.

Once she recovered enough to move back to Clarendon, her friend, a Texas Ranger named Jacob Dalton, had stayed by her side night and day. After a month, she could no longer stand the sorrow in his eyes when he saw her struggle to move. She'd finally ordered him to leave. Then a stream of nurses smothered her. Most of the hired nurses returned to Dallas on the train within a week, but Mary Ruth had managed to stay. She didn't mother, only bossed and lectured, while Nell ignored. In her mid-thirties, the nurse bore the height and strength of a man. She could carry Nell's tall body down the stairs when needed, as if Nell weighed no more than a rag doll. The nurse's one ability had doubled Nell's prison, but little more.

"I'll go put him in the study." The nurse moved toward the door. "If the last heart you broke isn't still in there whining. I've never seen a man take rejection so hard. He must have felt deeply for you."

"He hardly knew my name." Nell combed her hair with the brush Mary Ruth always left on the nightstand. "It was my money he felt the loss of."

"Maybe so, but I hate to see a man cry. I told him to stop, but he didn't listen, so I left him to his misery."

"Tell Gypsy to offer Number Twelve tea, and please, be sure the study door is closed before you come back to get me." Mary Ruth had forgotten twice in the past week. The nurse tended to forget orders she thought unnecessary. She didn't mind if visitors saw her doing her job, even if it did embarrass Nell.

Mary Ruth nodded once as she straightened her uniform. There was no need for Nell to say more. They both knew she didn't want anyone to see her being carried—not even the man she planned to marry. They also both knew that Mary Ruth considered the deception a bother and would forget the request as soon as it suited her.

As the nurse hurried downstairs, Nell pulled her hair up in a bun, making her look older, then rolled to the shadows of the balcony. She stared down into the huge, cavernous room below. The stranger openly appraised the place. The great room was a far cry from the gaudy red and gold of its brothel days. Nell had ordered most of the new furniture from catalogs. Now the room was tastefully divided into groupings. No line of chairs remained along the far wall where girls waited for their callers for the evening. Only two doors, besides the entry, led off the room. One to a small study. The other to the kitchen.

Nell remembered how the chairs had been all straight-backed cane when she'd been a child. Fat Alice didn't want her girls getting too comfortable while waiting for business. The old madam, who'd become her guardian after Nell's mother died, had also never allowed Nell in the big room during what she called business hours.

Today, the only personal touch to the room was Nell's pots of wild-flowers along the windowsills. If she couldn't go to the land, a little part of it would come to her. Though outside it might look like the last few days of winter, in the house it was spring.

The stranger below tapped riding gloves against his palm as he waited.

Gypsy, Nell's housekeeper, explained that since he came unannounced, he might have to wait a while.

Nell smiled. Old Gypsy might be almost toothless and spotted with age, but a hint of the hooker she'd been still lingered in the way she moved. She'd spent too many years in this house practicing her trade to ever lose the sway in her hips or the tilt of her head that told many a cowhand that he was about to be in for the ride of his life.

"I've come a long way," the stranger's words drifted up to Nell. "I hope the lady will take that into consideration and not keep me waiting long."

Gypsy put her hands on her hips. "Well, there ain't no charge for hoping, mister."

Mary Ruth reached the ground level before Gypsy could say more. Her crisp white uniform at least earned her a nod from the man, which was more greeting than he'd given the housekeeper.

The tall nurse stared eye level at the stranger. "You here about the ad?"

Of course he was, Nell thought as she watched him stiffen. No one came to this rambling old house by the tracks. She had trouble getting merchants in town to deliver goods, even though the place hadn't been a house of ill repute for years. Her doctor had to ride the train all morning to visit her once a month because the town doctor claimed to always be too busy to make calls out to the house by the tracks.

"I'm here to pay a call on Miss Nell Smith." Number Twelve's voice was deep and strong . . . and nervous. "My business is of a private nature." He lifted his head and stretched taller so that he could look down on the nurse. "Would you be so kind as to tell her Randolph Harrison is here to see her? I sent my card and introduction by post."

Nell thought of the letters stacked on her desk, but it was too late to sort through them and study the references of one from a Mr. Harrison. As for his business being private, everyone in town knew about the ad wanting a husband. Word was, men were laying bets at the saloon on how many men she'd turn down before she settled on one.

"She already knows you're here," Mary Ruth answered honestly. "She's not blind and deaf. If you'll wait in the study, I'll see if she wants to receive you."

Gypsy winked at the stranger. "You've made it farther than most. Some she turns down when she sees them walking up the path. One fellow, I think it was the fourth or fifth, didn't even get off his horse before she yelled for him to go away."

Randolph Harrison appeared bothered by the old housekeeper's attempt to be friendly. He handed her his hat and gloves without a word and walked into the study.

After securing the door, Mary Ruth climbed the stairs and carefully carried Nell, while Gypsy bumped the chair down the steps.

"As soon as this one leaves," the nurse said, "I'll put you down for a nap. With this much excitement, you'll need to rest another hour today."

"I'm fine," Nell insisted. She felt like she spent most of her life in bed.

Once Nell was back in her wheeled prison, both women fussed over her until she shooed them away. Nell nodded, and Mary Ruth opened the door. She braced herself for what she'd see. First he'd smile, noticing her face. Then he, like the others, would stare at the chair, and his greeting would change. He'd stop seeing her and only see a cripple.

She hated what came next. Pity. Every man who came about the offer to marry, in exchange for a full partnership in her holdings, looked the same. He wanted to help her, poor cripple that she was, but he wasn't sure he could tie himself for life to someone who couldn't walk. They'd ask questions about the accident, the future, the possibility of children. They'd even hint that the terms might need to be altered. After all, a partnership didn't have to include marriage. It wouldn't be fair to her, not knowing him. Maybe they should start with a business agreement first and see what developed.

Nell never allowed the conversation to progress further. She ended it. Better to reject them before they rejected her. She needed a partner but wanted a husband. She'd have both or nothing at all.

Holding her breath, Nell glanced up, expecting to see pity in Number Twelve's eyes. To her shock, there was none. His slate gray gaze studied her without any emotion. Either he'd learned to hide his feelings quite well, or he had none. She couldn't tell which.

"Miss Nell Smith?" His voice hinted of a formal education.

Nell offered her hand. "Mr. Harrison."

His grasp felt solid. He knew he was being tested. "I'm here in answer to your ad. I see now why you would benefit from a partner in running the several properties of your estate."

He didn't lean down but remained straight, his manner cold. "I believe you'll find my references satisfactory. Though it's been ten years back, I did the accounting for a large ranch in East Texas once."

She couldn't believe his total lack of interest in her condition. Was he being kind or indifferent? "And you'd agree to the terms?"

"Half your properties in exchange for managing the entire estate." He stepped a few feet away and lifted a book from her desk. He glanced at the spine and returned the book to the exact place. A man of order. "I believe those were the terms, and I consider them fair."

"And the marriage? You'd agree to this bargain for life?"

He hesitated only a moment, looking down at her chair before meeting her stare. "I assume you mean 'in name only' to the bond."

Nell nodded, not trusting her voice. She'd hoped the marriage would be on paper only, but had been afraid to make it part of the agreement.

He studied her with his cold gray eyes. "Until death do us part. You'll have my name and my word."

"Yes. Just like a real marriage, except I'd live here and you'd have your pick of the ranch houses to use as headquarters. I have seven properties in all: one farm, four working ranches, and two places I consider near worthless. We'd manage them jointly. This house and the land around it would not be part of the holdings."

"Bound in a full partnership for life." His hard voice seemed to carve the words in stone. "I'd like to set the rules and terms of the agreement before we marry. I've made a few notes about how often we'll meet and what will happen if we disagree on the management of your properties. I'd like everything clear between us before we go further."

Something in the way he said the words made her shiver. He was exactly what she'd hoped for. A man who looked like he could run her holdings. Intelligent. Well-mannered. Capable. So, what was wrong with him?

"Do I need to formally ask for your hand in marriage, or can the details be arranged along with the partnership?"

"I'll not marry before all agreements are signed. Without the proper papers, all I own would become yours with the marriage. I want to know this house and half of everything I have will stay in my name."

"Fair enough. Shall we send for the lawyers?" He didn't hesitate, only politely asked, letting her set the pace.

"I'd like some time to think about it, Mr. Harrison. To get to know you." Nell tasted panic. Always before she couldn't think of one reason to say yes; now she couldn't think of one to say no. "I'll make notes of my own before we talk again."

He raised an eyebrow, as if considering her request. "Would a week be sufficient? During that time, we can meet at your convenience to discuss details, and I would have the opportunity to visit each of your properties. I wish to put no stress on your condition."

He held the door for her as they moved into the main room, where Gypsy had set up tea for them. "Will you join me for tea, Mr. Harrison?" She needed time to think and also time to watch him.

"Thank you." He walked beside her, not offering to push her chair, for which she was grateful.

Before she reached the table, the front door jerked open with such force it almost rattled off the hinges.

Randolph widened his stance. Nell froze.

A broad shouldered, dust-covered Texas Ranger barged through the room like a tornado at full wind. "Nell!" he yelled. "I'm not having any of this."

Randolph stepped forward. "Now see here! You can't rush into a lady's home and yell at her. I don't care who you think you are."

Jacob Dalton glared at the man as if he were no more than a gnat pestering him. "Who are you?"

"I'm her future husband, Randolph Hamilton."

"Good!"

Nell had had enough of Jacob's bullying. "What do you think you're doing here? I told you I didn't need you mothering me."

He leaned down an inch from her face. "Well, someone needs to ride herd on you, Two Bits. I've had the job most of my life, and when I leave for a few months, look what happens. You go crazy!"

Mary Ruth rushed into the room like a palace guard protecting the queen. But before she could attack Jacob, Nell found her voice. "I'm doing just fine. I'm getting on with my life. Stay out of it."

I'll have to ask you to leave, mister." The nurse pointed to the open door as if Jacob would take such a hint. "I don't know who you are, but you're upsetting my patient, and I'll not allow it."

Jacob didn't seem to notice the almost six foot of nurse standing before him. His powerful body heaved in rage as he stared down at the thin, injured woman like he wanted to strangle her.

Nell gained control first. "What do you mean it's good that I'm marrying Mr. Harrison? If you approve, why are you yelling?"

Jacob straightened. "I said good because if he were already married to you, I'd have to kill him." He said the words too calmly for them to be a lie.

Mr. Harrison paled. Mary Ruth hesitated between helping him and protecting Nell.

When Harrison hit the floor, Nell motioned for the nurse to assist him.

The ranger stepped over the fiancé and opened a window. "You're not marrying anyone."

"Like hell I'm not. He's the twelfth one to ask and by far the best, if you didn't frighten him to death." Nell wished she could run. She'd put half a world of distance between her and Jacob Dalton. "I want to be married. Respectable. I've never had a last name except the one Fat Alice gave me when I went away to school. I'll give up half of all I inherited for it, and you're not stopping me, no matter how much of a big brother you think you are to me. I'm old enough and rich enough to get what I want in this one thing."

Jacob paced a few feet, then let out a long breath. He stared out the window as if seeing clearly for the first time in a long while. Propping his muddy boot on the window box, he almost sent a flowerpot tumbling. His big frame made the room shrink.

Nell watched him. A part of her would always worship the ranger she'd followed around when she'd been a kid running the streets. But she couldn't let him back into her life. She couldn't stand to see the sadness in his eyes when he looked at her. Even though he'd been miles away when her accident happened, she knew he blamed himself.

"All right," he said in little more than a whisper. "If marriage is what you want, then marry." He glanced at Randolph, still out cold. "But not him."

"Then who?" Nell glared at Jacob. She wasn't about to let him pick her partner.

"Me." His single word rattled across the room.

"You?"

He turned and straightened like a man preparing for battle. "I'm stepping into the line of men who've come knocking."

"Number Thirteen," Mary Ruth whispered.

Nell whirled her chair around and left the room.

CHAPTER 3

Jacob Dalton stood in the study doorway and watched the nurse carefully lift Nell from the wheelchair and carry her up the stairs. Nell didn't look in his direction, but he guessed she knew he watched.

To know that he saw her helpless would have hurt her pride, but he would be damned if he'd turn away. She needed to know he didn't care that she was crippled. He'd been her friend and protector most of her life, and he'd be it now if she needed him. The chair wasn't part of her. It was only something she used, nothing more.

When Nell and the nurse disappeared into the bedroom at the top of the stairs, he yelled, "I'm not leaving, Two Bits, so you might as well talk to me!"

"My name's not Two Bits," she yelled back.

At least there was nothing wrong with her lungs. She might have come home from that fancy school back East all looking like a lady, but get her mad, and the scrapper came out.

"Go away, Jacob Dalton. I'm not talking to you about this. It's none of your business what I do."

He walked into the entryway, his voice shaking the windows. "You don't have to talk to me. You just have to marry me. Near as I can tell, that ends most of the talking between men and women!"

Old Gypsy, who Jacob swore must have come with the house when it was built, poked her head out from the swinging door that led to the kitchen and covered her ears. She took one look at Jacob and turtled back behind the door before he even had time to growl at her. The old hooker turned housekeeper was just one of the strays Nell had collected, but Jacob wasn't about to allow her to collect a husband just because she thought she needed a last name.

"Go away, Ranger." Mary Ruth appeared on the landing, her nurse's apron worn like armor. "Miss Nell is in no mood to consider any more proposals today."

Jacob opened his mouth to argue, but reconsidered. Maybe he should give Nell time to think about it. Maybe *he* should think about them marrying. After all, the idea had only been in his brain a second before he voiced it. To him marriage had always rated up there with yellow fever. Something he didn't want to catch, or be around too many people infected because they felt the need to spread the disease.

The nurse pointed at the door again. A habit she had that was starting to bother him, and he'd only known the woman a matter of minutes.

Maybe he should go. He could take a bath and cool off. He'd lost count of how many days it had been since he'd had time for a proper bath, unless getting caught in the rain counted. Nell could probably smell him from the second floor.

He sniffed at his shirt. Not that bad. He smelled like his horse . . . on a hot day . . . after a long ride. There were worse smells. Glancing back into the study, he noticed the dandy who'd fainted was sitting up, rubbing the back of his head. Randolph Harrison must not be all that used to being threatened.

Jacob stomped back into the room and offered his hand to the man.

Hesitating, Randolph finally grabbed hold and allowed Jacob to pull him to his feet.

Jacob slapped him on the shoulder so hard he was afraid the man might crumple again. "No hard feelings, mister."

Randolph looked at him as if he were staring at madness in motion. He made a weak effort to dust off his trousers without taking his eyes off the ranger.

Jacob herded Randolph a few steps to the entry and yelled up the stairs, "Nell, me and Number Twelve are going over to the saloon to have a drink. I'll be back after I've cleaned up."

"I hope you drown!" she screamed back. "And take Number Twelve with you."

"I'm coming back. Not hell or high water will stop me, and you know it."

"You're not invited back unless he comes with you, Jacob Dalton. I'm not seeing you unchaperoned."

"What?" Jacob had been with her for years without anyone chaperoning them. What did she think? That he would attack her now that she was crippled up? "I swear, Two Bits, you must have scrambled some brains when you tumbled in that carriage. You know I'm not going to hurt you." He looked at Number Twelve. "And if I was going to knock some sense into you, what good do you think this guy would do? He couldn't stop me."

Randolph paled, as if fearing he might be asked to do just that. Jacob was not only almost a head taller, his muscular body doubled Randolph's lean form.

"At the most, he'd trip me on the way to strangling you, Two Bits."

"Don't call me Two Bits!" she shouted. "And don't come to dinner unless you bring the man I'm considering marrying."

Randolph swallowed hard, looking very much like a man who wished to change his mind about the proposal.

Jacob smiled and slapped Number Twelve on the back. "You hear that? We've been invited to dinner."

Nell watched from her upstairs window as Jacob and the stranger walked to their horses. Randolph didn't look near as good standing next to the dusty ranger as he had when he rode up alone. He suffered in comparison.

She rolled back a few inches from the window, thinking not many men would stand up to Jacob Dalton. Not many men ever had. For as long as she could remember, he'd been her ideal of what a man should be: strong, honest, trustworthy. She reconsidered. Stubborn, loud, bossy.

She'd worshiped him as a child, loved him as a schoolgirl, and needed him as a friend. But she'd not marry him. Not ever.

Lifting her chin, she refused to allow a single tear to fall as she watched him swing onto his horse like a man born to ride. He pulled his hat low against the sun and waited for Randolph to mount.

"He frightens me," Mary Ruth whispered from just behind Nell.

"That would probably please him to hear." Nell smiled. "He thinks he's tough."

"And he isn't?"

Nell laughed. "Oh, he's tough all right, but no one could have a better friend."

The nurse looked confused. "Why don't you marry him, then?"

"Because," Nell pushed herself back to her bed. "He should have a wife who can have his kids and make a home for him. He needs someone who can love him with the kind of wild passion he deserves and not be afraid to stand up to him when he takes a wrong turn." She pushed herself from the chair, her legs holding her only long enough for her to shift and lower herself to the bed. "He doesn't need me."

"Well." Mary Ruth tucked Nell in. "Maybe you need him."

Nell shook her head. "Even if I wanted to marry him, and I don't, I couldn't tie him down." She didn't add that even if she did marry him, she could never hold a man like Jacob. Not now. Not with a bullet lodged in her back.

He might be a big, tough man, but he couldn't stand to see her in pain. And pain had become a part of her life.

Mary Ruth moved around the bed, making Nell comfortable. "You rest now. All this excitement is hard on you, I know." The nurse insisted Nell take three short naps each day.

"Tell Gypsy to help Marla fix supper. With the men coming, she'd better triple the usual amount. I don't know how much Mr. Harrison eats, but Jacob can put food away faster than a horse." Nell closed her eyes, suddenly tired. "And tell her to make a skillet of cornbread as well as hot rolls."

Mary Ruth closed the door as Nell whispered, "Jacob loves cornbread."

CHAPTER 4

SUNLIGHT SLICED THROUGH THE STALE AIR AS JACOB DALTON walked across the sawdust-covered floor of the town's biggest saloon. He motioned for the bartender to bring two drinks and took an empty table near the back. Number Twelve in Nell's line of suitors followed, taking the other seat.

They drank and watched the crowd in silence for several minutes before Jacob asked, "What brings you to this part of the country, Harrison? You're not a cowhand. And not many pass through here for the scenery."

Both men smiled at Jacob's attempt at humor. Miles of flat land dusted by rolling tumbleweeds could hardly be called scenery. There was a beauty to the land that Jacob saw after years of riding across it, but he knew the stranger wouldn't see it.

Jacob couldn't help but think the man had an honest air about him, but there was something cold in his eyes. Something hidden away. His clothes were well made but worn. His hands had tiny scars and calluses, not the ink stains of a bookkeeper. His body looked almost prison thin. Maybe he'd been ill. Maybe he'd been poor and too proud to ask for a handout.

Number Twelve lowered his empty glass. "You're right, Ranger. I find little interesting in the life of a cowhand, and this land looks like God ran out of ideas, but it'll do for ranching. My talent lies not on a horse, but with figures. I can tell you the success or failure of a business by the numbers, not the men who ride for the brand."

Jacob smiled. He'd seen Harrison's kind before. The pencil pushers who told ranchers they only needed so many men to run so many cattle. The weather, or terrain, or threat of range wars didn't matter to them. All that mattered to Harrison's type was that the number at the bottom of the page was written in black.

"That why you think you'd be the right man to manage Nell's holdings, Number Twelve?"

Harrison's eyes narrowed. "That's why I know I'm the right man, so there is no need for you to be Number Thirteen on her list. She won't need another after I've had time to talk with her and explain what I plan to do, to merge her little ranches into one." He hesitated, then added. "It's Rand, by the way. Not Number Twelve."

Jacob had to give the stranger credit, once he recovered from the threat of dying, he seemed willing to stand up for his rights. Or maybe he thought he'd be safe here in the bar with twenty witnesses around. "All right, Rand, what about Nell? How does she fit into your numbers?"

Harrison shrugged. "I see the marriage as a business deal. She needs a manager and wants my last name. My name's all I have left to sell. She'll give me the start I need, and I'll give her respectability. With a little luck, in ten years I'll double her holdings."

"And walk away?" Harrison didn't look like the type who'd be happy in a small town.

"No," Harrison answered. "Not unless she wishes to end the contract. I'm giving my word, and I'll hold to it. She'll have my name for the rest of her life if that is what she wants as part of the bargain."

"But not your love?"

Harrison played with his empty glass. "I don't believe in love, sir, or witches or fairies, or the man in the moon. I live by facts and figures. A marriage in name only suits me fine."

"No love, no children?"

"No heart to engage, none to break. I have no interest in children of my own."

His stare met the ranger's. The cold gray of a winter morn colored his eyes, leaving no doubt that he meant his words.

Jacob offered him another drink, but the bookkeeper refused. He wasn't sure if Randolph Harrison wanted to keep his head clear or if he didn't have the money to buy the next round, so he'd not take the offer. Either way, Jacob's measure of the man rose a notch.

They watched the crowd in silence. Typical trouble brewing for a Friday afternoon, Jacob thought. A few cowhands looking for excitement after a boring week of work, two gamblers looking for suckers, but most men just drank, hoping to watch whatever might happen. Jacob figured out a long time ago that the best nights in the bar always happened when he wasn't there. Somehow in the telling the next morning everything always sounded grand, but in the living, it dimmed.

He glanced around, noticing no blood sprinkled in the sawdust. Either the town was settling down, or the saloon owner had just completed his annual sweeping. Settling down would be his guess. There were a few trouble spots along the frontier line, but for the most part Jacob was seeing most of the Wild West in dime novels and not in real life. The Indian Wars were over, and most of the range wars were settled. Before long he'd be able to walk the streets without a gun strapped to his leg.

One of the barmaids walked near their table. Her green dress, which had been washed so many times it looked dusty, brushed the arms of their chairs. The material lingered a moment as if hoping to be invited to stay.

After making no progress flirting with Harrison, she moved to Jacob. It took her a while to recognize him beneath all the dirt and beard. "Howdy, Ranger, want some company?"

Jacob shook his head. "Got one too many women on my mind already," he answered, then thanked her for the offer. Barmaids and bartenders could be a great help, an extra set of eyes and ears when needed. Jacob guessed he knew a hundred barkeeps and saloon girls in little towns across Texas.

Before Jacob could think of anything else to talk to Harrison about, the sheriff walked through the batwing doors. Parker Smith was a skinny fellow, years past his prime, but still lethal with a Colt. Jacob liked him and knew him as an honest lawman who always tried to do his best. But Parker was crippling with age, starting to slip. He no longer rode out to the ranches to check on rustling. The rangers were aware of his shortcomings and tried to cover if they knew trouble might be riding his direction.

Sheriff Parker walked up to their table, and Jacob stood, his hand already outstretched.

"Sheriff, good to see you again," Jacob greeted him warmly.

The old man smiled. "About time you got to town, Dalton. I was worried that you might not be here in time to straighten Nell out this time."

"I'm not sure I can," he answered honestly. "You'd think that wheelchair would slow her down and keep her out of trouble. I thought I told you to keep an eye on her."

"It's a full-time job, son, and I'm not as fast as I used to be. That's why I called you for backup."

Randolph Harrison stood slowly and faced the sheriff. The two lawmen turned, looking as if they'd forgotten him sitting at the table.

Jacob made the introductions, leaving out how he and Rand had met.

After Harrison and the sheriff shook hands, Jacob suggested Parker join them. As the men took their seats, the old man's wise eyes caught Jacob's for a second, then darted to Harrison and back.

Jacob read the message plainly. They'd both noticed the stranger's alarm. Randolph Harrison was edgy, near panic. He'd wiped his hands on his legs before taking Parker's hand. He kept his eyes low, never rising past the star on Parker's vest. He mumbled his name almost as if he hoped the old man wouldn't catch it. Both Jacob and the sheriff had learned from experience that men nervous around a badge usually had a reason to be.

"Welcome to Clarendon, Mr Harrison," Parker said casually. "Where do you hail from?"

"Back East," Rand answered without looking at either man.

"Nice country back East," Parker answered. "I know a lot of folks who come from the same place."

Jacob smiled, knowing in this part of the county it would be impolite to pry into a man's past. Half the folks settling Texas were running from something. Debts, family, the law.

But the seasoned sheriff was like an expert fisherman. It might take him some time, but he'd eventually reel in the man's secret. One of the reasons he kept a lid on trouble in town was his ability to spot it riding in.

Jacob stood, knowing Harrison might say more without an audience. "I'm heading over to the barbershop to see if baths are still a quarter." He scratched his beard. "I might even get a shave." Jacob looked at Number Twelve. "I'll meet you here in a few hours, and we'll head to Nell's for dinner. If she won't talk to me without you around, then you're coming with me."

Harrison didn't comment. He'd pulled a notebook from his vest pocket and seemed intent on writing something down.

Smith jerked as if their conversation had just registered. "Nell's having company for dinner?" He stood and nodded toward Rand. "I'll visit with you later, Mr. Harrison. I need to get over to Nell's and talk myself into an invitation. If she's having company, Marla's probably cooking something special, and she'll need to know to fix for one more." He grinned. "That cook is an angel; she always sends a plate of homemade rolls home with me for breakfast."

The sheriff frowned. "I almost forgot I've got official business with her today. Got a telegram from Sheriff Riley over in Cedar Point. Claims there's a man on his way here who says she promised to marry him in writing."

Jacob shook his head slowly.

"My feeling exactly. Our Nell might want a husband fast, but she's not fool enough to promise anything before she can weigh the full measure of a man with her own eyes."

"When we left, that bossy nurse was putting her down for a nap. So you might wait an hour or so. What do you plan to do if this mail-order husband shows up before then?" Jacob raised an eyebrow.

"I'll meet this fellow, Walter Farrow's his name according to Riley, when he steps off the train. If he thinks he's going to bully our Nell, he's got another think coming." The old sheriff accepted a drink from the bartender, downed it in one quick swallow, and added, "See you at Nell's for supper."

Rand Harrison didn't look up from his notebook, but he nodded once in agreement.

Jacob frowned from Harrison to the sheriff. He didn't like the idea of having to talk Nell into marrying him in front of a crowd. She was hardheaded enough on a calm day when they had time and privacy. Now he'd have to do his talking in front of not only that mothering nurse but Harrison and the sheriff. With his luck, Marla, Nell's cook, and little Gypsy, would join them. Who knows, maybe Nell's fiancé by mail would show up.

He stormed toward the barbershop, thinking he might as well rent the town hall and hold a meeting. Nell probably wouldn't mind at all. She'd lived her whole life with the town watching and disapproving of her. She wouldn't care if they all watched. None of them had been willing to take a hooker's child in to raise when Nell's mother died, but they'd complained about Fat Alice offering her shelter. "No place for a child to grow up," everyone had said. Then, when Fat Alice had left her considerable property to Nell, who was little more than a girl, the town had talked for weeks. Jacob didn't want to guess what they'd said last month when she advertised from Amarillo to Dallas for a husband.

Not that any of that mattered, he thought as he stomped into the barbershop, waking Jessie who napped in his barber chair. Once he married Nell, no one would dare show her anything but respect. He'd see to it.

"Afternoon, Dalton." Jessie climbed from his chair. "I sure hope you're here for a bath. I smelled you coming when you were half a block away." The barber walked around Jacob as though he were a horse to buy. "And we'd better get some of that hair off your face and shoulders or folks will be yelling that a bear's in town dressed up like a ranger." He giggled at his own joke, making a rattling sound like he was stuttering his way through a hiccup.

Jacob growled, knowing the barber would repeat his words to everyone who stopped by the shop. "I didn't come here to talk, Jessie. I just need a bath and a shave." He lifted his saddlebags. "I brought clean clothes, but I'd like to leave the ones I'm wearing if you've still got someone who does laundry."

Jessie took no offense at the ranger's bad mood. "I'll put a pot on to boil while you haul water from the well out back. By the time you fill the tank, I'll have enough hot water for you to wash the first layer or two off. But it'll take a day or two to get your clothes washed."

"Fair enough." Jacob dropped his bags and grabbed the buckets.

Thirty minutes later, Jacob sat in a steaming tub. He dropped his head beneath the water, then rose up and shook water across the storage room Jessie called his bath chamber. Jacob had too much on his mind to relax, so he took to scrubbing.

Nell filled his thoughts. What worried him more than he wanted to admit was that he feared Nell may have given up on her idea to run her own ranches. Before her accident, she thought she could do anything a man could do. Now she seemed to have decided that she needed one.

He could see why she'd like someone like Harrison. He was thin, but not a weasel like Jacob thought might answer her ad. He acted and talked like a gentleman and seemed honest with Nell about what he wanted and was willing to give to the partnership. Jacob would have been forced to strangle any man who had shown up with flowers and candy.

He smiled, guessing how Nell would have reacted to such a fool.

Jacob always sized up his opponent. Randolph Harrison had a straightforward look about him except for the few moments he'd squirmed in the sheriff's presence. He didn't want love any more than Nell claimed to. He would be a hard worker, Jacob guessed. Probably better with figures and management than Jacob could ever be. Nell didn't need a fast gun or a good tracker now. She didn't need him.

Jacob dumped the last bucket of hot water over his head. Apparently, Nell didn't want him running her ranches any more than the idea appealed to him.

"But," Jacob mumbled aloud, "Nell deserves more than a man with granite in his gaze." Hell, Jacob thought, she deserved more than even he could offer. She wanted respectability. She wanted marriage. He could give her that as well as Harrison.

Jacob hurried. He scrubbed his body raw, dressed in the only clean clothes he owned, then rushed Jessie through both a haircut and shave. In less than two hours he was back in the saloon ready to pick up Harrison and go back to Nell's. They might be far too early for supper, but that would give him time to talk to Nell. If she was still asleep, he'd wait.

He walked through the bar twice, even checking under the tables in case Number Twelve had taken to drink after he left. But Harrison was nowhere to be found.

The barmaid walked past him, smiling at the change in his appearance. "Evening, Ranger." She flirted, brushing his clean jawline with the tips of her fingers. "Want some company now? You sure do smell good." She rubbed the tip of her nose along his throat. "Dalton, I swear you're one fine-looking man when you take a notion to be. We could go upstairs for a spell. Just spend some time together, with or without clothes."

"No, thanks." Jacob removed his hat and acted as if they were just passing time. "You wouldn't happen to know if the man I was having a drink with earlier went upstairs?" Harrison hadn't looked all that interested in finding entertainment for the afternoon, but maybe he'd changed his mind after Jacob left. The girls here considered themselves barmaids by profession, but a few didn't mind earning extra money if the opportunity presented itself.

She shook her head. "He left a few minutes after you did. I was standing by the door and noticed he rode out toward Fat Alice's place." She giggled. "Hope he knows that house isn't in business anymore."

Jacob shoved his hat on. "I'll remind him right before I kill him."

CHAPTER 5

NELL TRIED TO PAY ATTENTION, BUT RANDOLPH HARRISON HAD been talking for an hour, and all the numbers were starting to melt together in her brain. At first, she'd been impressed at how he researched and planned out details of organizing her ranches. The idea of having a team of men who moved from place to place when needed to help a small stationary group at each property made sense. The hands assigned to just one ranch would learn that place and how to run the most cattle on that land, while being able to pull in help when needed. She also liked the idea of not having to be constantly hiring and laying off cowhands. When times were slow, the team could move from ranch to ranch doing needed repairs or building and improving each property.

The way Mr. Harrison had it figured, when the extra men were not needed, he'd have a list of things that could be tackled at any time, like adding extra wells and building new fences and corrals. When they were needed, they'd move in fast, in a large enough number to solve any problem before it got out of control.

"More tea?" Gypsy asked for the fourth time. She appeared so pitiful trying to stand still beside the tea set. The old woman preferred wearing her housedress to clean, but when company was expected, Nell encouraged her to wear a proper dress. She never stopped pulling at the material, as though the wool slowly smothered her. She reminded Nell of one of those tiny bugs that skims across the top of a lake, never landing, never pausing for more than a moment.

Standing still and being polite were as foreign to Gypsy as a corset. She liked cleaning and kept the house spotless, but she usually regarded dust and visitors with the same contempt. Nell thought the old hooker looked worried that her young employer might be overdoing, as Mary Ruth always called it when Nell stayed out of bed a moment longer than the nurse thought proper. At least Gypsy knew better than to mother Nell.

Unlike Marla the cook, Gypsy had come with the house when Nell inherited. Fat Alice tried to find all her girls respectable jobs, or husbands, but Gypsy didn't seem to belong anywhere but here. So she'd stayed when Fat Alice closed the business and even after the old madam passed away.

"Sure you don't want more, Mr. Harrison? I could go warm it up again." Gypsy lifted the pot and prepared to dart to the kitchen.

Harrison shook his head. Gypsy turned to Nell.

"No, thank you," Nell said, as if it were the first time she'd asked.

In truth, Nell welcomed the distraction of Gypsy's questions. She hoped Mr. Harrison would change the subject. She wanted to say that she cared about the ranches, though at the moment didn't want to think about them in quite so much detail. If she married him, Nell would have to limit their meetings to an hour once a month or he'd surely bore her to death.

He wasn't bad to look at, in a slender, pale kind of way. His face had good lines, and he held himself straight and tall. He'd wear a uniform well. She could almost see him in one as he stood waiting to continue.

She nodded politely, and the lecture continued on what breed of cattle would be best for this part of the country. One thing to his credit, he'd done his homework. He knew cattle, even if he didn't look like he'd ever worked a herd from the back of a horse.

When he paused, Nell asked, "Tell me a little about yourself, Mr. Harrison. Were you ever in the army?"

He looked down, avoiding her gaze for the first time. "No," he said softly. "I'm afraid I have very little to tell. I have no family and no place I call home. I've worked hard at every job I've had and traveled enough in my life to want to settle down. You'll have no unwanted relatives or past debts fall at your door if we marry." He raised his eyes to meet her stare. "I promise you."

She had no doubt he meant every word, but she realized he had told her little. Maybe he didn't like talking about himself or discussing such things with an audience. Nell smiled at Gypsy. The housekeeper dusted the teapot as if it had collected a layer of dirt in the hour it had been in the room. "Gypsy, would you please remind Marla to set the sheriff a place? I'm not sure I let her know."

Gypsy looked relieved to have something to do. She lifted the tray, then set it back down and picked up only the pot. "I'll reheat the tea while I'm doing the telling." She smiled. "So I may be a while."

A pounding sounded from the entry before she could exit through the kitchen door. She fluttered like a lost butterfly between whether to answer the knock or rush to deliver Nell's message.

Rand solved the problem by standing and taking a step toward the kitchen. "I'll inform the cook," he announced in his take-charge voice. "Gypsy, would you mind getting the door?"

Nell closed her eyes. Thank goodness. Peace. He'd left, taking his endless numbers and figures with him.

But peace only lasted seconds, for there was no mistaking the stomp of boots coming her direction. Nell didn't open her eyes. She simply waited for the storm that was Jacob Dalton to blow across her.

"Where is he?" Jacob demanded as he stepped into the great room that centered the house.

"Who?" she asked as she opened her eyes to a rare sight: Ranger Dalton all clean and combed. She couldn't hide her smile as she realized why Mr. Harrison had offered to inform the cook and not answer the door. He must have guessed Dalton would show up.

"Number Twelve." Jacob circled the room, glancing into the many small alcoves that had been built for private conversations when Fat Alice ran the house. Now, all the areas were lined with books or plants.

The teacups rattled in the corner as Gypsy set the pot back on the tray. "Would you like some tea, sir?" She asked just as Nell had taught her.

Jacob turned to the old prostitute. "Are you drinking again, Gypsy? Your hand looks none too steady."

"No," she whispered. "But I'm thinking about it. My nerves may need a sip. It's been a long day, and I don't see no end in sight."

"Well, the day I start drinking tea, I'll buy you a pint." Jacob smiled at her. "Would you mind closing the door on your way out? I'd like a few words alone with the lady of the house."

Old Gypsy glanced at Nell. Her eyes were full of compassion and need to protect her mistress, but her feet were heading for the kitchen door.

Nell tried to smile like she meant it. "Go ahead, Gypsy, set the dining table. I'll be fine with Jacob. We'll catch up with each other."

Gypsy paused at the door. "Should I send Mr. Harrison back in?"

Nell and the ranger both shouted, "No!"

Jacob smiled as he moved his chair close to where Nell rested on the couch. Her legs were covered with a quilt. Knitting lay neglected in her lap. She looked like a fine lady, but he knew the wildcat beneath the act. He knew the girl had more heart and courage than anyone around. He'd seen her fight, and love, and hurt. He recognized all her moods and planned to use that knowledge to his advantage now. The one word she'd said when Gypsy had asked if she wanted Harrison had told him all he needed to know. The bookkeeper would be on his way out the door in no time.

"You're not talking me into anything," Nell said as he propped his hat on the arm of the couch. "So get any ideas you've planned out of your head."

"How are you?" he asked as if he hadn't heard her.

"I'm fine," she lied. "I have less pain every day, and I can stand for a short time. How are you?"

"Fine," he echoed. "I was in El Paso starting a leave when I heard you'd gone nuts." He said the words as calmly as if they were talking about the weather, then grinned when her head snapped around to stare at him in anger.

"I didn't go nuts. I'm moving on with my life."

"Not without me."

"Yes, Jacob, without you. You need to find some good woman and settle down. Have half a dozen kids. Be sheriff of some town if you're tired of running back and forth across the state. Get on with your life and stop thinking you have to be my guardian angel. I'm grown now. I don't need you anymore."

He surprised her by saying, "You said you loved me. In fact, I remember the exact words. You said you'd love me all your life."

Nell glanced down at her knitting. "I was thirteen at the time. And I'm sure it wasn't a month later that I swore I'd hate you till I died."

When she looked up, he stared at her . . . frowning with one of those looks that had always made her squirm when she'd been a kid. Like he knew she'd done something and all he had to do was figure out what. She grinned, remembering how she ran away when Fat Alice had sworn to send her back East to school. Jacob had tracked her down, dragged her to the train, and threatened to paddle her behind all the way to Kansas City if she got off before she reached school. That first year she'd stayed in school half out of fear that he might carry out his promise and half out of fear that he might give up on her and not fight with her if she acted up one more time.

"I'm too old to spank." She winked at him. "And too rich."

"You're not too old," he grumbled. "And I don't care how much money you have."

"I know," she said. "You're the one man I know who isn't offering to marry me for my money."

He took her hand. "And you're the one person in this state who has never been afraid of me." He lowered his voice. "If you want a name, Two Bits, take mine, because I swear I'm never going to offer it to anyone else."

She didn't know what to say. She knew he meant it, even though she wished it wasn't true. In a few years Jacob would be thirty. If he'd planned to marry, wouldn't he have found someone by now? She could love him no more if he were truly her big brother, but she couldn't marry him. He saw her as a little girl, as a crippled friend, maybe as an obligation, but not as a woman.

Before Nell could think of how to answer Jacob, Gypsy banged her way through the kitchen door. "Trouble's coming in the back! That meddling sheriff's here, and he's got some dressed-up toad of a looking fellow with him."

Nell couldn't help but laugh. There had been a time in the history of the house that announcing the law coming would have sent folks scrambling, but not now. Parker Smith was a regular, particularly at mealtime. He was one of the few people in town who Nell could call a friend.

Jacob stood as the sheriff shoved a man almost twice his size into the room. The stranger banged his valise on every piece of furniture he passed as he complained loudly about being hurried.

"Evening." The sheriff tipped his hat as he herded his charge forward. "I know I'm a mite early for dinner, but I wanted to get business over with first. Nell, do you know this man?"

The stranger straightened, pulling his vest back over his middle and combing thin strands of hair across a shiny head. Cutting Nell off, he snapped, "Of course she doesn't know me on sight, Sheriff. We've only corresponded by post." He dusted the sheriff's grip from his sleeve. "And I'll thank you to stop treating me like a criminal. I happen to be Walter Farrow, Miss Nell's intended."

Nell swore she heard Jacob growl something about fiancés popping up like weeds. She offered her hand to the stranger, more interested in his pitch than angry at his lie.

To her surprise, he bowed low and kissed her hand with lips soft and wet. She fought down a giggle, thinking his kiss reminded her of a slippery frog's belly. Gypsy hadn't been far off in her appraisal of the man. If he hadn't had a firm grip on her fingers, she would have jerked her hand away.

When he straightened, the stranger bellowed, "Walter Farrow, attorney at law, at your service, Miss Smith. I've been awaiting our meeting for some time, and may I say your beauty is far greater than even my imagination hoped. I'm so glad we finally meet face-to-face after sharing so much by mail."

Sheriff Parker Smith stepped beside the man. "This fellow claims you promised to marry him."

Walter glared at the sheriff. "I have the documents with me, sir, and I'll thank you not to question my word. I'll have you know I've been a member of the bar in Dallas for almost twenty years."

The man left Nell speechless with his intensity. His sudden turn from being so syrupy to her and then so angry with the sheriff startled her.

Despite his age, the sheriff puffed up to fighting stance. "So there will be no misunderstanding about my intent, I'm not questioning your word, mister, I'm calling you a downright liar."

Nell was having too much fun to interfere with the truth just yet. Her days were usually filled with quiet boredom; now she felt as though she watched a grand play unfolding before her.

The huge toad pulled in his stomach and tried to barrel his chest, but the effect did little to help. The sheriff only moved closer. Nell knew Parker had long ago figured out that the Colt on his hip made him any man's equal in a fight. The question remained: Did Walter also understand?

Randolph Harrison and her cook, Marla, slipped out of the kitchen. They both watched the sheriff and his companion with curiosity and apprehension. Marla paused, ready to dart back into safety. Randolph had removed his coat, and his sleeves were rolled to the elbow. He looked far more human, Nell thought, almost comfortable in his surroundings. The bookkeeper might have paled next to Jacob, but compared to Walter, Mr. Harrison seemed a knight in shining armor.

Nell glanced at Jacob, wondering at his sudden silence. To her surprise, he only looked mildly interested. Like her, he seemed to be watching to see what happened next.

Walter Farrow lifted his briefcase to the table, rattling the forgotten tea service. "I contacted Miss Smith and offered to buy one of her properties that I believe, due to a misunderstanding, should have been in my hands already. She answered back by post that none of her land was for sale but that she would be willing to talk with me." He produced a blue piece of paper with Nell's signature and seal.

Everyone looked at Nell. She nodded. "I remember such an offer. It was for the old Stockard place. You said your uncle owned it and you felt he meant to leave the property to you and not Fat Alice."

The sheriff shook his head. "That place ain't been nothing but a hideout for coyotes and outlaws for twenty years. Stockard moved to a shack in town a few years before he died when an opening came up for town drunk. He used to try to sell folks sketches he scribbled out on paper for money to buy whiskey. I think he even tried to sell his land, but no one would offer him a dime for it."

"We got one." Gypsy hurried over to the stairs and pointed to a framed scribbling about halfway up. "We got what you were talking about, Sheriff. An almost painting Alice used to call it. She traded it for food to last him through the winter."

"If it hadn't been for Fat Alice, he would have starved to death in the mud." Parker continued, "No one was surprised he left her his land. Place probably wasn't worth the plot Alice bought to bury him in."

Walter Farrow appeared bothered by the interruption and showed no interest in the painting, even when Nell tried to offer it to him. He simply pointed at the Sheriff and added, "Be that as it may, Sheriff, Stockard left the land to Fat Alice, who left it to Nell, and I plan to own it. With her rejection of my offer to buy the land came notice that she was looking for a husband. I took the clipping as an invitation. I wrote back listing my qualifications and offered to marry her. I may be several years older, but I've a wealth of business sense to offer a young bride." He puffed out his chest, once more straining the buttons of his vest. "And, after several letters, she accepted."

"What?" everyone said at once.

Jacob glared at Nell. "Isn't there a limit to the number of fiancés you can have, Two Bits? Husbands aren't like dolls you can collect."

She rolled her eyes, bothered more by his teasing than Walter Farrow's statement. "I have never collected dolls, but I might consider husbands."

The big man lifted a stack of papers from his case and shuffled through until he found several blue sheets of paper, all with envelopes neatly attached. "Same stationery, same seal, same signature. I have her promise to marry me if I travel to Clarendon and find her unmarried. The Stockard place will be put in my name as part of the marriage settlement." He turned to Nell. "Are you still unmarried, Miss Smith?"

"Yes, but . . ."

Walter smiled. "There are no buts. We've an agreement. All that remains is to find a preacher. I'll not hear of further delays. We both agreed in writing."

Jacob moved closer to Nell, his ever-protecting role in full play. Harrison shoved away from where he'd been leaning on the wall beside the kitchen door and asked to see the papers.

Perturbed, Walter passed them to Harrison without introduction. He didn't seem to care who saw the papers; after all, they were his proof. "I believe you'll find the papers in order, and any lawyer will tell you the agreement is binding."

Nell watched Walter, trying to guess his game as she said as calmly as she could, "I wrote no such letters. Except for the first letter asking about the Stockard land, I've never corresponded with you, sir. I only agreed to talk with you because the land had once been in your family."

"Maybe you were on pain medicine?" Walter debated. "I've heard the drugs for pain can make you forget all manner of things. With a bullet still lodged in your back, I can only imagine what you've had to endure."

He spread his hands wide as if in court as he addressed the others. "Or maybe you've reconsidered my offer since you've sobered up. Living in a house of this kind might drive anyone to drink. I have no idea of your circumstance, but I have the letters. And, despite your shortcomings, I'm still willing to hold to my part of the agreement. We can be married by nightfall, my dear. A woman like you can not afford to be too selective or wait too long. There are those in this world who might try to take advantage of your condition, and I plan to see that does not happen."

"A woman like me?" Nell wished she had a gun within reach. The man seemed to think she'd been one of the working girls in this house before she inherited.

Walter lifted one fat finger. "A woman with a questionable past.

Which," he hurried on, "I am prepared to overlook and never mention again."

The sheriff shook his head and backed out of the way. Nell could take care of herself. She might not have the use of her legs, but there was nothing wrong with her mind. If she said she didn't write the letter, Walter was a fool to question her word. And as for questioning her past . . . he might end up a dead man.

Randolph Harrison held up the two blue sheets of paper. "The writing is the same. The signature on the second is a little shaky, but both are on the same paper and have her seal. The second does promise to marry him if he's willing to travel here and finds you still single."

No one appeared to be listening to Harrison. They all stared at Walter Farrow as if fearing he might strike like a snake at any moment.

Nell lifted her chin. "I don't abuse drink or drugs, Mr. Farrow. Though this house had a shady past, I assure you, sir, I do not." Her hands formed into fists around the yarn in her lap. "And, Mr. Farrow, I did not dictate, or write, the second letter." Her gaze bore into him. "So, what is your game?"

Walter looked offended for a moment before he realized no one in the room would buy into his plan. "I came to marry you," he said without conviction. "It pains me greatly that you no longer hold to the bond we made by mail." His face reddened as his voice rose. "You don't know who you are dealing with if you think you can back out on our agreement. No one, not even a cripple, swindles me!"

She saw it again. The flip side of Walter Farrow. One second cold and calm, the next threatening.

Nell glanced at Jacob and realized he simply waited for her to nod so that he might have the pleasure of clobbering Walter Farrow. She guessed that if Farrow even mentioned taking her to court for breach of contract, everyone in the room would take turns killing him.

She fought to stay in control. "I'm sorry for your inconvenience, Mr. Farrow, but there is nothing I can do. I fear the *cripple* isn't marrying today." If he'd have used any swear word, he couldn't have hurt her worse, but by tossing it back to him, she proved no word would crush her.

She reached for the letters, and Harrison handed them over. After one glance, she knew the problem. "Gypsy, could you asked Mary Ruth to come downstairs?"

Gypsy nodded and ran from the room as if wanting to complete her chore before she missed anything.

Everyone waited in silence as footsteps thumped down the stairs.

Harrison picked up a paper that had fallen from Farrow's case and began reading it as if to pass the time.

Mary Ruth made it halfway across the room before she saw the blue
stationery. Her face paled, but she didn't look down. "You needed to
see me?" she asked Nell in a voice that always seemed winter cold. "I
thought you said I had the night off. I haven't had any time for myself
in a week."

"Yes," Nell agreed, hating how Mary Ruth always reminded her
that she was an employee. "You do have the night off. I only need to
bother you a moment to ask one question." Nell turned the letters in
her hands so that the nurse could read them. "Did you write these letters, and this other one, to a Walter Farrow in Dallas?" The question
was direct.

Mary Ruth looked at the letters as if needing to read each completely
before answering. "At your request." Anger built in her words. "I wrote
them at your request."

"The first was at my request," Nell agreed. "But why did you write
the others?"

Mary Ruth soldiered on. "When you placed the ad for a husband, I
guessed you would get no proper gentleman applying. I thought, since
Mr. Farrow wrote about buying land, he must be a man of some
means. He said he was a lawyer, so he'd be educated." Mary Ruth
looked angry that she was being asked to explain.

"Go on," Nell said.

The nurse lifted her head. "Since you were offering marriage in the
ad, I saw no harm in offering it in the letter. I thought by the time he
arrived, you would have either found someone you liked, or you would
be willing to accept his offer. Either way, the letter sounded perfectly
logical to me. A person in your condition can't afford to be too picky.
Offering the Stockard place, which the sheriff said was worthless,
seemed only fair. I was acting in your best interest. For your own
good."

Nell nodded as if understanding the nurse's reasoning. "All right. I
see how you might have thought you were helping, so I'll provide the
price of your ticket back to Dallas. I'm afraid there will be no reference, however."

Mary Ruth's eyes bulged. "You're firing me?"

"You are already fired. You were no longer in my employment the
minute I realized you signed my name to a letter I never wrote or
asked you to write. I'll give you ten minutes to pack your things and

be out. A final train leaves for Dallas at dusk. You can wait for it at the station."

"You can't fire me. I was only doing what was best for you. You need me. You can't even get up the stairs without me. Who will bathe you? Dress you?"

"I'll manage." Nell's face warmed. She didn't want to talk about all the things she couldn't do. Not in front of everyone. She only knew she would not be treated like a mental cripple. She would not become a child in a world of adults just because she could no longer walk.

Gypsy sensed her mood. The old hooker stepped up beside Mary Ruth. "I'll help you pack. I figure you only have about nine more minutes left, and if I was you, I wouldn't want to be late leaving. It might not be healthy even for a nurse."

"I'll not stand for this treatment. I'm a professional."

Gypsy leaned into the nurse's side. "You bet you are, honey. Maybe you shouldn't let her talk to you like this. Maybe you should quit?"

Mary Ruth looked from Nell to Gypsy as if considering the fact that insanity might be spreading. "You'll never get another nurse to come here. I was the last one willing to even think about this job. You've fired too many of us. In a matter of days you'll be crawling around on the floor in filth wishing you'd taken Mr. Farrow's offer." She glanced at Walter Farrow and ran from the room with Gypsy in her wake.

Walter folded up his case. He straightened his clothes and faced her. "I am sorry for the awkward beginning, Miss Smith, but I assure you I believed we had a straight business deal when I arrived."

"A deal you intended to see that I held to," Nell said.

"Only because I believe it would be in your best interest."

He saw the anger in her stare and quickly added, "Both our interests. I don't suppose you'd reconsider selling me the Stockard place?" The smiling side of him was back. "I truly am in need of land, and I will give you a fair price. I'd like to keep the place in the family."

"I didn't know Henry Stockard had family," the sheriff mumbled. "Seems like he told me he'd tried to contact them a few times, and a lawyer sent a letter back saying they were all dead."

"We hadn't spoken in years. My mother would not tolerate his drinking," Farrow answered. "He was my mother's brother. I find it irresponsible of him not to leave the land to someone in the family."

"Like you," Parker guessed.

"Like me. In fact, I have evidence that he may have been under the influence of strong drink when he made out the will."

Parker smiled. "Henry was 'under the influence' every day that I knew him, but that didn't mean that he was fool enough to leave what little he had to a family that disowned him."

"That's not the point. I mean to have the land back. I'll buy it if I have to. I brought an offer with me in case I found you already married. Maybe you'd be willing to sign it with witnesses so there will be no misunderstanding this time." He seemed to hint that he still believed he'd been tricked.

Nell noticed Randolph Harrison still reading through the papers. "I'll have my accountant look over the papers." She raised an eyebrow at Harrison, and he nodded slightly, accepting her job offer. "If Mr. Harrison agrees, we will set a price."

Walter Farrow looked bothered but agreed and promised he'd check back as the sheriff and Jacob showed him the door.

Nell leaned forward as Harrison sat down across from her to explain the papers. "I'll pay you a fair price," she said, "if you will give me your opinion."

The thin man smiled. "I'll charge you a fair rate and dinner as a retainer. But why trust me and not Mr. Farrow? I'm as much a stranger as he, and we're both offering marriage because of the land."

Nell winked at him. "Because I know Marla asks everyone who walks into her kitchen to help, and you were willing to roll up your sleeves and give her a hand. I believe you're the kind of man I can trust." His last statement had proved it, but she didn't say more.

He smiled then. "I really had little choice. You see, I'm hungry. If I help, maybe we'll eat sooner."

"And can you cook, Mr. Harrison?"

"Very little, I'm afraid. But I can help. My mother was a boarding-house cook until the day she died. Every time I passed through the kitchen, I was drafted into peeling or washing, or cutting something. I didn't realize how much I missed her until I started peeling potatoes a few minutes ago in your kitchen. I had the strangest feeling of being home."

Nell touched Mr. Harrison's hand in comfort. Jacob and the sheriff stepped back into the room.

"He's gone," the sheriff said, dusting his hands. "But, I fear, like mold, he'll be back one rainy day."

Mr. Harrison stood and released her hand.

She didn't miss Jacob's lifted eyebrow, but she said nothing. The information about Mr. Harrison was his to tell, not hers.

CHAPTER 6

Jacob Dalton walked into the evening shadows of the porch and pulled a thin cigar from his vest pocket. He smoked little, even when he was in town and could buy tobacco, but he needed time by himself, and the cigar seemed as good a reason as any. The night was cool, the sky clear for a change. Winter's breath still hung in the air, but it wouldn't be long until spring. Jacob always loved the way spring rode the wind into this part of the state.

As he lit up, the thin ribbon of smoke blended with the odors drifting from town. Dinners cooking, the oily smoke from the last train, horses, and more . . . people. He'd spent so much time alone that all the familiar smells of town now bothered him.

He looked inside as though the window were a picture that had come to life. Everyone had moved from the dining table to more comfortable chairs by the fireplace. He saw Gypsy, curled in an overstuffed chair in one of the corners, sound asleep. Her duties as housekeeper didn't seem to extend to cleanup after dinner. Jacob couldn't help but wonder if Nell knew her story. She'd lived in this house all Nell's life, but there'd been a time when her home was a colorful wagon traveling between Galveston and Houston. Rumor was, back then, that her people had been gold smugglers. They'd been robbed one night while on the road. Gypsy, even though almost grown, was so tiny she hid in a cabinet. All her people had been killed that night, and Jacob heard that she wandered from one fort along the frontier line to another doing laundry and other services until she reached here. Fat Alice gave her the first home she'd ever had.

Jacob smiled as he watched. Old Gypsy only had two speeds, jumpy and asleep, but Fat Alice must have known Nell would make sure she continued to have a home here.

Rand Harrison, however, was another story. He looked out of place helping Marla clear the table. Rand must have said something to the shy cook, for she smiled and nodded. Jacob studied him while Harrison couldn't see him watching. All the pieces of Randolph Harrison didn't fit together. His manners were very proper, cold, but not unkind. Yet tonight he said little and never tried to press his point about wanting to marry Nell. In fact, he paid more attention to Marla and the food than he did anyone else at the table.

Maybe he was simply hungry, Jacob decided. Not that Marla was homely. The cook was a fine-looking woman, but Jacob couldn't help but wonder if Harrison would be as friendly when he found out what everyone, except the few people inside Nell's house, called Marla. She'd had a little trouble getting started as a cook. Everyone in town referred to her as Last Meal Marla because her first few employers died.

The sheriff had rolled Nell's chair to the desk, and they were busy looking over the blue letters Walter Farrow had left behind.

Jacob knew he'd join them in a few minutes, but right now he wanted to be where he felt the most comfortable: alone. It had been his life so long he couldn't imagine any other way to live. To Nell and the sheriff he was just someone who passed through now and then. But they were all the family he had. They'd probably be shocked to know how much they meant to him and how often he talked about them when rangers sat around campfires telling of their families.

Leaning against the porch railing, he stared into the night sky. Chasing a gang of bank robbers through Big Bend Country was easier than having dinner in a dining room. He hated trying to follow conversation when he really didn't care where it was going most of the time. Or worse, managing to follow it and finding out the discussion went nowhere. The sheriff loved to tell one story after another, and Nell had the nerve to encourage him. At least Harrison wasn't much of a talker. The man's good traits were piling up. Jacob had trouble not liking him.

The door behind Jacob opened. He straightened as the sheriff and Harrison walked out.

"We're heading back to town," the sheriff said when he saw the ranger in the shadows. "You coming?"

"No." Jacob tossed his cigar. "I think I'll sleep in Nell's barn if she has no objections. Don't want to get too comfortable. I only have a few weeks off."

"It'll be cold out there." Parker pointed to the large barn where Fat Alice used to let the cowhands stable their horses. The barn not only protected the animals against the cold but kept Fat Alice's customer list private.

Jacob shrugged. "I'm used to the cold. It won't bother me near as much as the noise at the hotel."

Parker walked down the steps, his legs stiff with the movements. "I talked Mr. Harrison here into boarding at Victoria's. The beds are always clean, and the meals are filling. Nell offered him the job of straightening out her books while she makes up her mind about marrying him. She even insisted on paying him in advance."

Jacob extended his hand to Harrison. "I wish you luck," he said surprised at how much he meant the words. If Nell wouldn't consider *his* offer, she could do a lot worse than Harrison for a bookkeeper, or a husband.

"Thanks," Rand answered. "Does that mean I'll live past my wedding day if she picks me and not you?"

Jacob grinned. "It means, if she picks you, that you'll live until you break her heart."

Rand stiffened. "I told you once, Ranger, I've no heart to offer and ask none as part of the bargain. But, after meeting Miss Nell, I think we can be friends as well as partners. That's all either of us want from the arrangement, I believe."

Jacob shrugged. "Maybe you're right. Try working with her for a few days on the books and see if you still feel the same." Jacob grinned from Harrison to the sheriff. "And don't forget to ask how she got along with the last bookkeeper."

Parker waved his hand over his head. "Now that ain't fair, Dalton, and you know it. He healed up just fine."

Harrison frowned. "Who healed up?"

Jacob shook his head. "Just ask, but wait until after you've finished your breakfast."

Harrison followed the sheriff while asking questions about Nell's last bookkeeper, but the old man only laughed and said accidents happen.

Jacob watched the two men climb into an old buggy the sheriff used when his arthritis was really bad. After he tied his horse onto the back, Harrison sat straight and tall as he took the reins. Parker looked like his bones were slowly curling him into a ball. Within a minute they'd disappeared into the blackness between Nell's place and town.

Jacob went back in the house to say good night.

Gypsy was halfway down the stairs with a load of bedding, and Nell waited in her wheelchair. Jacob noticed the small couch had been turned toward the dying fire in the drafty old room.

When he entered, Jacob also didn't miss the exhaustion in Nell's eyes as she looked up from her desk. He slowed, memorizing the way she looked at him. The way she always looked at him. Her eyes seemed to welcome him home. Even when she was angry at him about something, she took him in from head to toe as if making sure he'd come back whole.

"Mind if I bunk in your barn?" he said as he neared.

She smiled. "It's yours. Or I'll have Gypsy make up one of the rooms upstairs for you. The one you used when you brought me back here only needs dusting, and it'll be ready."

Gypsy mumbled about being overworked as she reached the ground level with her load.

Jacob shook his head. "Too many ghosts walking around up there." He moved closer, knowing where she planned to sleep tonight. Gypsy or Marla couldn't carry her up the stairs. The big open room was already growing cold with the night air and by morning would be chilled, even if Gypsy woke up every hour to feed the fire. The couch wouldn't be a good place for Nell.

He leaned over, placed one arm around her shoulders and slipped the other between her knees and the wheelchair. "Let me walk you to your door, miss."

Nell started to argue, then lifted her arms to circle his neck. He swung her up and walked toward the stairs. He'd carried her like this before in the first weeks after the accident. He knew how to lift her so that she didn't suffer too much pain.

"If you take me up, you'll have to carry me back down tomorrow morning."

Jacob smiled. "I'll do that if you'll feed me breakfast. When I'm gone, I miss Marla's cooking."

"So, you'd leave me upstairs to starve if it weren't for my cook?"

"Pretty much. Or, marry you off to Walter Farrow."

Nell tapped her fist against his chest. "He was a terrible man."

Jacob laughed. "True, but he loved you sight unseen." He slowed, in

no hurry to reach the top of the stairs. "At least as long as you came
with land." They passed Stockard's painting halfway up the stairs.
"Maybe you should have tossed in that painting his uncle did. Then he
would have fought a little harder for your hand."

They paused, looking at the ugly drawing.

"I always thought it looked like dying flowers fuzzy with decay."

Jacob turned his head to the side. "I thought it was an ocean washing on a dirty beach."

"It's midnight in the mud," Gypsy yelled, "and worthless."

Jacob laughed. "Then Walter must have loved you."

"He loved my land sight unseen," she added. "Why do you think he
was so interested in the Stockard place? It's probably the worst ranch
I've got. It's small, rocky, and full of rattlers. I've heard the stream
dries up by midsummer, and the water in the well isn't always fit to
drink."

Jacob shoved Nell's bedroom door open with his shoulder. "I don't
know. Some say Zeb Whitaker hid out there for a while. Maybe Walter's looking for the old buffalo hunter's gold."

Nell turned her head away from him.

"I'm sorry," Jacob said, realizing his mistake. Nell had been shot
because of the lost saddlebags of gold. Zeb Whitaker had always
claimed three women robbed him after they knocked him out and left
him for dead in the middle of nowhere. Only all three women swore
they never took a single coin. They'd all three married good men and
were Nell's adopted family. She took it personal when Zeb and his
gang came after them. The old buffalo hunter died searching for his
lost gold.

"There's no need to say you're sorry," Nell whispered. "It's not
something I forget about. Every day I think about what my life would
be like if I hadn't borrowed the buggy Lacy always drove to visit
Bailee and Carter's ranch. Zeb and his men thought they were shooting at Lacy, not me, but I can't help but think, what if I'd driven
slower, would the buggy have overturned? Or, if I'd been going faster
could I have somehow outrun the bullets? Sometimes I even panic and
think, what if Lacy had been there? She could barely handle a horse.
She might have died."

Jacob carried her to the side of the bed but didn't lower her. His
arms held her to him a little longer. "If you'd been going slower, they
might have had time to aim and pump more shots into you. If you'd
been moving faster, the fall when the buggy rolled might have killed
you."

Nell's laugh had no humor. "So, you're telling me I'm lucky."

"No," he whispered against her ear. "I am. You're still alive."

Nell leaned back and stared at him.

He saw confusion in her brown eyes, maybe a little anger, and hope, as well. Maybe if he could ask her to marry him, he could tell her how much she meant to him. Surely she knew she was a part of him, his past, his future. He couldn't imagine them not being friends.

Gypsy clambered into the room with her load of blankets, and they both looked at the old woman as if neither wanted to face what they saw in the other's eyes.

"I'll turn down your bed," Gypsy said as she hurried around Jacob to complete her task, then rushed to the wardrobe for Nell's gown. "I watched the nurse enough times. I should know what needs doing at bedtime around here."

"Lower my legs," Nell ordered Jacob. "Let me show you how I can stand."

Slowly, Jacob did as she asked.

"Now, step back and give me room."

He stepped just far enough so that he wasn't touching her, but stood ready to grab her if she began to fall.

Her fingers rested on his arm from time to time to steady herself, as Nell began unbuttoning her top. "I'm not helpless anymore, Ranger Dalton. I can dress and undress myself. It may seem a small thing, but not to me."

She set the last button free and opened her blouse, then slowly tugged off one sleeve at a time. Her movements were like a circus performer balancing on a wire as she moved.

Jacob raised his eyebrow at the sight of an ivory colored camisole lined in lace. The silk was so thin he could make out the shape of her breasts beneath the single layer of fabric. He wasn't all that familiar with ladies' underthings, but guessed this one was expensive and made just for Nell.

She laughed as she unbuttoned her skirt and let it fall. "Don't look that way, Jacob. You know full well that I'm far more dressed even in my undergarments than any of the girls who haunt these hallways."

He'd never known Nell to be modest. In fact, a few summers when she'd been a kid, he'd had to pull her naked from the river because she wanted to swim in the moonlight, and Fat Alice had been afraid she'd drown. She'd been beanpole thin and slippery as an eel.

How could she be modest growing up in a whorehouse? But he'd hoped that finishing school back East had taught her a few things about what not to do in front of a man. When she'd been so near death those first few weeks after the accident, Jacob had stayed by her side. He'd helped with her care, including changing bandages over most of her body.

But caring for a wounded girl was a far cry from staring at a fully grown woman in lace within arm's length of him. When he managed to find his voice, he said, "But the ghosts don't have much flesh and blood beneath their skimpy attire."

She laughed, and he finally managed to raise his eyes to meet hers, then felt his face warm at the realization that she'd noticed where he'd been staring.

"Tell me, Jacob, is it my flesh or my blood that makes you gawk?"

He grabbed the nightgown from Gypsy and lifted it over Nell's head. "I wasn't gawking. I was just noticing how pale you've gotten," he said, angry at himself. He thought of adding *and rounded* but figured it would be safer not to mention any curves he noticed. "You get any whiter and folks will think you're one of the ghosts around this place."

Nell poked her head through the gown opening and moved her arms into the proper holes with his help. As she buttoned the cotton gown to her throat, she swayed slightly, and he steadied her with a touch at her waist.

Her body let him take her weight, and he carried her the last few feet to her bed. "How long can you stand?"

"You've seen my only act, I'm afraid. Within a few minutes my legs give way beneath me."

He covered her as he knelt by the bed. "You'll get stronger."

"Maybe. Maybe not." She looked tired. Her long brown hair spread across the pillow as she turned her face to the side and closed her eyes. "You don't have to offer to marry me, Jacob; just be my friend."

He kissed her forehead. "I am, Two Bits. I always will be. We'll talk about getting married in the morning."

She was already asleep by the time he stood and walked from the room.

He strolled to the barn deep in thought, then took care of his horse before bedding down in the loft where he had a good view of the front of the house. A light burned low in her room, and he wondered if she'd call out for Gypsy in her sleep. He knew the pains sometimes came late in the night.

He frowned. If he planned to talk her into marrying him, he'd have his work cut out for him. She was dead set against it, and he didn't

have a clue how to court a woman. He thought about the day and decided he probably didn't get off to a very good start. She'd done
everything to discourage him except shoot at him.

But on the bright side, she was still speaking to him, and she did let
him sleep in her barn.

He covered his face with his hat. "Hell," he swore to himself. "I
should have kissed her on the lips, not the forehead." If he wanted her
to think of him as husband material, he had to stop treating her like
she was still a kid.

One thing he knew for certain, he decided as he remembered the lace
covering her breasts. She was no longer a kid.

CHAPTER 7

As ALWAYS, NELL SLEPT SOUNDLY FOR A FEW HOURS, THEN AWOKE when she attempted to roll over. Next she spent an hour trying to get comfortable again. Moving pillows. Adjusting covers. Listening to the clock tick away the night. She hated the darkness when she hardly slept, and when she did, the old nightmare returned to frighten her once more.

The dream started out the same as every night. She was driving a borrowed buggy on a rough road. Her thoughts were full of worry about her three dear friends. They were being threatened by an old buffalo hunter who thought they'd stolen his gold. She held the reins easy between her fingers as she planned how to help them. One of them was safe in town, another hidden away. Bailee would be the easiest to get to on her farm outside of town. Nell pushed hard, wanting to get to her friend as fast as possible.

Then, without warning, shots rang from nowhere. For a moment, she thought someone must be target shooting or hunting. Suddenly, bullets pinged against the buggy, spooking the horse. Frantically, she tried to drive as it rained bullets. She ignored the first sting on her arm. One more plowed into her back a second before the horse missed a curve in the road. Then, she was tumbling . . .

Nell always woke before the tumbling stopped. She had a fear that if she didn't, she'd die.

She struggled through the rest of the night, losing the battle to sleep more often than not. Lying in the darkness before dawn, she tried to ignore the pain. Sometimes she played a game. She'd pretend that the ambush never happened and there was no bullet lodged in her back. In her mind, she'd jump from the bed and run across the room to open the huge bay windows. Curling up in a blanket, she'd sit on the sill while she watched the sun rise. With her feet ice cold, Nell would dart down to the kitchen and make hot tea.

Once the water boiled, she'd snuggle against the cooking hearth, like she had a hundred times in boarding school, her legs curled beneath her, while she warmed and listened to the house awaken. She'd hear Marla up dressing, getting ready to start the bread, and Gypsy snoring away in the room beyond the back porch.

Nell loved everything about the morning. The steamy water she saw herself hauling upstairs for her morning bath. The smell of breakfast. The way houses creaked with age as they warmed to the day.

Fighting tears, she returned to reality. She couldn't watch the dawn, and there would be no hot tea until someone remembered to bring it to her.

Nell pulled herself up as the night turned from black to gray. She wanted to be fully awake to face the day, like an old warrior preparing for battle. A tiny part of her believed that if she didn't stand ready at dawn, she'd miss a whole day of her life. The fear might have been born that first month after she'd been shot, when all hours blended in pain. Each time she could get her thoughts together enough to speak, she asked the same question, "What day is it?"

Those around her always seemed to pick a day at random, for when she closed her eyes for only minutes, they'd change their minds and name another.

She shoved the covers aside and slowly scooted her legs to the floor. With her hands on the iron railing, she moved from the bed to the invalid's chair. The movements might look like only a small victory, but Nell considered it a mountain conquered when she no longer had to call for assistance to use the chamber pot.

If Gypsy had left the wheelchair near, she might have been able to twist enough to get in it. But the housekeeper had rolled the chair where Mary Ruth always insisted it be . . . out of the way in case Nell cried out in the night and the nurse had to rush across the room in the shadows. The chair by the window might as well have been a hundred miles away. She'd never be able to walk to it.

Nell struggled back to the bed and reached for her brush. Hopefully, Gypsy would wake up in time to help her dress before Jacob came in from the barn. Nell felt like swearing. She'd been so tired last night, she hadn't told Gypsy or Marla to sleep across the hall. They were probably both downstairs drinking coffee, totally unaware that she was awake.

Leaning onto her pillows, Nell listened, waiting for the sound of footsteps on the stairs. They'd check on her as soon as it was light, she told herself, hating her helplessness.

In the silent dawn, Nell heard the sound of a rider coming from the direction of town. It took her a moment to realize that whoever it was traveled fast. A dangerous thing to do in the shadows. During the day, riders passed by the house heading for the ranches past the tracks, but the trail was rarely used after dark. The ground wasn't level and curved enough times to be dangerous at night unless the traveler knew the path well.

She pushed herself up as she realized the rider must be heading straight toward them. What might have happened that could be so important someone in town had to notify them at once? Dalton. If there was trouble in town, Parker would send for the ranger who slept in her barn. Jacob had backed the old man up a hundred times over the years. Maybe he was needed now.

Nell knew Jacob well enough to bet he'd already be on his feet, probably with his gun in his hand.

She expected the rider to slow, pull up his horse at the broken gate, but he didn't. The horse thundered past her window at full speed.

Nell clawed at the sheets, wishing she could see out.

A shot rang out in the gray dawn with the sharp pop of a whip. Glass shattered and echoed across her bedroom.

Nell jerked, remembering how, months ago, the same sound rang in her ears a moment before pain exploded through her body.

She'd felt helpless that day. As helpless as she did now.

Other shots rang from the barn in rapid succession as the intruder rode past the house and barn. Then she heard Gypsy scream and footsteps tapping up the stairs. A heartbeat later, the front door sounded like it had been rammed, and heavy stomps took the stairs in great strides.

"Nell!" Jacob yelled from the hallway.

"Yes." Nell tried to call back, but fear choked her answer.

Then, as always, he was there, her own private Texas Ranger ready to fight whatever frightened her. His big Colt was in his right hand, his rifle in his left. "Are you all right?" he asked as he crossed to the window.

"I think so," she answered, realizing his boots crunched glass when he moved from one window to the other. "What happened?"

"Someone rode past and fired at your window. I returned a few shots, but I don't think I hit him."

Light filled the room enough now to see his movements. He looked angry, deadly, but Nell was glad to see him. He bent over her wheelchair at the window, then laid his rifle across the arms of the chair and holstered his Colt.

He turned up the lamp Gypsy left burning low, then crossed to Nell. "Are you sure you're all right? There's glass everywhere."

"I'm fine." She spread her hands out over the covers, expecting to touch pieces of the window.

Gypsy and Marla ran into the room buzzing like horseflies in a cow lot. They both asked the same questions, echoing one another before Nell had time to answer. Gypsy got her robe and Marla found her slippers, but when Nell asked for her chair, Jacob shook his head.

He lifted her up and carried her downstairs, ordering Marla to run through the trees to town for the sheriff and telling Gypsy to roll the chair after them.

Nell started to tell him that she preferred to dress before going down, but the words froze in her throat when she saw the bullet hole in the wicker of her wheelchair.

"Jacob?" She gripped the lapels of his unbuttoned shirt. "Jacob, someone . . ."

"I know," he answered before she could finish. "Someone tried to kill you. They couldn't have seen clearly enough to know that you weren't in the chair." He hesitated. "But the rider was definitely aiming at your window."

She tried to think of who might know that normally she watched the sun rise from the exact spot where the chair had been. Everyone, she realized or anyone who passed by the house. From dawn until dusk that spot had become her place to watch the world go by. Even the people passing in the trains leaving town might look over and see her sitting in her window.

Nell leaned her head against Jacob's shoulder and let his arms surround her. She might be fully grown, a woman of means who knew her own mind, but right now she needed to be protected. The only safety she'd ever known had been with him near. He'd always been the one rock in her ever-shifting life.

"It'll be all right, Two Bits," he whispered in her hair. "I won't let any harm come to you."

They'd reached the main room, but he still held her tight. For a few minutes, she curled into his arms, closed her eyes, and let the world go away. He'd always been near when she needed him or couldn't make sense of life. When she'd been a kid, everyone she'd ever known had let her down. Then, Jacob came along, little more than a kid himself, but thinking he was all big and grown. He'd made her believe in the goodness of people.

He lowered her to the couch by the fireplace. Gypsy covered her legs with a blanket while Jacob built the fire.

Once he finished, he stood and faced her. "As soon as the sheriff gets here, I'll saddle up and see if our early visitor left enough tracks to follow. If he headed away from town, I'll follow him. I'd have trouble tracking him if he rode in, but it looked like he was heading away."

"Why would anyone shoot at me?" Most of the folks in town didn't bother speaking to her, but they didn't wish her dead, or at least she didn't think anyone did.

Jacob lowered to one knee in front of her and pulled a small pistol from his boot. "I don't know, but whoever rode by and fired that shot was on a mission. It wasn't an accident No drunk riding home from a wild night. No young cowhand testing his gun. I watched him coming. When I realized he was headed here, I stepped from the barn, thinking he had a message to deliver."

The pistol felt warm as he placed it in her shaking hands. "Only he didn't see me. He was staring up at your window as he rode by at full speed. He got off one shot before I saw the gun. He didn't have time for another. When I returned fire, he leaned low, and his horse ran like ground lightning across the open range behind the house."

"It was too dark to see him. How will you ever find him?"

"I know two things about him. He's a good shot, too good not to have been trained to fire from the saddle, and he rides like he was born on horseback."

Nell smiled. "I guess that eliminates two people in town. Randolph Harrison and Sheriff Smith."

Jacob squeezed her hand. "You know of any reason why someone would want you dead?"

She shook her head. "Maybe it's just a case of mistaken identity like the last time I was shot. Maybe something about me reminds people of a target."

"Know anyone else in a wheelchair who lives out by the tracks?" He smiled, looking almost as if he believed she might say yes. "Our visitor was firing at you, no one else. Promise me you'll keep this gun close. Odds are it won't stop anyone, but at least it will sound an alarm."

"I'll do that," she answered as she slipped the pistol into the drawer in the table beside her. She'd handled weapons several times over her life and never thought much about it. But since the accident, they'd made her a little nervous. She knew it wasn't the gun that had hurt her, but the man behind it, yet somehow she related the pain to the weapon.

Jacob twisted and sat on the floor beside her knees. His long legs stretched toward the fireplace, his shoulder touched her leg. His nearness and the comfortable silence between them slowed her pounding heart. She brushed her fingers over his sun-lightened hair, wishing she could find the right words to thank him.

The fire popped, and she could hear Gypsy talking in the kitchen, but for just a moment the world stilled as she moved her hand through his hair. Something passed between them, a feeling, a bond. Neither had the words to say, but they both needed to know the other was near.

The sheriff walked through the front door without knocking. Jacob stood and stared down at her, his face unreadable as his big hand plowed through the strands of hair she'd just straightened. Then, almost by accident, she saw something in his eyes. A longing she'd never seen. A need.

"What's going on here!" Parker yelled to no one in particular as he neared. "Marla interrupted my breakfast to tell me someone's shooting at you. Who in the hell would want to do that?"

Jacob gave the sheriff his full attention. "Let me know, and I'll make sure they reach hell by nightfall." He was back in full control, two hundred pounds of Texas lawman.

Parker walked around Jacob like he was no more than a noisy tree and went straight to Nell.

Jacob moved to close the door the sheriff left open, but before he could reach the knob, Rand Harrison darted through.

"You're here early," Jacob grumbled. "I thought accountants had banker's hours for starting work."

Harrison didn't look frightened by the ranger's frown. "I heard about the shooting. I'm here to help. Is anyone hurt?"

"No, no one is hurt, and yes, you can help," Jacob answered. "Can you use a gun?"

Rand nodded. "If I have to. I'm not fond of them."

Jacob glanced at Nell. "There seems to be an epidemic of that around here. I don't care if you like them or not. Would you use one if need be?"

"I would." Harrison stood at attention.

"Good, I'd like you to stay here until I get back. I'm going to track the rider. It'll be full daylight by the time I get my horse saddled."

"Wait." Parker leaned and poked his finger through the bullet hole in the wicker of Nell's chair. "I've got a few questions."

Jacob looked bothered, but he gave the sheriff his due. This was his territory. He had a right to take charge.

"Did you see the shooter?"

"Yes, but it was dark." Jacob knew what the old lawman wanted, so he might as well give it to him as fast as possible. "He sat tall in the saddle. Thin. Λ big hat, shoved back on what could have been black or brown hair. It was too dark to make out his face. He fired one shot with a rifle. A man who can aim at that speed is trained."

"Or lucky," the sheriff mumbled. "We got a few cowhands in town who are out of work and needing money something terrible, but I don't think they'd fire at a woman. Maybe he could have been trained, but why'd he be here?"

"I'm guessing he was on a mission, because he didn't ever look my direction until I fired on him. Then he leaned low, blending with the horse, and rode out. He was out of range before I could center him in my sight."

"Any chance you hit him?"

Jacob shook his head. "I doubt I could even pick him out in a crowd unless maybe he was riding. He could sure handle a horse."

"Great," Nell whispered. "Brag on my assassin. He sounds perfect."

Gypsy rushed from the kitchen with a tray of mugs. She handed Nell the only cup of tea among the coffee cups. "Not too perfect. He missed."

Nell thanked her for the tea and looked at the old hooker turned housekeeper. Gypsy had on the same faded dress she'd worn for the past three days. She had dressed in her underthings and gowns for so many years that it never occurred to her to not sleep in whatever she happened to have on. The idea of changing clothes at dawn and dusk seemed a waste of time to her. Nell had bought her several new dresses, but she claimed to be saving them in case she had to go to town. Which she never did, except after dark once in a while to buy a bottle of whiskey she said helped her sleep.

While everyone in the room theorized as to why anyone would shoot Nell, Jacob reloaded his rifle from a chest of supplies next to Nell's desk. Fat Alice had always kept a stock of arms for protection, and Nell had continued the habit. He handed Harrison a rifle and handgun from her stash.

Rand looked at the weapon, not handling it with the ease Jacob had, but familiar with it.

Jacob raised his rifle to his shoulder and faced Nell's twelfth suitor. "I'm asking you straight out, Harrison, and I want you to tell me the truth. Will you stay here until I return? I'd feel safer knowing that you were near."

"You mean in town?"

Jacob shook his head. "I mean here at the house. I'd feel better if I knew either you or Parker guarded the place. Whoever that rider was, it won't be long before he figures out that he missed. I wouldn't be surprised if he dropped by for another shot."

Nell had been quiet long enough. "Don't I have any say about this, or are you just inviting men to stay with me without even asking for my opinion?" She knew Jacob made up his mind about a man quickly. The ability to pick who he could trust had saved his life more than once, but she needed time to decide who she trusted.

Jacob glanced at her, then turned back to Harrison. "It won't be an easy assignment. She's likely to make you sleep on the porch, but I have to know she's safe, and the sheriff's responsibilities are to the town. I may be gone for a few days. If I hit trouble, it could be a week."

"I'll check on the ladies every night about suppertime." Parker nodded his thanks to Marla for a fresh cup of coffee. "I'll spend as much time as I can out here. Between us, we'll keep an eye out for trouble."

Harrison nodded toward the women. "Not one of these ladies looks helpless," he said to the ranger. "I could sleep in the barn. But I'll stay only if Miss Nell agrees. It's not your decision to make, Ranger. It's hers." There was no doubt in his tone that he was talking about more than where he'd sleep.

Jacob opened his mouth to argue, but Nell spoke first. "All right. You can stay. You'll already be here most of the day working on the books. There's no need for you to sleep in the barn, Mr. Harrison. After all, we're almost engaged. Gypsy can set you up a bunk in my office. I think if there is a floor between us we'll still be respectable."

"Almost engaged," Jacob mumbled. "I'll be back as fast as I can."

He didn't look at Nell as he stormed from the room with the sheriff close behind. As he walked, Jacob listed things he wanted changed as fast as possible. The gate fixed and locked. The window upstairs replaced before nightfall. All doors to the house kept bolted at all times.

When they were out of hearing range, Nell glanced at Randolph Harrison. He must feel like he'd been drafted into the army. He examined the six-shooter Jacob had left out of the chest of weapons, then began loading it from a box of shells in the storage cabinet. He handled a gun well, but didn't look like he enjoyed the task.

"I'm sorry," she whispered.

Harrison looked up as though surprised anyone else was in the room. For a moment, he didn't say anything, then he cleared his throat. "I'm honored to help." He straightened. "But I hope there will be no need." Crossing to the door, he started to put the weapon on a high shelf, then changed his mind and put it within easy reach for someone in a wheelchair.

Nell smiled. In his simple action he'd told her that if trouble came, he knew she'd be willing and able to back him up. "You've already been of great service by offering. Jacob would never leave me unless he believed I'd be safe. I'm not too worried about being killed. In truth, I'm more interested in why anyone would want to."

"You're a rich woman," he said flatly.

"Not so rich," she answered. "I'd give it all up if I could walk again."

"We can't rewrite what's happened to us." Harrison refilled her tea and passed the cup to her. "No matter how much we'd like to."

They drank in silence as Gypsy went upstairs to bring down Nell's dress, and Marla whispered she would pack the ranger a knapsack. Nell watched the bookkeeper as he studied the fire. He didn't seem to feel the need to talk this morning as he had yesterday. Maybe if they weren't talking about the ranch, he felt he had nothing to say.

The time alone with him wasn't unpleasant. Neither was it as comforting as being with Jacob. But it might be, in time, when she knew Mr. Harrison better. She could get used to a marriage with times like this built in. At least she wouldn't be alone.

But she couldn't see herself ever running her fingers through his hair. In fact, she couldn't even picture Mr. Harrison with a hair out of place. He kept to an order in everything he did.

She studied her twelfth prospect. He wore the same suit he'd worn yesterday, but his collar was fresh. His shoes were far from new, but he'd blacked them and polished the leather recently. He'd probably be the kind of husband who wanted dinner exactly at six and who walked with a cane each night after eating just because that was what he thought proper. She'd seen men like him when she'd been back East. Men who never raised their voices, who weren't given to excess, and who shaved their faces clean every morning. Men of order.

She smiled. Too bad there weren't a few more such men in Texas.

Sheriff Parker banged his way through the door, swearing that if it weren't for his bad leg he'd be riding out with Jacob.

Nell thought of yelling for him to close the door but watched Mr. Harrison silently stand and close it without commenting.

When Parker reached the center of the room, he looked up. "Oh, Nell, Jacob wants to see you for a minute on the front porch. He made a point of telling me he planned to have a word with you alone." Parker headed for the coffeepot.

Gypsy crossed from the stairs and wrapped a shawl around Nell. With the housekeeper holding the chair and Harrison offering his arm to grip, Nell slowly stood and shifted her feet until she could lower herself into the wheelchair.

She thanked him without meeting his eyes while she wrapped the shawl around her body then tied it behind her waist. "Everyone, please, move into the kitchen. I can smell Marla's rolls, and they are best eaten hot. I'll say good-bye to the ranger and join you in a few minutes."

The sheriff was already at the kitchen door, but Harrison hesitated.

Nell gripped the wheels of her chair. "I can make it to the porch on my own. Don't worry, Mr. Harrison."

He bowed slightly. "Of course." If possible, he looked as embarrassed as she. "Please call if you . . . or the ranger . . . need me."

Nell tried to smile. "Thank you."

Without another word, she turned toward the front door that Gypsy held open. Nell accepted the flour sack filled with supplies for Jacob and put it in her lap as she propelled herself forward.

When she passed, Nell whispered to Gypsy, "Please close the door behind me." She wasn't sure what the ranger wanted to tell her, but she could never remember him feeling the need to say anything in private. Maybe he knew something about the shooter and didn't want to frighten the others. When she'd been a kid, he'd sometimes acted as if she were his partner fighting the bad guys. He'd often given her a mission, like asking her to keep her eyes open for something, a kind of horse, a man with a scar. She'd never known if his orders had been a game, or real.

Nell heard the door close almost as soon as she'd crossed the threshold.

Sunlight greeted her, but the day held no warmth. Jacob stood several feet away, tightening the cinch on his saddle. When he heard the door, he looked around. Worry lines wrinkled his forehead as he moved to stand in front of the porch railing. He was a handsome man, solid and brave, but for some reason he looked a little nervous for once.

"Now don't start lecturing me," Nell began. "I'm not completely helpless. I can take care of myself. And don't worry. I promise I'll keep the gun near me. If I answer the door, it will be in my pocket."

As she handed him the food, she noticed that with her on the porch and him on the ground in front of her, they were the same height. Nell couldn't help but smile. She'd only been eye to eye with him a few times in her life.

"I'm not worried about you," he said. "Parker will be close, and if Harrison steps out of line, you'll shoot him."

Nell crossed her arms. "Then why did you ask me out here in the cold?"

"I wanted to say good-bye." He looked more angry than friendly.

Nell didn't even attempt to hide her surprise. "All right. Good-bye. Be careful."

He pulled off his hat and stepped closer. "I will, but I need to remind you about something before I go."

"What?" Nell fought to keep from using a few of the swear words she'd spent four years at school trying to forget. Jacob was worse than ten parents. "I already told you I'll be careful."

"That wasn't it." He grinned.

Without warning, he leaned across the banister between them and kissed her on the mouth. It wasn't long, or hard, but it was a kiss. A real kiss. Not a brotherly kiss or a friend's kiss, but the kind of kiss a man gives a woman.

Only their lips touched. She could have pulled a fraction of an inch away and broken the kiss. But she didn't. His mouth was warm and bold against hers. About the time she got used to it, he stepped back.

Nell couldn't find words. She could barely hang onto a thought. Jacob Dalton had kissed her.

He plowed his fingers through his sunny hair and smiled. "I've been wanting to do that since I got here."

Then, without another word, he walked to his horse, swung up, and rode away.

CHAPTER 8

NELL SAT ON THE PORCH UNTIL JACOB AND HIS HUGE BLACK horse disappeared from sight. The cold of the day crept into her, but she didn't want to go inside. She needed desperately, if only for a few minutes, to be alone.

Jacob had kissed her. Not because she'd asked him to, or in greeting as he used to do when she'd been a kid, or even on impulse.

He'd kissed her for no reason at all.

Nell touched her lips. She'd been kissed a few times at school parties. Thinking back, she decided she had been kissed better, longer, softer, with more passion. But she'd never been kissed like this.

There was something solid about it. A promise. A claiming.

Nell wasn't sure how she felt about that. She'd always thought of herself as independent. She wasn't sure she liked being claimed.

But he hadn't said a word. Only that he'd been wanting to do it for a long time.

He hadn't even been romantic. No evening shadows, no candlelight and music, no holding hands and tender words. What had he said? That he needed to remind her about something.

What? She wanted to scream. That he was a man? That he cared about her? That they were still both young? What had he reminded her of with one kiss?

Nell turned back to the house. Maybe he wanted to remind her that she was a woman, or maybe that she should wait for him to come back. It wouldn't matter, she told herself. She'd wait. She couldn't think of marriage while her life was being threatened. But waiting wouldn't change anything. She still could not marry him.

She found everyone crowded around the kitchen table, eating Marla's breakfast rolls out of the pan. Nell smiled. She'd never have one of those proper families where people ate every meal at the dining table like she'd been taught in school. Thank God.

Gypsy made room for her as everyone told Nell their new theories as to what might have happened. As always, Marla was quiet but turned red when Mr. Harrison bragged on her cooking.

Gypsy decided the shooting might have been meant for her. After all, she'd lived in the house longer than anyone else, and when she was here alone, she used to take naps in a chair upstairs by that very window. "Maybe some fellow's got it in for me," she speculated with her mouth full. "I ain't spent much of my life trying to make friends. I got more jilted lovers than dogs got fleas."

The sheriff pointed his finger as if giving a lecture. "No one's trying to kill you, Gypsy. You're pretty much doing that job all by yourself. Drinking the cheap, rotgut whiskey sold out the back door of the saloon will eat you from inside out."

"Well, Parker, if that stuff is poison, I'm racing you to the grave." Gypsy laughed. "My people live a long time unless a bullet gets them. How long you figure sheriffs live?"

Parker twisted up his mouth. "I aim to stay alive long enough to let the whiskey pickle me so when they dig me up in a hundred years, there I'll be, same as the day I died."

Gypsy made a face. "Yeah, old and ugly."

Everyone laughed as Marla brought out another pan of rolls from the oven.

Nell was thankful the sheriff didn't tell the bookkeeper Marla's nickname. It had haunted her long enough. When Nell first returned, after the accident, the sheriff had shown up on her doorstep with Marla in tow. He'd whispered that no one in town would hire her, and she wouldn't leave Clarendon. Just the thought of going to apply for a job frightened her near to death, Parker explained. She'd never find the nerve to travel to a town where she didn't know anyone, so Parker helped by asking around, and this was the last house.

Nell welcomed her in, figuring she couldn't be as bad a cook as Gypsy. Marla, though four years older than Nell, had always been nice when they were children. She'd even whispered a hello when Nell saw her on the streets the few times Nell had come home from school, which was more than most people did. Knowing how shy Marla was made the greeting mean more to Nell. If Marla was down on her luck, the sheriff was right in guessing that Nell would be willing to help.

"Thanks," Nell said as memory faded and the worries of today returned. Marla passed her a plate with a roll made of bread and meat. "I love these. I truly do."

"I know," Marla whispered back. "That's why I make them so often."

"We all love them, deary." Gypsy reached for another. "You're a better cook than I ever was a hooker."

Marla turned away but didn't lower her head as she used to do when Gypsy talked of her former occupation.

Nell remembered what the sheriff had said that first morning he'd brought Marla over. "She can cook like a dream, but she's had a run of bad luck. I hired her to cook for the jail, and the last four men she fed got the death penalty. They call her Last Meal Marla. She also cooked for Old Ralph over at the hotel. He died three days after she went to work for him, but it was more his heart than her food, I figure."

The sheriff didn't have to say more. As in most small towns, it only took a few times before folks made up their mind about people. If Marla cooked for fifty years in this town there would be some who wouldn't take a bite.

Nell hired her on the spot and offered her room and board with a fair salary. Within days, she joined the family.

While everyone talked, Nell rolled a few feet backward and checked the baking soda tin where Marla kept the grocery money. Despite her bank account and the property she owned, the grocer still wouldn't allow her to buy on credit. He also wouldn't deliver, so Marla made at least two trips a week to the store for supplies.

"I've already checked," Marla whispered from just behind Nell. "We've enough to make it another week and still feed extra mouths."

Nell nodded. "My stash upstairs is also almost gone."

When she ran completely out of household money, she'd have to go into town. Nell knew she would be the freak everyone watched. Last time Mary Ruth had lifted her from the buggy to her wheelchair when they'd stopped at the bank. Several people had commented at the sight of a woman carrying another woman even if Mary Ruth was a nurse. One had even hinted that maybe a man hid beneath the uniform, for Nell Smith, at over five feet seven, would be no light load.

The only other time she'd gone to town, her friends Carter and Bailee had come from Cedar Point by train to help. Carter had carried her to a bed made in the wagon because she couldn't stand the pain long enough to sit in a buggy. He'd lifted her out carefully when they'd gone to the bank and carried her down the street to first the lawyer, then the doctor. Everyone called her Poor Child as if she'd stopped being an adult when she lost the ability to walk.

She couldn't ask her friends to come again. They had children and a ranch. Nell looked back at the table. Except for Mr. Harrison, no one could lift her, and she couldn't ask him to pick her up. She'd just have to hope the money lasted until Jacob returned. He'd carry her with ease while she did her business in town and she'd be willing to bet no one would talk behind his back.

Each time, she was torn between drawing more money out, or leaving it where it was safe. If she took too much home, she knew she would just be asking to be robbed. If she took too little, she'd have to make the embarrassing trip more often.

"I've got most of my salary stashed under my bed," Marla whispered. "You're welcome to use it."

"Thanks," Nell answered. "We'll make it."

They returned to the others. Now that everyone had finished breakfast, they huddled like generals preparing for battle. Nell tried to convince them that the shooting might have been just a one-time thing that would never happen again, but no one listened. They planned to be ready.

The sheriff left to check in at his office and returned two hours later to say that he'd ordered the glass for the window, but the hardware store owner said he had no one who could deliver it or put it in. Parker quoted the bothersome owner as saying that most folks had men around who could do such things. Then the sheriff looked guilty that he'd relayed such a hurtful message.

Gypsy swore and stomped. Mr. Harrison simply stood up from the desk where he'd been working and said, "I'll go, if you have no objection, Miss Nell. It's time I took some air anyway. I'll prepare a note stating that I'm your bookkeeper. If you'll sign it, that should be all the hardware store owner needs."

Nell nodded, surprised he'd offer. "Marla will give you our cash funds. I don't know how much you'll need, but I'm sure it will be enough." She didn't want to start worrying about money for food yet, but the glass was cutting into what cash they had on hand.

A minute later, Harrison handed her a neatly written note and a pen. "I'll be back before the sheriff finishes lunch."

To Nell's total surprise, Marla grabbed her bonnet. "May I go with you? I need a few supplies."

Harrison headed for the door. "I'll have the wagon ready in five minutes. I want to stuff it with straw to protect the glass."

"I'll be ready," Marla whispered.

The sheriff filled his plate from the pots left warming on the stove and joined Nell in the great room. While he ate, he talked about the time he'd been shot and Fat Alice had patched him up in the very spot where he now was having lunch. "She had a rule." He laughed. "A man got a free drink for every slug dug out of him."

Nell tried to listen, but her thoughts followed Marla and Mr. Harrison. If she wasn't safe in her own house, would they be safe in town or on the road? In a wagon the trip didn't take long. Nell had a feeling she'd count the minutes until they returned.

She was relieved when the sheriff suggested they sit on the porch while he smoked his cigar and they waited.

She guessed he also worried, though that didn't seem to slow his talking. While she sat in her wheelchair with a blanket over her legs, Parker paced back and forth. He told her it would be spring before long, and she needed to think about stocking the ranches with cattle and men. The sheriff talked as if he'd ranched for years and not spent his life behind a badge.

"There's trouble festering in town. Too many men out of work. Too many looking for a quick way to get rich. You'll need to be real careful who you hire."

"I will," she said, only half listening.

Most of the land she'd inherited had been either abandoned or neglected before it came her way. Nell had heard a few old hands still lived off some of the land, running a few head of their own but not working the ranch. If the men who'd offered to marry her knew what bad shape the ranches were in, all would have probably run faster than they did.

Harrison would know soon enough of her troubles; then he'd probably be on the next train out.

Remembering former suitors, she asked, "Has Walter Farrow left yet?"

The sheriff shook his head. "He's hanging out talking to whoever will listen. He checked out of the hotel this morning and moved into that old house that used to be his uncle's. Everyone in town knows

Henry lost it in a poker game, but evidently the paperwork was never filed, so there's no one to tell Farrow he can't live there."

An hour passed, and finally the sheriff stopped talking and stared down the road. He'd asked Nell ten times if she was cold, and each time she'd lied and said no. She couldn't go inside when Marla and Mr. Harrison were still gone.

Gypsy banged her way through the door with the afternoon tray of drinks and cookies. Nell took a cup to keep her hands warm. The sheriff didn't even answer when she offered him a cup.

"You can ride on in," Nell said. "We'll be all right here. You could be back in a matter of minutes."

Parker didn't answer.

"It could be a hundred things holding them up. Maybe the glass wasn't ready like the hardware store owner said. Some folks will say anything to make a sale." Nell stared at the sheriff's back. "Or maybe Marla took longer picking up supplies than we thought she would. You know her; she won't ask a question with anyone else in the store. She probably walked up and down the aisles waiting for her chance."

She went over every reason she could think of for her own sanity. "Maybe the wagon lost a wheel. That road is terrible. Or maybe the horse threw a shoe. Mr. Harrison might have taken him over to the blacksmith shop and had to wait in line. You know Saturday's always busy in town."

Gypsy shook her head. "Or maybe somethin' happened to them."

Her words hung in the air. No one said a word. Nell refused to consider Gypsy's possibility. It made less sense than shooting at a woman in a wheelchair.

In the silence, Nell thought she heard the jingle of a bridle. She leaned forward a few inches and slipped her right hand into the pocket of her jacket. "Let it be Marla," she whispered to herself. But just in case, she'd be ready.

The sheriff also shifted, resting his hand on his sidearm and leaning back into the shadow of the porch so that whoever neared wouldn't see him right away.

The jingle came again.

Nell didn't breathe.

Then she heard something she'd never heard before.

She heard Marla laugh.

CHAPTER 9

JACOB DALTON TRACKED THE MAN WHO'D SHOT AT NELL FOR FIVE hours before the trail disappeared. He didn't think the stranger had any idea he was being followed, but luck was with the shooter. The ground grew rocky, and the rider switched directions. Though the horse's tracks should have been easy to follow with the ground still damp from rain, herds of deer or cattle had wiped them in places.

By nightfall, Jacob wasn't sure he still followed the shooter. There had been a dozen places the man could have turned off on rocks or into shallow streams. When it finally grew too dark to track, Jacob made camp between a stand of trees and a formation of rocks. Here, he'd be out of the wind, and smoke from a small fire wouldn't be noticed in the shadow of the trees. He hadn't seen any sign of a ranch since early that morning, so he doubted anyone would pass close during the night.

He took care of his horse, then ate half the food Marla packed for him and saved the other half for breakfast. Rolling in his bedroll, he leaned against his saddle and relaxed for the first time. A weapon lay within inches of either hand.

All day he'd tried to concentrate on tracking and on trying to find a reason anyone would want Nell dead. The shot hadn't been at the house. He'd bet his career as a ranger that the man aimed at the outline of the wheelchair in the window. The chair where Nell always sat.

But who? Surely someone didn't still think the place was a whorehouse. As far as he knew, though people objected to a young woman inheriting, no one else fought for the old madam's money. No one would benefit from Nell's death. He'd heard Nell say once that she'd filed a will asking for all her property to be sold and the money passed to her friends if something happened to her. None of her friends would ever do her harm, and no one else would benefit.

Fat Alice, despite what a few good folks in town suggested, was highly thought of by most. She ran a clean house and in the town's early days acted as hospital and doctor many times. She always let anyone traveling through without money for a hotel stay in her barn, and more often than not served breakfast before sending them on their way. She'd done her best for Nell, and for that one kindness, Jacob figured she'd get to heaven.

Alice died working one spring while Nell was away at school. The undertaker, her last customer, did the service free.

Since Nell inherited, the house had been painted and cleaned up inside and out. Gypsy had lived in a back room until Nell came home. She'd fed the horses and kept the place clean more because she didn't have anywhere to go than because she wanted to stay. When Nell asked her to remain, she'd stayed drunk for three days to celebrate. Then she'd started cleaning and, near as Jacob could tell, she hadn't stopped yet.

Though some folks wished the house and its memories would go away, Jacob couldn't see anyone trying to make it happen.

The shooting couldn't have been random. That was why Jacob had to try to find the shooter. He didn't like the idea of leaving Nell alone with Number Twelve, but he had no choice. Finding out why someone wanted to kill her had to rank as more important than worrying about who she planned to marry.

He swore at the moon. Why couldn't she have been happy with how things were? Why'd she think she had to have a husband? It made no sense.

Jacob laughed. Neither did the kiss, he thought. Nell couldn't have looked more shocked if he'd pinched her. Maybe she didn't think of him in the way a woman thinks of a man who might kiss her.

He didn't like the idea that him kissing her was probably the last thing on her mind. But he knew it had to be true. When he'd offered marriage, she didn't consider the possibility for even a minute. And in truth, the thought hadn't crossed his mind, either, until she'd gone crazy and put out an ad for a husband. He and the kid had always been friends. She'd probably be more receptive to the old sheriff's proposal of marriage than his.

But friends could become lovers. Couldn't they? He wasn't sure. In truth he couldn't remember hearing about it ever happening. A man doesn't talk to a friend the way he talks to a woman who might be crawling into his bed. If they married, Nell wouldn't be able to claim she didn't know him. She'd seen him at his best and worst.

And he'd seen her grow up. When he looked at her he couldn't help but see a little of Two Bits, the child who stole his heart. Only lately, the person before him was a mystery. How did such a skinny kid grow into a woman curved in all the right places?

Jacob tossed another log on the fire and listened to the wind. An animal moved somewhere in the trees, letting out a soft call of alarm. He knew nothing would come close with the fire burning, but still, he brushed the handle of his Colt as he went back to thinking about Nell.

She tasted great. He couldn't remember other lips being so soft. Closing his eyes, he tried to remember the last time he'd kissed a woman.

Before Nell's accident, he realized When she'd sent him a telegram that her friends were in trouble, he'd been seeing a widow in El Paso from time to time. He'd heard that he wasn't the widow's only caller, but he didn't much care. She'd been friendly, offering samples of her charms, but not willing to give in completely until he offered marriage. And, even if he'd thought marriage might have been a good idea, her six kids quickly sobered him up.

After Nell had been hurt, Jacob never returned to the widow, even though he'd pass within a mile of her house once in a while.

He didn't want to spend too much time wondering why.

The wind carried the sound again. A cry like a small animal might make if caught in the beak of an owl.

He closed his eyes and told himself to get some sleep. He'd ride out at dawn, but if he didn't pick up the trail, he knew he would be headed home by noon. He wanted the shooter, but the prospect of making it in for supper tomorrow night seemed promising.

The noise came again. Stronger. Louder. Some animal sounded like it suffered in the trees just beyond his fire.

Jacob rolled to his feet, wide awake. With his Colt ready, he moved into the shadows. He'd free the creature if he could, but if not, he'd at least set it free from pain. Jacob could take as much pain as the next man, maybe more, but he couldn't stand to see animals suffer.

The trees grew close together, winding down into a dried-up creek bed. Jacob moved through the darkness as soundlessly as an Apache.

The cry tore at his nerves. It sounded almost like sobbing, the kind of bawling all animals, including humans, do when they know death is near.

Jacob circled first one tree, then another, moving blindly toward the racket. He stepped over a stream no wider than his hand.

The ground rose on the other side of the creek bed. He hesitated, guessing he must be a quarter mile by now from his camp. For a moment, he listened. If the cries had been a trick, someone might plan to steal his horse. Dusty would be pitching a fit about now. The horse hated anything on two feet except Jacob, and sometimes Jacob wasn't too sure Dusty liked him.

Jacob heard nothing. Only the sound of sobbing now. Human sobbing!

He ran as the trees thinned and a clearing appeared. In the pale moonlight, he made out the shape of a woman. Short. Rounded. Her head bowed low as she cried.

Slowing, he tried to figure out how to approach without frightening her. Maybe she was lost, or her horse had thrown her.

"Miss?" he said. "Miss, are you all right?"

She looked up, her sobs silenced by her sudden intake of breath.

He saw the fear in her young face. Panic made her eyes wide and liquid.

"It's all right," he hurried to add as he holstered his Colt. "I'm a Texas Ranger. Is there something I can do to help you?"

His gaze darted around. Maybe someone had robbed her and her parents. Her parents might have been killed or gone for help. She looked too young to be left out here alone. She might be fifteen or so, almost grown but not quite. Even in her coat, he could tell she was well rounded, a plump body to match her plump cheeks. "Are you hurt?"

She shook her head, curls bouncing around her face.

He moved closer while she shoved tears away with her sleeve. "Do you live around here, miss?"

She shook her head again.

He studied her, wondering if she could talk. Her clothes were well-made and relatively clean, except for her sleeves. She hadn't been lost long. He saw no ropes or gag, so she hadn't been kidnapped. There appeared to be no bruises or cuts, so she hadn't been mistreated in any way that he could see.

"Do you have any supplies? Water? Food?"

She looked at her hands, and he knew the answer.

"How'd you get here?" He stood five feet away. Close enough to see her in the moonlight, but not so close he'd frighten her. "If you don't mind telling me." They had to be fifty miles or more from any town, and if there had been a farm near, he would have seen some sign of it.

She took a deep breath and looked at him as if her answer wouldn't matter, but she'd tell him anyway. "My pa drove all night and most of a day to drop me off here. He says hell will freeze over before he comes back." She hugged herself. "It's getting cold, but I don't think that will happen, do you?"

Jacob smiled. "No, I don't." He'd seen some crazy things, but this beat all for parents trying to teach their children a lesson. Near as he could tell she had no supplies, not even a canteen, and no weapon. "You hungry?"

She nodded. "I haven't eaten in days. I left this clearing a few times to get a drink and once to stand under the trees when it rained. The water in the creek is mostly mud."

"How long you been here?"

"This will be my third night." Her eyes were swollen from crying. "I don't think he's going to come back to get me. At first I didn't want to walk, because I was sure he'd be back. But my hope's fading."

Jacob didn't want to have her start crying again, so he said, "I've got a little food and good water back through the trees. If you want some, you're welcome to it."

She stood slowly, leaning back to shift her center of gravity.

He fought to keep his face frozen as he realized the girl was pregnant . . . big pregnant. He offered his hand and carefully led her through the trees. She waddled like a duck beside him, holding a hand over her middle as if protecting a treasure.

Jacob was too busy silently swearing at himself to talk to her. He seemed to be developing a habit of saving young girls. First Nell, now this one. Couldn't the Good Lord take pity on him and send a dozen outlaws to him instead?

The girl started sniffling again like a little round train chugging through the trees.

Two dozen outlaws, he thought, with guns drawn, would be an easier find.

When they reached his camp, he made a seat for her on a log and handed her the sack of food. She ate the rolls first and then finished off the meat and apples while he built up the fire.

"Want to tell me where you live?" he asked as he passed her his canteen. He didn't like the idea of delay, but he couldn't leave her here. He'd have to see her to safety before continuing on. A day lost, or even a few hours, would probably mean he couldn't catch the shooter.

"On a farm," she answered, then let out a little cry. "Am I still in Texas? He didn't take me to the Oklahoma Territory, did he? Our farm's in Texas."

"That narrows it down considerably." Jacob shrugged. "And you've got to cross the Red River to set foot in the Territory, so we're still in Texas."

She looked like she might cry so he asked, "How about telling me what direction we need to head out in the morning? With the rain two nights ago, I doubt I'll be able to find any tracks your pa's wagon might have made. If you give me the town closest to your folks' farm, I can take you back there, and they'd see that you get home."

He hadn't helped matters by asking questions. A fat tear rolled down her cheek. "I can't go back. My pa told me if I tried coming home with this bastard still in me, he'd kill us both."

Now Jacob understood. "What about the baby's father?"

She shook her head. "I wouldn't tell my pa who he is, and I won't tell you either. Not even if you lock me up."

He smiled. "I'm not in the habit of arresting young ladies for being pregnant. All I meant was that maybe the father of your child will make things right."

To his surprise, she raised her chin. "I asked the boy I thought I would love forever just like he claimed he loved me. He said he'd swear nothing ever happened, so I guess his forever ain't as long as mine. His pa found out and claimed he'd see me dead before he'd let me marry his only son on account of I'm the dumbest one in my family." She swallowed and added, "And it's a big family. Eleven brothers and sisters, not counting steps and halves."

She rubbed her eyes. "I've been trying to think of something to do. If I somehow find my way home, pa will kill me. If I go to Teddie, his pa will kill me. It's been three days, and all I've figured out is I must not be bright enough to live. My stepma tells me I'm not worth feeding. I thought she hated me because I look like my ma, but lately I've figured out that maybe she just hates me."

"You got a lot of people wanting to kill you for such a young girl."

"True." She sighed. "Before you came along, I'd decided to fool them all and kill myself. Only, I couldn't think of a way that wouldn't hurt. That's why I was crying, on account of being a coward."

Jacob had to smile at her logic. "How old are you?"

"I'll be sixteen next fall," she answered with a yawn. "If I live that long."

He handed her his only blanket. "How about we turn in and talk about it in the morning."

She slid off the log and curled into a ball. "All right. I've been too cold and scared to sleep. The night's long when you're afraid to close your eyes."

As she settled, he asked one last question. "Want to tell me your name?"

"Wednesday," she mumbled. "Wednesday May. I was born the first Wednesday in May. My mom wasn't big on thinking of names."

"Good night, Miss May."

"Good night, Ranger."

CHAPTER 10

NELL SAT ON THE PORCH MOST OF THE AFTERNOON, A WINCHESTER across her legs in case trouble rode in before Jacob returned. Part of her hoped he lost the trail. She didn't like to think of him out there alone, maybe riding into an ambush. If the man who'd fired at her bedroom window had been such a good shot and, according to Jacob, a great horseman as well, wasn't there the possibility he might be able to set a trap and catch even a Texas Ranger off guard?

Closing her eyes, she pushed the image of a wounded Jacob out of her head. She couldn't bear thinking that he might suffer the same pain she had when she'd been ambushed. The memory of lying in the sun waiting for them to come closer to kill her. The feel of her own blood soaking her body. The knowing that she was helpless and could do nothing to change her fate. All crossed her mind as she waited.

A vision of him spread on the ground like a broken doll flashed across her mind once more. Nell forced it aside. His life was one of danger. He knew what he was doing. He'd be fine, she told herself. He always had been. *Think of something else . . . of anything else.*

The feel of his lips pressing against her mouth consumed her thoughts. The memory seemed so strong, she could almost feel his lips touching her now. She wondered if he were thinking of her and the kiss they'd shared at the same moment. Somehow, Nell knew this time was just like when she'd been a child and had needed him. She'd sensed him on his way long before she could get word to him.

A noise pulled her from her thoughts. Mr. Harrison and Marla carried the new window upstairs hours ago and were now working on fixing the gate. It surprised Nell how they worked together so smoothly and in silence most of the time. Marla usually started supper by now, but today she stood beside Harrison, holding the gate in place, waiting for him to finish tightening the new latch.

They were a matched set, Nell thought. Both tall and thin with ebony hair shining in the sun. If they married, their children would be beanpoles with straight black hair. Not that Harrison and Marla would ever even talk, much less fall in love and marry. Both had little to say.

Nell had never heard Marla say two words to any man, or any boy in their younger days. She wasn't sure Marla said more than that to Mr. Harrison, but it didn't stop them from being a team.

Harrison removed his jacket and collar. His undershirt was stained with sweat, and Nell guessed without asking that he had no other shirt. How proper he'd been only twenty-four hours ago when he'd arrived. She now guessed most of his stiffness had been fear, and the fainting spell probably more hunger than panic over the ranger's threats.

The bookkeeper straightened, lifted the tool box, and walked with Marla to the porch. Nell didn't hear either of them speak as they neared. Marla disappeared into the house, but he halted, one foot on the step, the other remaining on the ground.

"I think the latch will hold," he said, rolling his sleeves down. "Anyone planning to ride by now will have to stop to open the gate or risk a broken neck jumping the fence."

"Thank you." Nell didn't know what else to say. She knew he was trying to help out, still hoping they'd make a bargain of marriage, but he'd done far more than necessary. She would have been happy if he'd just managed to straighten out her books. Despite his silent nature, she'd learned a great deal about the man today. He liked to keep busy. He was kind. He must be, for Harrison put in the window with the sheriff telling him how it should be done, without once suggesting Parker help more and talk less.

Mr. Harrison wiped his throat with a handkerchief embroidered with an *H*. "I enjoyed the work. It's been a long time since I've worked outside. It felt good." His pale skin had reddened in the sun.

"Ask Marla to get the aloe cream down for you." Nell looked down, embarrassed at having stared. "It'll help with the burn."

"I'll do that." He stepped up on the porch and studied her a moment before adding, "If the ranger hasn't returned before nightfall, I'll go back to the boardinghouse and collect my things. If you've no objections, I'll use the team that's still hitched up so I'm only away a short time."

Nell had been watching the road and almost didn't answer. "That's fine. It is kind of you to offer to stay." The image of Jacob hurt, lying in the dirt, wormed its way back into her mind.

"You're more than welcome, Miss Smith." Harrison studied her.

Nell knew she acted strange. He probably thought her ill. She looked into his eyes for the first time. Something about him seemed very formal, but a secret lay beneath his guarded eyes. She no longer believed it had anything to do with her. "Mr. Harrison, you may use any of the horses or wagons you wish. You've no need to ask my permission. Fat Alice said she kept them in case she had to move in the middle of the night. I'm afraid they are in desperate need of exercise. I can't get Marla to take even the buggy when she goes to town."

"She's afraid of horses," he answered more to himself than her.

Nell raised her eyebrows. She'd never noticed, and the shy cook had said nothing when questioned. "How do you know?"

He set the tool box in its usual place near the back of the porch. "I saw the way she cut a wide path around them when she climbed in the wagon." Before she could ask more, he added, "Oh, by the way, I talked to the mercantile owner as well as the hardware manager. As of tomorrow, you'll have credit from both, providing I produce a signed note from you with a list of those authorized to charge. They asked that you pay the bill at the end of each month, and I assured them that as your bookkeeper I'd be by in person to do exactly that."

"You're joking?" No one living out by the tracks had ever had credit. "How did you talk them into such a thing?"

He smiled. "I told them I didn't look forward to boarding the train to Cedar Point every time I needed to buy your supplies."

Nell was almost speechless. "And they thought you were serious?"

He turned slowly, looking her directly in the eyes. "I was serious. If I'm to be your bookkeeper, even for a short time, my job is to straighten out your accounts." He grinned. "And both those men needed straightening. They realized I could have taken the train to Cedar Point, bought supplies, and been back before dark."

Mr. Harrison said the words so simply, no one would have argued that he meant them. She'd tried to convince the town's merchants to allow her to have an account. She'd even had the sheriff talk to them. "You threatened them?"

He shook his head. "No, miss. I just stated a fact. There's a difference, and they knew it. When Marla walked in for supplies, they were right in thinking she wouldn't board the train, and old Gypsy, even if she took the wagon to town, wouldn't travel all day to pick up supplies." He raised an eyebrow. "But I would have, and they knew it. I gave them a day to check with the banker to make sure you have plenty in your account to cover usual items. Tomorrow Marla may put her purchases on your bill and not have to worry about having enough cash."

Nell smiled. "Mr. Harrison, I could kiss you."

He stiffened. "Please, Miss Smith, not until we're officially engaged."

Now Nell laughed. She admired Harrison, but he would never be the type of man with whom she'd fall in love. But, as he'd pointed out, love wasn't always a consideration in a bargain of marriage.

Ill at ease with so much conversation, he excused himself and went inside to wash up.

When Harrison was gone, Nell straightened in her chair, trying to keep her back from aching. She wondered if he were being polite, or if the thought of her kissing him, even as a thank-you, might be repulsive to him. She'd noticed some people didn't touch her. It seemed as if they thought they might catch whatever she had that kept her from walking. She thought of reminding them that one doesn't catch bad luck.

The sheriff's buggy rattled across the breeze, announcing his arrival even before he was halfway to the house. He climbed out with stiff legs and grinned when he saw her on the porch. "I brought your mail out," he yelled, as if she couldn't hear him from ten feet away. "And three boxes of stuff you ordered. I swear, I used to think of myself as the pony express delivering mail out here, but these days I'm more like a pack mule. Ever' time I stop by, they've got boxes stacked up for you."

For a second, Nell gripped the arms of the chair as if to rise and help. Then, in less then a blink, she remembered. Funny how sometimes for a fraction in time, she would forget her limits. She felt like a prisoner who couldn't remember the doors were locked.

Sheriff Parker brought each box and placed it in her lap so she could open them one at a time. Gypsy wandered out of the house to help.

The first box held material. Soft white cotton for gowns and aprons. Solid blue fabric to bind the flour-sack squares they'd quilted when the weather had been bad. Fine lace she'd bought for no reason at all.

"I'll add it to the stash of material we've got," Gypsy said as she carried the box inside.

The second box was crammed full of seeds and small gardening tools that Nell could use to tend her pots. By summer she dreamed of lining the porch with flowers.

The third box was bulky but didn't seem heavy. Inside the packing, Nell found a tea set made of white china with flowers on the pot and cups. When she pulled the pieces out, the sheriff looked like he'd wasted his time bringing the box out. Even Gypsy mumbled that they had a perfectly good tea service she'd been doing her best not to break.

Nell hardly noticed their complaints. She handled each cup and saucer with care, letting her fingers slide over the tiny roses painted into the china. Then, reluctantly, she asked Gypsy to put the set away, and she resumed her watch. She didn't know why she'd ordered the tea set, maybe just because she could. There had been so few times in her life when she'd had enough extra money to buy something she didn't need.

Having afternoon tea had been one of the few things she'd loved at school. Being an outsider, Nell usually wasn't invited to the parties or for weekends away, but everyone at the finishing school was not only invited but expected to attend afternoon tea. And there, Nell could pretend that she wasn't so alone.

The sheriff had just returned from filling his third cup of coffee when she heard another wagon. They both sat in silence as Walter Farrow rounded the last bend and neared the gate. He pulled the reins and waited for someone to unlatch it. When no one came, he stumbled his way out of the wagon and opened the gate himself.

He took one step to climb back on the bench seat, then reconsidered and led the horse into the yard. Walter Farrow's skill with handling a wagon was minute, and his observation abilities even less. He didn't notice the sheriff and Nell on the porch until he walked almost to the steps.

"Mr. Farrow," Nell greeted him.

The big man removed his hat. "Miss Smith, I hope I'm not interrupting, but I felt I must come by and apologize for my behavior yesterday."

"No need." Nell couldn't keep herself from brushing her fingers over the rifle in her lap. "I consider it just a misunderstanding." She really couldn't blame Farrow when it had been Mary Ruth who wrote the letter encouraging him to come, but he seemed a slippery sort.

Maybe it was his greasy hair and sweating face. She didn't have a reason, but Nell didn't like him.

He smiled as if all had been forgiven. "You're most gracious, Miss Smith." Farrow took the first step onto the porch as Sheriff Parker Smith stood.

"Oh," Farrow said. "I see you already have company." One bushy eyebrow rose halfway to his hairline. "Or is the sheriff a relative? I assumed you had no kin, but now I realize you both have the same last name."

"Smith is a common name," Parker mumbled.

Nell couldn't help but smile at the old man. He wasn't about to tell Farrow that she didn't have a last name. Parker stood at the top of the steps blocking Walter's way, even though his body was half the width. If Farrow wanted to step onto the porch, he'd have to go around the sheriff or mow him down with his big belly.

Farrow backed down and turned his attention to Nell. "I was hoping to talk with you about the Stockard place. I'd like to go out and take a close look around, but after yesterday I wasn't sure you wouldn't have me arrested for trespassing."

"I might have," Nell admitted. "But you're welcome to look around as long as you understand that I haven't decided to sell the land."

He nodded as if expecting her answer. "I've spent the afternoon talking with the county judge. It seems my uncle didn't list his house in town in his will. I don't believe he thought he still owned it. The judge believes I may inherit that property as next of kin."

"I'm glad." Nell couldn't manage to sound like she meant her words.

Farrow looked frustrated. It was clear that she didn't plan to discuss anything with him, or even invite him to sit for that matter. "Well, I thank you, and I'll be on my way."

"I'll close the gate behind you." The sheriff started toward the wagon. Farrow had no choice but to follow.

As soon as the man was out of sight, Parker returned to his chair and mumbled, "I don't trust that man. He's no rancher. What would he want with the old Stockard place? It's nothing but a skeleton of an old farm that ain't good for nothing but raising rattlers. He's up to something. I heard someone say he's already starting to hire cowhands. Now what does a man without land need with hands?"

Nell guessed she'd be seeing Walter Farrow again. That type of man didn't give up until folks started seeing things his way.

"What do you think, Mr. Harrison?" Nell hadn't turned around.

She knew Harrison stood behind her. He'd slipped into the shadows of the porch while Farrow had been talking.

"If you've no objection . . ." Harrison nodded slightly. "I think I'll make use of one of those horses in the barn and ride out to the Stockard land. I'd like to know what Farrow finds so interesting."

She turned then, smiling back at him. Randolph Harrison had read her mind. If she could have, she would have done the same thing. Farrow was looking for something, and for some reason he thought it was on the old forgotten ranch.

An hour later, as the sun set and the sheriff talked, Mr. Harrison left to get his things. He returned with his valise and joined the sheriff and Nell on the porch until Gypsy told them dinner was ready. Though the food was wonderful, as always, no one made much effort to keep the conversation going. They all realized Jacob wouldn't be coming back tonight.

After dinner, Nell fought to keep from falling asleep in her chair. Finally, the sheriff said he'd better get back to town. Harrison walked him to the door, assuring the old man that he'd keep guard.

When the bookkeeper returned, Nell realized she would have to sleep downstairs. She couldn't ask him to carry her. She wasn't sure he could lift her. If she'd been standing, she would have been within an inch of his height, and he was so thin he couldn't be strong enough.

"Would you like me to help you to your room?" He broke the silence.

"I'll be all right down here," she lied, knowing that she'd have to have her privacy. "I'm afraid I'll have to ask you to sleep in the barn."

He nodded his understanding as Marla slipped from the kitchen. "If you'll allow us, Marla and I came up with an idea that might work if you'd like to sleep in your own bed."

Nell looked from one of them to the other, wondering how either had ever talked enough to come up with an idea. "I'm all right. I'm listening." She'd love to be in her own room, if only for a few hours.

Marla rolled her to the foot of the stairs. When Nell stood, Marla shoved the chair away and locked one hand on her elbow and the other on Mr. Harrison's arm. He did the same as they bent on either side of Nell. Their arms made a chair as Nell slipped a hand on each of their shoulders and lowered herself.

Slowly, they straightened, each taking half her weight. "We thought this would be easier on your back," Harrison said, his face only a few inches from hers. "Now you can sit straight as we move up the stairs."

In an easy rhythm, they climbed the stairs one at a time. Nell was almost in tears by the time they reached the top. The discomfort in her back had been minor. Her relief that she'd have a measure of privacy seemed a great gift. "Thank you," she whispered as they lowered her to her bed.

Before she realized what she was doing, she kissed them both on the cheek, then laughed when they both looked embarrassed. Before anyone could say a thing, Gypsy rattled the wheelchair into the room, complaining that the thing got heavier every night.

"I'll move my things and sleep across the hall," Marla whispered. "Just in case you need anything in the night."

"And I'll be downstairs sleeping where I've got a clear view of the stairs," Harrison announced. "You can rest easy, Miss Nell. No one will climb those stairs tonight without me noticing."

Nell decided she liked Randolph Harrison more the longer she knew him. But, when she looked up at the man who had proposed to her yesterday, he was staring at Marla.

CHAPTER 11

Jacob stared at the girl waddling behind him and swore under his breath. He couldn't leave her. She claimed she couldn't go home. In fact, she wouldn't even tell him where she lived. With her along, he'd never catch the shooter unless the man accidentally broke both legs and crawled directly ahead of them. Once, he'd suggested she wait for him in the clearing where he'd found her. He promised to pick her up on his way back. She'd cried for an hour.

There was no option left. He'd have to take her to Nell's place. Another town might be closer, but there would be no guarantee that anyone would accept her. Times were hard enough for most folks without feeding strays. She looked more kid than adult. Someone might be willing to take one child to raise, but not two.

"Wait!" she yelled. "You're moving too fast."

Jacob slowed. At this pace, her baby would be walking before they made it to Clarendon. He stopped, checking Dusty's saddle and pretending to be busy until she caught up. "You sure you don't want to ride?"

She shook her head. "It'll be too bumpy." They had been traveling an hour, and she'd already asked twice when they would stop.

He knew it wasn't her fault. Carrying all that extra weight and with legs no longer than a goat's, he couldn't blame her for complaining. Pulling his bedroll down, he laid it over the saddle to use for padding. "I'll walk beside you, holding the reins. We'll go slow."

She frowned. "I'd fall off a horse that big."

"I'll tie you on," he suggested, fighting the urge to add, *And gag you.*

She tumbled over a rock and would have landed on her face if he hadn't caught her.

"Look." He felt like he was trying to reason with a squirrel. "We'll never make any time like this. I crossed a road yesterday. It didn't look much used, but maybe we'll get lucky and see someone pass. If you'll climb up, I could walk twice as fast. You're safer up there than tripping over rocks walking."

"I can't see my feet. It's not my fault." She shook tangled reddish brown curls that were starting to look like roots growing from her round face.

Jacob tried another angle. "I'm out of food, and if we don't hurry, we'll starve before we reach any civilization."

"You don't have anything in your pack?" She'd complained about the breakfast of coffee at dawn. "I thought you were saving it."

Jacob grinned. Finally, he had her attention. "I didn't plan to be out more than a day or two. You ate my supply of food last night. All I have left is black coffee."

"All right," she whined, "I'll try it, but I've never been much for riding a horse. It may make the baby come."

A thought occurred to him. "Your mother did tell you what to do when the time comes?"

Wednesday nodded. "She said scream."

"Great." Jacob decided, once he got her settled, he'd search for Wednesday's parents and arrest them. They were either too dumb or too mean to be running around free. "If you'll ride, I think I can get you home. Nell will know what to do when the labor starts. The cook will bake you something special. She makes apple dumplings that melt right down your throat."

Wednesday looked interested.

"If you ride, we could make it by suppertime. I'll bet there's cake left over from Sunday dinner." She took a step toward the horse, and he added, "Nell's cook makes the best cakes in the county. Usually by evening, they're half gone, and there's extra icing on the plate if you like it piled high on your slice."

Wednesday raised her arms, and he lifted her onto the saddle. Using the ends of his blanket, he wrapped her so that she'd stay up, even if she had no skill. He also wanted to brace her back, since she'd been acting like it ached all morning. "I'm not sure I can strap the stirrups up enough for you to put your feet in." He'd had the saddle made for him without any thought that someone shorter might ride in it.

"Is your wife tall, Ranger?" Wednesday had a death grip on the saddle horn but seemed to be trying her best not to look frightened.

Jacob realized he'd called Nell's place home. In truth, he thought of it as just that. When other men talked of heading home, he thought of getting back to Nell and her place by the tracks.

"She is," he answered, thinking of Nell's long legs and how she used to do her best to outrun him when she was in trouble. He noticed Wednesday staring at him and added, "When she was your age, she could ride like a man."

He didn't want to tell the kid about the mess over Nell getting married. Wednesday had enough problems of her own. But, with luck, they'd see Nell soon. "My wife," the words rang strange to his ears, "took a fall last year that left her in a wheelchair."

Wednesday's cheery face melted. "I'm sorry."

Jacob worked a rope around the saddle, binding her like a pack to the animal. "I just wanted you to know so you won't be shocked when you see her."

"You sure she'll let me stay?"

"It's the only place I can think of to take you. Nell will put you up for a few days until we figure out something or get word to your folks."

"I'm dead to my folks," she answered as if simply stating a fact. "I'll never go back."

Jacob shook his head but didn't argue. He remembered times he thought his parents had been hard on him, but they'd never disowned him. Though they'd been dead since the year before he joined the Rangers, he felt like sometimes they were still watching over him, worrying about him. He missed the way his parents loved one another, the way his mother sang and his father complained about the weather. He missed the way he always knew they loved him.

Jacob calmed his horse. He held the lead close to Dusty's head as he began walking. If Wednesday would keep quiet, they might have a chance at getting back. He glanced up and noticed she had already nodded off as the motions of the horse rocked her to sleep.

His thoughts turned to Nell. She never had a parent's love. She never talked about her mother, not once, but she talked about Fat Alice plenty. The old madam might never have hugged the child she took to raise, but she took her responsibility seriously. He wondered if at any time in all her life, Nell had ever known she was loved. It might not seem like an important thing when you know you've been cared about. But, if you've never known love, would you even know to want it? Maybe that explained why she hadn't made it part of the bargain for marriage.

About midmorning they reached a road, little more than ruts that could have been made by a small wagon train heading from Fort Worth north. Jacob hoped the tracks were made by a supply wagon running from one of the old forts to another. If so, it might still be used from time to time, even though most of the forts operating had train stations nearby.

Wednesday began a long list of endings to a sentence that started with "I'm so hungry I could . . ." Then she listed all her favorite foods.

When she went back to complaining about being so uncomfortable, Jacob was actually glad. All her talk made him hungry. He tried to guess how long it would take them to get home, but he didn't see any way they'd make it, at this rate, by supper. If he had to, he'd walk all night, and with luck they'd make breakfast.

They stopped just after noon by a stream thirty feet from the road. He stood watch while she took a nap and Dusty grazed.

Jacob was saddling up when he saw a tattered old buggy rattling along the road. He ran to flag it down before he could see who drove it. At this point, the distraction of a highway robber would be welcome.

A white-bearded country preacher poked his head around the side of the buggy. Jacob smiled. There was no mistaking the man's occupation. He had a Bible in one hand and a .45 in the other. "Are you in trouble, son?" His voice boomed as if he were speaking to the multitudes.

Jacob held his hands wide and walked closer. "I am in need." Before he could say more, Wednesday waddled toward them.

The preacher laid down his gun. "I can see you are. Lucky I came along." He stepped from the buggy, the Bible held toward heaven. "Praise the Lord I made it in time before another one of God's children was born a bastard." He motioned Wednesday closer. "Afternoon, my name is Brother Aaron. I'm a sworn man of God, licensed to marry and bury folks." He looked at Jacob. "That'll be a dollar, son. In advance of the ceremony just in case one of you changes your mind halfway through."

Jacob couldn't manage enough spit to swallow. He took a step backward and raised his hands again, realizing he much preferred the gun pointing at him than the Bible.

"Are you going to do right by this little lady, sir? It looks like you robbed the cradle, and before spring she'll be rocking one." Brother Aaron raised his eyes to heaven again. "Lord, I'm not here to judge sinners, just help them get to going on the straight and narrow. If it weren't for sinners, you wouldn't need no preachers, so thank you, Lord, for putting these two fornicators in my path."

Wednesday finally figured out what the preacher hinted at. She found her words with none of the hesitance Jacob had. "I can't marry him, preacher. He's already got a wife, and she's in a bad way."

Brother Aaron shook his Bible and his fist at the sky. "Lord, you do try me greatly sometimes. I'm not judging this sinner who takes advantage of young girls and beats his wife, but Lord, if you could strike him dead, I'll do the funeral for free."

Wednesday started giggling. Jacob had enough. He stepped forward. "I didn't take advantage of this girl, and I've never hit any woman in my life." He took a step closer to the buggy. "And only a few preachers."

Brother Aaron lowered his arms and looked at Jacob. The old man might be twice his age, but Jacob saw a challenge in his eyes.

Jacob opened his jacket so the man could see the Texas Ranger badge on his vest. "I found this girl yesterday, lost and hungry. I need your help to get her to safety before she delivers that baby."

The preacher cocked his head and looked back at heaven. "Thank you, Lord, for not listening to me." He smiled at Jacob. "How may I be of service? I believe in always helping those in need."

"If you'll let her travel in your buggy, we could make much better time." Jacob studied the buggy, hoping the rattling trap would take the weight of both the preacher and Wednesday.

The preacher nodded and offered his hand.

"And if you've got any food you'd share," Wednesday added another sentence to Jacob's request, "she'd be most grateful."

Brother Aaron looked worried, but he pulled a tin from beneath the seat.

Jacob didn't bother to ask if that was all he had. "When we get where we're going, Reverend, I'll see you're stocked for the rest of your journey."

"I'm afraid I'm on a long quest," the preacher whispered as Wednesday climbed in the buggy with his food.

"You'll have all you can carry," Jacob promised. "It'll be the least I can do to thank you. Now, if we hurry, we can be home in time to have our knees under the table for the blessing."

Brother Aaron patted Jacob's shoulder. "You're a fine man. I'll follow you."

Jacob rode far enough ahead of the buggy that Wednesday's chatter buzzed around him, but he could not make out the words. It didn't matter. In the hours he'd been with the little mother-to-be she'd repeated everything she knew at least three times. He knew all her brothers' and sisters' first names, but she wouldn't tell him their last. She also claimed she didn't remember what town was closest to their farm since her family moved often.

They stopped hourly for Wednesday to run over to the bushes, but still made it to Nell's just after sunset. When he saw her sitting on the porch, all he could think of was how she always ran toward him when she'd see him ride in. He'd grab her and swing her up and around, both of them laughing. When she'd been little, she hadn't weighed a thing. When she'd come home from school, she'd been a tall, striking lady, but she still ran to him.

She didn't run now, and his heart ached as he jumped from his horse and hurried up the walk toward her.

Nell smiled. "About time you got back."

He swung one leg over the porch railing and covered her hand with his. "You miss me?"

"Not a bit, but Marla's been tossing food out since you left. Every meal she cooks thinking, like an old cat, you're bound to show up." She leaned closer to him. "You didn't get the shooter, did you?"

He shook his head. "I picked up something along the way and had to turn around."

Nell glanced at the buggy pulling into the yard.

Jacob laced his hand in hers, thinking about how easily they'd always touched. He'd hardly been aware of it until now.

She tightened her fingers as the preacher stepped out in his black funeral coat with his Bible clutched against his chest. "You're not rushing me, Jacob. I told you I want time to make up my mind about marriage."

He laughed. "I wouldn't think of it. I met Brother Aaron along the road, and he helped me transport the little lady I came across in the woods."

The reverend helped Wednesday out of the wagon and offered his arm.

"Who is she?"

"She's lost. Her parents kicked her out. Near as I can tell, she has nowhere to go and no one to help her."

Nell grinned. "But you. You always were a sucker for trouble."

"No more than you. I remember you picked up every stray that wandered near this place when you were a kid. You even had a hospital for bunnies in the barn until one Sunday Fat Alice was short a few chickens for dinner."

Laughing, Nell agreed. "I cried for a week."

They watched Wednesday slow her progress up the walk.

Nell leaned close to him and whispered, "She's afraid."

Jacob brushed his cheek against her hair, wondering when it started smelling so good. "She should know not to be afraid of you. I told her all about you."

"She's not afraid of me. She's afraid I'll turn her away."

Nell gripped the railing and stood. "Welcome." She smiled through the pain. "Won't you both please come in? Supper is almost ready."

Jacob swung his other leg onto the porch and put his arm around her. He held her against his side so he could take some of the weight off her legs.

Nell straightened, no longer fearing she would fall as Jacob made the introductions. Then, without asking, he lifted her and carried her into the house. The preacher helped Wednesday up the steps and followed.

Jacob held Nell as she introduced Brother Aaron and Wednesday to the housekeeper, Gypsy. "Marla's in the kitchen. You'll meet her when we all gather round the table."

Wednesday's eyes were huge as she tried to look at everything in the room at once. "I've never seen so many books," she said as she peeked into first one alcove, then another. "I reckon that's why you got Mr. Harrison here for a bookkeeper."

Nell smiled. "I've had lots of time for reading lately."

As soon as Gypsy said her hellos, she went to the porch and rolled Nell's chair to the dining table. In an almost angry tone, she announced they would wait no longer, dinner was finally ready to be served.

Nell laughed as Jacob carried her to where her wheelchair waited at the head of the table. "The only person a hooker hates more than a lawman is a preacher," she whispered. "The lawman might fine her, but the preacher will get her run out of town."

Jacob turned his head so that his words brushed Nell's ear. "And both are here for dinner tonight." He smiled, deciding he liked having these conversations with Nell, like this, so close. But he couldn't help wondering why she wasn't yelling at him. Usually by the time they'd been together for five minutes one of them was angry.

He frowned. Come to think of it, the one angry was usually him.

Lowering her into her chair, he saw Randolph Harrison come out of the kitchen with a huge platter in either hand. "He's still here?"

"You asked him to stay, remember?" Nell winked. "And he's proved a great help."

Jacob forced a nod at Harrison as the man pulled out a chair for Marla.

"Thank you for staying, Harrison." Jacob offered his hand. "I'm much obliged."

"It was my pleasure." Rand's handshake was firm, but his eyes were guarded. "Miss Nell has offered me a job until she decides on my proposal."

Before Jacob could get started on reasons Harrison should withdraw his offer, Nell told him of Farrow's visit. The conversation turned to the threat on Nell's life and why Farrow wanted the Stockard place. They all talked as the preacher ate and Wednesday dozed in her chair between bites.

CHAPTER 12

AFTER SUPPER, NELL ASKED MARLA TO SHOW THEIR NEW GUEST, Wednesday May, upstairs to one of the empty rooms. The girl seemed sweet and naive, but Nell didn't miss the fear in her eyes every time someone came through the door. More had happened to her than she told Jacob.

In one way, Wednesday reminded Nell of herself. Every now and then the girl would look around the room until she located Jacob. Whether he liked it or not, he was her hero. Her place of safety. Just like he'd been for Nell all these years.

Until her mother died, Nell couldn't remember a soul paying any attention to her. She'd wandered around, learning early to stay out of everyone's way, including her mother, who drank more hours than not each day. The men who visited her mother called Nell Two Bits because for a quarter she would disappear.

She remembered thinking that her life probably wouldn't change much when she moved in with Fat Alice. But Nell hadn't planned on Sheriff Parker and Jacob Dalton taking an interest in her or on Fat Alice taking her responsibility as guardian to heart. Like all kids, she fought the changes, but Jacob was always there to set her back on the straight and narrow.

"Want me to carry you up?" Jacob broke into her thoughts. He loomed tall as a tree in front of her. He stood with his feet wide apart, his right hand resting on his gun belt, an inch from his Colt. Nell wondered if the stance had become habit or was a precaution he always took when he sensed danger near.

"No." She didn't want the day to end. A new nurse had telegrammed that she would arrive tomorrow on the noon train. Like all the others, she'd fuss over Nell and remind her not to overdo, and watch her like a hawk. But for tonight Nell tasted freedom.

She glanced around the room. Harrison had returned to his desk to work on the books. He'd had little peace to concentrate in the two days he'd been here. With three women in the house, one was always thinking of something she needed him to do. Nell had to give him credit. The man never complained. She also thought he looked a bit healthier after two days of food. She wouldn't ask about his past. It was enough that he planned to make the best of his future.

Marla was either still upstairs or she'd returned to the kitchen by the back passage. If so, she wouldn't come out until time for bed. If she did, she might have to talk to someone. So, for a few minutes, the house seemed quiet.

"Where's Gypsy?" Like a cat, Gypsy usually found her favorite chair and napped until bedtime.

"While you were saying good night to Wednesday, I shook her shoulder and told her to go to bed." Jacob smiled. "Her snoring was keeping me awake."

"And the preacher? Where did he disappear to?"

"Brother Aaron drove into town, saying he needed to check out the number of sinners about."

Nell smiled. The preacher reminded her of a painting she'd seen once of Moses. All he needed was a staff and a few inches' length on his black coat. "He'll have no trouble finding them this time of night. Parker's always complaining about how the town is filling up with trouble. Maybe, with spring, they'll find work and be gone."

Jacob looked restless. "I'm surprised we're alone. You'd think with all the strays you manage to pick up that you'd never have a minute's peace."

"Me, picking up strays?" Nell winked at him. "I seem to remember you brought the last couple in."

He didn't argue as he poked at the fire. After a long silence, he said, "I was hoping to get to talk to you, just you and me, but I can't think of the words, and I'm too tired to start an argument."

They were alone for the first time since he'd offered to marry her. She needed time to talk him out of the idea of the two of them. If he could understand her reasons, maybe they could still manage to be friends. Nell couldn't imagine what life would be like without Jacob to lean on. But, like him, she knew if either of them brought the subject up, they'd start yelling at one another, and she didn't want that either tonight. Tomorrow would be soon enough.

"How about we declare a truce for tonight?"

"I'd like that."

He paced over to the window, then stirred the fire again as if it were cold. He was not a man who took to indoors easily.

"Would you take me for a walk?" Nell startled him. "I'd like to see the stars from somewhere other than my porch or window."

He nodded. "I think that sounds like a fine idea." Without a word, he wrapped her shawl around her shoulders and lifted her out of the chair.

"I'm not sure where to touch you, Two Bits. I don't want to hurt you."

Nell laughed. "As long as you don't drop me, we're fine." She rested her head on his shoulder as he stepped off the porch and into the night. The sliver of a moon offered just enough light to see the path that led behind the house.

"Want to go to the windmill?" he whispered against her ear.

When she'd first moved in with Fat Alice, there had been so many rules, Nell had been fighting mad most of the time. Her ranger would come by the front porch, lift her onto his saddle, and head for the windmill. While his horse drank, then grazed on the buffalo grass growing knee deep by the runoff tank, she'd tell Jacob her problems.

Her ranger, she thought. That's what he'd always been. She didn't have to answer. He'd known the windmill would be the perfect spot.

The blades flashed silver across the moonlight as he climbed the incline. Water was piped downhill to the house and the garden from this spot. In the spring there were always butterflies and flowers around. But in winter, when the temperature dropped to below freezing, someone would have to climb the hill and break the ice on the tank where extra water ran off so the animals could drink. For Nell, it seemed an ever-changing place. She'd even had a bench built near the trees so she would have a calm place to read. But by the time the bench was finished, she'd learned she might never have the strength to climb the hill.

"I always liked this place," he said as he lowered her to the bench. "In daylight, you can see the town with all the people moving around, looking like toys, but at night the campfires and flickers from windows remind me of a bunch of fireflies."

"Those first few days after I was hurt, I used to dream about sitting here." She pulled her shawl tighter.

"Cold?" he asked as he straddled the bench and moved against her back.

His knees were so high, she used them as armrests. As she leaned back against his chest, his warmth surrounded her. Though they always hugged and sometimes touched, she never remembered him holding her as close as he did now. She could feel his heart beating against her shoulder.

For a while, they just enjoyed the night. The stars came out. The long whistle of the train blew below, announcing the last stop for the night. A voice carried on the air, sounding like a call, as if some mother was standing at her open door a half a mile below and yelling for her child to come in for the night.

She didn't want the peace to end, but she didn't know when she'd get another chance to talk to him alone.

"Jacob?"

"Hmm." He moved his cheek against her hair.

"We need to talk."

"All right," he answered absently as he watched a bat circle, blinking in and out of the moonlight. "How do you get your hair to smell like that?"

Nell grinned. He wasn't going to make it easy. "I order my shampoo from a place in Kansas City," she answered. "But that is not what I wanted to talk about."

He shifted. "I'm sorry to dump Wednesday and the preacher on you. I had to take her somewhere, and the preacher sort of came along. I figured he'd be on his way after supper, but it appears he plans to stay awhile."

"The preacher can take care of himself, and he's welcome to stay in the barn, but what are we going to do with the girl?"

"I'm glad you said 'we,' because I'm out of ideas."

Nell poked him in the ribs. "Your only idea was to bring her here. Not much of an idea. What was plan B, leave her in the woods for the bears?"

"No, I like bears too much for that. Though, come to think of it, she does appear to be eating enough to hibernate for a spell." He watched Nell laugh, then added, "I thought as soon as it settles down here, I'd send out a notice. Some sheriff somewhere is bound to notice one little round pregnant girl missing. Then I'm going after the father of her baby and beat him until he comes to his senses and marries her."

"Maybe she's better off without him." Wednesday refused even to tell Nell her last name, much less anything about the father of her child. "He sounds more boy than man."

"Well, from what I've heard of her parents, she's not going back to them. Any father who'd leave his child out in the middle of nowhere isn't much of a parent. She's better off without them."

"I agree, but she's too young to work and support herself, much less a baby."

Jacob fell silent for a while, then said in a low, serious tone. "Well, then I'll have to take her back to the stump where I found her."

She poked him again. "You'll do no such thing. She can stay here, at least until her parents realize they made a mistake and take her back."

"I've got to find them first," he mumbled. "It could take a while."

"I'll manage."

He closed his arms around her gently. "I had a feeling we'd figure out something. I'm glad we had time to talk it out."

"That's not what I need to talk to you about, either." She could get used to him being so close. Nell had a feeling she'd never outgrow her need to be near him.

"All right, we got all night." He brushed his arms over hers, warming away the chill with his touch. "We may not get any sleep, but holding you like this, at least I know you're safe."

She took a long breath and twisted slightly so she could see his face. Her ranger was a handsome man, even with a shadow of stubble along his jaw and his hair looking like it hadn't seen a comb all day. "Why'd you kiss me?" It hadn't been the first question she'd planned to ask. There were so many more, so much to say. But somehow, it tumbled out first.

His brows wrinkled together. "Why do you think I kissed you?"

"To irritate me," she fired. "Because you feel sorry for me. Or maybe you haven't kissed a woman in a long time and I was available. Maybe you thought Harrison was watching."

Laughing, he asked, "Do I get to answer, or just pick one?"

She waited, her head high, her gaze staring blindly at the flickering lights from town. What did it matter which one he picked? All would hurt her pride.

"All right." He sounded angry. "I could care less if Harrison, or the whole town for that matter, watched. I've kissed a few women in my time, but not one because a clock was keeping time. I wasn't even thinking about feeling sorry for you. And I never heard of a man kissing a woman to irritate her."

"Answer my question."

"I wanted to kiss you, Nell. Hell, you're a beautiful woman when you're not yelling at me. Can't a man want to kiss a beautiful woman without having to give an explanation why?" He leaned back, allowing air between them. After a minute, he added, "All right, that's a lie. You're a beautiful woman even when you are madder than the devil at me. I've been noticing that fact for a while."

"I want the truth. Stop stalling."

Jacob moved close to her once more. "I didn't want you to forget that I asked for you. I know I'm older than you, and you probably think of me as your big brother, but I don't think of you that way. Not anymore."

"Since when?"

"Since I kissed you." He laughed. "I thought I'd wake you up to a few facts, but it seems to have backfired. I was a little unprepared for how good it felt. Shocked me."

His confession surprised her. "Didn't you like kissing me?"

"I haven't thought of much else since. I liked it. Didn't you?"

Nell shrugged. "I'm not sure. It happened a little fast to form an opinion. I haven't had much practice grading kisses. I'm not even sure I'll know when a good kisser comes along. Not that it matters. The man I marry will agree that we will be wed in name only."

Jacob swore.

She turned a little more toward him, her knees bumping against his leg. "Jacob?"

"What?" He looked at her then. Even in the shadows, she felt his angry gaze on her.

"Could we try it again?"

"I don't know," he said without conviction. "Don't see much point if it's a skill you plan to abandon shortly." He leaned closer until she felt his words caress her face. "Why would you want to even bother?"

Nell closed her eyes, waiting . . . knowing that he'd grant her request.

The kiss came far softer than she'd ever thought a kiss could be. Feather light against her mouth, then drifting along her cheek, light as a wisp of hair.

"I don't want this one to be too short for you to form an opinion." His words brushed her ear a moment before his lips drifted down her throat.

He tortured her with gentle pleasure, and she memorized each sensation running through her body. This memory would have to last her a lifetime.

His whiskers tickled along her jaw as he moved once more to her mouth. This time, the kiss pressed against her lips as his arms circled round her, holding her as if she were a treasure.

"Kiss me back." His request blended between them as she opened her mouth, welcoming the taste of him.

"Stop bossing me around," she whispered against his mouth, then kissed him fully.

"You got it," he finally managed to answer.

His finger slid into her hair and tumbled the pins free. His kisses came warm and inviting, a hypnotic pleasure she'd never expected.

Finally, he pulled back just enough for her to feel the cool air between them. She fought for a moment to keep her balance, not from fear of falling off the bench but from fear of falling in love with the man who lived inside the ranger.

"Now, maybe you'll remember being kissed." He rubbed his cheek against her hair. "Did I tell you I love the way your hair smells?"

"Yes."

He brushed his lips against her ear, tickling it with his breath.

"I'm still not going to consider marrying you, Jacob Dalton."

"Yeah, I know." He moved slowly across her cheek. "But you at least are starting to see that there's a man behind the badge."

She didn't comment that for her there had always been a man behind the badge. She turned her face so that her lips were only an inch from his and waited for another kiss.

This time his mouth was familiar against hers. In the short time they'd been at the windmill he'd learned what she liked, how she liked to be kissed. Or maybe she'd simply realized that any way he kissed her was just fine.

"Again," she whispered when he pulled away.

He leaned forward, his words mixing with his kiss. "Stop bossing me around."

Then she forgot what they were talking about as she drifted in pure pleasure.

"We'd better go in," he finally whispered. "It's getting cold."

"I don't feel cold." She took a breath, trying to steady herself.

"Neither do I," he mumbled. "All the more reason to go in."

He lifted her but didn't move toward the path. She wrapped her arms around his neck and laid her head on his shoulder. There were a hundred more things they needed to talk about, but she didn't want to spoil the evening. He might not know it, but he'd given her a gift as rare as diamonds tonight.

He'd treated her like a woman.

CHAPTER 13

THE HOUSE WAS QUIET WHEN JACOB CARRIED NELL INSIDE. SOME-
one had put out all but one light, and the fireplace glowed more with
embers than a fire. Jacob, as he always did, took in his surroundings
with a glance. The one thing he'd learned to hate as a lawman was surprise, but as earlier, everything seemed in place.

Rand Harrison's night of guard duty was over. The bookkeeper had
probably moved his belongings to the loft. Now that Jacob was back,
everyone understood all men would sleep in the barn. The preacher, if
he planned to return, hadn't done so yet. They would have heard his
buggy rattling from town. Jacob couldn't help but wonder if he was saving lost souls or joining them.

"Where is everyone?" he whispered, enjoying a few more minutes
alone with Nell. "I figured someone would still be up."

"I'm sure Gypsy's snoring away. She complains about life being
hard now she has to be up before noon," Nell whispered back as if they
might be caught if they woke anyone. "Marla and Wednesday must be
upstairs. I told Marla to put the girl's room at the end of the hall where
it's quiet. The child looked so tired she slept halfway through supper."
Nell's words brushed against his ear. "Marla said she'd sleep across
from me until the next nurse arrives tomorrow."

"When's Dr. McClellan planning to come?"

"I got a note from Theda saying they would try to be here by the end of the week. They've been in Houston learning new procedures to use during surgery."

Jacob fought the urge to hold Nell tighter. "He's not thinking of operating on you, is he?"

"No. It's still too dangerous. But they will stop by on their way home. It'll be good to see them again. Did you know they married two months ago?"

Jacob laughed. "I'm not surprised. She's a good nurse, and he's the best doctor around."

"I agree. At first I was worried because the doctor in town didn't have time to check on me, but now I'm glad. Dr. McClellan is worth waiting for."

"You think a lot of him."

"I trust him."

Jacob moved as silently as he could up the stairs. He was in no hurry to leave Nell. If she'd ask him, he'd hold her like this all night. He just *thought* he'd had trouble forgetting the kiss from a few days ago. It'd take the rest of his life to forget the way she'd kissed him tonight. If she'd been any other woman . . . he corrected himself. Nell wasn't any other woman. No matter what his body told him he'd like to do with her, he never would.

He'd spent his life learning to be tough. He could stay in the saddle from dawn to dusk. He'd fight the weather and hunger if he had to. He'd even learned to work through pain and do his job. But none of that mattered right now. Because for the first time in his life, he had to figure out how to be gentle with Nell.

Hell, he thought, half the time when he touched her he was more worried about breaking her than helping her. The doctor and his bride might be right for one another, but in some ways Jacob and Nell couldn't be more wrong. He wouldn't even know how to begin to love her.

"The house is filling up." Nell's cheek brushed his jaw as she laughed, having no idea how her nearness tortured him.

He grinned, knowing she loved this little game she played of whispering.

"Before long it will be as crowded as it was in the old days."

"Half as crowded," Jacob corrected. "Only one to a bed."

They crossed the landing, and he tapped the door open with his boot. He was smiling at her and for a moment didn't see Marla sitting on Nell's bed crying. The thin woman looked like a willow rocking back and forth in sorrow.

Nell recovered first. "What is it, Marla? Has something happened?" The cook seemed to curl into a ball. Even her tears fell silently.

Jacob lowered Nell to her chair, then moved to Marla's side. "What's wrong?" He wasn't sure why he waited for an answer. The woman had never said a word to him. In fact, he'd asked the sheriff more than once if she ever talked to anyone except Nell. From what he'd seen, she had nothing much to say to even old Gypsy.

Nell's hand touched his arm, and he moved back a few feet, knowing they'd get no answers with him so near.

"Please," Nell whispered as she rolled her chair parallel with Marla. "Take your time, but tell me what has you so upset."

Marla wiped her tears.

Nell patted the cook's hand gently as she added, "Now take a deep breath, Marla, and tell me what's happened."

The frightened cook raised her head. "You've got to see it," she whispered.

Nell nodded. "All right. Show me."

The cook crossed to the door and motioned for Nell to follow. They moved silently down the hallway, with Jacob staying several steps be hind. It wasn't easy, but he tried his best to make six feet and two hundred pounds of muscle disappear.

He barely heard Marla say, "I doctored her the best I could. She wouldn't let me tell anyone, but she fell asleep, so I thought you should see."

Marla pushed open the door to what had to be Wednesday's room at the end of the hall.

Jacob heard Nell's soft cry a moment before he reached the opening and saw for himself.

Wednesday lay on her side with her back to the light, looking almost like a child in the big bed. The covers were turned down and her back exposed to the lamp's low glow.

Jacob gulped down an oath and took a step closer, wishing he could turn away. Welts crossed back and forth along her white skin. Big, bloody welts an inch wide.

He grabbed the doorframe to keep from slamming his fist into the wall. He'd grumbled about her complaining all day thinking that she must be whining. Now, he wondered how she could have stood being wedged in his saddle or even riding in a buggy.

"I had to soak most of her underthings to get them off. The blood had dried them to her skin." Marla let out a little cry. "She must have been stripped for the beating and then forced to dress without being doctored."

He made himself see all the damage. The places her young skin had been torn apart and scabbed over. The spots where yellow pus festered just beneath the surface of her flesh. The bruises that would eventually heal, the broken skin that would scar. He needed to see it all, so he could remember when he found whoever had hurt Wednesday.

Nell rolled closer and gently placed the sheet over the girl's back.

Without anyone saying a word, Marla pulled Nell's chair backward into the hallway. Jacob closed the door so softly it didn't make a sound. The three of them moved down to Nell's room.

"Who could have done that?" Nell's anger didn't surprise him. "Her father? Could he have hurt her that badly and then left her?"

Marla shook her head as she knelt in front of Nell. "I said I wouldn't tell, but I'm afraid some of the blisters are already infected, and I'm not sure what to do."

Jacob stood in the shadows by the door. With her back to him, the cook seemed to have forgotten he was there. He wanted to move closer, but he couldn't risk Marla being too shy to finish.

She continued, "I had to beg her to let me clean it. At first I thought it was only a scrape on her shoulder. I thought I'd put on a little of the cream the doctor gives me for my hands. Then I saw her back."

"Who?" Nell asked again. "Did she tell you who beat her?"

Marla's thin hands shook.

Nell's voice softened. "It's all right, Marla. We'll find whoever did this to her. What matters is that she's safe with us now. Just tell me who hurt her."

"Her stepmother," Marla cried. "Wednesday said the woman would have killed her if her father hadn't taken her away. That's why he left her in the woods, so her stepmother couldn't find her. He must have thought it was her only chance."

Nell glanced up at Jacob, tears in her eyes. "They can't come take her back, can they?"

He shook his head, knowing that legally they probably could. He wanted to find the parents, but maybe not searching would keep Wednesday safe. If he sent no telegrams out, no one would know that she was here. Nell's place wasn't on any main road. Even if the father changed his mind, he'd have a hard time tracking them here.

The lawman in him wanted to see justice, but he knew that even if he could get proof of the beating to a judge, nothing would be done. Some folks might even say that she'd given them good reason to beat her, and there was no law against disciplining children, even harshly. At most, the parents would probably be fined. Which would make them even madder at Wednesday.

He moved out of the way so that Marla could leave without looking at him. Sheriff Parker told him once that Marla grew up an only child of a widowed mother who made her living as a cook. Parker said the mother had been a bitter old woman who blamed all her troubles on men and believed a good daughter was a silent, hardworking one. Jacob felt sorry for Marla. He wondered, if in her way, she wasn't as scarred as Wednesday would be when she healed.

Jacob closed the door. "Want me to lift you into bed?"

Nell shook her head. "I'm too angry to sleep."

Jacob moved to the chair by the window. He wasn't sure it would hold his weight, so he lowered himself slowly. The thing looked more like a pillow someone had tied ribbons around and tried to make it look like a chair.

Nell rolled to the other side of a small table across from him. For a few minutes, they both watched the night sky. Neither bothered to turn on a light other than the small lantern Gypsy always left burning when she turned down the bed. But even in shadow, Jacob could see the sorrow on Nell's face.

"What do you want me to do?" He leaned forward, bracing his elbows on his knees. "I could try to find the parents. There's not much officially I could do, but I could threaten them with prison."

She reached for his hand. "Do you think they'd come for her even if they knew where she was?"

Jacob shook his head. He thought of adding that he hoped not, but things were bad enough without Nell having to worry about what might happen if they showed up.

"She can stay here with me." Nell lifted her head.

"She needs you," Jacob said. "You can offer her a safe place. Not even the law can do that."

They were silent for a while. He turned her hand over in his and brushed her palm with his thumb. He liked the way her hand fit, her long fingers lacing easily between his.

"Thank you," she said.

"For what? For bringing trouble to your door?"

"No. For letting me help. It makes me feel like, if I can do her some good, I'm not worthless."

He shifted on the frilly chair, frustrated that he couldn't say what needed saying. He stared out the window, hoping he could make her understand before he turned and looked at her. "You really have no idea how priceless you are, Nell."

Her smile was sad. "I'm afraid I'm far more aware of all the things I can't do."

"You don't realize what you do or how much you mean to so many people." He gripped the arms of her wheelchair and pulled it as close as their knees would allow.

She shrugged and didn't meet his gaze. "My money may help, but most of the time people would get along just fine without me. I offer nothing meaningful."

"Yes, you do," he answered, brushing his fingers across her jaw until she looked at him.

"Oh, yeah?" She tried to smile. "Name one."

"You offer the only beauty in my life."

Before she could respond, he kissed her lightly, then stood as if he'd shown her a side of himself he hadn't meant to.

"I'd better be getting to the barn. I want to check that gate before I turn in, and I plan to rattle every door, making sure they're all locked."

"Jacob?" He was almost across the room before her voice stopped him.

"Jacob," she said again in little more than a whisper.

He turned, figuring she'd laugh at him. He and Nell had talked more about feelings tonight than they had all the times they'd been together over ten years. At this rate he'd probably turn into a poet or some fool thing within the week.

"Thank you," she said.

"You're welcome," he answered and hurried out the door.

He was halfway down the stairs when he realized he had no idea why she thanked him or why, in hell's name, he'd said you're welcome. He should have thanked her for the evening. Sitting out by the windmill was a time he'd think about in the months ahead when he was out on the road alone. Maybe she was thanking him for the kiss.

Moving into the night air, he shook his head. She hadn't thanked him for kissing her before. And, to his surprise, it was something he was getting used to doing regularly. Before he knew it, he might just develop kissing as a habit.

Jacob smiled and ran his thumb over his lips as he walked toward the barn. The thought that kissing her might feel so right hadn't occurred to him before. He wouldn't mind it becoming a habit.

Glancing up to her window, he noticed Marla's shadow standing beside Nell's chair. They probably couldn't see him in the darkness, but he could tell they were talking, and he was glad Nell had others to worry about besides herself.

Almost to the barn, Jacob stumbled over the preacher. Like a drunken brawler, Brother Aaron came up swinging and quoting scripture.

Jacob dodged him and disappeared into the blackness. Tonight, all he wanted to do was find a quiet place to think. He'd apologize to the preacher in the morning.

CHAPTER 14

FROM THE LANDING AT THE TOP OF THE STAIRS, NELL STARED DOWN at the open room below. Her dining table, to the left of the study, was already loaded down with breakfast. On Mondays, Marla always made pecan pancakes. Gypsy and the cook usually took their breakfast in the kitchen, and Nell ate her meals by the window in her bedroom. Only today, and every day that she could from now on, Nell promised herself she'd dress and eat downstairs. At least while she had someone to carry her to ground level.

This morning, Marla filled the table with dishes for company, extra bowls of eggs, ham, and bread just in case her pancakes weren't hardy enough. She'd left a chair empty and made gravy, knowing the sheriff would probably show up.

Mr. Harrison had already taken his seat at one end of the table. He studied the paper as though he found it fascinating. Nell noticed he glanced up and smiled when Marla refilled his coffee. Nell couldn't tell if Marla raised her head enough to smile back. Harrison's shirt looked freshly washed, and Nell guessed Marla had done it for him late last night, then dried it by the stove.

Nell listened as the preacher told Gypsy about his fight with the devil in the dark. The old man reminded her of an actor onstage making his words come alive. Gypsy stared at him with wide, almost colorless eyes.

"He came at me while I was sleeping beneath the stars," Brother

Aaron's voice rose, "with eyes as red as fire and smoke coming out of his nose. The first thing he did was strike me with his head. I'm sure he thought to kill me with one blow. Rage circled like a storm around him when he noticed I didn't die, and he hurried off, hoping to escape before I woke up enough to fight back."

"I think I've seen that fellow you're talking about," Gypsy answered as she leaned on the corner of the dining table while the preacher pulled out one of the chairs. "He used to come in some nights, back years ago. Big guy with meanness scribbled all over him."

The preacher was far more interested in his story than in her comments. "He must have been ten foot tall and broad as a door." Brother Aaron waved his hands wildly. "He was out to get me, I tell you. If I'd have been a weaker man, I'd have died of pure fright." The reverend raised his shaggy white hair to reveal a knot on one side of his forehead. "But I'm stronger than he thought. I lived through the war, and the devil will have to send an army if he plans to take me away from my quest of saving sinners."

Harrison raised his gaze from the paper he'd been reading, and the preacher's voice grew louder to include the swelling crowd. "Lord . . ." Brother Aaron looked to heaven. "I'm ready to come home whenever you call me, but I'll not let the devil draw me down. This warrior of your word will fight as long as there is breath in me. I'll give up sleep if I have to so the devil will not be able to come on me unannounced."

Gypsy glanced up as if expecting to see who he was talking to.

"Lord," Brother Aaron continued, "I know the devil got a hold on me because of the drink, and I'm mighty sorry about that. But I swear to you, just like I did back in Abilene, that I'll never touch Satan's nectar again."

In confusion, Gypsy's brow creased into a hundred wrinkles.

"Liquor," Harrison clarified, looking slightly bored.

She nodded and turned back to the preacher. "Did the devil get you drunk before or after he tried to kill you?"

Her question pulled the preacher out of his conversation with the Almighty. "That's it!" he shouted. "I would never have taken a drink if it had not been the devil offering it to me. He must have been planning to kill me and put the drink in front of me so I'd be too blind to see his plot. Oh, he's far more evil than even I thought. Drink made me let down my guard."

"I've said the same thing myself on occasion." Gypsy offered the preacher a cup. "You want a little hair of the dog in this coffee? I keep a bottle in the kitchen for breakfast and mornings after I've had a hard night fighting the devil."

Jacob opened the door and entered as the preacher pushed back from the table and jumped up. "Get thee behind me, Satan!"

Gypsy looked around him. Then she smiled at the ranger, her attention redirected. "Morning, Dalton, you want coffee?"

Jacob pulled up a chair next to Harrison. Both men nodded their greeting.

Harrison pointed with his coffee. "The reverend was telling us that he ran into the devil last night in the dark outside the barn."

Nell laughed from above. Mr. Harrison wasn't buying into the preacher's story, but Gypsy circled the old man asking to see the bump again. She wanted to touch where the devil hit him.

Jacob didn't comment but stood and walked to the bottom of the stairs. "Are you ready to come down?" He grinned. "I'd be honored to escort you."

"Yes, please," she answered and watched him take the stairs two at a time. "I'm afraid I might miss some of the reverend's story."

"I doubt that it's possible for anyone within a hundred yards to miss his sermon. I heard his story from the road."

When he lifted her out of the chair and into his arms, she brushed his sand-colored hair off his forehead and noticed a bruise at the hairline. "You have a run-in with the devil as well?"

He winked. "I'll never tell."

As he carried her down, the preacher whirled around with his eyes closed, his great black coat flying like wings. "I understand, Lord. I get the message. You're speaking to me loud and clear. The path is before me, and I'll not hesitate. You've brought me to this place for a reason."

Everyone waited, having no doubt the preacher would tell them the news when he finished. Jacob reached the bottom of the stairs but made no effort to cross the room.

Brother Aaron opened his eyes and smiled at Nell. "The Lord hath made it plain to me that I'm needed here, and here I'll stay until my work is done."

Jacob frowned. "You wouldn't know how long this tour of duty will be, do you, Reverend?"

The old man shook his head and returned to his place at the breakfast table. "A man builds up a powerful hunger talking to the Lord."

Nell patted the ranger's shoulder. "I've room for one more. At least for a while. There's plenty of hay in the loft, and I can afford the food."

"I'd argue, after listening to him snore half the night," Jacob whispered. "But another gun might come in handy if our night shooter returns."

"You think Brother Aaron would kill someone?" Nell whispered as Jacob slowly crossed the room with her.

He turned so that his lips brushed her ear as he answered, "The old man told me yesterday at one of our many rest stops that he fought under General Lee during the war. He said he was with the man from secession to surrender. Told me he was shot three different times. The last time he was in an army hospital for six months. That's when he decided, if he lived, he'd head west, spreading the word to sinners. He planned to work his way to California, but Texas has kept him busy for twenty years."

Nell looked at the reverend again with renewed respect. "You think he's telling the truth?"

"About the war, yes." Jacob was so close he could have kissed her cheek with little effort. "About the devil living in Texas? No."

Nell brushed Jacob's hair back once more, fighting the urge to kiss his bruise. "I'm not so sure. There are sides of you, Jacob Dalton, that I didn't know existed. It might be interesting to see if there is a halo or horns beneath all that hair."

"Does that mean you'll reconsider my offer of marriage?"

"If I do, will you agree that if I don't pick you as my husband, you'll be nice to the one I do choose?"

He frowned. "I don't like the idea that someone else is even in the running."

"Jacob, you're not in the running unless you agree." She saw a fire deep in his eyes and knew she'd put it there.

"All right," he agreed, still holding her gaze. "How about I agree that I won't kill him? Would that be enough? I don't know that I can go so far as being nice. It goes against my nature."

She laughed. "Fair enough."

He walked slow enough that Gypsy had time to bump the wheelchair down the stairs. Jacob sat Nell at the head of the table, and they both turned to watch Wednesday slowly making her way toward them. The journey wasn't easy for someone who couldn't see her feet.

"How's our little pregnant weekday?" Jacob asked.

"Much better today, I think." Nell smiled as the girl waddled along. Wednesday wore a morning shift, the kind women often wore around the house when no company was expected. Nell had ordered the thing months ago, thinking she'd like it, but she'd never worn it. The garment reminded her of something halfway between a dress and a gown, not dressy enough to be seen in public, not comfortable enough to sleep in. However, now that she saw it on a pregnant woman, Nell was glad she hadn't thrown the dress away. Wednesday must have hemmed it up a foot to make it fit her height.

The little mother-to-be reached the bottom of the stairs, took a deep breath, and hurried across the room as Marla set the girl's milk on the table. "Morning, Ranger." Wednesday took a drink of the milk and left a thin white line on her upper lip. "You were right; I slept like a log in your wife's house."

"Wife?" Nell asked Wednesday, but watched Jacob. "Moving a little fast, Dalton? I just agreed to consider your offer two minutes ago."

"I may have jumped the gun, but I didn't really say we were married. She misunderstood."

"But . . ." Wednesday started.

"Lord!" The preacher raised his hands and shouted to the ceiling. "You've placed me in a house of wayward souls." He looked around the table. "Is no one married at this table?"

Silence. Marla slipped into her place with her head down. Wednesday seemed busy filling her plate with eggs. Harrison looked like he'd lost interest in the conversation, and Jacob frowned, as usual.

"No," Gypsy finally spoke. "But I'm willing if you're offering, preacher. I've always had a fancy for white-haired men."

Nell fought down a giggle. In her day Gypsy had a fancy for all men with hair, and a few without, but that was the past, and the house was respectable now. "Brother Aaron, the men sleep in the barn."

He raised his fork. "And the devil lies between them and the women."

"Maybe that's why we need you, Reverend," Harrison said calmly. "To act as chaperone."

"What's a chaperone?" Gypsy asked as she poured cream gravy over her pancakes.

Brother Aaron grinned. "That, Mr. Harrison, will be my mission. I'll guard the virtues of these fair ladies with my life."

"It's a little late for me." Wednesday downed half her milk. "But I thank you for the offer."

"Not for me." Gypsy smiled. "I've been waiting years for someone to guard my virtues."

Nell had never felt so much like laughing since her accident. She glanced across the table and met Jacob's gaze. To her surprise, he winked at her. She couldn't help but wonder if the devil in the darkness Brother Aaron had fought with last night might be planning to get past the guard tonight.

She smiled back, thinking how nice sitting with him out by the windmill had been.

He'd done it again, she thought. He'd made her feel like a woman. Only now she knew a secret that she hadn't guessed before. Maybe she was the one who made him feel like a man.

Lively conversation whirled over breakfast. Harrison, now that Jacob had returned, could get on with taking care of Nell's books. The first thing he wanted to do was ride out to the Stockard place. Walter Farrow would be showing up again any day, and he'd expect Nell to have a price ready.

Remembering Farrow's threat killed her appetite. Nell didn't like the man, but that wouldn't keep her from selling him the land if it truly was no good for ranching or farming. Sheriff Parker told her once that outlaws sometimes hung out at Stockard's place. It was hard to reach, so lawmen didn't often make the trip out that far from town. Stockard's cabin had been built on a hill, not down in the valley where it would be safe from the weather. Parker said by the time he could ride up to the front door, anyone could have seen him coming far enough away to be long gone out the back.

Even the man who'd ambushed her, Zeb Whitaker, was reported to have spent a winter hiding out there. Zeb had been an old buffalo hunter who, once the herds were gone, had made his living robbing folks. Talk was, years ago he'd killed a man and stolen two saddlebags full of gold. Only while he tried to get away, his horse broke a leg. Zeb found himself on the run and on foot. After walking for two days, he passed a wagon with three young women in it. He decided to just take their wagon, claiming they were near dead anyway.

He probably would have gotten away, but he picked the youngest one to take with him as a bed warmer. Lacy, Nell's best friend, hadn't been any older than Wednesday at the time. Angered, the women fought back, clubbing the old buffalo hunter and leaving him for dead. When he came to, his gold was gone.

Nell knew all three women, and she believed none of them took the gold, but Zeb kept trying to track them down and get it back. Or maybe, as one of the women once told Nell, Zeb just needed someone to hate, and he picked them to blame for all his troubles.

Smiling at Jacob, Nell remembered how he'd shot Zeb. The ranger had been there for her and her friends the night Whitaker had thought to kill them all.

"What's so funny?" Jacob asked.

Everyone else at the table seemed too busy eating to respond.

"Nothing," she said. "We'll talk about it later."

Jacob nodded. She didn't miss the promise in his eyes.

Harrison stood and picked up his plate. "I'd better be on my way if I want to get to the Stockard place and back by dark. The sheriff said this morning he'd ride out in his buggy as far as the road goes, then I'll make the rest of the trail alone."

"I'd like to go with you," Jacob said.

Both men glanced at Nell. There was no need for more conversation on the matter. They both knew someone had to stay near her.

Harrison raised an eyebrow as he said, "You'll stay with her until I get back?"

Jacob nodded, recognizing his own words. "I'll be here until you return."

A few minutes later, Jacob and the preacher followed the bookkeeper out while Marla and Gypsy cleaned the table. Nell, for lack of anything else to do, showed Wednesday the material she'd ordered all the way from Kansas.

"I can sew," Wednesday volunteered. "My ma says I sew better than anyone in my family, including my grandma."

"Would you like to help me put a quilt together?" Nell asked. "Quilting is something I can do from this chair."

"I wouldn't mind." Wednesday seemed happy to find some way she could be of help.

"Anything else you'd like to make, you're welcome to the material. I think I've ordered far too much."

"You mean it?"

Nell smiled. "I mean it."

An hour later, Wednesday and Nell were having a great time. Gypsy finished her chores and sat nearby. Her hands were too crippled up with arthritis to sew, but she seemed to enjoy the company. Within minutes, she fell asleep in her favorite chair.

The preacher returned, claiming the sunny day was getting the better of him. He walked around picking up first one book, then another, until he finally settled on the newspaper Harrison had been reading at breakfast.

He walked out to the porch, reading as he moved.

Nell wasn't surprised to see that he'd strapped an old Walker Colt to his side. She guessed Jacob had talked to him about the danger the women faced.

Around midmorning, Marla brought tea and stayed to join them for a cup. Brother Aaron took his to the porch.

Though Marla could cook anything, she couldn't sew. Her dresses were store-bought, and most were worn thin from washing. She seemed fascinated with the way quilt pieces fit together.

Wednesday hadn't lied about her skills. Her short little fingers worked a needle faster than Nell had ever seen, and her stitches were straighter than any sewing machine could have made. The girl never seemed to look at her hands as she talked and worked nonstop.

"How'd you learn to do that?" Nell finally asked.

"It was either sew or go outside and work in the field." Wednesday didn't look up from her work as she squared the corners where two pieces slipped together perfectly. "As I got better, I found out I really liked it." She leaned closer to Nell. "I could make Mr. Harrison a new shirt out of this cotton, if you like. He's about the size of my second brother, so I don't need to measure."

"All right." Nell wondered what it was about Harrison that made the women want to take care of him. She knew they all liked the ranger, but Marla hadn't asked to wash Jacob's clothes, and Wednesday hadn't offered him a shirt. Even Gypsy was always filling Mr. Harrison's cup and slicing him an extra-large dessert. Nell stopped sewing. Hadn't she done the same thing? She'd offered him a job when she knew he needed one.

She grinned. It's a wonder the man wasn't the best-dressed, richest, fattest man in Texas if all women reacted to him the way they had. She couldn't put her finger on what it was about him that drew women. He was polite, a little standoffish. Quiet, but when he talked, it seemed like he'd been asked to swear on a Bible to whatever he said. His only passion was his work, which he couldn't wait to get back to. In three days she'd learned to trust him. He was a fine man.

The games she'd played with Jacob when she kissed him needed to stop. Nell had to be sensible. Jacob was a man full of life. He needed a wife who could love him with a wildness of passion she'd never be able to offer with her light kisses. Mr. Harrison would much better suit her as a husband. He knew business and figures. If she married Jacob, he'd be constantly torn between riding off to do his duty and staying home to help her. Harrison was looking for the security of a home and a business that needed work. Jacob would see the same fate as a prison.

Accidentally stabbing her finger, Nell fought to keep from swearing. The hurt inside was far deeper than the prick. She had to think with her head, not her heart. She remembered how one of her teachers used to say that knowing what was right and doing what was right don't always run on the same track.

Well, she knew what was right for Jacob, and that was for him to walk away from her and get on with his life.

The clank of Sheriff Parker's wagon drew her attention. Thankful for the distraction, she asked Wednesday to open the door so she could greet him on the porch. She hadn't expected him back until near suppertime, but maybe he picked up more mail after he saw Mr. Harrison to the turnoff to the Stockard place.

His old wagon rattled and squeaked so loudly she thought she could hear it coming almost from the time the sheriff left town. She waited on the porch for him.

As soon as he came into sight, Nell knew something was wrong. "Wednesday!" Nell tried to keep her voice calm. "Would you go find Jacob and tell him I need him as soon as possible?"

Wednesday looked confused but waddled off toward where Jacob had been working with the horses in a field past the barn. They'd all seen him from the window earlier.

Brother Aaron stood from the porch swing and moved to Nell's side. Without taking his attention off the approaching wagon, he whispered, "He's moving too slow not to be trying to transport something lightly. I fear we have trouble arriving."

"I know," Nell answered, straining to see if it could be Randolph Harrison riding in the buckboard. The bookkeeper said he was meeting Parker. She calculated the hours. Three, maybe four, since Mr. Harrison left. He'd had time to reach town and from there ride out to the turnoff to the Stockard place. But, she reasoned, he hadn't had time to get there and back. If Harrison was in the wagon, something had happened to him before he got to the Stockard place. But what?

The only enemy she could think Harrison might have would be Walter Farrow, and he could handle himself well enough to stay out of the bossy man's way. Also, even if they met in town, Farrow seemed more like a man who might take an enemy to court, not call him out.

The sheriff drove as if trying to make the trip as easy as possible on his cargo.

"Can you see anything?" she asked Brother Aaron.

The preacher shielded his eyes. "There's something in the back, but

I can't tell what. I'll go down and open the gate so he doesn't have to stop."

Nell tried to remember to breathe as the sheriff pulled his wagon up in front of the house. She could see blankets in the back. And a body, covered completely. It had to be a body.

Grabbing the railing, Nell forced herself to stand. She'd forgotten to lock the chair, and it rolled backward, but she hardly noticed. "Mr. Harrison," she whispered. If he were dead, it would all be her fault. He wouldn't have been checking the ranch if she hadn't asked him.

Out of the corner of her eye she saw Jacob running toward the wagon. He must have come to the same conclusion.

"Morning," Parker said. The sheriff smiled as if nothing were wrong.

Jacob reached him. "What is it?"

Parker lowered himself from the bench seat. "Oh, nothing much. I just thought I'd bring out the new nurse."

Nell almost collapsed. It wasn't Randolph Harrison.

Jacob leaned into the buckboard. "Is she alive?"

Parker laughed. "I wouldn't bring you a dead one, now would I?"

The ranger didn't look like he appreciated the joke.

Throwing back the blanket, the sheriff added, "There was a train robbery northwest of Fort Worth this morning. I didn't get a lot of the details. Got my deputies collecting statements now. But from what I gathered, the passengers decided to buy samples from a liquor sales-man so they could steady their nerves. Drunkest bunch of folks I ever saw arrived on the noon train. I couldn't just leave a snoring woman laid out on the platform, so I brought her here."

"Lord! Lord!" the preacher yelled. "The devil's taken to riding trains."

CHAPTER 15

The nurse slept in the back of the sheriff's wagon like a logger after a hard winter. Jacob placed the blanket back over her face to muffle the sound. "She seems fine," he yelled at Nell, who stood watching from the porch.

Sheriff Parker grinned and whispered to Jacob, "If this were one of them fairy tales, she'd be Sleeping Ugly."

"How long has she been out?" Jacob swore he could smell her breath through the quilt covering her.

"Ever since I picked her up. She was the only single woman that got off, or rather got carried off, the noon train. I figured she had to be the nurse that Nell sent for to replace Mary Ruth."

Jacob tried to judge her weight by the bump she made in the blanket. He'd guess her almost double Nell's width, but the woman would be shorter by a head.

The sheriff read his mind. "We could let her sleep it off in the barn. I could borrow one of Nell's wagons for the ride back to town." He tried to make himself not sound like a coward. "It don't seem fair to wake a woman up after all she's been through this morning."

"Maybe we'd better ask Nell. I have no idea what to do with a drunk nurse." Jacob glanced toward the porch in time to see Nell start to crumple, her hands peeling away from the railing as she fell.

He ran around the wagon and was halfway up the walk when her legs no longer held her. She was alone. No one stood near enough to help.

Panic gripped his heart as he watched her melt like a rag doll. At first she seemed to drift to the planks. Then he heard her head hit the wood, a hollow, sickening sound. He would have taken a bullet not to have seen her fall.

In what seemed like a heartbeat, he leaned over her and lifted her into his arms. "Two Bits," he whispered, wishing her eyes would open. "Nell, are you all right? Answer me!"

She didn't move.

Suddenly, everyone surrounded him, buzzing like flies, asking questions, trying to get closer, trying to help. He didn't care what they had to say. He held Nell as gently as he could in his arms and stood. The only voice he wanted to hear was hers.

"Get her upstairs," Gypsy ordered. "I'll get cold towels. She always bumps her head when she falls."

"Should I go for the doctor?" Parker asked. "I could toss the nurse out of the buckboard and make it back in minutes."

"You know he wouldn't come." Gypsy swore beneath her breath. "That's why Dr. McClellan wants her to have a nurse. He knows the town doc never has the time to care."

Wednesday started crying as she waddled back and forth across the porch like a windup toy. The girl was starting every sentence with "I should have . . ."

Jacob knew he had to do something, anything, fast.

"Gypsy, soak towels in well water. That should be cold enough. I think you're right; she did hit the back of her head." He turned toward the entrance. "Wednesday, hold the door and then find Marla." He looked at Parker. "Help me get her upstairs, Sheriff."

Everyone ran at once, glad to have something to do besides panic. Parker walked ahead of Jacob as if clearing a path. Everyone but Gypsy climbed the stairs in slow motion.

About the time they reached her room, Nell moved in his arms, moaning as she reached for her head. Jacob took the first deep breath since he'd seen her fall. He rolled her slightly so that her head rested against his heart. "You all right?"

She rubbed her face against his chest. "I think so," she whispered as he laid her down on top of her bed. "What happened?"

He knelt on one knee. "You about scared the hell out of me! You should have . . ."

She closed her eyes and moaned in pain. He forgot what he'd been about to say.

The human flies were back, buzzing around Nell, taking off her shoes, pulling the pins from her hair, covering her with blankets, putting a cold rag behind her head. Suddenly everyone had something to do but Jacob.

Jacob stepped back, feeling helpless.

The sheriff lit the fire in her small fireplace as if there were a chill in the air.

Jacob crossed to the windows, surprised at how anger had replaced fear. He couldn't believe he wanted to yell at Nell for falling. Why had she stood in the first place? Didn't she know how fragile she was? Couldn't she think ahead? She might have been really hurt in a fall. Hell, she might be hurt right now for all he knew. Gypsy had said something about Nell usually bumping her head. Didn't the woman learn anything?

He stared out the window, forcing himself to calm. Yelling at Nell would do no good. What kind of fool gets mad at the fool who lets herself get hurt? They were dueling idiots.

Jacob watched the preacher help an unsteady nurse out of the back of the wagon as Brother Aaron tried to introduce himself to a drunk. She seemed more interested in straightening her hat than in talking to anyone.

"Are you married, woman?" Brother Aaron bellowed in his town hall meeting voice.

The stout woman in her forties nodded. "I've been wed three times and widowed three times." She hiccuped and tried to keep her words from slurring together. "I took care of them all until they decided to go meet their maker. When the last one died, I decided I might as well take up nursing. It already seemed my chosen occupation."

The preacher bowed. "It appears, madam, we are in the same business. We're both sending souls to heaven."

She took his arm and let him lead her up the walk. Just before they disappeared from view, Jacob heard the preacher ask the nurse if she'd like a cup of coffee before she went up to meet Miss Nell.

Jacob thought that would be a great idea. What good would a drunken nurse do Nell now? He'd already decided to tell Nell to send her back on the afternoon train. He smiled, remembering the preacher's night out and Gypsy's drinking almost every Friday night. They already had their quota of drunks around the place. The nurse would have to look for employment somewhere else.

He glanced back at Nell. A tiny blue bottle rested on her nightstand. Jacob knew what it was: opium. He wanted to ask how much she took each day, but his question could wait. Right now he was just happy to see she wasn't reaching for the bottle in pain.

Gypsy rolled the wheelchair in and shoved it near the window so it would be out of the way. When she passed him, the little woman patted his arm. Her light blue eyes were filled with tears. "She's going to be all right, Ranger. Just took a fall, that's all." He wasn't sure if she said the words to him or to herself. "I've tumbled down the stairs twice in the last year and look at me."

He'd rather not, so he pointed with his head toward the bottle. "How often does she take that stuff?"

"She is not deaf," Nell answered before Gypsy could say a word.

Jacob smiled, but his words sounded harsh. "Well, it's surprising, because she's certainly dumb."

Gypsy darted out of the way as if expecting something to fly between them at any moment. "I'll be in the kitchen helping Marla if you need me."

The sheriff ushered Wednesday out. "We'd best get downstairs. Miss Nell is fine; she needs a little rest," he said, sounding almost as if he knew what he was talking about. "You'll call us, Dalton, if she needs anything."

Jacob walked over to the door and slammed it closed. "I've got a few words to say to you, and now's as good a time as any."

Nell rose to her elbows. "I'm not listening to anything when you talk to me in that tone. Go away. I have a headache." She closed her eyes as if to make him disappear.

Jacob crossed to her bed and sat down beside her. "You'll listen to me if I have to tie you to the bed."

She opened one eye as she folded her arms across her chest. "All right, Dalton, say what you have to say."

"I don't want you thinking you can stand when no one is near to catch you. I want you to promise me you'll not try. Promise me there will be no repeat of what I saw today." He took a deep gulp of air, wondering if she had any idea how close she'd come to scaring him to death. He'd rather face down a band of horse thieves than see her fall again. "You are never to do such a thing again."

"Or," she said calmly.

Or I'll what? he thought. She was too old to threaten. Too much a woman to punish. In a way what she'd done had been what she had always done. She'd taken a risk. He realized he loved and hated the same thing about her. She wouldn't be Two Bits if she wasn't a fighter, and a fighter would never accept being tied to a wheelchair, even if it meant that every time she stood, she took the chance of falling.

"End of discussion," he said, realizing he was making no sense. Her half of the argument had been one word. What bothered him most was that she'd won.

When he turned away, wanting to disappear before he made an even bigger fool of himself, she reached out and gripped his hand. He froze, not knowing how he'd explain his actions if she asked him to. How could he explain how much she meant to him?

"Jacob, I'm all right. I've got a bump on my head. That's all." To his surprise, she smiled at him. "I know you're worried, but I'm fine. We all get bumps from time to time." She brushed the bruise on his forehead.

He leaned down, his face only a few inches from her. "I was . . ." He couldn't find a word that expressed how he'd felt. He was not a man to admit to being frightened.

Her fingers brushed across his hair. "I know."

Jacob told himself he wouldn't get so close to her again. Last night had to be a onetime thing. She'd made it plain she wanted a husband in name only. "Do you have any idea how beautiful you look?" The words were out before he could stop them. He closed the distance between them and brushed his mouth lightly over hers. As she lifted slightly and kissed him back, their bodies touched.

He leaned lower, pressing his chest against the softness of her breasts. He could feel her heart pound as he tasted her lips once more, and her mouth opened in invitation. She wasn't going to make the "in name only" part easy for him, but he decided he'd take all the punishment he could before complaining.

She felt so right against him. Like a part of him had always been missing. He breathed her in, filling his lungs with the fragrance that was only Nell. Wildflowers, he thought. She smelled of wildflowers.

For a moment, she clung to him, drawing him closer; then she moved her hand from his hair and gently tried to push him away.

Jacob resisted, wanting more. The slight pressure against his shoulder was featherlight. He could ignore it. This was what he wanted. What they both wanted.

Then he realized what he'd been about to do and straightened. It took a while for his pulse to calm, for him to be able to look at her without passion in his eyes. "Are you all right? I didn't hurt you, did I?"

"You didn't hurt me," she answered, but her smile was sad. "I don't think we should be doing this . . ."

"Right," he answered not needing to hear the rest. *Of course we shouldn't.* How could he expect her to consider marrying him if he wasn't going to follow her first rule? Marriage in name only. She wanted his name, not his love. If a fall could almost kill her, what might lovemaking do?

He stood and did his best to smile before he left the room. It didn't surprise Jacob to find Gypsy outside the door.

The old woman started past him. "I'll set with her while she's resting," Gypsy whispered. "No matter how she hurts, it won't be long before she wants to get back up."

"You'll call me." Jacob felt helpless. "I'll carry her down."

Gypsy nodded. "You go down and try to sober that nurse up." She reached for the door, then glanced back. "And try not to scare her off before Nell gets a chance to talk to her. The nursing school told us they were scraping the bottom of the barrel to find one more graduate willing to come. The only reason we got this one was because she's so old none of the hospitals wanted to hire her."

Jacob walked down the stairs thinking they hadn't even had lunch yet, and he'd already had enough excitement for one day.

One look at Sheriff Parker's face told Jacob he was mistaken.

CHAPTER 16

Jacob saddled his horse. Every bone in his body wanted to stay with Nell, but duty called. When he'd signed on with the Texas Rangers he'd sworn to protect all the citizens, not just one, and if he didn't do his job now, more would die.

"You'll check on her." He shot the sheriff a grim look. "Twice, maybe three times a day?"

"She'll be all right. You've got your hands full of worry already." Parker reassured Jacob for the tenth time. "She's surrounded by women, plus she's got Harrison and Brother Aaron to look after her. Near as I can tell, everyone in this house is armed, so don't go thinking someone will just walk in and harm them."

"Maybe she'd be safer in town?"

Parker shook his head. "She wouldn't go, even if we both ganged up on her and demanded it. This is her home. How do you think folks are going to react if Nell moves all her gang to town?"

Jacob knew. Most folks wouldn't speak to Marla, much less Gypsy. They'd treat Harrison and the preacher like strangers. There wasn't a hotel big enough to hold them all, or that would let the men stay close enough to the women to be of any good if trouble came. Wednesday would be stared at. And worst of all, they'd pity Nell. She'd hate that.

Parker was right. She'd be safer here. "I wish I didn't have to leave," he said aloud. "It's been quiet for two nights, but that's no guarantee. I should have caught the shooter. Then all this worry over Nell would be over."

"You tried, son. That's the best you can do."

"I don't feel right leaving her."

The sheriff nodded. "I know, but there is no one who can do the job you can for fifty miles around. You're trained. If anyone can track the robbers, you can. You have to go."

He flipped open the telegram he'd received while Jacob had been upstairs. "The marshal out of Denton says they're headed this way. From all accounts there were six outlaws, all fully armed. If they get past us and into the Oklahoma Indian Territory, we'll lose them for sure."

Jacob strapped on his gear. "I know." He didn't need convincing. He knew his job. But for once, he wanted to complain a little.

Parker rubbed his face with the palm of his hand. "I didn't tell you all the facts this morning when I brought the nurse in. I didn't want to talk about it with the women around." He took a deep breath. "They killed six, maybe eight people this morning in the train robbery. It's no wonder everyone still riding came in drunk. I don't know how bad it was. They found six bodies where the gang stopped the train and another two men wounded but still breathing."

Jacob closed his eyes, not wanting to see in his mind what the sheriff described.

"Philip ran the telegram out as soon as it came in. He said he'd been listening to some of the other passengers' stories. One told about how the guards inside the mail car refused to open up once the train stopped. He said the gang pulled one after another of the passengers off the train and shot them in the head with each minute that passed before the guards opened up. They'd killed four before they killed the two guards." Parker looked like he was about to cry. "The last one killed before the guards gave in was a woman."

Jacob pressed his forehead against his horse's neck. He had to go. He had to leave Nell. And somehow, he had to stop the gang before they reached the border. Men like these couldn't be allowed to roam. This would be only the first of many stories if he didn't stop them.

"Ranger?" came a soft voice from the barn opening.

He looked up to see Marla standing several feet away. "Yes?" If she'd come out to the barn and spoken, she must need something important.

"I packed you supplies again." She didn't look at him as she held out a burlap bag.

He walked to the opening. "Thanks."

She disappeared a moment after he took the bag. Jacob smiled. At least he was making progress with one woman in the house. Marla had talked to him.

He turned to the sheriff. "Ask Rand Harrison to stay on the grounds once he gets back from the Stockard place."

"I will." Parker nodded. "I already told the preacher that if I see him in town I'll shoot him."

Jacob smiled. "That should keep him sober."

He handed the reins of his horse to Parker. "I'll only be a minute. I have to say good-bye to Nell."

Parker twisted the leather between his fingers. "She'll worry about you. She always does."

As Jacob walked to the house he thought about what Parker said. He would have never guessed Nell gave him more than a passing thought when he was out of her sight. She always looked glad to see him, but she'd never written saying that she missed him, even when he'd been away for weeks at a time.

When he entered the house, he wasn't surprised to see that she was up and waiting. He climbed the stairs. "How you feeling?"

"You're leaving, aren't you."

He nodded. "I have to."

"I know." She raised her arms.

He lifted her from the chair. "I'll carry you down one last time before I go. The nurse should be sober enough to carry you up tonight, or Rand will be home and he and Marla can do it."

She nodded, looking like she might cry.

He started down the stairs. "Promise me one thing, Nell. Promise you won't marry anyone until I get back. I don't know how long this will take, but I don't want to have to worry about you going crazy and marrying while I'm gone."

He expected her to remind him that she wasn't going to marry him, but instead she whispered, "I promise you'll be at my wedding. But do me a favor and come back safe and sound."

"It's only one band of outlaws." He managed to look offended that she'd even worry.

She smiled. "That's right, only one."

When they reached the bottom of the stairs, Jacob would have liked to kiss her good-bye, but everyone in the house except the snoring nurse on the couch watched. So he lowered her carefully and whispered, "When I get back, I plan to take you for a walk by the windmill again."

"I'll plan on it."

He kissed her cheek. When he straightened, Gypsy handed him his hat. He shoved the Stetson low and turned to the others. "Take care of Nell until I get back, or I'll . . ."

"We know," Gypsy snapped. "Or you'll shoot us all."

Jacob frowned. "The way this house is growing, I may have to reload," he mumbled. He'd become far too predictable. He stomped out of the house and down the walk. He wouldn't be able to leave if he looked back and saw tears in Nell's eyes.

Swinging onto his horse, Jacob saluted the sheriff, telling himself Nell wouldn't be crying for him.

After two days in the barn, Dusty was ready to run, and Jacob ate up the miles as he rode due east. If the outlaws were heading north, they'd have to cross paths. He'd spent years learning all he could about tracking. They wouldn't get by him. He had no idea how many were in the gang. The report mentioned there might be six. It didn't matter. He would have to stop them. There was no time to get more lawmen in the area, and if he'd brought someone like Harrison or one of Parker's deputies along, that would only be someone he'd have to watch out for.

Just before nightfall, he stopped on a ridge where he could see for miles in every direction. If the gang was riding hard, they'd stir up enough dust to be noticeable. If they stopped, he'd see their fires. He listed the facts he'd pieced together from the little he knew. First, they would own fast horses if they robbed a train, and be accomplished riders. Next, if two men guarded the mail car, there must have been something valuable inside. So the gang would be burdened with at least one, or maybe two pack animals. Probably mules. Their tracks would be easy to spot on the flat, dusty land he covered.

He'd crossed this part of the country several times. Near the Red River there were several spots to cross into Indian Territory, but a hundred miles south, the land was unpredictable. Unless the men knew the terrain, they'd probably stay close to one of the old cattle drive trails. They'd make faster time that way, and this time of year the chances of running into anyone were slight.

Jacob also knew one other fact. Whoever he was looking for wasn't some group of boys or down-on-their-luck farmers trying to get rich quick. These men, or at least some of them, were hardened killers. They were men who placed no value on life. They didn't get that way from their first robbery or murder. That kind of killing was burned into a man. He'd be willing to bet that most of the gang had already served time in jail, maybe more than once. If so, they'd have a hatred of lawmen built over time.

Pulling his badge from his vest, he slipped it into where he'd cut the stitching on his saddle a month after he'd bought it. If he ran into the gang, it might buy him a little time if they thought he was just a cowhand and not a ranger.

Watching the sky, he leaned back against his saddle. His muscles ached. The cold night air seeped into his bones, but he wouldn't light a fire. He ate a biscuit in the dark and took a long drink from his canteen. After midnight, clouds moved in, and he pulled his blanket over his shoulders and closed his eyes.

But sleep eluded him. Nell lingered on his mind. He couldn't get the vision of how she'd looked when he'd left her next to the fire. Or how she'd felt when he'd lowered his body over hers for just a moment before he'd realized what he'd been about to do. Or how she'd tasted when she'd opened her mouth and kissed him as if she'd hungered for him for years.

She'd promised she'd wait to marry until he returned. She hadn't promised to wait for him. He might not be the one.

Jacob tried to think how it would feel to watch her marry another man. For once in his life he'd thought of something he wasn't sure he could do. When had he decided she had to marry him? Maybe he had always known, even when she'd been a kid and asked him to wait for her to grow up.

He tried to think of something else. Everyone at Nell's place would be asleep by now. The preacher and Harrison would probably be in the barn. After all, there was no sign the dawn shooter would ever be riding by again. He hoped the nurse had sobered up enough to take care of Nell, and Wednesday, too. At least with Sleeping Ugly there, someone would know what to do if the baby came.

A coyote howled in the night, sounding as lonely as Jacob felt. He moved his finger close to the trigger of his Colt beside him. Without a fire, an animal might come close. It paid to be ready.

He drifted into a light sleep, dreaming that he lay beside Nell. They weren't touching, but he could feel her near. The memory of the smell of her hair, the way she breathed, and how her whispers tickled against his ear were as real to him as the coyote's howl.

·   ·   ·

Miles away, Nell lay on her back. The house had finally grown silent. Marla and the nurse had given Wednesday a bath and treated her welts. Nell heard the girl cry herself to sleep, but her tears seemed to come more from sadness than pain.

Gypsy had shown Mrs. O'Daniel to her room, and despite the fact that the nurse had slept half the afternoon away, she was snoring again within minutes of closing her door.

Mrs. O'Daniel had told them about the train robbery. Of how she'd tried to get off the train when she'd heard the gunfire and knew they were shooting some of the passengers.

"I'm a nurse!" she'd screamed and pushed her way to the platform.

But a lean robber who didn't look old enough to shave had held her back and forced everyone to stay in place. He said they'd kill anyone who got off the car, and when she heard more shooting, the nurse had no doubt he spoke the truth.

They all waited until the robbers had what they came for, then the bandits ordered the train to move on. Mrs. O'Daniel cried when she told of looking out the window and seeing the bodies.

Nell knew what Jacob was riding toward. Trouble. Big trouble. She'd talked to Mr. Harrison about it. He had offered to try to catch up with the ranger, but they both knew Jacob would want him to stay right where he was. Whatever Jacob faced, he had to face alone.

Nell stared at the ceiling. For once, something besides the pain in her back kept her awake. She pictured herself lying next to her ranger. "Details," she whispered. "Remember every detail."

His chest rose and fell with his breathing. He smelled of horses and campfires and fresh air. His hair looked coarse but was surprisingly soft in her fingers. His hands were rough, and when he tried to be gentle he touched her heart. His voice was so loud when he was angry, but she heard the laughter in it when he whispered.

"Remember every detail," she whispered, for with the details she'd somehow keep him alive. Nothing could happen to him if she remembered everything.

Closing her eyes, she imagined his lips touching hers. She listened to the pounding of his heart. The wall of his chest against hers. The warmth of him near.

Nell relaxed, slipping into sleep as her mind registered the faraway sound of a coyote howling.

CHAPTER 17

"WE NEED TO TALK, MISS SMITH." RANDOLPH HARRISON SAID THE words so matter-of-factly she knew she couldn't put him off any longer.

He'd been patient enough, she guessed. Marla and he carried her down the stairs, and he hadn't said a word. He talked mostly to Brother Aaron at breakfast without giving details of his trip to her worst property. He'd even stood watching as Nell took time to show Wednesday where all the knitting supplies were kept.

When Nell met his gaze, Mr. Harrison set his coffee cup down and once more waited.

"Very well, Mr. Harrison," Nell answered, her hands already curling around the steel circling her chair's wheels. "Shall we go into the study?"

He followed her in and closed the door. Sunshine flowed into the room, as bright and warm as a summer day. All the morning glories in pots along the windowsill were in full color.

"Spring is definitely here." He brushed one of the flowers with his fingertips as if it had been a lifetime since he'd touched one.

She didn't mention how little it mattered to her. The days were pretty much the same, cold or hot, bright or cloudy. Yet she couldn't help but notice the difference in him since he arrived four days ago. He looked more solid, probably thanks to Marla's cooking, and his face was now tanned. Again, she wondered where he'd been before he came here, but she didn't ask. He had a right to his privacy. What mattered was what he did with his time now, and as best she could tell, he was well on his way to making himself indispensable to her.

Nell rolled to the desk and waited, wishing she didn't have to deal with business. Settling the new nurse, taking care of Wednesday, and worrying about Jacob seemed like enough to deal with for the day.

Last night, when Harrison returned late, it was enough to know he was safe. She'd asked to delay any discussion about the Stockard place until morning. He'd nodded politely and disappeared into the kitchen, knowing that Marla would have kept his supper warm.

Nell thought she'd heard them talking once when Gypsy opened the kitchen door, but she couldn't be certain. It occurred to her that the proper bookkeeper and the shy cook would probably have little to talk about.

"How is Mrs. O'Daniel this morning?" he asked more as conversation than true interest.

"I don't think she's over her fright from the robbery, or maybe it's the whiskey she drank yesterday. When Marla stepped into her room at dawn, the nurse told her to inform me that she'd be taking today off, but she'd like to visit with me when I awoke."

"And did she?"

"Take the day off?" Nell asked. "Yes."

"No," Harrison corrected. "Did she talk with you?"

Nell nodded. "I tapped on her door an hour ago. She was still in bed and, to tell the truth, the woman was as white as the sheets. But she wanted to go over her duties and then thanked me for the job."

Nell shook her head. "I thought she was going to cry, but she didn't. She seemed so grateful when it is I who should thank her for coming all this way."

"Jobs must be hard for a widow her age to find." He sat behind the desk.

"Especially one with her unique ideas. She tells me I'll be starting exercises twice a day tomorrow and as soon as it warms a little, she plans to take me into the water. I told her the nearest water is two miles from here, but she didn't seem to think that would be a problem."

Rand relaxed his arms on the desk as if it had been his for years and not days. "Do you think that will work? Exercise in the water?"

Nell shrugged. "Nothing else has. I'm willing to try it. All the others seemed to think I needed more rest."

He smiled, one of his rare grins. "I hope Mrs. O'Daniel can swim, because I doubt the woman will float."

Nell thought he had a pleasant face when he smiled. "She says standing shoulder deep in water will take most of the weight off my legs and help me build the muscles back a little at a time. Her first husband, McGovern I think she called him, came back from the war in the back of a wagon. Folks told her he'd never walk again, but they swam every night in the Gulf of Mexico until his muscles finally grew strong enough to hold. She said he was running the day he died."

"What happened to husband number one?"

Nell smiled. "She said gambling killed him. Apparently, he didn't see that there were already three aces on the table when he showed his hand."

"Too bad the water didn't improve his sight," Harrison said. "This theory of hers might work, if you don't float downstream." He shuffled papers on the desk, putting little faith in the nurse's idea.

"And if I did," she teased, "would you jump in and save me, Mr. Harrison?"

He shook his head. "No. I can't swim."

She had no doubt he was being honest. Her ranger would have said he'd have tried even if he couldn't swim. With Harrison, life would always be constant, even. With Dalton, it would be unpredictable.

"Shall we get to work?" Harrison asked as though they'd wasted enough time simply talking. "There is much we need to cover this morning."

Nell nodded, wondering if the man would ever allow anyone to know him well. He'd been in her house almost four days, and she knew little more about him now than when he'd introduced himself.

As he explained all that he'd found on the Stockard place, she tried to focus. This was her land, her money, her future income. She couldn't afford not to know all about it. But thoughts of Jacob drifted like tumbleweeds across her mind. He'd been gone almost twenty-four hours. Had he found the train robbers? Was he still safe?

A strange sensation settled over her. An ache deep inside. She'd missed him before, thought of him often, but never like this. Never as if a part of her were missing. The longing wasn't for something she wanted, but more for something she needed.

"I drew a map of the property." Harrison broke into her thoughts. "It is my estimate that about thirty percent of the land could be used for farming, but it would take a dozen men a month to clear it of brush and rocks. Another twenty percent had enough grass and water to be used as range. But it wouldn't take long for the cattle to move across the grass. With your other land, there would be no need to move the cattle to Stockard's ranch. If you ran a few head on the place and there was a drought, the cattle on the property would have to be absorbed into the other ranches."

"So, you're telling me half is worthless and the rest is poor."

He nodded. "A man would have to be a fool to offer more than half the going rate for land like I saw yesterday. If you add in how far out it is from town and the signs that the water will disappear in a drought, a half-price offer for the ranch would be worth considering."

Nell leaned closer to Harrison. "And Walter Farrow wants to offer us the going rate. Twice what it's worth."

Harrison lowered his voice. "Either he's crazy, or I didn't see what was so valuable about that property."

"Maybe it's not the property." She tried to remember what the ranch had looked like. She'd gone out to the place years ago when Stockard had been ill. "I rode in a supply wagon once to deliver food and medicine to the old man. Fat Alice was worried about him." Nell winked. "Fat Alice worried about all her paying customers, and somehow Henry Stockard always managed to come up with enough money to come to call. Near the end, I think she must have just cared about him."

Mr. Harrison shook his head. "He might have raised money from gambling, but not from any profit made on the land."

"He might have rented out his little house in town."

"Maybe."

Nell could still remember the earthy way Henry's half-dugout, half-cabin had smelled. "I don't recall much about the land, but I'll never forget the feeling I got almost the minute I turned off the main road." She hesitated, not wanting Harrison to think her silly. "It was like someone, or something, watched me. No, not just watched, more like stalked me. Fat Alice said no one but Stockard lived on the place, but I sure had the feeling someone else was out there hidden among the rocks."

Harrison looked surprised. "Strange. I kept looking over my shoulder yesterday. I couldn't shake the feeling I was being followed." He brushed the back of his neck. "I could almost feel them breathing down on me."

"You think it could have been Walter Farrow following you?"

"It could have been. He's staying in town, and I rode through there, so he might have seen me and followed. But why? You told him he could go out there. He must have known I'd be checking out the place."

When Nell didn't comment, Harrison added, "The sheriff says as far as he knows, no one has been on the ranch since the old man died."

Nell agreed. "The last time Fat Alice checked on him, Stockard was too weak to protest, and she brought him to town. He died in the doctor's office a few days later of pneumonia. His will was on file in town, and everyone knew, besides the land, he didn't own anything anyone would want. Fat Alice never even sent someone over to clear out his belongings that I know about."

"Then why," Harrison grinned, obviously loving a mystery, "is his shack boarded up?"

"You mean locked up?"

"No, boarded up. I didn't have the tools to break into it, but whoever nailed the boards across the door and windows didn't want anyone getting inside without some effort."

"And who could have done it?" Nell asked. "Alice, maybe, but why? Who'd she want to keep out?"

Harrison shook his head. "My guess is she might have wanted to keep something locked away inside. I circled the dugout. It'll take a hatchet to get into there. I couldn't even find a loose board to pull off so I could take a look."

Marla entered with coffee. Then, at Mr. Harrison's invitation, stayed a minute to discuss the plans for the day.

Harrison wanted to go to town for supplies and to make sure the title to the Stockard ranch would be ready to transfer if Walter Farrow made an offer. He planned to make another trip out to the land but didn't want to be away from the house that long until Jacob returned.

"I could get into town and back in an hour," he suggested.

This time Nell wasn't surprised Marla wanted to go along with him. Marla was turning into his shadow, she thought, or maybe it was the other way around.

Nell knew Gypsy would be busy with wash until midafternoon, so that would leave her to entertain Wednesday and the preacher. She predicted the day would be full of chatter.

When she joined Wednesday, Nell found her busy sorting fabric. The girl smiled up at Nell as though she'd found a pirate's hidden treasure. Nell had a habit of ordering material by mail from a store in Kansas that sent out samples several times a year. By the time the purchases arrived, she'd forgotten what she planned to do with most of the fabric. But Wednesday had ideas. The best of which was making Nell dresses that didn't have to go over her head.

"If you'll let me," she giggled, "I'll make you one and show you how much easier it will be for you to get dressed. It'll be my way of paying you back an ounce for your pound of kindness."

Nell acted like she was thinking about it. "Well, all right, but you'll have to make everyone else something new, too. It wouldn't be fair otherwise."

The girl laughed and began chattering about ideas she'd already thought of. Gypsy needed a dress that pulled on quick as an apron so when company knocked she could slip it on and run for the door. Marla needed something that looked good on her slender frame.

"This could take some time," Nell finally found a break to comment. "You might have to stay quite a while. If I like the dress, I'll want another."

Tears filled Wednesday's eyes when she smiled.

Nell pulled an unfinished quilt over her lap and began to embroider stitches across the seams as she listened to Wednesday's plans for each piece of material.

When Mr. Harrison stopped by to tell her he was leaving for town, she pulled him aside and told him to buy material for baby things. He looked at her as if she'd asked him the impossible.

"I'll try," he said, then hurried away before she could think of any more dragons that needed slaying.

Nell returned to her sewing, but by lunch, she'd enjoyed as much of Wednesday's talk as she could endure. They ate on the porch with Gypsy and the preacher. As the others cleared away the dishes, Nell asked the girl to take her sewing and go up to keep Mrs. O'Daniel company. The nurse must be lonely in her bedroom.

Nell slipped into one of the window coves and opened a book.

The house hadn't been quiet for two hours when the preacher came in to wait for dinner. He said he'd been studying all day and wondered if he might practice a sermon on her. Everyone else passing through could claim to be busy. Nell was trapped. After an hour of acting like she was hanging on every word, her only saving grace was that she wouldn't have to hear it again when he preached from the pulpit.

He'd been to town to turn in his request to preach some Sunday, but hadn't heard a reply.

Nell swore that Gypsy announced dinner was ready before Marla even cut out the biscuits, so they could gather round the table and the reverend would have to stop practicing. They'd all noticed the man couldn't seem to get wound to full speed while he ate.

So they sat talking at the table, all wondering from time to time why dinner hadn't been served. Finally, Marla brought it out and seemed surprised everyone was already around the table.

Exhausted, Nell forced herself to stay downstairs as long as possible. She knew if she went to bed, she'd only worry about Jacob, so she spent an hour reading to everyone after supper, then let Harrison guide her to the study to go over some of the records he found.

It was almost midnight when Harrison and Marla carried her up to bed. Alone, she sat in the darkness and wondered where Jacob was.

He was all right, she decided. She would have felt it if he'd been shot.

Shadows deepened as the house grew quiet. One hour slipped by, then another, as she strained to hear any sound announcing Jacob's return.

"He's safe," she whispered in the darkness of her room.

She listened again but heard only silence.

CHAPTER 18

When Nell opened her eyes, morning spilled across the room in bright colors of reflected light. She'd overslept and missed the sunrise.

In the months since the ambush, she'd learned to move slowly when she first awoke. The last thing she needed was a jab of pain shooting through her body when she wasn't wide awake enough to fight it.

So she lay still, bracing herself before she faced another day.

A voice seemed to drift from nowhere. "Roll to your side, dear, before trying to sit up. It'll put less pressure on the small of your back."

Nell did as the voice ordered, then pushed herself to a sitting position. A squarely built woman in a navy blue dress with a starched white apron faced her. "Remember me?" The nurse laughed and waved. "I'm Mrs. O'Daniel, and I'm happy to be at your service."

Nell had talked to the woman several times yesterday, but the Mrs. O'Daniel she'd seen in bed suffering from a hangover looked nothing like the proper woman before her now. Only hours ago, the nurse hadn't been able to focus, and her hair was a bush of tangles and curls around her plump, pale face. Now all signs of disorder had been forced back into a bun at the base of her neck. This morning there was no hangover. The woman who'd looked like she might fall apart had vanished and been replaced by a chubby woman who stood straight as a drill sergeant but smiled as warmly as an old maid aunt.

"Good morning," Nell managed as she lowered her feet to the floor.

Mrs. O'Daniel handed her a glass of water. "I'd like to get a few details out of the way, if I may, before we start our first day together, my dear."

Nell nodded, not trusting her voice.

The nurse stood as if at attention. "I'd like to rearrange this room for you. The wheelchair needs to be beside your bed and the lamp far enough away that it won't get knocked over. After moving some of the furniture, you should have something to hang onto when you move about."

Nell saw the woman's point, except for the "moving about" part. Standing and taking one step had been the sum total of her "moving about" for six months.

"Next, starting today, you'll be on a routine. Regular meals, regular sleep, regular exercise. As soon as it's warm, we'll swim in the afternoons, but for now you'll have a hot bath and a rubdown a few times a week."

"You sound like I'm a horse." Nell smiled, thinking she'd make Jacob laugh when she told him of the nurse's orders. In truth, she was willing to try anything. Dr. McClellan would be here soon, and she wanted to show him some progress.

Mrs. O'Daniel didn't smile. "Your housekeeper laid out your clothes, miss, and I've put your brush near enough." She moved the straight-backed chair she'd been standing in front of closer to Nell. "If you'll hold onto this, it will make standing easier while you're dressing. I'll see you in thirty minutes." She turned and opened the door.

"Aren't you going to help me dress?"

Mrs. O'Daniel stared at her. "If you can stand on the porch all by yourself, you can dress yourself. I've put everything you'll need in front of you."

The door closed before Nell added, "But I fell."

Thirty minutes later, Nell was ready for a nap. She'd struggled with dressing and combing her hair. At first she'd thought to put it up, but soon found it took far too much effort. She braided it in one long braid and braced herself on the chair back while she reached for a ribbon.

Mrs. O'Daniel returned with the chiming of the clock. "You look grand, my dear."

Nell wanted to call her a liar, but she smiled at the nurse's effort to compliment her on effort at least.

Mrs. O'Daniel straightened the room as she talked. "Everyone is waiting breakfast on you, miss. I'll help you downstairs." She carried a wide leather belt. The buckle was sturdy and the leather pliable from use. Without comment, the nurse buckled it loosely around Nell's waist. "I know it's not much, Miss, but it will hold."

Nell raised her arms so the nurse could carry her, hoping the stout woman could manage it. She looked like she might weigh as much as the last nurse, only Mrs. O'Daniel was not only ten years older but more than a head shorter than Mary Ruth had been.

To Nell's surprise, Mrs. O'Daniel put one arm around Nell's waist and gripped the belt. She braced her other arm in front of Nell to help her stand.

With a little effort, Nell stood beside the woman and placed one arm across her thick shoulders.

"Now hold your body straight and do the best you can to walk, miss. Don't you worry about falling. The grip I've got on this belt won't let you go. We'll move as fast or as slow as you like. Speed isn't important, progress is."

Nell nodded and gripped the back of her chair with her free hand.

Moving across the room, Nell reached for support as she passed furniture. It took them twenty minutes to get to the landing. Though Nell moved in small steps, her feet took very little of her weight. She was almost walking, she thought. Almost.

When Harrison and Marla saw her at the top of the stairs, they both ran to help. Mrs. O'Daniel informed them that they weren't needed. She moved so that Nell could hold the railing with her free hand. "We're going down these stairs together. One step at a time. Anyone near her but me will just be in her way."

Nell lifted her chin, not wanting to admit how frightened she felt. Her knuckles were white as she gripped the banister, taking one step down, then Mrs. O'Daniel waited while she got another firm hold and they managed another step.

Halfway down, Mr. Harrison moved in her path. "Let us carry you the rest of the way," he asked. "You've done quite enough for today."

Mrs. O'Daniel looked at Nell. "You're only halfway through," she said. "These stairs will never be longer or harder than they are today if you reach the bottom."

Nell tried to smile. "I want to go the rest of the way," she whispered.

Harrison moved aside. His face was set with no display of emotion, but she didn't miss the worry in his gray eyes. He joined the others watching from the bottom of the stairs.

The preacher mumbled a prayer, and Wednesday paced as Nell held fast to Mrs. O'Daniel's shoulder with one hand and the stair railing with the other. Sweat ran off her forehead, but she forced her head high. The nurse was giving her a chance to fight, and fight she would. One step at a time.

Mrs. O'Daniel's breathing sounded like a train pulling into the station, but she held on tightly to the belt. Nell leaned into her, knowing the woman would hold fast.

One more step.

Nell's shoe turned, making her foot slip sideways. Mrs. O'Daniel held on, giving her time to straighten and find her balance again.

One more step.

Nell closed her eyes, remembering all the times at school that she'd walked down the stairs alone to go to dinner. She'd written Fat Alice long letters about her friends at school, but in truth, she'd been alone. No one wanted to be friends with a girl they knew nothing about, and if they'd known her past, they wouldn't have offered anyway.

One more step.

She'd told herself then that their whispers didn't hurt. She told herself now that the pain didn't matter. She would survive.

With the last step, everyone cheered, and she realized she'd reached the bottom of the stairs. She was no longer that frightened child; she was surrounded by friends. Nell felt exhausted and thankful when Gypsy slipped the wheelchair against the back of her legs and she could sit down.

"You did a grand job," Mrs. O'Daniel whispered as she unbuckled the belt. "A grand job indeed."

"Thank you," Nell answered out of breath.

For once she let the housekeeper push her to the table.

Mrs. O'Daniel took the seat Harrison pulled out for her. Now that she was sober, she seemed all business, which was something he understood. She ate in silence, then pushed her plate aside and pulled out her watch. The timepiece was huge, the kind of pocket watch a man would carry.

As she drank her second cup of coffee, Nell couldn't help but wonder which of Mrs. O'Daniel's husbands had left it to her. Smiling, Nell remembered the watch she'd given Jacob a few years ago for Christmas. He'd told her it was the best gift he'd ever received.

After Nell downed the last of her coffee, she felt more like facing the day. "What's the plan, Mrs. O'Daniel?" She liked the way the nurse seemed to know what she was doing. Most of the others had been happy to read while Nell stayed in bed. All had insisted she take frequent naps.

"We'll walk down to breakfast every morning from now on. And every day you'll stay out of that chair a little longer until one day, you'll climb the stairs alone and the wheelchair will be pushed into a corner to collect dust."

Nell wasn't sure she believed her words, but they offered Nell something she hadn't had in six months: hope.

Mrs. O'Daniel worked upstairs rearranging Nell's room for most of the morning. She sent Gypsy and Marla bumping their way downstairs with the bedroom rug and ordered Mr. Harrison to bring up two more ladder-back chairs. When she finally came downstairs, she had the belt with her.

Nell smiled. "I have a feeling I'm going to grow to hate that thing."

Mrs. O'Daniel was all business. "It's time for your work, dear. Gypsy tells me you like tea. Would you like to walk to the kitchen for a cup or out to the porch to stand in the sun for a few minutes?"

The nurse offered her arm for Nell to pull up on. "The porch please," Nell answered. She'd not whine, no matter what the nurse suggested. After the stairs, a walk to the porch didn't seem all that hard, but her legs felt weak.

To her surprise, the trip was not as bad as she feared it might be. Nell was learning to trust the stout little woman. True to her word, Mrs. O'Daniel moved slowly, allowing Nell to find her footing with each step but not letting her put much weight on her legs.

When they reached the porch, Nell closed her eyes and smiled into the warm sun. She took a deep breath, smelling rain in the air. Looking north, she noticed clouds rolling in along the horizon. A storm would be upon them by nightfall.

Mrs. O'Daniel stood like a rock beside her. "One more step each day, miss. Just one more step, and before you know it, you'll be walking."

The preacher hurried up from the barn. "I thought I'd go into town after lunch and have a talk with a few more of the churches. Let them know I'm offering to preach next Sunday to whoever asks first." He stopped a few feet away. "It's been months since I've stood at a real pulpit. Most places I come to are lucky to have a barn or a tent they use for services."

He held the door open as Nell and Mrs. O'Daniel walked inside. When Nell lowered herself back into her wheelchair, the nurse whispered, "Before supper we'll do the same thing."

Sheriff Parker rode out from town to join them for lunch. The moment he saw Mrs. O'Daniel, he smiled, knowing he'd have someone new to tell his stories to. Nell pumped him for any word about Jacob, but all he knew was that a posse hired by the railroad rode out from Fort Worth a few hours after the robbery. They'd have little chance of catching the bandits unless weather or Jacob slowed them down. He told Mrs. O'Daniel about how he and three other lawmen rode into the Indian Territory after a gang of outlaws who'd rustled a hundred head of cattle. The outlaws had caused so much trouble that the Apache living near the border gladly handed them over. Unfortunately, no one seemed to know what happened to the cattle.

Sheriff Parker agreed to stay at the house while Brother Aaron made his trip into town. After lunch, he helped Harrison round up the stock and get them inside the barn. By the time they returned to the house, rain was tapping at the windows.

Harrison lit a fire more to chase away the gloom than for warmth. Wednesday claimed her chair where the light was best for sewing. Nell read a book, while Harrison worked at his desk. She looked up when the clock chimed four and noticed that Mrs. O'Daniel, Gypsy, and the sheriff were all asleep. The rhythm of the rain blended with their snores.

A few minutes later, Mr. Harrison knelt beside her to show her the figures he'd totaled on last year's running of the properties. "I've seen barn raising that made less noise," he whispered as he pointed with his head toward the snoring section of the room.

She smiled. "I've read the same page three times. It's hard to concentrate."

He laid his hand over hers. "How about we disappear to the kitchen? I think I smell Marla's cobbler."

She rolled backward until she was several feet away from the nappers, then turned her chair around and passed through to the kitchen as Mr. Harrison held the door open.

Marla was starting supper and happy to have the company. They drank tea and ate cobbler around the kitchen table.

After finishing his second serving, Mr. Harrison told Marla she'd better make another one, because he didn't think there was enough left to serve for dinner.

Nell laughed. "Well, there might be enough if you and I skipped dessert tonight."

He frowned.

Marla reached for the apples.

Nell couldn't believe she'd eaten two helpings herself. When she'd taken her meals upstairs, more often than not, the tray came back to the kitchen untouched.

Maybe it was all the exercise.

She looked at Harrison and Marla talking quietly about how much the preacher ate. Or maybe, she reconsidered, it was the company that made her hungry. Randolph Harrison seemed more relaxed around Marla than he did when he was with the others. He was still very proper, but he didn't seem quite so emotionless. With the shy cook he let his guard down a little.

She thought again about what a good husband he'd make and wondered if he realized, as she did, that there were only three days left until she'd promised to give him an answer. She knew if Jacob was still gone, she'd have to ask Mr. Harrison to wait a little longer for the answer.

Nell told herself it was because she'd promised Jacob she'd wait until he returned, but deep down she knew it was more.

CHAPTER 19

THE RAIN POUNDED JACOB DALTON SO HARD HE FELT LIKE IT might cut into the oil-soaked slicker he wore. Still, he forced himself to push onward. In order to catch the outlaws, he had to move faster and longer than they did. These men had killed six innocent people two days ago, and he had to do everything in his power to see that they didn't get the chance to take any more lives.

With the clouds so heavy above, he had trouble telling the time. It looked like just past twilight, but he guessed it had to be before six in the evening. A pocket watch was tucked away inside his coat. Nell had given it to him a few Christmases ago, but he didn't dare take it out and risk ruining it in the rain. What difference did the time make anyway? He wouldn't stop until it was too dark to see, and he'd eaten the last of his food, so there would be no supper to look forward to.

He rubbed his whiskery chin. The shortage of food was shy Marla's fault. Her cooking was so good he hadn't wanted to ration it out. He'd pay for the few good meals he'd had from her supply bag by going without until he got back home.

He knew there were a few strips of jerky in his saddlebags, but after eating Marla's cooking, they didn't seem very appetizing.

Home. There he went again, calling Nell's place home, like he had a right to claim it any more than he could claim he belonged anywhere. But it wasn't the house, or the town he'd be riding back to. It was Nell.

A half hour later, Jacob pulled his hat low and studied the horizon, watching for any sign or movement. The rain had slowed to a drizzle, and the terrain had changed from rangeland to rocky, uneven ground. In the distance, distorted by moisture in the air, he thought he saw a trail of smoke pushing toward the clouds. Someone had lit a fire in the back of a small canyon where they'd probably be out of the wind and most of the rain.

That someone might be who he had been looking for.

He rode on, knowing he'd probably find a farmer or maybe some travelers, but Jacob hoped that for once he'd get lucky.

The wet earth muffled any sound as his horse closed the distance to the smoke. A hundred yards out, Jacob could make out a campfire. He tied Dusty in the shelter of a mound of rocks about twenty feet high and pulled his rifle from the saddle.

It was fully dark before he moved toward the fire. By now he was soaked to the bone and hungry, but he couldn't wait to know who warmed by the campfire. If he'd stayed with his horse for the night, whoever camped might be gone at dawn.

Twenty yards out, he stood in the open, still as a cottonwood. On a clear night, they could have seen him in the moonlight, but tonight he'd stay a part of the darkness until he was within a few feet.

He made out six men. Two rolled in blankets close to the fire. Two squatted with cups cradled in their hands. One man worked with the horses several yards away, while another seemed to be examining the packs. He'd been right. If these were the robbers, they were traveling with two pack mules.

Were these the men? Jacob didn't want to jump to conclusions. They might just be cowhands stuck out in the storm. After all, they'd built a fire.

Or they might be the robbers and guessed anyone trying to follow them would hole up out of the rain and not be fool enough to try to track them.

Cowhands would have known to tie their horses closer, keeping the animals sheltered from the rain. It might have meant building a smaller fire, but without horses in this part of the country, a man could die.

Jacob took another step. He had to be sure. Then he had to figure out a way to take all six gunmen without getting himself filled with bullet holes.

He smiled, remembering what he'd told Nell when she'd worried about him. He'd said, "It's only one gang," like he saw no problem. Right now he'd give a month's pay to have one other person with him.

If he opened fire, he could kill two, maybe three before the others took cover. Then he'd face a shoot-out in the dark with no one to cover his back.

Silently, he circled round to the horses. His one chance to catch them was to make sure they couldn't ride away. The animals were skittish from the storm. He whispered to them and patted each one. The man who'd checked on them had gone back to the fire, and from the sound of it he was arguing with the two drinking coffee about doing more than his share of the work.

By the time the horses settled, all the men had turned in for the night. They'd left a guard, who found a dry spot near the edge of the cliff and looked like he was dozing. He was a big man who sat cross-legged with his slicker over him like a tent.

One by one, Jacob untied the mounts. When he reached the mules, he saw the mailbags from the train and two locked Wells Fargo boxes. The robbers hadn't had time to examine their loot. They also must not have planned ahead, for repacking whatever was locked away in the boxes would have been much easier to carry.

The animals were strong, but they'd been greatly mistreated. Jacob felt sores on the mules' backs where they'd been whipped, and one had a jagged cut on his side where one of the boxes must not have been strapped on tight enough. Jacob ran his hand along the animal's neck, wishing he had some way of doctoring the wound.

He led the mules off first, wanting to get the injured animal to more shelter. It took him almost an hour to make it back, but he wanted to get the mules far enough away so that they wouldn't be found easily. He tied them between huge cottonwoods so they'd be out of the wind.

Then he returned to the camp and carefully moved three of the horses away.

The guard still remained on the corner of the ledge, a blanket now wrapped over his head. Jacob guessed he was supposed to wake someone else to relieve him of duty, but he'd fallen asleep. No one would stand guard on a night like this any longer than demanded.

Jacob took the last three horses in a different direction. He rode one and led the other two so that he could cover more ground.

When he returned one last time to the camp, he felt like a walking dead man. The constant rain had drained him, but he knew it would also help him, because the robbers would have no idea where to look for the horses. They'd been fools to use what little dry ground they had for themselves. They should have pulled the horses in closer. Even the noise the mounts made as he moved them was muffled by the storm and the blanket over the guard's ears.

Jacob took one last look at the sleeping guard and moved back into the blackness. He knew that at first light, when the others discovered the horses were gone, the guard would be dead.

And then there would be five.

Jacob returned to his mound of rocks close enough to the outlaws to see their fire. He lay among the rocks, no longer caring that he was wet. He lowered his hat and tried to remember how nice it had been out by the windmill that night with Nell. It seemed like a lifetime ago.

It seemed he'd just closed his eyes when a single shot rang out.

Raising to one elbow, Jacob saw the gray dawn spreading through the fog. Lowering his hat back in place, he tried to relax. It would take them some time to figure out what happened. They'd probably make coffee, maybe breakfast if they had any food. Then, they'd talk about what to do.

Jacob tried to work through their logic. They'd have to leave one, maybe two men to watch the loot. At first they'd think that the horses probably got spooked by the storm and wandered off. Maybe they'd decide one had jerked out a stake, leaving the others free to move away.

He smiled. If he were lucky, they'd blame one man and shoot him. Then there would be only four.

After a few circles, they'd spread out, heading in different directions, and that would be his time. Hidden among the rocks, he was close enough to the camp that they'd all soon be past him in their search. Then, all he had to do was take care of those left in camp first and wait for the others to return one by one.

It seemed simple enough, but Jacob had to take into account that he hadn't slept more than a few hours in two days. His bones ached from the cold, and he was so hungry he could eat one of the mules.

He watched from above as the men circled the clearing beyond their camp. When they met up an hour later, he saw what must be the leader pointing for each man to take a different direction. The land here was uneven and spotted with cottonwoods as well as bushes big enough to hide a horse. On foot, the men would probably never go far enough to find any of the mounts.

Only one man walked back toward the camp, which surprised Jacob. It told him two things: the leader trusted the one man, and he still didn't suspect that someone might have taken the horses. If he'd even guessed there might be someone watching, he never would have left the camp and the loot to one man's care.

Jacob made sure he was in the clear, then he climbed down from the rocks and moved toward the camp. He figured the leader had planned some kind of signal for the others to return. If so, it was probably one gunshot. So that left out shooting the man in camp as an option. The last thing Jacob needed was to shoot one man and have the other four come running with guns ready.

In the daylight, Jacob had no cover, so his only armor had to be guts. He walked into the camp like he was just out for a stroll.

The kid by the fire jumped two feet when he saw Jacob, spilling his cup of coffee all over his leg.

"Sorry." Jacob smiled and raised his hands high. "I didn't mean to frighten you, kid. I just saw your smoke and hoped you could spare a cup."

The boy of about fifteen reached for his gun, but Jacob just kept talking. "My horse went lame two days ago, and I've been walking ever since. I thought I'd find a farmhouse, or at least a road, but you're the first sign of life, except jackrabbits, I've seen."

The kid raised his gun. "You'd be wise to keep walking, mister."

Jacob glanced at the coffeepot. "All right, son. I don't mean to bother anyone. I'm just a cowhand looking for work." Jacob stared into the boy's eyes. He was wild, but not a killer. Not yet. Jacob would bet his badge this member of the gang hadn't done any of the killing. "You wouldn't offer me a cup of that coffee would you, son? Then I promise I'll be on my way. I'm near starved and so cold I'm not sure I'll ever get warm."

The boy pointed with his gun. "You can have one cup, but drink it fast. My pa and his friends will be back with the horses soon, and they don't like strangers."

Jacob lowered his hands and reached for the pot. "Much obliged." He knew he was fast enough to draw and kill the kid, but Jacob waited, hoping for a few answers.

"You traveling with your family?"

The kid sat down on a log without putting his gun back in its holster. "Yeah. My pa. Only family I got. My ma died last year."

"Where you heading?"

"You ask a lot of questions, mister. What d'you care?"

Jacob poured himself a cup of coffee, noticing that it was thick as mud, but he didn't care. "I was hoping you all were heading someplace where you know there's work. I've been out of a job most of the winter."

The kid shook his head. "We ain't looking for work." The boy reached over and offered Jacob a biscuit that was hard as rock.

Jacob decided to play it safe. One too many questions might get the kid scared enough to set off the alarm. "That was one mean storm last night, wasn't it?"

"Yeah. Our horses must have got spooked and ran off. They're probably not far, and you'd be wise to be long gone before my pa gets back. He's been in prison most of my life and, like I told you, he don't take to strangers."

Jacob stood, careful not to look in the direction of the bags. They were in plain sight, but he knew if he even glanced that way, the kid wouldn't be able to let him go. "Well, I'll be on my way. Thanks for the coffee. You're a good kid."

"No I ain't," the boy mumbled and looked away from Jacob for a few seconds.

That was all he needed. In one quick jump, Jacob grabbed the gun from the kid's hand and slammed it up against the boy's head. The kid didn't even have time to groan before he tumbled in the mud.

"Sorry," Jacob mumbled, knowing that he may have just saved the kid's life.

He tied the boy up and gagged him, then carried him back to the rocks. Carefully lowering him between two boulders, Jacob guessed the kid would be scared to death if he woke up. But when this was over, at least the young man would be alive.

Which, with any luck, Jacob thought, so would he.

CHAPTER 20

Jacob Dalton made it back to the outlaws' camp and finished off the last of their coffee while examining the mailbags and the two Wells Fargo security boxes. The train robbers must have been riding hard, for nothing seemed to have been opened. They'd been prepared to travel when they'd hit the train. Most of the saddle packs were filled with supplies enough to last a week.

He circled the camp, widening his search with each pass, until he stepped outside the shelter of the cliff's ledge. Cold rain soaked him so completely he could feel his flannel shirt sticking to his body even beneath his coat, but he didn't slow. Ten feet outside the camp he found the body of the man who'd been on guard the night before. The outlaw couldn't have been more than twenty and had taken one shot in the head. He had no weapon on him, and his pockets were turned out. His partners in crime apparently hadn't been satisfied with splitting his share of the loot, they robbed him in death as well.

The boy Jacob had left tied up said his father was one of the men looking for the horses. What kind of father allowed his son to watch such a senseless killing? Jacob asked himself as he dragged the man's body toward the fire.

Lifting the boy's slicker, Jacob slipped it over the dead man's shoulders, then leaned the body on a bedroll so that it looked like the boy had fallen asleep by the fire while the others were gone. He found the kid's hat and shoved it low over the dead man's face. Anyone walking up might think the body was the boy sleeping, if they didn't look real close.

Jacob built up the fire so that it blazed between the dead man and whoever might be approaching. With any luck, the posse that would be following the men had kept moving during the night and were now close enough to see smoke if there were a break in the storm. The wood he used was wet, so steam rose along with the smoke.

Jacob smiled. He could use a little help right now, but it wasn't something he usually planned on.

Checking the camp, he memorized it in case he had to act fast with no time to survey the area. The returning members of the gang might come through the trees, but he'd bet anyone on foot would take the easier path up from the clearing, even if they had to circle around. If they came from the north they'd have to climb down from the twenty-foot cliff. From the south, trees made the ground uneven and dangerous in the mud. They'd have to return to camp from the east.

The rain came in spurts. A cold early morning drizzle washed the world to gray. Jacob stepped beyond the shadow of the cliff to wait for the first man to return. A few feet beyond the overhang to the west, the ground disappeared. The fog was so thick Jacob couldn't tell how far the land dropped away. He kicked a rock off the ledge and listened for the sound of impact. One second, two. Ten, maybe fifteen feet, he'd guess. If this didn't turn out the way he planned, he might have to make the jump to escape. He couldn't run through the clearing; they'd have an easy shot before he could make it to the rocks where the boy waited.

His odds were four to one, but he had surprise on his side, at least until he was forced to fire a shot or one was fired at him. He had to win, Jacob thought, or else the kid might die. No one would find him tied up in the rocks. Even if he regained consciousness and managed to get the gag off, no one would hear him yelling in this rain.

The question crossed his mind of why he cared so much about the kid. Maybe for once he wanted to prevent an outlaw instead of just catching one. The boy didn't have much of a chance in life with a worthless father, but maybe Jacob could give him that one opportunity, and who knows, maybe the kid would be smart enough to take it.

A movement came from the clearing. One of the men had given up and was coming in. Jacob watched him head straight into the camp with his head down against the storm.

"Hell of a rain," the man yelled as he swung water from his hat and squatted in front of the fire. Balding, he looked to be in his forties. "Hell of a morning." He swore as he lifted the coffeepot and found it empty. "Can't you do anything right, kid? Why didn't you make more coffee?"

The outlaw started around the campfire, raising the coffeepot like a weapon. "Your pa weren't around to teach you nothin' when you were growing up, but I'll teach you something you'll not likely forget."

He raised the pot in the air and took aim at what he thought was the sleeping kid's head.

A moment before he swung, Jacob stabbed the barrel of a rifle in the small of the man's back.

"Don't make me waste a bullet killing you," Jacob said in little more than a whisper.

The outlaw didn't move.

"Drop the pot and raise your hands real slow."

The outlaw coiled and hissed like a snake but followed orders. Within minutes, Jacob had him tied and staked to a tree near where the horses had been left in the rain the night before. He didn't bother worrying about the knots being tight as he had with the boy. Without a slicker or coat, the outlaw's filthy clothes blended to gray in the rain. No one would see him, even if they passed within a yard of him.

"You're a dead man, mister."

"Maybe so." Jacob didn't argue.

"You don't know who you're dealing with. I'll kill you real slow until you beg for it to be over. We planned this for years while we was in prison, and one man don't have a chance against us."

"We'll see," Jacob mumbled as he worked. Every outlaw he ever caught thought he was too mean to die.

The man swore until Jacob stuffed a gag in his mouth and pulled his hat down low over his face. Jacob circled one final rope around the tree and across the man's throat. If the outlaw struggled, the rope would rub his neck raw within minutes.

Jacob moved back to the camp and made coffee, hoping the smell would distract the next outlaw long enough for him to move up behind. He had three more to catch, and his only ally now was the rain.

Walking back into the shadows, Jacob waited. He could feel the storm more outside the cliff's shelter—the wind, the cold rain, the lightning close to the ground—but he didn't dare stand too near to the fire. One look at his size, and the outlaws would know a stranger was in camp.

An hour passed, and he guessed the other three had found shelter somewhere. They were probably waiting out the rain before continuing their search or returning to camp.

Despite the coffee, lack of sleep started to wear on him. Jacob closed his eyes and thought of Nell. She always laughed at his stories and thought his life was such an adventure. She had no idea. Trying to get his mind off the cold rain, he thought of the big main room in her home and how the fireplace warmed the whole house in winter. On a rainy day like this, Nell would probably read to everyone. She had a talent for making a story come alive. He could almost hear her voice now. She used to read the dime novels after supper. Gypsy would always flutter her eyes when Nell read the words "soiled dove," which would make Jacob laugh and usually stop the reading for a few minutes.

A voice with an Irish accent returned Jacob to the present. "Get up, ye lazy good for nothing boy!"

Jacob opened his eyes and tried to see through the rain to the fire. A big man stood over the body of the dead guard.

"Get yer lazy bones up or I'll shoot you like I did Willie this morning, I swear. A man who canna do his job has no business being in a gang."

Jacob had let the man get too close to the fire before he moved from the shadows. Now, if he tried to cross the area between them, the Irishman would see him. He had to pick his timing with great care.

The outlaw's voice grew as he kicked at the dead man beside the fire. "Ye ain't worth nothing, and I'm sorry to call ye son, I am. Wake up."

Jacob took a chance and circled the fire. All the outlaw had to do was look up, and he'd be caught.

Jacob drew his gun. If the man raised his head, the ranger would have to fire, even though it might bring the other two still out in the rain running, for this outlaw looked deadly even from a distance.

Lucky for Jacob, the outlaw's anger focused on what he thought was the kid beneath the slicker. He kicked at the bedroll again. "Wake up!" he yelled. "I should have left ye to starve to death for all the good ye are too me. Yer ma probably died just to be rid of ye."

He knelt and jerked the hat off the man lying by the fire. It took him only a moment before he recognized the dead guard. With lightning speed, he pulled his gun and swung around.

Jacob had found the safety of the trees by then and was moving as fast as he could away from the fire.

The outlaw's oaths rumbled through the air like thunder. Jacob didn't know if he were calling his son's name or that of one of the other outlaws. It didn't matter. If he didn't shut up soon, all the men would be back in camp. The few trees wouldn't hide Jacob for long, even in rain thick as soup.

"Where are ye?" The man yelled as he crossed from one tree to the other, his gun leading the way. "I know you're out here."

The ranger waited for an opportunity. He listened to the man's footsteps. His heavy breathing gave the outlaw's fear away.

The Irishman laughed suddenly and fired, then swore and began to move as before, one step at a time, through the trees.

Jacob waited, knowing he stood almost close enough to touch the outlaw's shoulder.

The man took one step nearer, then he turned toward the fire and yelled for whoever was out there to show himself. "I'll kill you in a fair fight," he shouted as he pulled a long knife from his boot.

Jacob saw his chance and rushed him from behind. The ranger was close enough to knock the gun away a second before the man could turn and fire at him. A round sounded from the six-shooter a moment later, but the barrel was pointed skyward.

The shot seemed to echo off the canyon walls as Jacob threw his body into the outlaw. They tumbled in the mud.

This time the outlaw he fought was close to Jacob's size and a seasoned fighter. He gave as much as he got. The mud made maintaining their footing hard, and every time one stood, the other knocked him down. Jacob delivered a few hard blows that should have broken bone, but the outlaw kept coming like a fevered animal too angry to think of his own safety.

As he fought, thoughts skittered across Jacob's mind like ground lightning. In a short time, others would be here and the odds would only get worse. If he didn't win, if they killed him, there would be no one else to stop them. The men would be into Indian Territory and out of reach of Texas law. If they killed him, none of them would be able to find the boy, even if they found the horses. The boy might die, tied up and hidden between the rocks.

Jacob fought like a wild man, until he felt the blade of a knife slide across his ribs.

He stepped away. In the blink of lightning, he saw the flicker off a knife in the outlaw's hands. The man smiled, knowing he'd taken the advantage.

"Don't know who ye are," he hissed, "but one thing's a fact, stranger. You're a dead man."

He lunged forward, swinging the blade close to Jacob's arm. Before

Jacob could recover, he swung again, cutting into the material of his coat and drawing blood.

"I ain't in no hurry, stranger. I'd just as soon cut ye ten times and watch ye bleed out."

Jacob dove at the man, knocking him off balance at the same time he felt the blade shoot into his shoulder, hot as a bullet. Slamming a fist into the outlaw's face, Jacob heard bone break and knew they were now even.

The Irishman swore and backed away, dropping the knife as he stumbled to keep his footing.

Jacob rolled toward the weapon, aware that he was close to the overhang.

Voices sounded from behind him. "We found the mules!" one yelled.

"Why'd you fire?" another shouted. "Ain't you got the horses?"

The Irishman rushed for his knife, grinding his foot into Jacob's hand as he reached for the blade. "Over here!" he called to the others. He lifted the knife to Jacob's throat. "Got me something that needs killing."

Hearing the rush of hooves and men, Jacob knew he had only seconds. He put his free hand on the Irishman's boot and shoved hard as he rolled away from the knife.

The outlaw stumbled, then widened his stance, preparing to fight once more.

Only Jacob didn't stop. He rolled over and over, ignoring the pain each time he landed on his left shoulder.

Three rolls. Four. He reached the edge under the cliff where the ground dropped. Then, as silently as if he'd vanished, Jacob plummeted.

He tumbled, taking what he thought might be his last breath. If rocks lay below the cliff, even falling ten feet would kill him.

But to his surprise, he landed almost soundlessly in thick, wet grass. He heard the swish of tall buffalo grass as his body sank a few inches into the mud.

Jacob didn't move. He heard the men shouting above, but the fog hid him from view. One claimed he was dead. The Irishman ordered them to fire rounds. Bullets tapped the mud around Jacob, but none landed close.

The Irishman shouted for the other two to load the mules. Despite the rain, they needed to move out fast.

"If there's one man out here, there might be more," someone said.

"What about the horses?" another yelled.

"Can't waste any more time looking for them. With the mules to carry the loot, we can walk out of Texas in a few days. Once we're in Indian Territory, we'll buy horses."

"I found Charlie," the first voice called. "You want me to untie him?"

The Irishman laughed, "Leave him. I shot him by mistake. He's dead."

If the other two outlaws thought the Irishman's comment strange, they didn't say anything.

Jacob could hear them moving, loading the mules. He could hear them talking but couldn't make out the words. Even without hearing, he knew they were leaving the boy, not taking the time to look for him. The remaining three must be thinking they'd just double their earnings with the boy, Charlie, and the guard dead.

By the time all was silent, the rain had slowed to a drizzle. Jacob tried to stand but found himself almost too weak. His shirt and coat were soaked in blood, and he realized he was doing exactly what the Irishman had planned for him to do. He was bleeding to death.

Slowly, he crawled back up the embankment a few inches at a time. His left arm was worthless to pull him up, but he could use it to hold to the earth so that he didn't slide backward. Rocks cut his hands and pestered the cut along his ribs, but Jacob blocked out the pain and kept climbing, making only a few inches of progress at a time.

When he reached the campsite once more, the outlaws had been gone so long the fire was almost out. They'd left their saddles and most of their supplies. The fog had cleared enough for Jacob to see Charlie still tied to the tree, his head now forward, stretching the rope about his throat. He no longer cared if he choked.

Jacob took a few minutes to bind his shoulder and ribs with a shirt he found in one of the packs and chewed a few bites of jerky. Then, with evening drawing near, he made his way across the small clearing to the rocks where he'd hidden the boy.

It took all his strength to pull the boy up with one arm. The kid was wiggling and fighting all the way. When Jacob finally got him back to what was left of the campsite, he sat the kid down and pulled the gag away. The boy stared at him as if he thought Jacob were the devil.

"What's your name?"

The kid glared at him.

"What's your name?" Jacob asked again.

"Hank," he finally said. "And you better let me go, or my pa will kill you."

Jacob shook his head. "Look." Jacob fought to keep from passing out. "My name is Dalton. I'm a Texas Ranger. I've been hunting you for three days. Two of the gang are dead, neither by my hand. Your pa and the other two are heading north toward the Red. They left you behind but took the loot."

He looked over, expecting the kid to say something, but he just stared.

"The way I see it, I'm too wounded to hold you here. If you go with your pa and the others, it's only a matter of time before the law catches up with you. If you stay with me willingly, I'll do what I can for you. I can't promise you won't get jail time, but if you weren't the one who shot those people back on the train, I think I can keep you from hanging."

"You going to untie me?"

"When I have your word you'll go back with me."

Jacob reached for the knife he'd used to cut the makeshift bandage, but when he leaned forward to cut the ropes, the world began to spin. He tumbled without hearing the kid's answer.

CHAPTER 21

Nell awoke late in the night. The rain had stopped. Rolling slowly to her side, she stared out the window, realizing the silence must have awakened her. Unbeckoned, her thoughts filled with Jacob. He'd been gone five days now. That wasn't long, she reminded herself. He'd said he might be gone a week, maybe more.

Listening, Nell tried to hear something, anything. Nothing. Gypsy was the only one of the women who snored, and she slept in one of the rooms off the kitchen.

The silence should have reassured her, but it didn't. Something was wrong. She could feel it as easily as she felt the night wind drifting from the open window Mrs. O'Daniel had insisted be left ajar. Fat Alice used to say that once in a while she heard a shadow move. Nell swore she heard it now.

A stair creaked. Someone crept about. Maybe Wednesday making a midnight run to the kitchen, or the nurse checking the house.

Suddenly, Nell realized pain hadn't awakened her. Something else had. She took a deep breath, trying to remember what she'd heard the moment before she'd passed from sleep. But all she could think of was the rain that had pounded the house for two days and how now she almost missed the sound.

The same rain must have made her ranger's life hell. Jacob always said he didn't mind the weather, but more than once she'd seen how tired he looked when he rode in after a storm.

She forced herself to relax. Every door was locked, every window on the ground floor double-checked. Brother Aaron probably still snored on the porch where he claimed the wicker chair was far more comfortable than the barn floor. She'd seen Harrison bed down near the loft door in the barn. She guessed he wanted a clear view of the house and grounds if anything unexpected happened during the night.

She was safe, Nell reminded herself again.

Another step creaked slow and low as if someone were putting his or her weight on the wood as carefully as possible so as not to cause a sound.

"Who's there!" Nell called softly as she fought panic.

No answer.

"I said, who is out there?" She waited. Anyone on the stairs should have heard her. If she said the words any louder, she'd wake everyone in the house.

Again, no one called in return.

"Mrs. O'Daniel!" Nell screamed.

Footsteps, running fast, rattled down the stairs as she screamed again.

She rolled to the side of the bed and felt for the arms of her wheelchair. She knew she could never reach the stairs in time to see whoever ran, but she had to do something. She could not lie still and wait for trouble to reach her.

A light flickered on in the hall, then another outside the barn.

Wednesday reached Nell first, scrambling in her bed like a frightened child. "Miss Nell," she cried. "Someone was coming up the stairs! I thought I was dreaming until I heard you yell. You heard it, too, didn't you?"

Nell put her arm around Wednesday and held her tightly as much to calm her own fear as to help the girl. Mrs. O'Daniel rushed into the room with her hair tied up in rags. "What's happened?" she demanded. "Is someone harmed?"

Nell heard Harrison and the preacher bang their way through the front door and storm the stairs.

"Is everyone all right?" Harrison yelled. "May we come up?"

Nell almost laughed and gave her permission. Jacob Dalton would have never asked such a thing if he thought there was trouble on the second floor, but Harrison would be proper to the end.

Harrison stood in the doorway holding the barn lantern in one hand and an old Walker Colt in the other. Brother Aaron appeared sleepy, taking a few steps into Nell's bedroom and glancing around as though expecting to see a wild animal lurking in the shadows.

Both men looked like deer who'd stumbled into a bear cave. Nell could see that they both thought they were definitely somewhere they didn't belong.

"We're fine." Nell pulled her blanket up not because she felt exposed, but because she guessed the men felt uncomfortable seeing a lady in her nightclothes. "Someone was on the stairs a few minutes ago. Both Wednesday and I heard them. When I called for Mrs. O'Daniel, they ran down."

Mrs. O'Daniel paled. "Someone was in the house." She looked at the preacher.

"They didn't get past me. I sleep with one eye open most of the time."

Gypsy and Marla thundered into the room, shoving the preacher closer to the bed. The old man still had all his clothes on, but he buttoned his coat as if he could ward off sin with fabric armor.

Harrison seemed to relax and take charge. "Were either of you on the stairs a few minutes ago?"

Marla and Gypsy shook their heads as if their chins were connected with an invisible string.

"How about you?" He turned to Mrs. O'Daniel, who shook her head in double time.

"Not me," Wednesday offered before she was questioned.

Nell decided it would be a waste of time for her to say anything.

Harrison lifted the lantern. "Everyone stay here." He moved toward the door. "I'll check things out."

No one argued. In fact, he would have had trouble finding a second to follow.

He disappeared. A few moments later, they all heard his footsteps descending the stairs.

Gypsy turned up Nell's night-light and paced back and forth across the room. Wednesday curled closer to Nell. Mrs. O'Daniel glared at the preacher, mumbling something about being married enough times to know that trouble usually wore trousers.

"You don't think it's my pa come to get me, do you?" the girl whispered. "I don't want to go if it is. He can't make me, can he?"

"No," Nell answered and gave the girl a squeeze around the shoulders.

"I don't want to go back," she repeated. "Not ever. I want to stay here with you."

Mrs. O'Daniel pulled her robe tighter around her ample chest. "It might just be one of those men who likes to look at women sleeping. We had a fellow like that in Fort Worth once. He'd find an open window and poke his head in, hoping to see a woman in her nighties."

Brother Aaron frowned and glanced at Mrs. O'Daniel's hair with rag ends sticking out like rolled barbed wire. "I bet he was disappointed more often than not."

"I wouldn't know." She raised her chin. "He leaned in once too often, I heard, and a widow slammed a cast-iron skillet into his face. Folks said he didn't have enough nose left to sneeze."

Wednesday giggled, lightening everyone's mood.

"That's not true," the preacher debated.

Mrs. O'Daniel hugged herself. "Is, too. I heard he got religion soon after that, though most folks can't stand the sight of him for more than a graveside funeral."

Nell joined Wednesday's laughter.

"I'm coming up!" Harrison called as if everyone might have given up worrying and gone to bed while he was checking out the house.

He tapped up the stairs, then seemed to stop halfway before climbing the last few steps.

"I think I've solved the crime," he announced with a smile.

Everyone gave him their full attention as he walked to the center of the room.

"The lock on the back door had been broken. It must have happened during the storm earlier tonight, or one of us would have heard something. Marla, did you notice anything when you locked up?"

The shy cook shook her head.

Harrison continued. "Well, it must have happened sometime around midnight, because the storm settled about one."

Everyone nodded, following his logic.

"Only one thing was stolen."

"Stolen," Nell whispered. She couldn't imagine what would be valuable enough to commit a crime to get from her house.

Harrison looked straight at Nell. "The painting Henry Stockard gave Fat Alice. The one hanging halfway up the stairs."

No one said a word for a moment, then Gypsy mumbled, "We've been burgled by the dumbest thief in the world."

No one argued.

Harrison moved closer to Nell when she asked, "Do you think it could have been Walter Farrow?"

He shook his head. "Why? You offered him the painting his uncle did when he was here. Why would he turn it down and then come back almost a week later to steal it? I'm not even sure he's still in town. Looks like he would have been back out to check on what we want for the land if he is still interested."

Gypsy had listened in. "Walter Farrow doesn't strike me as a man who cuddles up too closely with reason."

The others moved to the hallway to take a look at the space where the painting had been as if they might find another clue. Harrison stayed behind with Nell. "I'll board up the back door before I return to the barn."

Nell looked up at him. "Would you sleep on the sofa downstairs, just for the rest of the night?"

Harrison rested his hand on her shoulder. "Whoever it was won't be back. Not tonight. I think he got what he was looking for."

Nell knew Harrison was right, but she didn't want to admit how frightened she'd been. All her life she'd been brave. She'd run with the wind behind her and dared anyone to stop her. And now . . . now she feared a breeze.

"I'll move my bedroll in and sleep where I can see both the kitchen door and the front entrance. No one will climb the stairs again tonight without my seeing them." He smiled and handed her his old Colt. "Keep this nearby. If you even hear something strange, shoot toward the window. I'll come running." He winked at her. "Don't worry about the glass, I already know how to repair it."

Nell smiled, grateful he understood. She could hear the others in the hallway discussing the crime. "Thanks," she whispered. What was it about her life? Men kept handing her guns. First Jacob and now Harrison.

"You're welcome," he answered.

And right there and then, Nell decided she liked Randolph Harrison. He wasn't helping her because she was crippled or because he hoped to be her husband, or even because he worked for her. He helped her simply because they were friends.

Brother Aaron cleared his throat from the doorway. "I think we'd best be letting Miss Nell get some sleep."

Harrison removed his hand from Nell's shoulder, but he didn't look as if he thought he'd been doing anything he should repent for. He turned away as Nell slipped the gun he'd given her between the sheets. He was right about one thing; she'd feel far safer now knowing she could at least defend herself, even if she couldn't run away.

Harrison bowed at the door. "Until tomorrow."

"If we're lucky," she answered and tucked her feet beneath the covers.

Nell listened as the house settled. Mrs. O'Daniel poked her head in to see if she wanted a hot cocoa. When Nell declined, she heard everyone else move downstairs. It was hours before dawn, but the house was awake. And Nell heard Wednesday tell everyone that since they were awake, they might as well have something to eat.

Leaning on her pillows, Nell wished Jacob were here. He'd probably think it was funny that someone stole the ugly painting. As she slipped back into sleep, she thought of how he'd kissed her by the windmill and how she'd wished he'd touched her. She would have liked to curl up in his big arms and feel his body pressing against her. She slept soundly, safe and wrapped in the dream of being in Jacob's arms.

Just before dawn, Nell pulled herself into her wheelchair and rolled to the window. Mrs. O'Daniel had done a grand job of teaching her how to shift her weight, and she loved the small ounce of freedom she now had to move about her room. The chairs were shoved away from the window so she could roll right up to the edge.

She pushed the window wider, ignoring the chill as she took a front-row seat to watch the dawn. All others in the house were asleep. They'd probably talked and drunk cocoa for an hour or more before turning in. Now the house was so still, not even the air moved about.

Just as the sun cleared the horizon, Nell heard a horse coming from the back trail that led away from town. She rolled to the side of her bed and pulled the old Colt out. As she'd been taught by Jacob years ago, she checked the gun to make sure it was loaded, then returned to the window.

Two horses broke from the line of trees. One rider, one pack horse loaded down.

"Hello the house!" the rider called. He pulled up as courtesy required on farms and ranches when the traveler was unknown. "Hello the house!" he called again.

Nell rolled as far as she could to the window and answered. "Ride on in."

The man tugged the reins of the pack horse and came in slow and easy.

Nell kept the gun ready. She couldn't see a weapon, but she'd had enough trouble of late to take precautions. As the rider neared, she saw he was little more than a boy. Almost a man, but muscles as lean as rawhide.

His pack was loaded down with rain slickers crossed over his cargo to keep it dry. There wasn't enough light for Nell to see clearly, but one animal looked to be the midnight color or Jacob's mount Dusty, the other horse a paint.

Nell heard the front door open and knew Harrison was awake. She also guessed that he'd meet the visitor with his rifle in hand.

"Morning," the boy said as he swung down at the end of the walk. "I hope I'm at the right house." He moved to the other horse and began pulling rain slickers away. "I haven't heard a word from the ranger for hours, but he must have told me the route ten times."

Nell's heart caught in her throat as she recognized Jacob's body crossed over the saddle.

She heard the clank of a rifle hitting the porch. A moment later, Harrison was by the boy's side, helping lower Jacob to the ground.

"Mrs. O'Daniel!" Nell yelled as she rolled backward as fast as she could. "Mrs. O'Daniel, come quick."

The nurse and Wednesday came running as if last night's robbery had only been a drill and they were now well-trained troops. The nurse had removed the rag twists on her hair and clawed her way into her dress as she walked.

"I have to get downstairs." Nell cried as she rolled toward the stairs.

"I'll get the belt," Mrs. O'Daniel said.

"No, just brace me. We can make it." Nell was already pulling up on the banister. The nurse had no choice but to circle her waist and help her. They'd made the trip every day, but never without the belt for security. But safety wasn't in Nell's thoughts now.

She ignored the pain as she moved down the stairs as fast as she could, but they already had Jacob inside by the time she reached the bottom. He trailed blood behind him as they half carried, half dragged him.

Wednesday bumped the wheelchair downstairs behind them and had it ready within seconds. Everyone in the house was up now and running around wildly.

Once in her chair, Nell took a deep breath and took charge. "Get him to the study. We'll use the desk. Marla, put water on to boil. Gypsy, bring the medicine kit and all the bandages you can find. Mrs. O'Daniel, check his wounds. If I know Dalton, it took more than one to bring him down."

She was proud of her little army. They stripped off Jacob's coat and shirt as well as his boots. He looked like he wore a pound of mud and almost as much blood. Gypsy grabbed a rag and began to clean, while Mrs. O'Daniel examined the wounds.

"He needs a doctor for that shoulder," she said when she finally glanced up. "I can take care of the cuts on his arm and hands, but the shoulder wound is deep, and the cut along his middle would prove bothersome."

Harrison lifted Jacob's head and forced a few swallows of whiskey down his throat. "The preacher's already gone for the doc. I told him to bring the man even if he had to talk him into it at gunpoint." He looked over at the boy who'd brought the ranger in. "How'd this happen?"

The boy backed away. "I don't know, I swear. I just found him like that. He told me to take him west. He said just before I got to town I'd see a house off by the train tracks and I was to take him there. He made me swear."

Nell gripped the boy's hand. "Thank you," she said. "You did a good job." She turned back to Jacob, but she heard Marla whisper to the boy that there was coffee and food in the kitchen if he was hungry.

"Thank you," he answered. "I haven't had anything since yesterday morning."

Nell looked at the kid again. "What's your name?" She tried to keep fear out of her voice. Talking might help her keep from worrying about Jacob.

"Hank, miss." He looked frightened. "He's going to live, isn't he?"

Nell wished she had an answer. "Go get some coffee and warm up. You did a good thing bringing him here."

Hank smiled.

The doctor arrived with Sheriff Parker on his heels. He quickly shooed everyone out of the study except Mrs. O'Daniel. He didn't look like he wanted to be in Nell's house, but a Texas Ranger was down, and it was his duty to do all he could.

"But I got to ask him questions," Parker complained. "I got to know what happened out there."

The doctor didn't bother to consider the sheriff's demands. He only closed the door to everyone.

Nell's small army moved to the kitchen, where they crowded around the table and drank coffee. Everyone voiced a theory on what might have happened. The boy who brought the ranger in was silent. No one felt like eating except Gypsy, who said she needed her strength now that it appeared the household had given up sleep.

Harrison, in his usual take-charge manner, poured coffee and helped Marla fix a breakfast that Nell guessed no one would eat.

An hour passed. The nurse poked her head around the door and said the doctor wanted to speak to Nell.

Everyone moved back to the study door as if Nell were their collective name.

The doctor didn't comment, but he did direct his announcement to Nell. "He's going to be fine. Just weak from loss of blood. The cuts are not deep, mostly bothersome. I had to stitch up one on his arm and another on the back of his shoulder. I don't know for sure, but they look like knife wounds. He managed to wrap the cut across his ribs well enough that I think it's started to heal without stitches, but it'll leave an ugly scar."

The doctor smiled and added, "They'll match the others he's collected over the years."

He glanced up at the boy standing back close to the kitchen door. "If you hadn't got him home when you did, he might have bled to death. Even now there is some danger of infection. We had to dig rocks and dirt out of some of the smaller scrapes and cuts. I'll be interested to know what he had to go through after he was stabbed, but, son, you may have saved his life."

Everyone turned to the kid. No one seemed to be able to find words to say until Mrs. O'Daniel screamed. "That's him! That's the kid who wouldn't let me off the train when the firing started. He's one of the bandits."

CHAPTER 22

Jacob woke up slowly, one limb at a time. He opened his eyes, trying to think of the bright side. His left leg didn't hurt. That was it, end of the bright side. Every other part of his body felt like it had been in a meat grinder.

He stretched, realizing he was off the horse finally and, for the first time in days, he was warm. The boy named Hank had tried to hold him in the saddle and ride behind him, but Jacob was too heavy. Every time Jacob passed out, he hit the dirt.

Jacob grinned. He had to give the boy credit. When he'd tumbled, the kid had fallen off still trying to hold him.

When they'd found one of the other horses, Jacob had the kid tie him onto Dusty's saddle, hoping that even if Hank decided to abandon him, Dusty would eventually head to Nell's place. Jacob figured he was dead if they didn't make faster time than they could make riding double, so what difference did a little discomfort make?

His gaze shifted to the top of a bookshelf in front of him. Either the kid had made it, or heaven looked a lot like an old whorehouse.

"You awake?" Gypsy popped her head into his line of vision, her nose almost touching him, her breath working like smelling salts on his senses.

He wanted to push her away but wasn't sure he had the energy. "Yeah, I'm awake. I guess the kid got me here."

"Three days ago," Gypsy said. "Ever'one got tired of watching you sleep. They all left but me. I got housework to do. I don't have time to go off fiddlin' around in a town that don't got nothing I want. There's more folks pass by this house than I wanta talk to most days. Can't see going into town just to be bothered by crowds. "

"Where'd they go?"

"I told you, town. You must have fallen on your head once too often." Gypsy went back to cleaning the bookshelf.

He rubbed his forehead, thinking the old woman was probably right. "Any reason?" he mumbled, knowing Nell would not have left the house unless she had to.

"To see the kid who brought you in."

Jacob tried to clear the cobwebs out of his brain. Gypsy wouldn't fill in any details if he didn't ask. "Why's the kid in town?"

Gypsy tossed her rag down and turned back to Jacob. "The sheriff arrested him right after he brought you in. Mrs. O'Daniel fingered him as one of the train robbers. She said if it wasn't for Hank, she'd have been off the train when she heard the shooting start and probably killed dead a minute later." Gypsy shook her dust rag out the window. "But Sheriff Parker didn't seem to take that into consideration. He's got the boy locked away, and Brother Aaron says there's talk in town about hanging him straightaway without taking time for a trial."

Gypsy took a deep breath. "That's all I know. Can I get back to my chores? Oh, the doc said you're going to live. We was all real glad to hear that."

Jacob closed his eyes. "So am I." But he didn't smile. He was too worried about the boy. He didn't like the idea of the kid being in jail. Jacob hadn't saved him from the outlaws to watch him hang.

Jacob slept off and on until he heard the front door. He kept his eyes closed, listening to the preacher complain about the mud on the road and Wednesday say she was hungry.

Brother Aaron claimed if she ate any more, she'd pop, but Wednesday only laughed and said she had to eat because Mrs. O'Daniel said so.

A hand touched Jacob's and, without looking, he knew it was Nell. When he closed his fingers around hers, she jerked in surprise.

"You're awake."

He smiled up at her. "I'm awake."

She looked more beautiful than when he'd left. Her face was flushed with color, and her brown eyes were filled with worry. He'd always thought her pretty but never to the point that he couldn't stop staring. The memory of how she'd looked that first night in her underthings flashed through his mind. Her skin had been like cream, and he'd had no trouble making out the outline of her breasts. She had nice breasts, not too big, not too small.

Jacob swore and closed his eyes. He must have been out on the trail too long. This was Two Bits he was looking at. He'd known her most of her life. It was probably just the lack of blood to his brain that made him think of such things. If the outlaw had cut him one more time, Jacob would probably think Gypsy was good-looking.

Jacob glanced at the little pixie of a woman still dusting the shelves. Her gray hair was like a fuzzy dandelion ball around her head, and the skin on her arms kept wiggling long after she'd stopped. No, he decided, he'd never lose enough blood to find her pretty.

"Want a little soup?" Nell asked.

He looked back to her. "I want a lot of soup and a steak if there's one handy. Tell Marla she doesn't even have to cook it, just warm it up and I'll eat it."

Nell smiled. "You're definitely feeling better."

Two bowls of soup and half a pie later, Jacob stopped eating. He'd moved to the couch by the fire in the big, airy room to eat. The old nurse buzzed around him like a dragonfly.

"If you eat any more, you'll split your stitches." Mrs. O'Daniel checked his bandages as if she expected to see blood.

"I'm fine," he assured her. "You've got enough patients around this place. Don't think you can add me to your list."

Nell leaned forward and ran her hand over the bandage that covered his ribs. "Take care, Jacob." Her fingers brushed his skin above the cotton. "You've lost enough blood for a while. No more."

He met her eyes as her warm touch crossed his heart. He wondered how many times in the past three days she'd brushed her hand over his skin, maybe just making sure his heart was still beating, maybe feeling to see if he had a temperature. It didn't matter; he was sorry he hadn't been awake to enjoy her every touch.

Then, unexpectedly, he saw something in her eyes. She enjoyed the contact as much as he did. The knowledge that she saw him as a man as well as a friend surprised him.

Gypsy offered him a clean shirt, and Nell leaned away. The moment was gone.

The old hooker helped him into the shirt. "We had to toss all your old clothes."

Jacob tried to button it, but the bandages across his hands slowed his progress. Finally, frustrated, he mumbled an oath.

Nell leaned forward and began buttoning his shirt from the bottom. As she moved up, he took a deep breath, breathing her in and wishing he knew how to tell her he wouldn't mind if she reversed the action sometime.

"Thanks," he managed to say when she'd finished. He no longer tried to keep his thoughts away. He didn't care if she could read what he was thinking when she looked at him.

"You're welcome." She smiled.

The thought crossed his mind that she might be thinking the same thing. But she didn't say anything. She just moved away and picked her sewing back up.

Jacob glanced around the room at the others, wondering if anyone had noticed him staring at Nell. The ranger decided he agreed with the old hooker; sometimes there did seem to be a crowd always around.

He would have liked to talk to Nell or Rand Harrison in private, but there wasn't much chance of that. After an hour of milling around, the preacher, Wednesday, and Gypsy moved to the dining table to have a snack. Jacob caught Harrison's eye. "Fill me in on what's happened here since I've been gone."

Harrison sat beside Nell. As Jacob expected, the bookkeeper answered without adding any unnecessary details. He told of the robbery in the house and of Hank's arrest.

"How's the boy holding up?" Jacob asked.

"Not well." Harrison shook his head. "I talked to Parker, and he said one of the deputies got a little rough with him last night. Claimed Hank tried to jump him, but Parker admitted the deputy's sister had been on the train, and the robbers scared her half to death. The kid's lip is swollen and one of his eyes blackened. I got him to lift his shirt so Mrs. O'Daniel could make sure he didn't have any broken ribs."

Jacob nodded. He'd seen the way prisoners were sometimes treated in small jails before.

Harrison continued, "When Mrs. O'Daniel saw Hank this morning, she cried, then demanded to be allowed to look after his wounds." Harrison showed no emotion as he added, "She feels bad for turning him in since he may have kept her alive during the robbery and probably saved you."

"But he was part of the crime," Jacob admitted. "And I promised I'd stand by him if there's a trial."

"The sheriff said they caught three others. They were almost at the Red River." Nell broke her silence. "They had the loot but only one mule. Another mule had died. One of the posse rode in a few days ago to get a wagon. He said they just followed the circling buzzards and found the dead mule, then the tracks where the outlaws were dragging the loot was easy to follow."

Harrison continued, "Parker thinks the posse will lock the gang up in his jail for a day or two, then head to Fort Worth for trial. He doesn't want them staying here any longer than necessary. A lot of the town had kin on the train, and Parker fears the hanging will outrun the trial."

An uneasiness settled over Jacob. He knew his job, back the law, but he didn't like the idea of Hank being mixed in with the three out-laws still alive. The boy could have run a hundred times instead of bringing Jacob back here. Hank could have collected the horses, left Jacob for dead, and ridden to join his pa and the others. Or he could have ridden west and disappeared without a trace. He was old enough to hire on as a cowhand with only a few lies.

But he hadn't. He'd brought Jacob home.

"I need a little fresh air. Harrison, will you join me?" Jacob stood slowly, testing his legs as he nodded once to Nell.

She turned her chair toward the dining area, but he didn't miss the question in her gaze.

His body felt stiff, but he managed to walk to the front door. Harri-son opened it for him, and they stepped into the sunshine.

When they were alone, Jacob said, "Thanks for taking care of Nell while I was gone."

"I didn't do it for you."

Jacob smiled. "I know."

For a few minutes the two men stood in silence. Finally, Jacob added, "About the boy, I've got to ask you something I have no right to ask."

Harrison leaned against the railing. "You're wanting to know if I'll help you break him out if a mob forms."

Jacob raised an eyebrow. That was exactly what he planned to ask. He couldn't believe Harrison guessed.

The bookkeeper shrugged. "I was thinking the same thing, but I would have never mentioned it to a Texas Ranger."

"Smart idea." Jacob laughed. "If you help, it might be dangerous."

Harrison crossed his arms over his chest and stared down. Jacob wasn't sure Harrison would go along with any plan. After all, they would be breaking the law. Any other time, he'd stay in the jail and protect the prisoner, but he wasn't sure he had the strength to ride. In a week, maybe less, he'd be able to fight any mob that came along, but right now, he wasn't sure. "All I'd be asking you to do, Rand, was cover my back if the time came. Nothing more. Nothing illegal."

Harrison took a breath and said in a low voice. "I was in Kansas once when a drunken mob decided to break into the jail and hold a midnight trial on a man who'd murdered his wife. They rushed the guard. Got a prisoner out with nothing but threats. I rode up just as they dropped him from the second floor of the saloon. His neck snapped when he reached the end of the rope. They went back to drinking, figuring they'd done their duty. The prisoner swung there till dawn."

The bookkeeper looked up at the ranger. "The next morning we found out that the mob opened the wrong cell that night. They hung the wrong man."

No hesitation shown in Harrison's gaze. "I'll not help you let him escape, but I'll do whatever it takes to see he has a fair trail."

Jacob nodded once.

The door opened, and Nell, flanked by her nurse, stepped out. "Afternoon, gentlemen," she said. "We're out for our walk."

Jacob couldn't believe it. The nurse might be holding her tightly about the waist and letting Nell lean on her for balance, but Nell was walking. He watched her grab one hand to the railing as she moved in baby steps along the length of the porch and back.

When she reached them, she looked exhausted, but she smiled, "Mrs. O'Daniel says another few days and I can go swimming."

"You look grand," Jacob said, and before he realized everyone was watching, he leaned and kissed her cheek.

"Now none of that," Mrs. O'Daniel yelled in his ear. "Neither one of you are solid on your feet."

She was right, he realized, and was thankful when Harrison moved to his side. Jacob placed his hand on Rand's shoulder. "How about we go back in?"

Harrison understood and slowly walked inside with Jacob leaning on him for support.

Three hours later, when Jacob awoke from his nap on the couch, Wednesday was keeping watch over him.

"Hello." He smiled. Nell might look more beautiful, but Wednesday only looked rounder. "How are you, Miss May?"

She giggled. "I'm fine. They told me to keep an eye on you while I sew. Miss Nell is napping. Mr. Harrison is working on the books."

"Where are the preacher and Mrs. O'Daniel?" Jacob asked, realizing keeping up with everyone in this house wasn't easy.

"They went back to town. Mrs. O'Daniel is worried about a cut over that boy's eye. She wanted to ask the doctor to check it." Wednesday looked down at the sewing. "I was in the kitchen, but Marla ran me out, telling me you needed watching more than she needed talking to."

Jacob laughed, remembering how much the girl talked. "How about we go in the kitchen and see if Marla has anything to eat? I'm starving."

"Me, too," Wednesday said as she set down her sewing.

Once they were at the kitchen table, Wednesday did most of the talking while Jacob ate everything Marla set in front of him. He felt sure the shy cook didn't really want him taking up room in her kitchen, but as always, she didn't say anything.

After a while, Harrison joined them for a cup of coffee while he unfolded the weekly paper.

"Feeling better?" he asked Jacob as he sat on a stool beside where Marla was cutting apples.

Jacob nodded. "Much. Good food is all I needed." He glanced up to see Harrison smile briefly at Marla.

"She's quite a cook. That's a fact." He straightened out his paper on the corner of the cutting board.

The thin cook's cheeks were as red as the apple peels she sliced. Then, to Jacob's total surprise, Harrison held his palm up beside the bowl, and Marla sliced off a piece of apple into his hand.

The action was a small one, looking as though she'd done it many times before. No big deal. A silent request granted.

Harrison ate the apple and read. Jacob wondered if he tried the same action would he lose a finger.

Wednesday chatted on about how frightened she was after the robbery, and Jacob watched the bookkeeper and the cook over the rim of his cup. Neither showed any sign of even being aware that the other one was in the room. But, after a few minutes, Harrison, without even glancing up, repeated his request. An apple slice landed in his hand.

A few hours later at dinner, Jacob managed to sit at the table without too much pain. He talked with Parker about all the news and told the sheriff how Hank had helped him. But, despite all he needed to tell the lawman, Jacob kept an eye on Marla.

She moved about as silently as always. Once everything was in place, she slipped into her chair beside Gypsy and ate her meal without looking up from her plate more than a few times.

Jacob was about to decide he'd been seeing things earlier in the kitchen, when Marla stood and began serving dessert with coffee. Harrison, at the other end of the table, also stood and collected plates.

He never looked at Marla, yet he silently helped her and she thanked him with a brief nod when they passed one another.

Jacob pushed away from the table and excused himself. He'd eaten dessert in the kitchen as his appetizer. He walked slowly to the front porch, stretching his muscles and wondering how many days it would be before he felt like himself.

The night was warm for a change. Spring couldn't be far. That was one thing he liked about this part of the country. The seasons changed all at once sometimes. He'd seen spring poke through snow and winter freeze leaves still green on the trees.

Relaxing on the porch swing, he lit a thin cigar and watched the night sky.

The door opened and closed, but he didn't stand to peer around the corner to see who followed him out. He knew.

Nell rolled slowly toward him in the shadows. He watched, hating her chair. She'd once moved so gracefully on her long legs; now the jerky movements of her chair seemed so out of place.

"Want some company?"

"If you don't mind the smoke."

She pulled her chair beside the swing. "Did I ever tell you that I took up smoking my last year of school?"

"No." He smiled, wondering if she were lying. When she'd been a kid, she'd sometimes think of the worst story possible so when he discovered the truth about some little something she'd done, he wouldn't think it was so bad compared to the tale.

"Several of the girls did." Her voice was low. "We'd climb up in the attic and open an old, forgotten window. Then we'd all sit around shivering while we smoked. I never got the hang of it, but I liked the smell."

"You did?"

"Sure. It reminded me of busy nights in the old days when it always seemed like all the men smoked and all the women laughed. Fat Alice would make me go to bed early, but I could hear the partying happening below my room up in the attic."

"I forgot you lived up there when you first came."

"Fat Alice had my meals sent up with extra water and food so I'd have no reason to come down after dark. It wasn't long after I came that she closed the business, and I guess you could say she went into private practice. Only her longtime customers were allowed to call."

Nell brushed the bandage over the back of his hand. "Does it hurt?"

He stretched his fingers. "Not much." He ran one finger over her palm, watching her long fingers curl slightly to his touch. "I'm glad to be back."

"Jacob." She moved her hand up his arm. "Do you think you could ever see me as a woman and not just some kid you protected?"

He leaned closer. "I do think of you as a woman. Hell, Nell, half the time I'm thinking of you, I'm trying *not* to think of you as a woman."

Even in the shadows he saw her smile. "Why?"

Jacob took a long breath. He didn't know how to answer her. He thought of himself as a man of action, not words. But she needed the words. "Sometimes, when I'm out sleeping alone under the stars, I feel like I'm the only man alive. There's a kind of loneliness that settles over me that aches all the way through my bones. When I get like that, I think of you. Not the kid I've known, but the woman who ran to me that day at the train station when you came home that last time from school. You were all woman, and I couldn't believe you were running with your arms wide open toward me."

She was still smiling.

"I swung you around in my arms wishing the whole world could see what a fine lady you were and wishing you'd never let go. I have to remind myself you're my friend and maybe I shouldn't be thinking about you like I do sometimes."

He heard the lock click on the sides of her chair and watched her use the arms to stand.

"Will you hold me now?" she whispered as she extended her arm.

He circled her waist with his hands and gently sat her beside him. Lifting her legs over his knee, he pushed the swing in motion.

For a long while they moved gently with the breeze, cuddled against one another.

"Nell," he whispered. "Would you mind if I kissed you again?" He thought about just leaning over, but after she'd told him she wouldn't marry him, he didn't know how she'd feel about him kissing her again.

She hesitated and finally whispered, "Would you mind touching me first?"

Jacob froze. That wasn't the answer he'd expected. "All right," he said for lack of something better. "Where would you like me to touch you?"

He expected her to hold his hand or put his fingers to the side of her face. After all, she was quite a bit younger than him, and maybe that was what she thought a man and woman should do first. He hadn't been around women enough to know what they wanted. Maybe when he'd kissed her before, she'd thought he was leaving out a few steps along the way.

She lifted his hand and laid it over her left breast.

Jacob didn't move. Touching her here hadn't been in the top ten places he would have guessed she'd wanted to be touched.

"I know you can't feel much through your bandage and my dress, but can you feel my heart beating?" She placed her hand on top of his.

"I can," he lied, for his heart pounded so hard he wouldn't have heard thunder in his ear. And what he felt beneath his fingers had nothing to do with her heart.

She took a deep breath, her breast rising and falling in his hand. He thought of telling her that what they were doing was far from proper, but then she might suggest stopping.

He leaned forward and touched his lips to hers and heard her moan softly. He'd meant only one light kiss, but a hunger rushed through his blood, and he deepened the kiss.

When she answered his need, Jacob closed his hand around the softness below layers of cotton and felt her moan of pleasure against his lips.

This definitely beat holding hands.

CHAPTER 23

Nell curled beneath the covers and closed her eyes even before Mrs. O'Daniel had time to turn down the wick on her nightlight. She needed to be alone with her thoughts. She wanted to remember every detail of what she and Jacob had shared on the porch. The way he'd kissed her so tenderly took her breath away, and the way his hand had warmed over her breast made her feel alive.

She'd been afraid to ask him to touch her, but she wanted him to see her as a woman, and just kissing might take forever before he woke up to the fact. He treated her like a kid one minute and like some kind of china doll that might break the next. Nell grinned. She'd given him something to think about tonight. She could almost picture him downstairs on the couch trying to figure out what happened in the shadows of the porch.

He probably believed it was the man who made the advances. She fought down a laugh. Her ranger had a lot to learn. Maybe he never married because he didn't understand how much a man needs a woman? Well, he was about to find out. Even if she couldn't marry him and have his children, she'd develop the hunger in him. Once he realized he needed a woman, it wouldn't take him long to find one.

She didn't want to admit how much the thought of him with another hurt. Nell had to think of his happiness. Jacob had spent all his life learning to be tough; it was time he developed a taste for love.

She checked the Colt beneath the extra pillow on her bed. Tonight she'd be safe, but she'd never forget to check before she fell asleep. Mrs. O'Daniel's rubdowns and baths relaxed her enough to help her rest, and the exercise exhausted her during the day. Since the nurse came to live with Nell, she'd been sleeping more, eating more, and beginning to hope that someday she might walk. She could hardly wait until Dr. McClellan saw her progress. Nell had often felt guilty when the doctor and his nurse made the train trip down to her and she remained the same. Even though they never complained, she felt she was wasting their valuable time.

Nell fell asleep dreaming of what life would be like if she could walk. If she could just walk a few steps by herself, she'd never take it for granted again.

Deep in her dreams, she heard a voice.

"Miss Nell?"

She rolled over, the sound pulling her awake.

"Miss Nell?"

She stretched and felt a hand touch her shoulder.

Nell's dreams vanished as she opened her eyes and saw Wednesday's little round face.

Wednesday tried to smile, but fear filled her eyes. "Miss Nell, I think I'm leaking."

Nell rose to her elbows and tried to see in the darkness. "What?" Maybe she was still dreaming.

Wednesday looked embarrassed. "I can't seem to stop. Water's coming out of me."

Nell had no idea what was happening but tried not to look as frightened as the girl did. "I'm sure it's all right. Get Mrs. O'Daniel."

Wednesday nodded, happy to have a plan. She waddled off to the nurse's room. A few minutes later, Mrs. O'Daniel tromped down the stairs at full speed. When she hit the ground floor, she yelled, with no regard to Jacob sleeping on the couch, "Marla! I'm going to need water. Gypsy, wake up! We've got a baby coming, and I'm going to need lots of towels and sheets."

Nell stood and pulled her robe around her, then sat in her wheelchair. She rolled to the landing as lights were lit downstairs. Jacob had sat up, the firelight flickering off his bare chest. "Anything I can do to help?" he bellowed as Mrs. O'Daniel ran past him with a load of towels.

"No. Go back to sleep and stay out of my way," the nurse answered.

He shrugged and turned his back as he lay down.

Nell wanted to yell for him to go get the preacher and Harrison but realized this emergency was one for the women in the house. The men could be of no help. The men might as well sleep.

She rolled down the hallway. When she reached Wednesday's door, the girl stood beside her bed, crying softly.

Nell went into the room and took her hand, surprised to find it cold as ice.

Wednesday sniffed. "Mrs. O'Daniel told me to change my gown and get into bed, but I'm too scared. I hurt all inside. The pain comes and goes."

Nell didn't know what to say. The girl had a right to be afraid. Almost half the women in the cemetery had died in childbirth. It wasn't an easy thing for any woman, and Wednesday's body didn't even look fully grown.

"I'll help you all I can," Nell whispered. She wished she could do something more.

The girl nodded, then turned her back and pulled off her wet gown. Before she slipped on a fresh one, Nell had time to study the scars on Wednesday's back. Most were healed, but the marks of her beating would never go away.

As Wednesday awkwardly crawled into bed, Nell whispered, "The water you lost is natural. I read about it in a book at school. All mothers-to-be have it. The baby floats in a bag inside you, and the bag is full of water."

Wednesday's eyes widened in interest now, as if Nell were only telling her a fairy tale and nothing more.

Nell wished she'd paid more attention in her final classes. Many of the girls in her school were going on to be nurses, so she'd heard conversations about all kinds of things. "Next comes what they call labor. It's going to be hard work to move the baby out."

The girl didn't look like she wanted to hear more. "It ain't fair, Miss Nell. It hurt when I got pregnant, and now you're telling me it's going to hurt again. I don't like this. I don't want to grow up. I don't want to be a woman." She started to cry harder. "I don't know how to be a mother. I'm not sure I can do this."

Nell wouldn't lie to her. "We've got Mrs. O'Daniel, who told me a few days ago that she's delivered several babies. She'll know what to do." Nell thought of sending for the doctor. He'd been good to come when Jacob was brought in, but other times, he'd been reluctant to venture out to the house by the tracks. He might not consider this an emergency worth his time. "You're a very brave girl, and you're going to get through this."

Wednesday nodded, but she didn't look like she believed Nell was telling her the truth.

"I'll have Marla make you some tea. Would you like that?"

Wednesday nodded again, her eyes closed tightly as she gripped her middle. "It hurts something terrible, miss."

Nell took one of the girl's hands. "You help me know when it hurts. When it starts, you hold my hand real tight. Then I'll know."

Wednesday took a deep breath. "It's gone now."

Five minutes later, she gripped Nell's hand, and they both held tight through the next pain.

When the other women hurried into the room, Nell started to move back, knowing that her chair would be in the way.

"No, miss," Wednesday said. "Don't leave me."

Mrs. O'Daniel agreed. "I can work around you and that chair. We may need all the hands we got to get this baby born. You stay at her head, Miss Nell, and keep talking to her."

Nell wanted to say she really didn't want to be in the room. She'd never seen a woman in labor. But she couldn't back out now. When Nell glanced up, she saw her panic reflected in Marla's eyes. She, too, must have never witnessed a birth.

Mrs. O'Daniel came to the cook's aid. "Marla, I'll need you in the kitchen keeping water on to boil and coffee coming. Gypsy and Nell can help me here, but we'll need coffee to stay alert, and if hours pass, something that we can eat fast to keep going. The last birthing I helped with took almost two days."

The cook nodded. "I'll check in every thirty minutes or so. The kitchen's right below. Just stomp on the floor, and I'll come running to see what's needed." She vanished like a rabbit.

Gypsy moved to the nurse's side. "I've assisted a few times. I know what needs to be done."

Mrs. O'Daniel nodded and, for the first time that Nell knew of, smiled at the tiny old prostitute.

Wednesday held Nell's hand as the contractions grew closer together. Nell wiped the girl's ashen face and watched the clock. The pains didn't last long, and Nell guessed when each was half over. She'd lean close to Wednesday and whisper, "We're on the downhill slope now. Hang on. Hang on. The time's counting down." When the contraction was over, she'd whisper, "That's one less."

Wednesday would try to smile and nod as if she and Nell were playing some kind of game with the clock.

In less than three hours, Mrs. O'Daniel smiled. "Bless my soul, the baby's crowning. It won't be long now."

Suddenly, Nell felt like all the women were in a tornado. Wednesday might be the one having a baby, but they were all working, helping, encouraging, and crying together.

Wednesday screamed, and Mrs. O'Daniel yelled, "Push!"

Then, like silence following a storm, it was over. Mrs. O'Daniel lifted a baby and handed the wiggling boy to Gypsy. Wednesday gave one more push as ordered, and then relaxed back against the pillows as if she'd run ten miles. Gypsy and Mrs. O'Daniel cleaned the bed while Marla brought in one of the dishwashing tubs to bathe the baby. She might not have been able to stand the labor or delivery, but she was fascinated with the newborn. She sang to him as she gently cleaned away blood and wrapped him in a blanket Wednesday had embroidered tiny flowers around.

Wednesday whispered as she waited for them to pass him to her, "He's real ugly, isn't he?"

Nell laughed. "I think all babies look pretty much the same."

"I don't mind." Wednesday smiled. "My ugliest brother was the nicest to me when I was little. It won't make me love him less if he's pig faced."

Nell watched in awe as Marla lay the baby in Wednesday's arms. Everyone was laughing and crying at the same time.

"He's beautiful," Mrs. O'Daniel announced.

"You think so?" Wednesday asked.

"Finest boy I've ever delivered. He'll grow up to be a handsome man."

Gypsy grinned at the wiggling bundle. "I can tell by looking at him that he's going to be the kind of man someday who'll take good care of his ma."

"Really!"

"Sure. I can see the truth of a man at birth when he's learned no lies. This little fellow is going to make you proud every day of his life."

The new mother smiled. "You think so?"

"I know so." Gypsy winked. "I got the gift in my blood for knowing such things."

Wednesday stared down in wonder, unsure what to do, then she pulled the baby close and kissed his head. "You sure caused a lot of trouble," she whispered, "for no bigger than you are. I don't know how it's possible, but I already love you, and I don't plan on stopping loving you till I take my last breath."

Nell laid her hand on Wednesday's arm. "You'll be a great mother." Wednesday looked down at the tiny baby. "You hear that? I'm going to be a great ma. I'll try not to ever yell at you, and I swear I'll never hit you with anything bigger than a twig."

Mrs. O'Daniel proclaimed it was the easiest delivery in which she'd ever been involved.

"I thought I was going to die," Wednesday whispered. "You mean it could have been worse?"

Nell had to agree with Wednesday. If giving birth could sometimes be harder, how could any women stand it?

It was dawn by the time the room was cleaned. Wednesday held her boy for a while, then carefully passed him to Nell. The little mother ate breakfast as if she'd been working in the fields all night.

Marla, out of nervousness probably, had not wasted her time downstairs. She'd made several of Wednesday's favorites.

Harrison and the preacher came in to look at the baby. Harrison seemed fascinated by the tiny hand that wrapped around his finger, but didn't say anything. Brother Aaron went on and on about the beauty of a newborn, pure and sinless.

Jacob came into the room next. He seemed far more concerned about Wednesday than the baby. He nodded toward the little fellow, but didn't want to hold him. Mrs. O'Daniel had to assure him twice that Wednesday had made it through the delivery without problems before he smiled. Unlike Harrison, the ranger was still unshaven and his clothes had been slept in, but he had more color to his face than he'd had the day before.

With Wednesday falling asleep, they all moved out into the hall. Mrs. O'Daniel said she would sit with the girl for a while and ordered all the others downstairs to breakfast.

Without asking, Jacob lifted Nell out of the chair and carried her down the steps.

"Your shoulder," she whispered, remembering his wounds.

"I'll manage," he answered. "You look tired."

She smoothed his hair back as he carried her. "And you look like you just rolled off the couch."

"I did. Tell me, darling, does this place ever calm down? I've had quieter nights sleeping out in the wilderness."

Nell laughed, more because he called her darling than any other reason. "At least it's not boring around here." She cuddled against his shoulder. "And you are right, I'm very tired."

When he sat her on a kitchen chair, he kissed the top of her head before straightening.

Everyone gathered round the kitchen table and ate breakfast out of huge bowls Marla pulled from the warming drawers at the top of the stove. They all laughed as though they'd been a family forever.

When they were all stuffed, Nell asked Jacob to carry her back upstairs.

He silently lifted her up and left the room. Harrison had already taken his cup of coffee to his desk and was hard at work. Gypsy and Marla were talking about taking a morning nap, and the preacher said he planned to keep watch from the porch, which meant he'd be snoring within minutes.

Jacob climbed the stairs slowly. "It's been a long night."

Nell rubbed the whiskers along his jaw. "Mrs. O'Daniel says Wednesday will sleep most of the day, or until the baby wakes her, wanting to be fed. He's a sweetheart, don't you think?"

"He must take after his father. No hair. No teeth. Red as a beet, and I'm not sure his eyes are open yet."

Nell fought down a giggle. "He's not a cat. Of course his eyes open."

Jacob didn't look like he believed her. He carried her into her room and gently laid her down.

As he tucked her in and leaned close to kiss her cheek, Nell tugged, pulling him atop the covers.

"Lie with me a minute before you go."

He raised an eyebrow as if to argue.

"Everyone else is already asleep except Harrison, and he'll never climb the stairs without making an announcement. Just lie next to me for a minute. I need to feel you near."

"You don't want to be alone?" he questioned.

"No, that's not it. I want to be with you."

Jacob stretched his arm, and she used it as a pillow, then he laid his free arm across her waist and stretched out beside her. His weight shifted the bed as he removed pillows and pulled the cover to her chin.

"Comfortable?" She whispered, fighting not to laugh.

He moved his chin against her hair. "Yes." He shifted again. "You?"

"Yes, thank you."

The sensation of having him near rocked her completely with the rightness of him beside her. She closed her eyes and drifted into sleep, knowing all the world was in balance for the first time in her life.

While she slept, he listened to her breathing grow slow and regular. He felt the slight movement of her body as her breath went in and out. She wanted him with her. She wanted him near, he knew. Then why wouldn't she marry him? He could get used to being beside her like this . . . well, not just like this, he reconsidered. Less clothes on maybe and definitely less covers between them.

The thought crossed his mind that she might be trying to make Harrison jealous, but that made no sense. Harrison wasn't the type to have such a feeling, even if he did love her, and he'd made it plain to Jacob that he didn't even believe in love. Near as Jacob could tell, the two of them never talked about anything but the running of the ranch.

Lines worried their way across his forehead. If he wasn't in the running for husband, then could she be just toying with him? He knew he was her friend and more. Surely the kisses they'd shared proved that. Half the time she acted like he was her Texas Ranger and not the state's. She wanted him near. She wanted his touch. He had no doubt about that.

He smiled. As long as he could give her what she wanted, he wouldn't complain. Even now the memory of her breast warmed the palm of his hand. He'd never known a woman to answer his kiss with such honest passion. The thought of her last kiss reminded him that sleep was the last thing on his mind.

Maybe she was just trying to drive him crazy one last time. After all, near as he could remember, she'd been having fun driving him to the breaking point most of her life.

But not like this. Not with passion.

"Nell," he whispered against her ear, figuring if he were wide awake, she might as well join him.

"Yes," she mumbled.

"Mind if I touch you again?"

"No," she answered. "I don't mind."

"I mean really touch you, darling, like I did out on the porch."

She stretched slightly and raised her arm above her head. When she moved again, he felt her body warm and soft beside him.

He moved his fingers from her waist to her shoulder. She felt so good. With only her gown and robe on, he could feel the outline of her body beneath, and every inch of it felt like perfection.

He slipped his hand beneath her robe and molded his fingers around the fullness of her. She felt like heaven, all warm and willing.

"I could get used to this," he mumbled against her ear. "Turn your head so I can kiss you."

She did as he requested. Her mouth was slightly open when his lips touched hers, and the pleasure of it warmed him several degrees. He took slow pleasure in exploring the kiss as his thumb crossed over the peak of her breast.

When he pulled an inch away, it took several minutes for his breathing to slow and his brain to form thoughts. He moved his hand back to her waist, fighting the urge to pull up her gown and feel her flesh against his.

"Good night," she whispered as if the kiss had been no more than a way to say sweet dreams. She moved so that the breast he'd been holding pressed lightly against his chest.

"Good morning," he answered and closed his own eyes, deciding she was definitely driving him crazy. The strange thing was, at this point, he didn't even care why.

CHAPTER 24

A FEW HOURS LATER, JACOB SLIPPED FROM NELL'S SIDE AND walked to the window. The sun was high, but he heard nothing moving in the house. He glanced back at Nell, not wanting to think about how good she'd felt beside him, how right. He'd fallen asleep with her in his arms, but a part of him never totally relaxed. Old habits were hard to break. He'd heard the rider coming even before anyone on the porch would have been able to see someone approaching.

From the window lookout, Jacob spotted Sheriff Parker, his old hat flashing white in the morning sun. As he always did on what he called his "good days," he forced himself to sit a horse. Unfortunately, with one glance anyone could see the ride gave him far more discomfort than riding in a buggy. His days in the saddle were nearly over, no matter how much he swore he still enjoyed the freedom of being on horseback.

Most men the sheriff's age could sit back and retire while their sons ran the family business, but with lawmen, there was no retirement. Most didn't live past their forties, and those who did usually switched to a safer career.

Parker had no family and nowhere else to go, as far as Jacob knew. He'd spent his life alone.

The ranger was down the stairs by the time Harrison let the lawman inside. While the sheriff poured himself a cup of coffee, Harrison explained why everyone else in the house was still asleep.

If the bookkeeper thought Jacob's being upstairs was unusual, he didn't comment about it.

"What did the little fellow look like?" Parker didn't seem to care what the answer would be.

"Pink," Harrison answered. "Tiny and loud, very loud."

Parker nodded as if he recognized the breed. "Yeap. That about sums it up. Except it takes quite a while to fix that noise part. Years, from what I can tell."

The sheriff rummaged through the bread tin until he found muffins to go with his coffee and asked Harrison and Jacob to take a seat. "We need to talk," he mumbled between bites. "While the women are still all asleep."

Jacob pulled a chair out and sat. There was no hurrying Parker; he'd tell what he wanted them to know in his own good time.

"First, I thought you'd like to know, Dalton, the posse brought in the three outlaws you let slip away." He said the words as if Jacob had simply waved farewell to the robbers and not been lying at the bottom of a gully after being stabbed and falling ten feet.

"I know." Jacob smiled. "Careless of me to leave them running around out there, wasn't it?"

Parker took his time nodding agreement and then continued, "One of the three fellows, Hank's pa, didn't look so good. I think he must have suffered as much as you in that fight you said the two of you had. Maybe more. Both his eyes are black and one, the left one as I recall, is swollen shut. He'll be lucky if it's open by the time they hang him."

"Real lucky." Jacob nodded, remembering how he'd heard bone break when he'd smashed his fist into the man's face. "He wasn't much of a pa to the boy. I heard him say he wished he'd left Hank to starve to death. From the little I remember, I think Hank's mother is dead."

The sheriff agreed. "When they brought him in, Hank's pa seemed more angry that the boy was alive than happy to see him. He's a mean one. Been picking at the kid all morning, like it gives him some kind of pleasure. The sheriff in Fort Worth thinks he may be one of several men who killed a few guards down in Huntsville and broke out of prison a few months back."

"I wouldn't be surprised." Jacob remembered how he fought and how the man smiled when he'd drawn blood. He wasn't just trying to knife Jacob in the fight, he was trying to cause as much pain as possible. Men like that take years to get so mean.

Parker took a drink and made a face. "Who made this coffee? Worst darn stuff I ever drank."

"I did." Rand Harrison frowned. "Everyone else was still asleep."

"Tastes like you boiled the beans in mud."

Jacob's patience for waiting grew thin. Time was short. "What else is new? You didn't ride all the way out here to complain about the coffee."

Parker took another bite of muffin, chewed for a while, then said, "The posse's got two men mending over at the doc's place. They got hurt in the fight when they took the outlaws. It might have been a dozen men to three outlaws, but the bandits didn't go down without a fight. One of the posse took a bullet to the leg, the other to the shoulder. As soon as they're able to travel, they want to take the train robbers back to Fort Worth, and I'm glad to let them. Trouble is, we got a problem."

"What's that?" Harrison appeared interested in the conversation for the first time.

The sheriff pointed his cup at Jacob. "It seems Dalton here brought the boy in. I can't release a prisoner of a Texas Ranger's to anyone without the ranger's permission. I can let them take the other three, but Hank stays in my jail until you give the word. The railroad man riding as head of the posse didn't like it much, but I can't change the law."

The sheriff leaned closer. "I've been told his whole posse is hired guns. If that's true, they'll lose money if they leave one here."

Jacob shook his head. "I don't want Hank tried with the others. He's not like them. He proved it by bringing me home when he could have left me along the road anytime."

"I know that. I'm even keeping him in a separate cell, though that don't keep his pa from screaming all kinds of insults at him." Parker shook his head. "But, no matter how you look at it, Hank is one of them. There ain't nothing no one can do about that. If they hang, he'll hang, too. That's the way the law works."

Jacob knew the sheriff was right. He didn't need a reminder. But the boy who'd handed him a cup of coffee that morning crossed his mind. That kid was more afraid of his father than of what might happen to him if he got caught robbing a train. Jacob would bet Hank went along with it all out of fear. That's why, when he had the chance, he stayed with Jacob and didn't ride north to find his old man.

"I'll not release him to the posse." He looked straight at the sheriff. "You know as well as I do that the odds are not good that the outlaws will even survive the trip back to Fort Worth. One of them makes the wrong move, and they're all dead. The guns guarding them get the same money whether they bring the outlaws in dead or alive."

"I know. And to tell the truth, most of the men riding are young and nervous. They're good men near as I can tell, but they're not seasoned enough to handle the outlaws. I'd guess they might shoot first and think later. They already see the prisoners for what they are, cold-blooded killers, so even the best among them probably won't lose any sleep one way or the other."

"Except for the kid," Jacob said. "From what I understand, Hank didn't kill anyone. He doesn't deserve to be shot down like a mad dog."

Parker nodded. "But he can't stay here. I'm worried that even a few more nights in my jail may not be good for his health. Two of the men killed during the robbery were from around here. There's talk about stringing them up now and saving time. I think we're safe as long as I've got the posse around to act as extra guards, but once they're gone, I'm not sure the boy will be safe, even behind bars."

"I'm not turning Hank over," Jacob said for the third time.

Parker shook his head. "You're not strong enough to travel yet or I'd suggest you take a back trail that would be hard to follow. If you tried going with the posse on the train, you'd probably pass out somewhere between here and Fort Worth, and then where would the kid be? I'm too stove up to go with you, and I'm not sure backup Rangers could get here in time."

The sheriff was right, but Jacob didn't want to admit it. His body hurt now from carrying Nell upstairs, and she weighed next to nothing. What if the boy turned on him and fought? He wasn't sure he could handle the kid in a fight right now, and he knew he'd never shoot Hank. Not after the boy saved his life.

Parker finished his coffee with a frown and stood. "I got to get back. You think on it, and maybe you'll come up with something. I've talked the posse into staying over at the hotel across from the jail, so won't be nothing happening tonight." He turned to Jacob. "If you're going to take the kid, I'd take him before the posse leaves."

Jacob nodded.

Harrison walked the sheriff out. When he returned, Jacob was already checking the gun cabinet.

"You think there's going to be trouble?"

"I know it's coming, and soon," Jacob answered. "I'm just not sure from which way it'll ride in."

"Sounds like we have a few days." Harrison returned to his study.

Jacob nodded. "Only when the posse leaves, I have to be ready. And, if I were their leader, I might consider having no one, not even Parker, know when I would be pulling out."

He made sure all the rifles were loaded, then pulled on his boots. By the time he'd walked to the barn and back, he felt exhausted. How would he ever be able to stand against a mob in the shape he was in now?

"Two days," he mumbled Parker's words. Maybe three. That's all the time he had to figure out how to help Hank. He'd promised the kid a chance, and he'd see the boy got it.

Jacob wanted to go back upstairs with Nell, but he knew someone would notice. He didn't much care what anyone in the house thought, but he figured Nell might. So, he lay back on the couch and tried to sleep.

An hour later he was still wide awake when he heard Marla tell Harrison lunch was ready. He and Harrison were the only two who joined Marla in the kitchen. She'd checked upstairs and told him everyone was still asleep, even the baby. No one had to check on the preacher; they could hear him snoring from the porch. He hadn't even stirred when the sheriff walked past him.

"You think everyone plans to sleep all day?" Jacob asked more for something to say than hope of an answer.

Harrison shrugged. "I'm getting more work done than usual with all the quiet." He smiled at Marla. "How about you?"

She lowered her head and didn't answer. Jacob thought he saw the hint of a smile. He couldn't understand why she'd talk to Harrison, who'd only been around for a few days, but in the months Jacob had known her the woman had never even looked at him.

Jacob finished his soup and moved back to the couch. He figured Marla would never talk with him around, but she might if he left. Sure enough, within a few minutes he heard her whispering to Harrison.

Then Harrison laughed.

Jacob couldn't help wondering what the shy woman could have said that was funny. He closed his eyes and pretended to be asleep. The preacher must have smelled food, for he banged his way through the door and disappeared into the kitchen.

Frowning, Jacob tried to roll over and lie so that nothing hurt. Trying to sleep in the big room was like sleeping in a train station. If he couldn't sleep here because of the noise, and he couldn't sleep with Nell because she was so near, and the barn was out, he might as well give up the habit of sleeping all together.

Jacob wasn't surprised an hour later when Walter Farrow showed up, but he continued to act as if he were sound asleep.

Harrison opened the door, but didn't invite the stout man in. Like sugar ants, Walter Farrow rushed inside anyway.

He huffed and puffed all around the study.

Harrison tried to explain. "We've had some things happen here and Miss Nell has not had the time to make a decision about the Stockard place."

"Did you remind her that I'm offering a fair price? She can ask anyone in town. She'll not make more on the land."

"I told her," Harrison answered firmly.

Jacob opened an eye and noticed Number Twelve was holding his own. The fat lawyer didn't frighten him.

"Did you tell her I'm waiting?" Farrow rose on his toes and rocked back to his heels. "I'm paying a great many expenses while she takes her time."

"She knows," Harrison answered. "But you are free to return to Dallas, sir. She'll inform you by post of her decision."

"No." Farrow stumbled for words. "I'll wait a few more days. I'd like to talk to her the next time I come. Tell her I expect to be received. I'll not allow her to treat me like someone who comes begging."

"I understand. I'll let her know your feelings."

"You do that." Farrow raised one finger. "Tell her I'm not a man to dally with. I have interests all over this state as well as friends."

Harrison kept his proper manner as he walked to the door. "I think it would be best if you wait until Miss Nell determines the time of the next meeting."

Farrow looked like he might argue. He glanced over at Jacob. "All right, but when I meet with Miss Nell, I insist on doing so alone."

"I'll inform her of your wishes." Harrison turned the knob. "Now, I must insist on you leaving before you wake anyone."

Walter Farrow lifted his head and marched out.

Pretending to awaken as the man departed, Jacob held his side and moved to the door.

"He's going to be trouble," Harrison said as they watched Farrow head back up the road to town.

Jacob agreed.

"He hinted that he might question the will again. If he does, he'll never get the land, but he could tie up all of Nell's holdings for a time." Harrison rubbed his forehead with his palm. "But, if I were betting, I'd bet he'll take more direct action, and I don't even want to think about what it might be."

"You think Nell should sell him the Stockard place just to get him to stop bothering her?" Jacob smiled. "Let the rattlesnakes feed on him out at the ranch he wants."

Rand shrugged. "Sounds good. I don't know what she'll do. It's not my decision to even offer advice unless she asks. I just wish I could figure out why he wants it so badly. I rode out there and couldn't find anything. The land's no good. Even the shack is falling down."

"Farrow doesn't strike me as the kind of man who would want to work to fix up a place."

"Exactly. So why does he want it?"

Jacob guessed, "Maybe because it was in his family?"

"Maybe," Rand agreed. "But I've been going through the accounts since Stockard died. The place never made a dime. I don't know how the old man lived out there as long as he did. Gypsy told me the painting on Fat Alice's wall was the only one that she knew about him painting. So Farrow's probably not going to find a gold mine of valuable art in that shack."

The men moved back into the house and were surprised to find Nell downstairs with Mrs. O'Daniel by her side. Both the women looked rested.

"Morning," she smiled.

"Afternoon," Jacob corrected, unable to resist tugging on one of her braids. He hadn't seen Nell in braids in years.

She made a face at him much like she had years ago when he'd done the same thing to bother her. "Mrs. O'Daniel says today is going to be my first swim. Would either of you gentlemen like to come along?"

Harrison backed away. "No, thank you. I have far too much work to do."

"What about Wednesday and the baby upstairs?" Jacob looked at the nurse as if she were forgetting her duty.

"They're fine. The baby took his first meal an hour ago. Gypsy and Marla will see that Wednesday has everything. What the girl needs right now is some time to get used to being a mother. She'll sleep when the baby does for a few days."

Mrs. O'Daniel turned to Nell. "But Miss Nell missed some of her exercise this morning, and the thing we need to do now is get caught up. I'm not one to neglect my duty, no matter what happens." She glared at Jacob as if daring him to question her, then smiled as Harrison offered to carry the bag at her side.

Jacob fought to keep from growling. What was it about women? They all seemed to like Harrison, making him laugh, offering him coffee, being nice to him. Sometimes he swore Nell even liked talking to the bookkeeper more than she liked talking with him.

"What can I do to help?" Jacob offered, thinking he might want to start trying a little harder to be friendly.

"I've already asked the preacher to hitch the big buggy that I saw collecting dust in the back of the barn. It will be easier for Nell to get in and out of than a wagon. Gypsy's packing towels in it now, and I'm wearing my swimsuit beneath my uniform." She looked at Jacob. "If you'll come along to help me get her in the water, that's all I ask. I can handle everything once we're in the water."

Jacob started to say he wouldn't let Nell go near the river without him along, but he decided he'd be wise to keep his mouth shut. He wasn't sure Mrs. O'Daniel was all that fond of him. If she thought he'd be trouble, she might insist she could handle Nell alone, and Nell was so determined to follow Mrs. O'Daniel's advice, she might tell him to stay put.

In less time than he thought possible, the four of them were in the buggy heading down to the river. The preacher and Mrs. O'Daniel rode in the front. Jacob and Nell were in the back.

He braced his arm around her so the sway of the buggy didn't hurt her. She seemed more excited than frightened. That was his Nell, he thought. Never afraid to face anything.

"You all right?" he asked as the buggy bumped along.

She nodded. "It took me a while, but I finally managed to sit. I hated it at first when I had to lie in the back of the wagon."

"Me, too," he added, remembering how she'd looked more dead than alive when they'd brought her home.

When the preacher reached the river, Brother Aaron pulled the buggy as close to the water as he dared. Nell stood on a blanket and removed her skirt, petticoats, and shoes. Her blouse hung down well past her waist, and her pantaloons were thick with ruffles.

"I've ordered a bathing suit," Nell told Jacob. "But it won't be in for at least a month."

Jacob wasn't sure what his job would be, so he tugged off his boots. "Does it come with a hat?" Not that he cared, he thought, but the hats on pictures he'd seen always looked strange.

"The water's going to be cold," Mrs. O'Daniel warned, "but it will do wonders." She pulled off her dress to reveal a bathing suit that covered her completely in dark blue.

When she turned to test the water, Jacob whispered, "She's going to scare the fish to death. We'll be picking them up off the top of the water in no time."

Nell laughed and leaned against him for support. "Come in with me?"

He frowned, but it was Mrs. O'Daniel who answered, "He's not going into this water until he's healed. I'll not have that shoulder getting infected."

"Sorry," he said. "You're on your own. I'll walk you in until the water hits my waist."

The preacher must have decided his duties were over, for he climbed up a small hill and sat down to read his Bible aloud. He was far enough away that the reading sounded more like rumbling than scripture.

Nell slowly moved down the bank, laughing as cool mud oozed between her toes. Mrs. O'Daniel tied the thick leather belt around Nell's waist and had a firm hold on her patient, even though Jacob was on the other side.

As water lapped against his waist, he stopped and watched her move on. True to her word, the nurse never let go. When she stepped into shoulder-high water, Mrs. O'Daniel widened her stance and told Nell to hold onto her shoulder and let her body float.

Nell did and laughed as she yelled back to Jacob. "I can move without pain." She splashed with her legs. "It feels so good."

He watched as she moved her long limbs gracefully in the water, dancing slowly around the nurse. When she tired, she floated free in the water.

For an hour, Mrs. O'Daniel held to the belt and instructed Nell to do first one exercise and then another. She never let go of her patient as Nell moved and splashed in the river.

Jacob walked back to the shore, dried off as best he could, and sat watching them. She reminded him of a little girl again, playing and laughing. For the first time in his life, he wished they'd been the same age. He would have liked to have been a kid the same time she was; then he wouldn't have always had to play the parent role.

"Now," the nurse finally shouted back toward the shore, "it's time to go."

Jacob waded out when he saw them returning. Nell smiled, but he saw the exhaustion in her eyes. Without asking, he lifted her and carried her to the buggy. She curled against him, feeling boneless in his arms. With towels and blankets wrapped around her, the preacher drove them home.

"Take her right upstairs," Mrs. O'Daniel ordered as she stepped in the doorway. "Marla," she yelled, "bring up the hot water as fast as you can and more towels. I don't want her catching a chill."

By the time Jacob got Nell upstairs, Marla and Harrison were lugging steaming buckets in and filling a hip tub by the fireplace. Even though the day was warm enough to open the windows, the fire was blazing in her room.

Harrison and Jacob went back downstairs as Marla stayed to help Nell with her wet clothes and Mrs. O'Daniel disappeared to change. Jacob could hear the women moving about and was glad Nell would be warm, for she'd shivered in his arms most of the way home.

Gypsy passed Jacob and frowned. "You'd better get out of those wet clothes, Ranger, before you even think about sitting on that couch."

Harrison smiled. "Yes, Ranger, we wouldn't want you catching a chill."

If Jacob had enough energy left, he would have taken a swing at the bookkeeper, even though the man did offer him a towel.

Jacob hadn't really thought about how wet he was. He'd been too worried about Nell. He changed out back in the mud room off the kitchen and washed up. The idea of a bath sounded good, but he knew if he got his bandages wet, Mrs. O'Daniel would have a fit.

Gypsy opened the door while he stood with only long johns covering his legs. She glanced up and down his long frame, stopping to study his bare chest.

"Did you need something?" he asked. "Or did you just come to stare?"

She shrugged. "I figured if I was goin' to get a look, I might as well have a good one. And I came to give you this new shirt Wednesday made for you, not that you don't look mighty fine without it." She batted her eyes in a gesture that once made her look pretty but now had a spooky effect. Then she crossed her arms and continued to gawk.

He wasn't sure if he should thank her for the shirt or arrest her for staring. The thoughts she had in her head would probably make him blush. He took the blue shirt and slipped one arm into the sleeve. The material was heavier than any store-bought shirt, and he guessed it would wear well.

"She double stitched all the seams."

"It fits," he said, surprised. Most of the shirts he bought in the general stores were too small. The sleeves were always an inch too short, the yoke tight across his shoulders. But this one . . . this one was made for him.

"Of course it fits. That girl is magic with a needle. She made Harrison a shirt he said was the finest he ever owned."

Jacob smiled. He hadn't had a shirt made for him since his mother died. "Tell her thanks."

"You can tell her yourself. She and the baby are coming down to supper in an hour."

"I thought women were supposed to stay in bed for a month after having a baby?"

Gypsy shrugged. "I don't know. Mrs. O'Daniel just said if she feels like it, she can come down for a little while."

By the time he finished shaving, it was almost dark, and Wednesday had changed her mind about coming down. She ate in her room with Mrs. O'Daniel and Gypsy watching the baby. Everyone was invited to join their little dinner party, but Harrison said he'd keep Marla company in the kitchen, and the preacher decided he'd better go to town and check out sinners.

As he left, he swore he'd not touch spirits while he was gone, but Jacob had his doubts.

When Jacob went upstairs to thank Wednesday for the shirt, he asked if Nell was awake.

Mrs. O'Daniel said she wanted to have dinner in her room since the night without sleep and then the exercise had tired her.

He went downstairs and offered to take Nell a tray. Marla didn't comment when he filled it with enough food for two.

As Jacob pushed her door open, he saw her sitting by the window. Her hair was combed down, flowing across her shoulders, and she was already dressed in her robe and gown.

"I thought I'd have supper with you tonight, if you've no objections." He set the tray down on the table beside her and pulled up one of the ladder-back chairs.

"I'd like that." She smiled. "But I may be too tired to be good company."

"Maybe you did too much," he worried.

"Wasn't it wonderful? I felt like I was walking."

He couldn't point out that she looked tired. She was too pleased with herself.

They ate and talked of all that had happened in one day. He stretched in the uncomfortable chair and thought how nice it was to be with her.

When Mrs. O'Daniel checked in to say good night and ask if Nell needed anything, she frowned at Jacob sitting by the window, but she didn't say anything except to warn Nell not to stay up late.

Jacob stood to leave. "Want me to carry you to bed?"

"I'd like that." She raised her arms.

As he lowered her in the covers, he decided it was time to get a few things straight before he kissed her good night.

"I've been thinking," he started, "as soon as things settle down and I know Hank is safe, we should get the preacher to marry us."

He felt her stiffen. "Oh," she said softly. "When did I agree to marry you?"

"Now don't start this, Nell," he tried to keep the anger out of his voice. "A woman doesn't go around kissing a man and letting him touch her, unless she's going to marry him. I'd say you've already said yes with your actions."

He knew she was just pestering him, like she'd done all her life, and he wasn't about to let her get away with it. "You don't sleep with a man and not marry him."

"Is that so? My mother did. Fat Alice did. Every woman I knew until I was half grown did."

"They don't count. You know what they were."

"They were women," she answered. "Or didn't you notice?"

"How could I not notice? Most of them walked around downstairs half naked. But I never climbed the stairs with a one, and you know it."

She grinned. "I noticed. But your being a virgin doesn't mean I'm going to marry you just because you touched me."

"I'm not . . ." He stopped. He had no intention of telling her about his past. He'd had a few women over the years who'd come willing to his arms. He hadn't paid them, and he wouldn't talk about them.

"I didn't think you could be naive and kiss like that." She laughed.

"And what do you know about it?" He wasn't sure he wanted to know. If he could take the question back, he would before she told him.

For lack of a plan, he leaned forward and kissed her. At first the kiss was hard, meant to silence her, but quickly it turned into something else. The taste of pleasure . . . of desire . . . of passion. The shock of it rattled him to his boots, and he reached down to dig his fingers in her hair as if he'd fall off another cliff if he didn't hang on tight.

She opened her mouth and welcomed him to deepen the kiss. Suddenly, he didn't care where she learned it. He just enjoyed it.

As carefully as he could, he lowered beside her without breaking the kiss and felt her mold against him. A hunger built inside him unlike anything he'd ever known. He kissed her long and lovingly as if his survival depended on it.

A need for her grew inside him, hungry for more of her even as they touched.

When he finally broke the kiss, he buried his face in her hair. "Marry me, Nell, or shoot me. I don't care which."

CHAPTER 25

Dawn crept into her room with the fog. Nell pulled herself up and stared at the open window. The air smelled of rain again. A part of her wanted to slip back under the covers and sleep another hour. She'd had a fight with Jacob last night, and an uneasiness pestered her dreams because of it.

He wanted her to agree to marry him. In fact, he seemed confused that she'd even hesitate. She knew him well enough to almost read his thoughts. In his mind he would be her best choice for a husband. He knew her, she trusted him. He'd also proven in the past few days that he was definitely attracted to her, though he hadn't said he loved her.

She smiled. But, then, there was his touch. It said volumes. His touch did something deep inside her, but was that enough to build a marriage on?

Her ranger had always been the one who thought he knew what was right for her, but now, Nell had to think about what was right for him. No matter what he claimed, he deserved more than she could offer as a mate.

Marla slipped silently into the room with Nell's tea. "I guessed you'd be awake," she whispered.

"Thanks." Nell took the cup. "Who else is up?"

"The baby and Wednesday. They've been awake an hour. And the ranger. I must have woke him when I started the fire. He's pacing around downstairs like a caged cougar."

Nell wasn't surprised. "What about Mrs. O'Daniel?"

"I think I heard her in her room." Marla glanced down. "Would you like me to help you dress?"

"Thanks," Nell answered. "What little muscles I have left are sore from the swim." She stood, a bit steadier than she'd been a week ago. "If you'll hand me my clothes, I can manage the rest."

One by one the layers went on. Marla had helped enough to know when to do things for Nell and when to let her take care of herself. Usually, Nell put her own hair up, but this morning she relaxed and allowed Marla to do it for her. By the time she rolled her wheelchair down the hallway, Nell looked every inch the proper lady.

"It may rain all day," Marla said from behind her. "If it doesn't, do you want to go into town to see Hank with us? Mrs. O'Daniel said yesterday that she'd be going, and Mr. Harrison offered to take her."

"I might," Nell agreed. She'd been worried about the boy since Mrs. O'Daniel described his wounds.

When Nell turned into Wednesday's room, the young mother greeted her with a grand smile. "He likes my milk," she said. "I was worried yesterday 'cause he wouldn't take much, but this morning he ate like a pig. Because of me, he's going to grow into a big man."

Nell laughed. "Good." She looked at the baby wiggling beside Wednesday. "You have to think of a name soon or some nickname will stick, and he'll never get rid of it. Believe me, I know."

Wednesday held his tiny hand between her finger and thumb. "I was thinking of calling him HD after Mr. Harrison and Ranger Dalton on account of them being the two finest men I've ever known."

Nell nodded. "I think that would be grand."

"How about DH?" Jacob's low voice sounded from the doorway.

Wednesday grinned. "You wouldn't mind if I used your name? He ain't got a pa to be named after."

"Yes he does." Jacob took a step into the room. "You just haven't found a man worth being his pa yet. But one day maybe you will."

Wednesday liked that answer. Nell and Jacob stayed while she ate the tray of food Marla had brought up, then she told everyone it was time for her and little DH to take a nap. Making a nest of pillows and blankets, she cuddled in with her son.

When they reached the landing, Jacob bent down to lift Nell. She was almost in his arms when a blue and white uniform stepped in front of them.

"Stop right there," Mrs. O'Daniel said in her all-business voice. "Miss Nell will walk down the stairs."

"But I'm . . ."

Nell let her arms slide down his chest. "I'll walk down," she added, ending any argument Jacob had planned.

He let go of her reluctantly.

While Mrs. O'Daniel strapped the thick belt around her waist, Nell watched her ranger hurry down the stairs. She knew he didn't want to watch her struggle with each step. Not when he could have carried her.

Mrs. O'Daniel was right about one thing. Each time she forced herself to move down and up the steps, it got a little easier. The nurse always let her set the pace, but Nell noticed the grip on the belt, though firm, no longer carried most of her weight. Each time her leg took a step, pain throbbed along her spine, but she told herself over and over she wouldn't quit until she passed out. She'd learned to brace for the pain. As long as she could stand ready against it, she could take it. The problem came in those times fire shot through her spine unexpectedly.

When Nell finally joined the men for breakfast, she thought of doing the same thing that Wednesday did and announcing it was time for a nap. Only, Nell knew if she wanted a nap, Mrs. O'Daniel would make her climb the stairs again. So Nell took the lesser of two evils and decided to work with Harrison on the books.

As the day passed, the rain continued. Jacob paced, edgy at being walled in. He finally decided to ignore the rain and go to the barn. To Nell's surprise Mr. Harrison joined him after lunch.

She read and forced herself to work on a needlepoint, while Gypsy slept in her favorite chair and Brother Aaron worked on a sermon at the dining table. Mrs. O'Daniel divided her time between Wednesday and the baby's care and Nell's exercises. Nell took her first few steps alone, without the belt. She held onto a chair to balance, but still for a few seconds she felt she was walking, even if Gypsy did remind her that she looked more like she was falling in the general direction she'd been planning to walk.

When Jacob and Harrison returned from the barn an hour before supper, Jacob seemed in a good mood. He talked and joked and, she noticed, paid very little attention to her. He was still angry she hadn't agreed to marry him.

When he went to the porch to watch the rain, Nell joined him. It wasn't like them not to face their problems head-on. She'd just have to make him understand that she needed time. And maybe, during that time, he'd see that she wasn't right for him as a wife and begin to look for someone else. She pulled her chair within a few feet of him, but somehow he still seemed distant.

Rain fell in a steady sheet off the porch roof. "It makes me feel closed in," she opened the conversation, their first alone since the night before.

Jacob didn't look at her as he watched it pour. "It makes me glad not to be out in it."

Neither of them said anything else. He seemed like someone she hardly knew. She watched him, wondering how this silent man could be the same man who'd kissed her with such passion. His hands, the same hands that had touched her so gently, now gripped the railing with an iron grip.

There was a gentleness inside him, but she felt like she had to fight to even be allowed to see it.

She'd had enough. "Are you going to ignore me for the rest of my life?" She decided she'd rather have him mad at her than not even seem to notice she was in the room. "Can't we have a calm discussion about what's bothering you?"

He didn't answer for a moment, and she knew he was forcing himself not to yell. "I'm waiting for you to come to your senses," he answered just as formally.

"And if I don't?"

"You will." He tossed his cigar into the rain. "I know you well enough to know that you never let anything come easy. If I have to, I'll fight for you as well as with you about this, Nell, but make no mistake, in the end it will be settled with a wedding. Ours!"

"You're not bullying me into anything, Jacob Dalton. I'm no longer a child." Nell tried to sit calmly in her chair, but she had never wanted to stomp away so badly in her life. "This isn't something you can just decide is good for me and make me go along with."

He stood over her looking like a warrior. "Stop trying to make me nuts. One minute you're cuddling up beside me all warm and willing, and the next you're telling me you might marry another man. I've had enough, Nell. It's time you made up your mind."

She lifted her chin. "I'll marry when I want to."

"You know you love me." He gave a quick grin as if trying on charm like he might a new hat. "Don't even try to say you don't feel something when you kiss me. You've always loved me. We've both known it."

She didn't buy the smile, so he went back to scowling.

Harrison stepped out on the porch, took one look at them, and turned around. The door closed behind him.

"Maybe I kiss every man like I kiss you," Nell said when they were once again alone.

"Have you kissed Harrison like you kissed me?" The ranger's hands gripped his gun belt.

"That's none of your business, Jacob. You're not my husband, or even my fiancé. You're only Number Thirteen in line to ask for my hand. Which, by the way, it took you long enough to get here. Were you hoping another might sweep my heart away, and you wouldn't have to bother with me?"

Jacob turned toward the front door.

"Where do you think you are going?"

"I'm going to go beat the answer about kissing out of poor Number Twelve." He said the words as if it were a chore he had to do. "Too bad, I really like the man."

Nell fought down a laugh. "You will do no such thing, Jacob. If you did, I'd never speak to you again, and that's a fact."

He smiled, for real this time, and walked to where she sat. He knelt down in front of her. "Why don't we settle this between us and marry? I got here as fast as I could when I heard you wanted to get married. You still want a last name, and it might as well be mine. I don't know why, but we're connected, we always have been. You're a part of me and I'm a part of you."

Nell raised her chin. Her pride wouldn't let her tell him the real reason she turned him down. He deserved more than she could offer. She'd never be able to love him the way he should be loved. She wasn't sure she could even be a real wife to him. What if their lovemaking brought her too much pain? How fast would his love die if he thought every time he touched her she was in pain?

Nell closed her eyes. She shouldn't have let him kiss her in the first place. She should have known better. But, just for a few minutes, she wanted to live the dream of being in Jacob's arms. Only, in the end, the pleasure they'd shared would cost them both dearly.

"I can't," she said brushing his hair with her fingers. "It wouldn't be fair."

He met her gaze and held it. "To who, Nell? To me or to you?"

"To you," she finally admitted. "I could never be the kind of wife you'd want."

He stood, suddenly angry. "How do you know what kind of wife I want? Now who's making decisions for the other?"

Walking to the far end of the porch, he leaned against the railing.

He seemed so powerful, so strong, but she was hurting him, and it ripped her apart.

"Jacob, can we go back to being friends?" She'd been miserable all day. It felt like it had been raining in her heart. "Can we *not* talk about getting married for a while?"

He slowly turned and walked back to her. "All right. Set the rules, Nell. I'll play your game."

She felt the chill of his words all the way to her bones. "I don't know the rules."

"Then how will I know when I step too far? I feel like you've drawn lines in the sand, and I have no idea where they are. I swear I seem to bump into one every time I talk to you."

She had no answer. Everything seemed so cold if she had to set down rules. But, he'd been right. He did seem to step over the line. It occurred to her that maybe, for Jacob, there was no line between them.

Gypsy stepped onto the porch, saving her from answering. The little woman hurried up to Nell and asked, "If you two are finished arguing, the rest of us would like to eat. Dinner's getting cold."

Nell nodded. "We're on our way."

This was Wednesday's first time downstairs. They should make the dinner special. "We'll talk about this later." She stared at Jacob, daring him to argue.

"We sure as hell will," he added and held the door as she moved inside.

She could feel his anger as she passed him. He was a straightforward man. Right and wrong were clear in his mind. Playing games was not something a man like him had ever done.

She avoided his gaze as they ate dinner. Marla had baked a cake and decorated it with sugar in honor of the baby's first party. Everyone brought presents. Marla gave Wednesday a comb and brush set with hummingbirds carved on it. The girl cried because she'd never had anything so nice. Nell gave her a Bible to write her son's name in. Harrison bought a windup top that clanked as it rolled around. The preacher gave her a handkerchief with fine lace to use when she wanted little DH christened. Gypsy gave her ribbons and a rattle made from a gourd.

Mrs. O'Daniel offered the most unusual gift, a tiny pouch to put a piece of the umbilical cord in. She said the Apache mothers wore them so they would always be connected with their sons. Jacob brought in a crib he'd found in the attic and repainted. But the air was so damp the paint hadn't dried, so with blue paint on his hands he promised he'd finish it again on a sunny day.

Everyone laughed and talked at once. Nell tried to push the argument with Jacob out of her mind. She would never hurt him, but she couldn't ruin his life.

When dinner was over, she didn't miss the look Jacob gave Harrison. Something was up; she could feel it. The men had spent most of the day busy and away from the house. Even the preacher seemed to have something on his mind. She'd seen the sheriff ride in twice, but he'd done his talking to the men in the barn.

The fact that Jacob had strapped his Colts on that morning had started her thinking, and now that they were moving toward the door, she knew something was wrong.

She rolled toward them. "What is it?"

"Nothing." Harrison was a lousy liar.

"We just thought we'd go into town," Jacob said without looking at her. "The rain seems to have let up, and I figure we'll be back in less than an hour."

"Both of you?" Nell tapped the arm of her chair, hating the invisible chains that held her to it.

"Brother Aaron said he'd sit on the porch while we're gone. He says if he hears even a mouse in the barn, he'll fire off a couple of shots. We'll be back at full gallop."

Harrison placed his hand on Nell's arm. "Don't worry about us. We'll be back in no time. We just want to check on Hank and talk to the sheriff."

His reassuring words did little to calm her. She guessed what they were about. They were going to help Hank, maybe even get him out of jail. She couldn't say more without worrying the others.

She met Jacob's eyes. "Whatever you are planning, I'll help if I can. You know that, don't you?"

He nodded and lifted a rifle. "I'm not expecting any trouble." His smile seemed a little forced.

Maybe he didn't expect it, Nell thought, but he would be ready if it came. That was Jacob's way.

"Don't worry, we'll be back in time to have another bowl of Marla's cobbler with you before we all turn in," he said as he moved toward the door.

"Be careful." She turned to Harrison, knowing Jacob was making light of whatever he planned. They wouldn't be going out in the rain if it wasn't something important. They wouldn't be leaving her. "Take care of him. He's not fully recovered from the knifing."

"I will." Harrison lightly kissed her cheek. "I promise."

Jacob had been pulling on his coat, and Nell thought he hadn't noticed Harrison's light kiss, until Harrison joined him at the door and the ranger mumbled, "When you get through covering my back tonight, I may have to beat some sense into you, bookkeeper."

Harrison didn't look the least bit frightened. "Maybe I'll get lucky and beat some into you, Ranger."

They were gone before she could hear more.

While the others talked and sewed baby things in a circle around the fire, Nell asked Mrs. O'Daniel to help her to her room. She got ready for bed but rolled to the window to wait.

The men had already been gone over an hour.

She listened to the clock chime once more. Two hours, she thought, realizing they'd told her once too often that they'd be home early. They'd both been trying to oversell a lie.

Trouble whispered in the wind tonight, and all she seemed able to do was wait.

CHAPTER 26

BECAUSE OF JACOB'S SHOULDER AND THE POSSIBILITY THAT HANK
might be coming back with them, the men took the buggy to town.
Harrison drove while Jacob leaned back in the seat, trying to stay out
of the drizzle. But the leather bonnet was old and sagged in several
places. Everywhere it sagged, it leaked, making tiny waterfalls.

Jacob Dalton had been in a dark mood all day and was tired of acting as if the fight he'd had with Nell didn't bother him. He hated being confused almost as much as he hated being angry, and right now
he was both.

"You want to talk about it?" Rand asked politely but without any
great interest.

"No," Jacob answered, not even trying to pretend that he didn't
know what the bookkeeper was talking about. The people inside the
house might not have been able to hear what he and Nell had been
talking about on the porch, but the windows probably provided a grand
view.

"She loves you, you know?" Harrison acted as if he hadn't heard Jacob's answer. "Everyone knows."

"I said I didn't want to talk about it."

"You're right," Harrison admitted. "I'd be the last person to talk
about courting a woman. I only courted one in my life, and she tried
to have me killed. So I'm no good at advice." He drove for a few minutes before adding, "But even I could give you a few pointers."

Jacob didn't really want to talk, but he had a feeling Harrison did. So he might as well herd the conversation away from Nell and him. "How'd the woman you courted try to kill you?"

"*Have* me killed," Rand corrected. "She wasn't the type of woman to get her hands dirty doing anything like that herself."

Jacob leaned up a little. "All right, tell me."

Harrison hesitated.

"Look, if my love life is in the pot for discussion, so is yours." It was so dark Jacob couldn't make out Harrison's face, but he had a feeling the bookkeeper was smiling.

"Fair enough," Harrison answered. "I'm the second son of a big cattle rancher down by Victoria. My father runs cattle over five counties."

"Start with the truth," Jacob said before he thought to stop himself.

Harrison laughed and didn't take offense. "Let me finish. After I was born, my mother had enough of my father bossing her around and moved to Chicago. When I was old enough, I saw him summers for a few weeks a year, and my mother hated even that. He wouldn't support her, and she had to work long hours to see that I got educated. Even though I was a baby when we left, my father seemed to take it personal. He never cared much for me."

"When my mother died, I had to quit school and go live on the ranch. My father treated me with indifference, but my older brother hated me. Since I hadn't grown up riding, I was of little use, until my father discovered I was good with figures. Then he wanted me with him, not to do the ranching, but to keep the books."

"Which made your brother angry to be splitting some of his old man's attention?"

"Right. To make matters worse, we both fell for the same girl. I don't know about him, but I still believed in love and fell hard."

"And?"

Harrison paused as if he'd never told the story before. "She came to my room one night. We made love in the dark without saying a word, but when it was over and she was curled in my arms, I whispered how much she meant to me. Something about the midnight stars and blue sky, if I remember correctly, I was only seventeen."

He handled the buggy with skill as he maneuvered around rivers of mud. "Before I understood what was wrong, she started screaming and accusing me of things. It seems she had entered the wrong room and now the deed was done, it was all my fault. My brother was the one who was supposed to get lucky that night."

"My brother rushed in, a gun in his hand and yelling at both of us.

All I remember was a lot of screaming and crying, and then the gun firing."

Jacob stopped the story. "Was your finger on the trigger?"

Harrison shook his head. "No, but I was trying to get the gun away from my brother. The bullet hit her cheek and left an ugly scar. I was arrested for rape and attempted murder. At the trial, I was foolish enough to think she'd tell the truth, and it would all be cleared up as a misunderstanding. But she didn't. She said I pulled her into my room, had my way with her, and then tried to kill her. She cried on the stand, begging the jury to give me the death penalty."

"And your brother," Jacob asked already knowing the answer.

"He stood with her, as did my father. I was given ten years of hard time. The first few years in prison, I didn't much care if I lived or died. I had no family, and the only girl I'd ever loved hated me. I worked on a gang building roads and fell asleep so exhausted at night I didn't even care that I was filthy and my hands were usually bleeding."

"What turned you around?"

"By accident, the foreman noticed my math skills, and I was moved to his office. He was promoted out of prisons to the state offices in Austin. Within a year I went from wearing prison blues to wearing proper clothes and accompanying him on inspections. He didn't want anyone to know I was serving time. He knew all about building things, but for me it was all about the numbers. When I got out, he offered me a job, but I wanted to make it on my own, leave all my past behind."

"Did you go back home?"

"Once. The train stopped in Victoria, and I spent the night at the hotel. While I was trying to decide if I should go out to the ranch or not, I spotted my brother in the hotel bar. He didn't recognize me and was so drunk I didn't bother introducing myself. I watched him losing at poker from across the room. He'd aged twenty years in the ten years since I'd seen him. Times were hard for me, trying to find work as a bookkeeper with my record. But, after watching him, I figured I got the lesser of the sentences."

"What about the girl?" Jacob asked as they pulled into town.

"My brother married her."

Jacob smiled, understanding Rand Harrison clearly for the first time. "So what's your advice for me?"

"Spend a little time courting Nell," Harrison said. "I don't think ordering her to marry you will work."

"You're probably right, but I don't have any idea where to start." He quoted Rand. "Saying something about the midnight stars and blue sky didn't work too well for you."

Harrison shrugged.

As agreed, they pulled up near the saloon. Before Jacob talked to Sheriff Parker, he wanted to see what the townsfolk were talking about. If there was trouble brewing, he'd learn about it here first and not secondhand from the sheriff.

They stepped out into the rain. Jacob went inside as Rand tied the horse.

The place was quiet except for a drunk trying to pick out a song on the piano. The ranger took a table near the back and watched the crowd. Harrison circled the room once before joining him so that if anyone was watching it wouldn't look like the two men came in together.

They'd made plans to meet Parker here when he made his last rounds. The sheriff had talked with them earlier and said the posse hinted they'd decided to leave tomorrow morning and that there had been no trouble.

"Maybe no one wants to start anything," Harrison guessed. "Mobs usually take hours to build up enough courage to act."

Jacob agreed, but he couldn't shake the feeling that something was about to happen. Three of the men from the posse were huddled over by the bar, and every time Jacob looked in their direction, they were watching him. The cowhands gambling tonight didn't seem at all interested in talking about the prisoners across the street. They seemed far more interested in losing their money and heading home.

Parker came in and joined them. "It's so quiet around here tonight I'm starting to get worried."

"I know what you mean." Jacob ordered a round of whiskey.

"The two wounded men from the posse left on the evening train with a buddy each riding with them. That leaves eight to haul the three outlaws back to Fort Worth. If they leave on the first train, they'll make it in before nightfall with any luck."

"Eight should be enough men to watch three prisoners." Jacob noticed two more men who looked like they were with the posse come in and join their friends at the table. They were all young and green, he noticed, wearing their deputy badges on their coats.

"Their captain, name of Kelly, wants to talk to you, Dalton." Parker said. "He still thinks you should let them take Hank in the morning."

"Not a chance," Jacob answered.

"I told him that, but he claims the kid will be better protected with them than he will be with you." Parker rubbed his whiskery chin. The stress of having the killers in his jail was starting to wear on him. "The captain wants to talk to you alone. Told me he wouldn't be needing me to come along, like I was one of his foot soldiers or something."

"Where does he want to meet?"

"Down at the end of the street in that little café close to the station. It's a rat hole, but he claims to like the chili. He's probably waiting there now." Parker seemed to chew on the words a while before he added, "He's been a great help to me these past few days. Takes his job real serious."

"But?"

Parker shrugged. "Nothing, just a feeling I get that he's a man used to getting everything his way."

Jacob stood. "Well, I guess I'll go over and correct that notion right now."

Harrison also stood, planning to follow.

Jacob raised his hand. "If he wants to see me alone, then I'll go alone." He didn't see any need to tell the others that the captain's reason probably had to do with offering a bribe. Jacob had dealt with some men who thought the law could be bought. He enjoyed straightening them out. "Rand, if you'll go on over to the jail with Parker and start getting the kid ready to move, I'll join you in no time." Jacob pulled a paper from his pocket. "I already filled out the forms and signed them. Have the boy ready to leave by the time I get there."

"What you going to do with the kid?" Parker asked.

Jacob shook his head. "For tonight, I'm not sure, but before the rest of the gang gets on that train, I plan to be out of range of any trouble. It may take me a while, but my plan is to get Hank to Fort Worth in one piece and to stand beside him during the trial. It's the least I can do for him."

Parker shook his head. "He's not in very good shape. My deputies swear they didn't touch him, but someone landed a few blows on him last night. I found him this morning on the floor of his cell. Whoever did it left a gag in his mouth so he couldn't cry out for help. He laid there in pain most of the night, I figure, and the doc wouldn't come treat him this morning. To tell the truth, he looked scared to death when I even suggested it. I think whoever got to him must have threatened to kill him if he said anything."

Jacob glanced at Harrison. "No matter what, we're taking him tonight."

Harrison nodded. "I'll do whatever I can for him while I'm waiting for you."

Trying to control his anger, Jacob walked down the street. The rain had finally stopped, but clouds still hung low, making the night soupy and black. Jacob couldn't escape thoughts of how the kid must have looked when the sheriff found him all bloody and gagged. He wouldn't be surprised if they'd beat the boy up, hoping he'd be too hurt to travel. Or maybe they let his father get to him. If the pa was mad about the boy not finding them, he could have done the beating. As big a man as he was, it wouldn't have taken much to leave the boy on the floor too hurt to move.

As Jacob walked, he noticed even the light in this part of town seemed dingy. The wooden walks in front of the stores were narrower and sometimes in poor condition. He found the place the sheriff had told him about and went in, anxious to get this meeting over with.

When he asked for a man named Kelly in the run-down café, Jacob was surprised to find him sitting at a table with Walter Farrow. They were a mismatched pair: Kelly tall and lean with a weathered face, Farrow rounded and pale. But their eyes were the same: cold and hard.

The leader of the posse stood and introduced himself as Anthony Kelly, an employee of the railroad. Jacob took measure of the man and guessed him to be far more than he claimed. He had the look of a Pinkerton, or maybe an ex-Pinkerton who'd left to make deals concerning protection on his own.

Walter Farrow tried to act as if he and Kelly were great friends, but his effort fell flat. He excused himself, saying he had to run, and hurried away.

Kelly offered Jacob a chair.

The ranger didn't miss the four men sitting two tables away watching as closely as if he and Kelly were a play. No one else was in the place, and Jacob wasn't surprised. The smell coming from the kitchen made him lose any appetite he may have had.

"We're in the same line of work, Ranger Dalton. Catching bad guys."

"It appears so."

Kelly laughed as if Jacob had said something funny and continued, "I understand you were hurt in your efforts to stop the outlaws."

"Correct." Jacob didn't like the way Kelly made it sound as though Jacob had failed somehow. If he hadn't taken the horses, the gang would have been well into Oklahoma Territory by now. But he figured Kelly knew the facts as well as he did. There was no use in talking about it. "The sheriff tells me you wanted to see me." Jacob got to the point.

"Right." Kelly straightened in his chair. "I want to offer you a little more time to recover. I'll take the bandit you brought in back with me to Fort Worth, and you can join us when you are feeling better."

"Thank you for the offer, but I'll handle my own prisoner."

Kelly leaned forward. "If money for the recovering is a problem, the railroad would be happy to make a cash offer to help. After all, we're much in your debt."

Not quite a bribe, Jacob thought. The man was smooth.

Jacob stood. "I didn't do it for the railroad. I did it for those people who lost their lives during the robbery. If you want to help someone recover, help the families of those folks."

Kelly rose to his feet. "I ask that you reconsider, Ranger. For your own safety."

"I don't have to," Jacob smiled. "I never considered it in the first place." He tipped his hat at the head of the posse and walked out of the café.

Walter Farrow was waiting for him on the walk out front. "Mind if I walk with you?" Farrow asked as he circled Jacob.

"You don't know which direction I'm going." Jacob headed away from the café door, and Farrow seemed to relax a little.

Farrow fell into step. "It doesn't matter. I just came out to warn you about something."

Jacob didn't slow. "All right. Warn me."

"I think the posse is planning to take the boy with them in the morning, no matter what you agree to."

"Tell me something I don't know."

"I can't say more." Farrow leaned close, his hand on Jacob's arm stopping their progress. "I just want to tell you to be careful. Remember that I warned you."

"I'll remember." Jacob started moving again, but slowed, wondering what the fat man knew. "Tell me, Mr. Farrow, how good a friend are you to Anthony Kelly?"

"We're men of like mind in that we both strive to accomplish our goals, no matter what the odds."

Jacob guessed Farrow would be of no help, and he didn't have time for his double-talk. "Good night, Mr. Farrow."

"Good-bye, Ranger." Farrow stopped walking and within seconds had disappeared into the blackness.

Jacob rested his hand on the butt of his Colt. At this end of town most of the bars were rough, and the smell of whiskey and urine hung in the damp air. He listened for the sound of other steps on the walk, but there were none.

He passed an opening into one of the saloons, and glanced in. The bartender and a girl dressed in red were playing cards at the bar. The barmaid waved at him, and he waved back, remembering her from a few years ago when she'd asked the sheriff for protection against a cowhand and Jacob had talked to the man.

The only other person he saw was a drunk passed out at one of the tables, looking as if he planned to sleep there the rest of the night. It was early yet; business might pick up when men kicked out of the better bars stumbled down the street looking for a few more drinks.

Jacob stepped off the walk into two inches of mud. He picked his steps carefully in the shadows between buildings. The last thing he wanted, he decided, was to slide in the mud and take a tumble. He cradled his shoulder now that no one was looking. He'd been acting like it didn't hurt all day. Just like he'd been acting like the argument with Nell didn't matter. Hell, at this rate he'd be on the stage in no time.

A moment later, he reconsidered his choice for the last thing he wanted to happen.

Men in black circled him, and he felt the crack of a bottle against the side of his head. The next thing he saw were stars in the cloudy sky as he tumbled.

CHAPTER 27

NELL WATCHED THE ROAD TO TOWN UNTIL SHE FELT HER EYES would cross. When the clock chimed ten, she knew something was wrong. They'd been gone three hours.

She rolled to the hallway and called for Mrs. O'Daniel. The nurse must have been up reading, for though already in her gown, she didn't look like she'd been asleep.

"Something's wrong." Nell tried to keep her voice calm. "Something's happened to Jacob. He said he'd be back in an hour. It's been three."

The nurse opened her mouth to deny the claim, but Gypsy started up the stairs. "I feel it, too," she snapped. "I can taste trouble on the back of my tongue and, once I taste it, I ain't never wrong. Mr. Harrison and the ranger would have been back if they hadn't run into something."

"Maybe it's just the damp air." Mrs. O'Daniel looked down at Gypsy. "Maybe the taste on the back of your tongue is something you ate or drank."

But all three knew it wasn't. Harrison had said they wouldn't be gone long, an hour, no more. Jacob didn't like the idea of leaving Brother Aaron alone with the women. He would have taken care of business in town and come back.

Unless something happened. Nell made up her mind. "I'm going to town."

"Now? At this time of night? I don't feel that is wise." Mrs. O'Daniel shook her head but was wise enough not to step in Nell's way.

"I'm going, with or without you, but your help would be greatly appreciated."

Marla had crossed the big room in silence. "I'll go with you," she said, looking up from the bottom of the stairs with eyes full of tears. "I can't stand to wait any longer."

The nurse tried to be the voice of reason. "It's misting out there. The road will be dangerous. Someone has to stay with Wednesday and the baby. We can't just leave them."

Their voices woke the preacher sleeping by the fire downstairs. He stretched and realized what was happening. He was a man in a houseful of women. He didn't say a word; he just began putting on his coat.

"You aren't strong enough to stand for long, even with my help. What kind of help could you be to the ranger?"

"Then I'll go in my chair." The wheelchair would only fit in the open wagon. "Brother Aaron, will you get the wagon ready?" She turned to the nurse. "And I'll go armed."

"This is madness," Mrs. O'Daniel said. "Doesn't anyone see that but me?"

"We all do," Marla whispered as she passed the nurse, "but we all also know something is wrong. If we stay here, safe and dry, while the ranger is in trouble, we'll never forgive ourselves."

"But if the wagon rolls or breaks a wheel in the mud, Nell will be trapped. None of you can carry her back home."

"I'll be all right." Nell lifted her chin. "At worst, I'll be soaked in the rain, but with luck I might be able to help Jacob. The way I see it, I only have to worry about getting *to* town. Jacob will be with me on the way home."

Wednesday opened her door. "I heard you all talking. I'd go if I could."

Nell smiled. "We know, but little DH needs you more right now." She turned to her troops. Brother Aaron had already disappeared to get the wagon ready. "Gypsy, I'm leaving you on guard. Sit at the bottom of the stairs with a rifle."

"I can't shoot nothing. Never had no aim." She doubled up her tiny fist. "Maybe I should go with you and fight."

"No. I need you here." Nell almost added that between the two of them, Gypsy and she couldn't probably fight a rabbit, but being willing to try counted for something. "If trouble walks through that door, just point and fire until all the rounds are gone."

The tiny old housekeeper frowned. "Then what do I do?"
"Reload."
Gypsy nodded.
Nell turned to Mrs. O'Daniel. "Get all you'll need from the kitchen. You and Wednesday stay upstairs while I'm gone." It was probably more precaution than necessary, but Nell didn't want to have to worry about those who stayed behind.

While Marla helped her dress, Nell planned where they'd go. The town was so small they should have no problem finding a Texas Ranger the size of Dalton. With luck he would be drinking coffee with the sheriff at the jail, and all this worry would be for nothing. Maybe he was just waiting out the rain.

Marla wrapped a velvet cape of deep blue around Nell and covered her hair with the hood, then circled her black cape around her.

The preacher backed the wagon up to the steps, leaving deep ruts with his wheels, but no one seemed to care. With only a two-inch bump to contend with, Nell pushed her chair off the porch and into the back of the wagon with ease. Mrs. O'Daniel oversaw the tying of the wheels so that it wouldn't roll and insisted Nell put a tarp over her shoulders and the chair. She might not be going on this wild run into town, but she planned to take care of her patient as long as possible.

Mrs. O'Daniel, Marla, and Gypsy helped push the wagon through the mud to the road where the ground was packed. When Marla climbed in beside the preacher, her skirts were muddy to her knees.

Gypsy stood on the porch watching and waving until they turned the bend and were out of sight.

They moved through the night in silence, no one mentioning what they might find when they got to town. The wind made the rain colder, and there was no protection in the open wagon except the tarp.

Not long after the lights from the house disappeared, a few lights from town twinkled in the distance. The preacher drove slow and easy, talking to the horses almost as much as he talked to the Lord. The wagon had been built for hauling, with wide wheels that held stable even on the slippery road.

Nell was shivering by the time they reached the jail. Several young men were hanging around on the porch as if waiting for something to happen. She could see through the window that a few more were inside, but none were shouting or causing trouble. They all stopped talking and watched the wagon pull up as close as Brother Aaron could to the steps.

Nell wasn't sure who they were, but she knew they were no mob waiting to cause trouble.

"Fellow brethren," the preacher boomed. "I've a sister here who wishes to visit the jail on this night. Will you help her down so she can go about the Lord's business?"

Nell shoved the tarp aside so that the men could see her wheelchair. None of the men moved to help.

Brother Aaron climbed to the back and untied the wheels of the chair. "Strong young men like you should be able to lift her chair and all onto the porch. If she could walk, I wouldn't be asking your help, but as you can see, she can't."

Nell pulled her cape around her, not wanting them to see her embarrassment. For the first time she saw the folly of her plan. "If you'll get Ranger Dalton, he'll lift me down," she asked as kindly as she could. She wanted to add that she didn't need their help, but for once, she did.

One of the men stepped forward. He wore a badge on his rain slicker proclaiming himself to be one of the posse. "A woman in your condition shouldn't be out on a night like this, miss. It's not safe."

Nell fought to hold her anger. "I know, but Brother Aaron convinced me we have to pray for the killers, even if we all are hoping they have a swift journey to hell." Nell lowered her voice. "I may not be able to do much, but I have to try. If you could ask Sheriff Parker to step out, please, I need to speak to him as well."

The preacher picked up on her crusade. "If none of you will help the sister to the jail, perhaps you'll join me in prayer for the sinners. We could kneel around their cells. I'm sure many of you know how to speak in tongues, and if you don't, only a few hours on your knees should convert you to the calling."

The man who'd admonished Nell moved closer. "I'd be happy to help you down, sister." He glanced at the others. "Frank, Mike, give me a hand."

Two of the men stepped over into the wagon's bed and lifted the chair while another two eased it onto the porch.

"You go on about your saving sinners, sister," one said. "We'll help you back in the wagon if we're still here when you leave."

"Bless you," Nell whispered from the folds of her cape. As Marla pushed her forward, Nell relaxed her hold on the gun that rested across her lap.

Once inside, the sea of men parted. By an old stove, Nell saw Mr.

Harrison with the sheriff. She let out a breath and realized how foolish she'd been to get Marla and the preacher out on a night like this.

But as she rolled closer, she saw the worry in first Parker's face and then Harrison's eyes. Something was wrong. She looked around; Jacob was nowhere in sight.

Sheriff Parker waved his hands and ordered everyone out of the office as Brother Aaron found his invisible pulpit by the window and started a prayer at full volume.

The posse grumbled but shuffled out. Parker closed the door and motioned for the preacher to continue. He filled two cups of coffee and returned to the back where Harrison stood and offered his seat to Marla.

When she sat, he stood behind her, his hands resting on the back of her chair.

No one spoke until the women drank a few swallows of coffee.

Nell leaned forward and whispered, "Is it safe to talk?"

"No one will hear us over Brother Aaron," Parker answered, "but we need to talk fast. What have your heard, Nell? Where is Jacob?"

Nell looked confused. "I thought he was with you."

The old sheriff shook his head, and Harrison related the last few words he'd had with Jacob.

Nell took another drink trying to make sense of what was happening.

"I waited here for half an hour, then thought I'd walk down to the café and see what was keeping him. The place was still open, but no one even remembered seeing the ranger. I checked in every open door between the café and the saloon where he'd left me. Nothing. Most folks were huddled inside waiting out the rain, so I returned here."

The sheriff picked up the conversation. "When Harrison showed up alone, I got worried that Jacob may have found trouble or passed out because of his weakened condition. The man would tell me he was fine even if he were bleeding all over my floor." Parker scrubbed his face with the palm of his hand. "I took a deputy and two lanterns on rounds. We checked every alley turning off of the main road. No ranger anywhere."

"What could have happened to him?" Nell whispered. Jacob couldn't have just vanished in the rain.

Harrison rested his hand once more on the back of Marla's chair. "Our hope was that for some reason he'd gone home. I even checked to see if the buggy was gone. We thought maybe he walked to your house. You showing up here crosses off that possibility."

"Who knows he's missing?"

"Pretty much all the men outside," Parker answered. "They were kind of waiting around to watch him take the boy out tonight. Most of them wanted to try to talk Jacob into traveling with them, but I figure they're about ready to give up and call it a night. They'll need their sleep come morning when they haul off these three." He pointed to the bedrolls in the left cell. Two of the men were snoring. The third was staring out the back window as if he expected help to show up.

"When Jacob and I parted at the saloon doors, he was going to meet the man in charge of the posse. A man named Kelly." Harrison rubbed his neck.

"Yeah," Parker added. "Only Kelly's been by here asking me why the ranger never showed up at the café. He says if Dalton doesn't claim Hank by morning, then the boy goes with the posse as part of the gang."

"I don't know where Jacob is, but I know he wouldn't want that." Nell had a feeling that if the ranger was able, he would have already been here.

"Exactly," Harrison said. "I've even got the orders releasing Hank back in the ranger's custody, but I don't think those men would let me have the boy on behalf of Jacob even if he signed the form."

"I would," the sheriff said, "if I thought you could get past them men. I got a bad feeling that these killers are going to get what's coming to them before they have their day in court. I don't much worry about those three, but the boy bothers me. He's not like them. He thanks me ever morning for the mush I feed them for breakfast. Can you believe that?"

"Maybe we could take him," Nell planned aloud. "Harrison, you and Hank could run for the wagon at the last minute after Marla and I are already in it."

Harrison shook his head. "The boy's hurt badly, and the doctor is too afraid to come over to even examine him. Too many people in town don't think he should dirty his hands. He's in no shape to walk out, much less run."

The sheriff agreed. "Even if you made it to the wagon, the preacher would never be able to outrun men on horseback in an old wagon."

Nell fought down tears. If Jacob were here, he'd barrel his way through all the trouble and act so tough no one would challenge him.

But Jacob wasn't here to help the boy. In a few hours the posse would be boarding a train with the killers and Hank if she didn't do something.

"We'll wait for Jacob," Nell whispered. They were all silent for a while. Brother Aaron preached on, getting more wound up about the demons of hell. At one point, a little after midnight, he opened the door and asked the men still on the porch to come in so that they could hear better.

They all declined.

One of the outlaws woke up and screamed that he was already in hell after listening to Brother Aaron for two hours. Then, yelling over the preacher, the prisoner listed all the ways he'd like to kill Brother Aaron. The preacher took the heckler as inspiration and marched on with his sermon.

A little after one, all but a few of the men outside were gone. The sheriff had taken pity on the prisoners and handed each a pillow to block out the preacher.

Parker leaned back in his chair. "One good thing, with the rain and the extra men guarding, we didn't have a mob outside shouting for revenge."

Harrison accepted his fifth cup of coffee from Marla. "If a mob had shown up, we'd turn Brother Aaron loose on them. He'd shout them down and see it as a full house to preach to."

Marla refilled the sheriff's coffee when he raised his mug. "You know, since you showed up, my coffee is getting better. I don't know what magic you did, Marla, but I could drink this all night."

Marla whispered, "I washed the pot." She smiled at Harrison when he laughed.

Nell had been thinking of a plan and decided now might be a good time to talk about it. After all, the preacher's voice couldn't last much longer. In the rainy night there was nothing more to do to find Jacob, but they could help Hank.

She held her hands out, and they all leaned in close, layering their hands over hers as if they were all in prayer. Not even the sheriff's deputy sleeping by the desk a few feet away could have heard them.

"I have an idea," Nell began, and the others looked at her, already with her even before they heard the plan.

When Nell straightened, they all lowered their hands and nodded once.

Mr. Harrison stood first. He walked over to the coat rack, picking up first his coat, and then layered Nell's velvet cape beneath it. Then he asked if he might make a final check of the boy. The deputy was too tired to walk with him to the cell. He just handed Harrison the keys. After all, the boy was in no shape to escape.

Next, Marla told the preacher to get the wagon ready.

Brother Aaron nodded and carried his sermon outside.

Marla rolled Nell back to the last cell as Nell demanded to say one last prayer to those she feared were about to die.

The sheriff yelled to the deputy that these folks were finally saying their farewells, and he thought everyone should help them along.

The deputy nodded and opened the door as Harrison walked out, tipping his hat and handing the keys back to the deputy.

A few minutes later, Marla pushed the wheelchair with an invalid wrapped in a velvet cape out the door. The sheriff dropped a paper on his desk, then oversaw the lifting of the chair into the bed of the wagon. He said his good-byes as the preacher tied the ropes in place. Then Brother Aaron stood in the wagon and blessed them all before pulling away.

Parker ordered the deputy and three of the posse to keep an eye on things because he thought he'd call it a night. The posse moved inside, huddling against the stove even before the sheriff was out of sight. As the door closed a cheer reached the street as the posse found the coffeepot full and hot.

None of them heard the back door open a few minutes later and a slender woman slip out.

Harrison was waiting in the alley with the buggy by the time Nell moved slowly down the two steps. She used the railing to brace herself and fought to keep from falling.

If he'd been a minute later, he would have had to pick her up from the mud.

He helped her inside the old buggy, wrapped his coat around her, and drove toward home.

She shivered against him, and he put his arm around her, but the bookkeeper didn't offer the warmth her ranger always did, and Nell couldn't stop the tears from silently falling as she worried about what might have happened to Jacob.

Harrison patted her shoulder. "You all right?"

She sniffed and nodded. "I would have never made it without the bars to hang onto. Then I only had one step through the door, and there was the rail waiting for me."

"Dalton would be proud of you," he said. "That one step may have saved a boy's life."

The others were unloading the wheelchair as Harrison pulled up to the house. He and Marla laced their arms and carried Nell all the way to the fireplace. Then Harrison and the preacher made a sling out of one of the blankets and lugged the boy up to the attic.

Nell watched them all struggling from her seat on the couch. Gypsy raced past them to make up the bed that had once been Nell's in the tiny attic room. Mrs. O'Daniel, her hair back in rag twists, was shouting orders as she climbed the stairs beside the boy.

Wednesday woke up and carried the baby downstairs so she could sit with Nell and ask questions while they watched everyone else go up and down the two flights of stairs. Wednesday spread a quilt over them both and huddled next to Nell with her baby in her arms.

Nell smiled and circled her arm around the girl's shoulders. She might be a mother, but a part of Wednesday was still a child herself.

Finally, Harrison and the preacher came down, saying they would take care of the horses. A few minutes later, Marla hurried past them to the kitchen to warm soup. The men were back from the barn by the time Mrs. O'Daniel came down with a report.

"He's weak," she said. "Don't look like he's had nothing to eat for a few days, or water as near as I can tell. He's beat up bad, bruises in the shape of knuckles all over his chest and back. His face looks like it must have hit the wall a few times. I got him to look at me a few times, but he turned away, acting like he didn't want my help." She shook her head. "I've seen that kind of blank stare before. In mothers who lose one too many babies, in widows after they bury their spouse. He's not thriving. He don't care if he lives."

Nell fought back tears. "He *will* live, won't he?"

The nurse shrugged. "Looks like I got my work cut out for me. He'll recover; I'll see to it if I have to force food down him. I figure I owe him one. He saved my life. Now I'll do my best to save his."

Nell knew she had to do her part, too. "Gypsy, burn his clothes tonight."

The housekeeper nodded. "I've already got them rolled up in a ball. I'll get rid of everything, even his boots. We'll have no trace he's here except in the attic."

Mrs. O'Daniel straightened. "I need to say something before this goes any further. I was against you going tonight. I always figured it was wrong to meddle with the law. But if I'd known they'd hurt that boy, I would have stormed the jail myself. Tomorrow, you'll find the ranger, but tonight you and the others did a good thing here."

"Thank you." Nell smiled at her. "That means a great deal to me."

Harrison and Marla carried Nell upstairs. She didn't miss that he held the shy cook's hand a moment longer than was necessary, but neither of them looked at the other as they left her room.

Nell heard the clock chime three, knowing dawn would come slowly without Jacob beside her.

CHAPTER 28

Nᴇʟʟ ʜᴀᴅ ᴊᴜsᴛ ꜰɪɴɪsʜᴇᴅ ʙʀᴇᴀᴋꜰᴀsᴛ ᴡʜᴇɴ sᴏᴍᴇᴏɴᴇ ᴘᴏᴜɴᴅᴇᴅ on the front door. She'd been talking with Harrison about where to look for Jacob and the hope that her ranger might have returned made her heart race.

Only it wouldn't be Jacob. He never knocked.

Harrison crossed to the study, while Gypsy went to open the door.

Nell wasn't surprised when Sheriff Parker and two other men rushed into the room. The entire household had been waiting for someone to call.

The two strangers nosed around like hunting dogs near a fox hole, but the sheriff removed his hat politely.

"I'm mighty sorry for the inconvenience, Nell, but these men are with the posse from Fort Worth, and they wouldn't leave with the others this morning. They seem to believe a man escaped from my jail last night, even though I have a signed paper showing that Ranger Dalton picked up his prisoner."

"They think the paper was false?" Nell tried to act calm as one man boldly opened the door to the kitchen, while the other poked his head into every little reading cove.

"Oh, they think the paper is real. They just don't believe the ranger ever came by for the prisoner. It seems they had men watching for him who claim he never showed up. But when I got to work this morning, the paper was on my desk, so he must have stopped by when no one was looking."

The older of the two men faced Nell. "The sheriff knows that would be impossible. One of my men would have seen him. We're searching your house, miss."

Nell lifted the huge Colt from her lap. "Not without my permission."

The stranger's eyes widened.

For a moment, Nell thought he might be dumb enough to go for his gun.

"I may be in a wheelchair, but I assure you I have no handicap when it comes to my aim. Ranger Dalton taught me to shoot before I was ten." She leveled the Colt to his heart. "Now, you've insulted the sheriff and myself. I suggest you start this visit over unless you'd like to be carried out of my house."

The stranger glanced at Parker, realizing he would get no help from that corner. "You'd let her shoot me?"

Sheriff Parker didn't hesitate. "And then testify on her behalf."

Nell fought down a smile as the stranger reconsidered his campaign.

"May we please look around your house and grounds for a member of a gang who may be a killer? We have reason to believe he is not in the custody of the ranger but has escaped."

"I'll know your name," Nell said.

"Kelly. Anthony Kelly, miss, and I assure you we mean you no harm." He looked at Parker. "Tell her, Sheriff, that we're not here to hurt her or anyone in her household. For all we know, the killer could be preying on this poor, helpless woman, holding her prisoner and forcing her to say what she's saying."

Harrison stepped from the study, a rifle resting in the fold of his arm. "No one is holding Miss Nell against her will. Do not also presume that she is unarmed or helpless."

Gypsy lifted the gun left by the front door and added, "I can never hit anything, but say the word, and I'll give it a try."

Kelly lost all his huff and puff as fear flashed in his eyes. "Stop this, Sheriff."

"Way I see it, this lady, all helpless, has a right to protect herself in her own house. I told you not to come in here pushing people around. Most folks in this part of the country don't take well to being bossed for no good reason."

Kelly knew when to cut his losses. "I apologize. In my anger and panic at fearing I may have let a killer go free, I stepped over the line. I hope you will accept my deepest regrets."

Nell smiled and lowered the gun. "I will, and I'll allow your man to search upstairs, providing he doesn't disturb anything. You are welcome to look through the barn and outbuildings, provided we understand one another that you will never storm my house again."

Kelly looked surprised that she would make such an offer. She caught the flicker in his eye and knew he was thinking that anyone allowing a search would have nothing to hide.

He nodded toward the younger man. "Sammy, look upstairs, but make sure you disturb nothing."

The man nodded and took the stairs two at a time. The first door he tried, everyone downstairs heard a woman's scream.

Sammy stumbled backward, almost tumbling down the stairs.

A moment later, Mrs. O'Daniel appeared, her robe wrapped around her like a towel. "How dare you come into my room while I'm dressing!" She looked down at the sheriff. "Sheriff, thank God you're here. Arrest this man!"

"I'm sorry, ma'am. I didn't see nothing, and what I saw I'm real sorry I looked at."

Kelly appeared irritated. "Get on with it, Sammy. I'll meet you at the horses in five minutes."

He touched his hat with two fingers as he glanced at Nell and disappeared back through the open front door. Gypsy waved him goodbye with the old gun still in her hand.

A few minutes later, Sammy climbed the small flight of stairs to the attic room.

Nell heard him open the door, then start apologizing again. He stumbled his way down to ground level. When he reached Nell he asked, "Did you know what you got in the attic?"

"What?" Nell closed her hand around the gun in her lap.

"You got a young woman with her dress open, and she's feeding her baby. Should she be doing that in public?"

"She was in the privacy of her bedroom." Nell tried to look angry. "I believe you were the one out of line."

Sammy's face turned scarlet. "I'm real sorry. I never seen a woman doing that before. Not all open like that."

He was out the door so fast, Nell didn't have time to laugh. A minute later she heard them ride away.

Mrs. O'Daniel and Wednesday appeared on the landing, both smiling.

"Well," the nurse finished buttoning her uniform. "We did our part."

"How did you think of it?" Nell had to ask.

Wednesday giggled. "Gypsy told us if a man sees a little skin, he don't see nothin' else in the room. So I set on Hank's bed with him right behind me and started feeding the baby."

"And I decided I'd get whoever came up the stairs rattled before he even got to the attic. I may have shown an inch too much, I fear, for the fellow almost tumbled down the stairs."

"Do you think we'll get arrested?" Wednesday asked.

"Not if they didn't find Hank, and even if they had, you could hardly be arrested for feeding your baby."

Wednesday smiled. "I'm going to go back up and sit with Hank for a while. It's something I can do to help, and it is a quiet place to feed DH."

Nell agreed and rolled into the study to do her part in helping Harrison plan their next move. They had to find Dalton.

The bookkeeper leaned over a map he'd rolled out on the table.

"Where could Jacob be?" She asked the question that she knew was on both their minds.

"He didn't ride out. Dusty's still in the barn. He's too big to be lying around in the mud. Someone would have noticed by now. My guess is the posse has him, or rather had him."

"You think they made sure something happened to Jacob so he wouldn't take custody of Hank by the time they picked up the other three outlaws."

Harrison nodded. "Maybe they kidnapped him, or left him tied up somewhere. Only somehow, they lost track of him and may think he actually got Hank out. Otherwise, they'd be beating it out of Jacob right now and not searching barns."

Nell looked up from the map. "You don't think they killed him, do you?"

Harrison shook his head. "No. They're the good guys, remember. But in this case we just met an overachiever in Anthony Kelly. They want to bring all the outlaws in and be the big heroes. Jacob helped them in the hunt, but he's getting in the way of their glory."

"So, if they don't have him, and he didn't ride away, he's where?"

"Somewhere in town. And my guess is about now he's waking up with one hell of a bump on his head." Harrison smiled down at Nell. "You want me to go to town and find him."

She nodded.

He reached for his jacket. "You know, Miss Nell, being your book-keeper is a busy job, but being your friend runs round the clock."

"Want to quit?"

He winked. "Not a chance."

CHAPTER 29

Jacob rolled out from under a bench. Clothes tumbled in an avalanche over him, and he swore as he opened his eyes and tried to focus.

Sitting up, he shoved all the fabric away and looked around, finding himself in the ugliest room he'd ever seen. The walls were painted, by someone possessing little talent, with birds and flowers. Cheap jewelry and hats hung on nails near the low ceiling. Clothes were piled everywhere, and perfume thickened the air.

"Morning, Ranger," a woman's voice squeaked.

Jacob looked around. It took him a few seconds to pick her out from all the colors. "Morning," he mumbled as he felt the knot on the back of his head. "Where am I?"

She smiled with stained teeth framed by dark red lips. "I found you last night in the alley, passed out cold. It smelled like someone broke a full bottle of whiskey over your head. I got Dave to haul you in here 'cause I feared whoever hit you might come back to finish the job."

"Thanks." Jacob stumbled over a mountain of clothes. "I think?"

She shrugged. "You were nice to me once, Ranger, and Pearlie don't forget. Dave said about an hour after we moved you in here, a pair of young fellows came in looking for you. They claimed to have seen you stumble off the walk, but we remembered noticing you pass earlier, and you didn't look like you were drinking. Dave didn't tell them nothin'."

Jacob tried to untangle his arm from a scarf that had grown attached to his shirt. "Have any idea what time it is?"

"After noon, I'd guess." She patted powder on her throat. "We opened early on account of so many people in town come to see the outlaws off this morning. Once the sheriff and that posse got them loaded on the train, everyone was wanting to drink and talk it over."

Jacob combed his fingers through his hair. He smelled of whiskey, perfume, and mud. "Could you do me another favor, Pearlie, and loan me a horse?"

"Dave's got one tied up out back. He won't need the nag till he rides home tonight. You're welcome to it till then."

Jacob thought of offering her money as thanks, but knew it would cheapen what she did. "I owe you one," he said. "Thanks for the favor."

She smiled. "Don't worry about it, Ranger. That's what friends are for."

Handing him his hat, she added, "We couldn't find your gun. Dave said it's probably lost in the mud."

Jacob brushed his empty holster, feeling strange without the Colt on his hip.

"Next time you come spend the night, Ranger," Pearlie's painted-on eyebrows danced, "try to be awake."

Laughing, Jacob promised, guessing that they both knew he'd never return.

He took a deep breath as he stepped out of her bungalow behind the bar, but most of the smells walked along with him. Crossing to the alley, he took the only horse tied there. He wanted to clear town as fast as possible before someone saw him and rumors started about him being a drunk. Or worse, if Nell found out where he'd spent the night. She was already mad at him. Any news might push her over the line into hating him, and that would probably ruin his chances of marrying her.

Halfway home, he ran into Rand Harrison driving Nell's buckboard.

"Morning," Harrison said as calmly as if they were simply passing.

"Not much good about it," Jacob answered. "They send you to look for me?"

Rand nodded.

"Mind if I take this horse back before I start explaining?" Jacob's head pounded.

"You think you can stay in the saddle?"

Jacob swung the horse around and let Rand worry about keeping up with him.

When they returned Dave's horse, Harrison looked at the run-down saloon. "You spend the night here?"

Jacob tied the horse. "Yeah. You planning on reporting to Nell?" He thought of threatening Rand if he did, but it didn't seem right to pester a man about telling the truth.

"No," Harrison answered. "You do enough to ruin your chances with her without me adding fuel to the fire."

When Jacob climbed in beside the bookkeeper, Harrison held his nose.

"Ride in the back, will you? You're offending the horses." Harrison thumbed toward the straw behind him.

Jacob stepped over and sat in the middle of mud-covered straw. He felt like a pig being hauled to market. He even smelled like one.

The bookkeeper laughed while Jacob told him what happened, then swore he could have guessed the entire story just from the look of the ranger.

Jacob saw no reason for humor. "I failed, Rand. I let that boy down. I gave him my word he wouldn't be on that train this morning, and I was out cold when the posse took him away."

"First of all," the bookkeeper twisted on the bench so he could see Jacob, "you didn't let him down. You were ambushed in the dark. Any man's going down if someone slugs him with a full bottle, even you. And, second . . ." One corner of Rand's mouth lifted slightly. "You didn't break a promise. He's not on his way to Fort Worth. Hank's in Nell's attic, tucked away in a bed with Mrs. O'Daniel fussing over him."

The bookkeeper shoved his hat back. "We got him out without anyone noticing and left your signed note on the sheriff's desk."

"What?"

Rand turned off the road and circled to the back of Nell's place. "I'll tell you all about it while you bathe in the horse tank out by the windmill. If I take you into the house smelling like this, the women will shoot me. I'll walk down to the barn and fetch a clean set of clothes I saw Gypsy place on your saddle yesterday."

Ten minutes later, Jacob stripped and fell face-first into the horse tank. He sank to the bottom like a rock and lay there for a few seconds, remembering that Mrs. O'Daniel promised to kill him if he got his bandages wet.

By the time he came up for air and scrubbed some of the whiskey and glass out of his hair, Harrison had picked up the clean set of clothes for him. The bookkeeper relaxed on the bench facing the house and told him all about what they'd done the night before. He gave every detail of how the preacher kept talking and how Nell gave up her wheelchair so they could roll the kid out right under the posse's noses.

"You should have seen her," Harrison said with pride. "She's quite a woman."

"I knew she would be, even when she was a kid. She used to look at me with those big brown eyes and make me swear I'd wait for her to grow up. To tell the truth, I didn't think it would be so soon."

Jacob pulled off the bandages and splashed water across his bruised and scabbed flesh. Then he reached for a towel atop the clothes, thankful there was no fresh blood coming from his wounds. He ignored Harrison's suggestion that the wounds have fresh bandages and tugged into clean long johns.

Harrison looked out toward the town, lost in his own thoughts.

Pulling on his clean Levi's, Jacob walked over to sit on the bench beside Harrison. He leaned his elbows on his knees as he dried his hair. "I've been thinking of what we talked about going into town yesterday. Maybe you're right."

"About what?" Harrison tossed him a shirt.

"Maybe I should court Nell a little. I guess I didn't figure I had the time with others standing in line. But, looking back, that may be just what she wants. Seems like I went from bossing her around to kissing her. Maybe there should have been a little of something else in between."

"I'm still standing in line," Harrison announced. "So don't start thinking that you have too much time. My offer to marry her any time she says the word is still there."

"Are you hinting I'm slow at this marrying game?"

"How long would you have waited to ask her if she hadn't placed the ad? A year? Five years? You would have left things like they were between the two of you until you both were old and gray."

Jacob scrubbed his scalp, wishing he could clear his brain. Harrison was right. He liked how it was between Nell and him for the most part. Sure, they fought and yelled, but he always knew they'd stay friends in the end.

Harrison interrupted his thoughts again. "I'll not take back my offer. I made it with honor. But I'll help you any way I can. Not because I don't want to marry Nell and own half her property, but more because I think she might be happier with you. The difference between the two of us, Ranger, is simple. I see it as a business, and you see it as a life. Even if I married her and lived with her for twenty years, I'm not sure she'd ever love me the way she loves you."

"You're a good man, Rand. She could do a lot worse than marrying someone like you."

The bookkeeper nodded. "Thanks. Coming from you that means a great deal."

"So, what's your first advice?"

"Be slow and gentle with her. No matter what happens, don't get upset and start going off half-cocked." Harrison frowned as if he were trying to get through to a bear. "Try being polite to her for a change. Don't rush her into anything."

"I can do that. How hard could it be?" Jacob ignored Rand's raised eyebrow and continued, "No matter what she says, I'll be nice. I'll be so damn nice she'll probably think I got brain damage from that bottle of whiskey colliding with my scalp."

Harrison looked like he had his doubts. "It won't be easy."

"I can do it. Bet you."

"What?"

Jacob realized having a wager might strengthen his resolution. He'd lost few bets in his life and none where he'd bet on himself. "A week of your pay against a week of mine."

"Fair enough." Harrison offered his hand. "With an extra week's pay I could buy another suit."

Jacob shook the bookkeeper's hand. "And I could get another Colt. Pearlie thinks mine is lost in the mud in the alley."

They walked to the house and went in the rear entrance. Jacob slipped up the back stairs to see Hank. He had to know the boy was all right before he made any plans about getting him to Fort Worth. Harrison said he looked pretty bad after the last beating.

Mrs. O'Daniel was guarding the attic door. "About time you showed up, Ranger. You missed all the excitement last night."

Jacob didn't want to talk about where he'd been. "How's the boy?"

Mrs. O'Daniel's face turned from anger to worry in a blink. "He's not doing so well. Oh, near as I can tell his wounds will heal, mostly bruises and a few cracked ribs, from what I can tell. But I can't get him to eat anything. He won't even take a drink unless I threaten to hold his nose."

"What's wrong?"

"He's hurting from the beatings, that's for sure, but it's more than just physical pain. I don't think he cares to live anymore. He lost his mother a while back, and the father who came after him didn't do anything but beat him down in body and spirit."

Jacob nodded. He's seen it that morning by the outlaw camp. Hank had fought to free himself, but not for his life. And when he'd come back with Jacob, the ranger knew it was more running from his pa than thinking he was heading toward safety. Hank saw Jacob as the lesser of two evils, and now he must think even the ranger let him down.

"What do we do?"

"If I can get him to eat, he'll heal enough to ride in a week or so. But why should he? What's he got to look forward to? A hanging. Life in prison. My guess is he'd have been a dead man if he hadn't helped with the robbery, and now he's a dead man because he did. Not much reason to keep breathing. I think, one way or the other, he believes fifteen is as old as he's going to get."

Jacob's head felt like a few thousand buffalo were stampeding across it, and now he had to figure out how to make a boy want to live. "Can I take a look at him?"

Mrs. O'Daniel nodded. "He won't open his eyes or even answer you."

Jacob nodded and slipped into the room. Wednesday was sitting in a rocker beside the bed. She rocked her baby and sang a song about the green hills of Ireland.

Jacob touched his finger to his lips and indicated for her to continue. He sat for a while, listening to the song and trying to figure out what to do. According to the law, he should take the kid in. Let the jailer worry about keeping him alive until the trial.

But why lock him in a cell? If he were dying, maybe all Jacob could offer him was a place to do it quietly. The kid deserved that much. Mrs. O'Daniel had a point. If his pa and the others were planning a robbery around the kid, they probably would have felt the need to kill him if he hadn't gone along.

Jacob studied Hank. He wasn't even shaving yet, though a few whiskers sprouted on his chin and upper lip. If he lived, he'd have a few scars from the beatings. The ranger wished he knew which men had done such a thing. He'd teach them a lesson they'd carry into hell.

Frowning, Jacob realized he was getting mad. He'd better start working on his temper before he even talked to Nell. There were lots of things that made him angry, but Nell always seemed to know where to light the match, and he swore she pestered him sometimes just to see how long it would take her to make him start yelling.

Well, no more. He would take Harrison's advice and be polite. He'd be gentle and not raise his voice. *Hell,* he thought, *I'll be so calm, she won't even recognize me.*

Hank moved in pain, shifting slightly beneath the sheet that covered his bandaged body.

Before Jacob could react, Wednesday laid her free hand on his shoulder and patted as softly as she patted her baby's back. "Hush now. Don't you cry. Hush now and rest."

Hank seemed to relax, and Wednesday went back to singing.

Jacob watched them. Both were little more than children who'd had their share of trouble for a lifetime. In the few hours they'd bonded, probably with very few words. He'd known Nell over half her life and he didn't understand her half as well as Wednesday seemed to understand what the boy needed.

He slipped from the room, figuring Hank was getting the best of care already. There was nothing Jacob could do for him.

He wandered down the hallway to Nell's room and was surprised to see her silhouette against the window. For a moment he watched her. When had she turned from the ugly duckling he'd known a few years ago? When had she grown from pretty to beautiful?

"You looking for someone?" he said in a low voice.

"Jacob!"

For a blink he thought she might rise and run to him. He almost opened his arms to catch her. He'd twirl her around with her skirts and hair flying.

Only she didn't move. She waited.

Jacob walked to her and knelt on one knee. "You're looking quite fair today." He smiled as her hand reached out to touch his face.

"I was worried about you."

"So was I," he admitted. "Not so much about myself but about what I didn't do that needed doing. I got knocked cold in a dark alley. I thought I'd let Hank down. Thanks for rescuing him for me. Harrison told me what you did." He didn't want to think about what would have happened if she'd fallen or been caught taking Hank from jail.

"It was nothing," she lied. "Only a few steps."

He stood and offered his hands. When she gave him hers, he pulled her slowly to her feet. He'd forgotten how tall she was, half a head or more above most women. But she still seemed small to him. He leaned down a few inches and touched his lips to hers.

Nell circled her arms around his neck and let him take her weight against his heart as she kissed him back.

He loved holding her like this, standing as if they could face all the world had to offer. But he was all too aware that he couldn't hug her too tightly or sway more than a few inches without feeling her stiffen in pain. She kissed him with warmth and the hunger of a woman, but he could never forget that he was holding glass.

Harrison had been right; if Jacob couldn't be gentle, he could never have her. He lowered her back to the chair. "We have to talk."

Jacob didn't miss the sadness in her eyes. "I know."

"What you did last night was a major crime. Folks just can't go into a jail and take someone out."

"We had your paper, signed and filled out."

"I know, and if it gets down to it, I'll swear I was with you, but I don't like lying, so try to stay within the general letter of the law from now on."

She nodded. "Just so you can always tell the truth, I'll try."

"Thanks. Now, no one besides that army downstairs is to know that I even came here. Is that clear? You have to act like you have no idea where I am. It's the only way to keep Hank safe. If anyone thinks I'm staying here, or even stopped by, they might be back, and this time the search will be complete."

She shrugged. "Who would I tell? If anyone asks, you were never here. Hank isn't here. Wednesday's not here. In fact, I'm not so sure I'm here anymore."

"Be serious." He scolded with a smile.

"I'll try, but I'm so glad you're home I accidentally forgot about being mad at you."

"Good. I've been thinking maybe we could start over like we're fresh out of the chute. I'll stop trying to make you marry me and start trying to be your friend." He smiled, proud of himself. "Would you like that?"

"Are we friends who kiss?"

He started to say, *Hell yes,* then thought about it and said, "If that's the way you want it."

She nodded. "And touch. Are we friends who touch?"

"I wouldn't mind that, if the opportunity came up. The feel of you is a pleasure that surprised me."

"All right. We'll start over as very good friends. Would you carry me downstairs before Mrs. O'Daniel comes in and insists I fight the stairs again today?"

He lifted her and kissed her as he walked across the room. Then he poked his head out to make sure the coast was clear and carried her downstairs. She was sitting on the couch when Mrs. O'Daniel came down from the attic.

The nurse frowned at them both, but it was Jacob she attacked. "I'll have a look at those wounds before you're off again, Ranger."

"They're fine." He tried to put her off.

"You can strip right here or in the mud room, but I'll check them now." The stout little woman might only make half of him, but she'd gotten her bluff in. Jacob swore all the way to the mud room, removing his clothes as he stormed.

Gypsy held the kitchen door for him. Jacob passed Harrison drinking coffee on the corner of the cutting board. Marla worked across from him. They both watched as if the ranger was the nightly floor show.

"Haven't you got some figuring to do?" Jacob snapped.

Rand smiled but didn't move. "Haven't you got some outlaws to fight?"

Jacob rattled all the windows on the back of the house when he slammed the mud room door.

Mrs. O'Daniel didn't hesitate as she opened the door and came right in behind him.

Jacob growled. He needed to move on, he decided. Too many people in this place had lost their fear of him.

CHAPTER 30

Mrs. O'Daniel took one look at Jacob's wounds and insisted on putting ointment over them. Then she bandaged the shoulder and swore he'd see more of his own blood if he bothered with the bandages again.

Jacob didn't complain. He understood the difference between a promise and a threat. Mrs. O'Daniel was making a promise.

Gypsy poked her head around the door and stared. Sometimes her round, water-blue eyes seemed to take up half her face.

"Get out," Jacob ordered calmly, for he knew the old woman wouldn't listen unless she wanted to. "I'd like to get dressed without an audience."

"I'm here to tell you that snake Walter Farrow is back sitting on my clean couch like he belongs. He's offering marriage to Nell again while you're out here getting pampered."

Jacob shoved to his feet and out of the reach of Mrs. O'Daniel. He took two giant steps toward the kitchen before he realized he wasn't supposed to be at Nell's house. He couldn't face the toad of a man, no matter how much he'd like to. Walter Farrow was the kind of gossip who'd tell half the town all he saw at Nell's place. He seemed to gather great delight in sticking his nose into everyone's business.

Harrison appeared at the mudroom door. "You'd better disappear." He smiled. "Because I doubt you'll be able to watch the lawyer without wanting to clobber him."

"Wait." Jacob kept his voice low as he slipped into the kitchen. "I have to see if Farrow shows his hand. He has no idea I'm anywhere close. If he does start waddling toward the kitchen, you can stall him while I slip out the back. With his width, he'll be lucky to get through the swinging door without a push from the other side."

"I wouldn't mind tripping him to see how many times he rolls," Mrs. O' Daniel mumbled as she disappeared up the back stairs.

Jacob motioned for her to be quiet as they moved toward the door leading to the main room.

When Marla looked up and saw Jacob crossing her kitchen, she smiled, really smiled at him for the first time. "Welcome back, Ranger," she whispered. "We were all worried about you."

Jacob winked at her, making her blush. "I only returned for more of your cooking."

She turned away, but not before Jacob noticed how pretty she looked when she blushed. He'd always thought of her as plain, but now, he reconsidered.

Harrison moved beside the swinging door and pushed it open slightly, then let it close. "Farrow's in there, all right."

Marla picked up a tray, and Harrison nodded once. When she shoved the door, the bookkeeper stood well out of sight.

When Marla returned, Harrison stopped the swing of the wood a few inches before it closed. Walter Farrow's back was in clear view.

Jacob shifted so he could see through the opening.

Nell didn't look happy that Farrow was there, but she wasn't pointing her gun at him, which surprised Jacob.

"You say you have word about Ranger Dalton?" Nell asked as she poured tea and offered him a cup.

"Yes, I saw him last night." Walter leaned forward to accept the sweets she held toward him. "It was late, and we walked together for a time." Farrow ate two cookies at once, chewing as he talked. "I knew you'd want to know that he was alive. I heard the sheriff and his deputy were searching for him last night and feared bad luck had finally found him."

"If you don't mind me asking, what did you and the ranger talk about during your stroll?"

Farrow straightened. "Despite his anger toward me in the past . . ." The fat man swallowed. "Which I believe is based more because I asked for your hand in marriage than anything else, I hoped, due to our pending business deal, to become both your friend and the ranger's."

Jacob leaned back from the doorway and decided this lawyer was the fattest chameleon he'd ever seen. How can Farrow show up acting all nice when the last time he called they almost had to run him off the place?

Marla handed Jacob a cup of coffee, then pulled a stool close to listen. The ranger didn't miss that she leaned her arm on Harrison's back as she tried to see through the crack in the door. Harrison didn't seem to notice, but he hadn't jerked when she touched him, either.

Nell's voice drifted through the opening. "I wasn't aware we had a pending business deal, Mr. Farrow. I'm worried about my friend, and if you have any information about him, I would greatly appreciate anything you can tell me. The sheriff and a man named Kelly have already been out looking for a boy Dalton may have taken from the jail last night, but I'm afraid I'm very much in the dark about what is happening in town."

"My news may not be good, I fear." Farrow patted her hand in sympathy, then took another cookie. "But I rushed to tell you all the same in an effort to show my good faith as a friend."

Nell sat so stiff in her chair she could have been made of steel. "Please, go on. Do you know if he's alive?" She gave no hint that she'd kissed her ranger minutes ago and knew full well that he was alive.

Farrow moved his cup to the table. "To my knowledge, Miss Nell, he's breathing. He was seen leaving a barmaid's quarters not an hour ago. My source was several feet away, but he reported the ranger smelled both of liquor and perfume. He looked as if he'd just awoken with his hair wild and his clothes wrinkled. The two of them must have had a wild night."

Something tumbled in the kitchen, but Nell ignored it. The happiness over Jacob being alive was cracked by the fact that he'd spent the night with another woman.

Nell considered where the information was coming from. It made no sense. Jacob wouldn't neglect his duty. He wouldn't have abandoned Hank for a night of drinking and womanizing.

Nell lifted her head. "I don't believe you, sir."

Farrow shook his head. "I was afraid of that. You're welcome to check it out for yourself. The barmaid's name is Pearlie, and she lives back behind a little saloon run by a man named Dave Digger. I questioned Dave, and he wouldn't tell me anything, but I could see it in his eyes. A lawyer is trained to tell when a man is lying, and I'd stake my reputation on the fact that Digger knew where Jacob Dalton spent the night."

"I think I'll wait to hear Jacob's side of the story. I'm sure it will not be the same."

Farrow reached in his briefcase and pulled out a gun wrapped in rags. "I found this a few feet from the woman's door along with a broken whiskey bottle. Your ranger must have stumbled on his way into her bungalow last night."

Nell took the Colt and turned it over in her hand. She didn't offer to give it back. "Is that all you came to tell me, sir?"

"No, Miss Nell, I wish to offer you my protection. I feel it would be my honor and duty to do so."

Nell almost laughed. "Your protection?"

"Yes. You see, I believe you have fallen into the clutches of evil men, and I wish to be of help."

"Evil men? You're starting to sound like Brother Aaron."

Farrow didn't see the humor. "I'm accustomed to recognizing the criminals among us. In my profession they are a necessary unpleasantness we must deal with."

He stood and straightened his vest as if preparing to face the court. "I have it on good authority that Brother Aaron has been run out of more than one town for being drunk while standing at the pulpit." Farrow paced before her, his hands locked behind him. "I checked some of the places he listed when he asked to preach last week at the church I've been attending while I'm staying in town. Not all spoke highly of the preacher."

He walked a few feet away, then turned back, shaking his head as if he hated passing along such sad news. "I make it my business to learn about people. Your bookkeeper, miss, has only recently been released from prison. Your housekeeper is an old hooker, and I believe your cook may have poisoned more than one man."

Now Nell did laugh. When she could catch her breath, she asked, "Is that all, Mr. Farrow?"

He seemed surprised at her request. "I've made inquires into your new nurse, but find nothing except that she's buried three husbands. Which I find suspicious, but not, in itself, damning."

"And me, Mr. Farrow? Did you find out anything about me?"

He nodded. "According to several in town you were a wild child after your mother died, but I'm willing to forgive that. Most folks said they didn't know you very well, that you kept to yourself. And I think you'll be glad to know that everyone I talked to said how sorry they were that you were confined to a wheelchair. I believe that if you would be so kind as to entertain the possibility of a marriage between us, my standing and name would offer you a comfortable place in the community."

Nell couldn't bring herself to thank him for what he thought she'd find good news. She changed the subject. "And you, Mr. Farrow? How spotless is your past?"

He didn't answer.

"You see, I don't need to do much checking on you. I can read most of it in your eyes. You let your uncle die alone and then decided you wanted his land. You think because you practice law that somehow allows you to play with the courts and with people. You like finding dirt on folks and don't much care how accurate it is. As for my standing in the community, I find I've become quite comfortable standing outside looking in."

"I've come here to help you." He stiffened. "A woman like you would be wise to accept my offer of protection."

"Why?" she asked calmly.

"Because I wish to be your friend, and in time I think you would find me a proper choice as husband. I know we got off on the wrong foot, but things can change. I can be a great help to my friends." A threat flavored his words with warning. "A woman alone, like yourself, needs protection."

Nell called for Gypsy. "Mr. Farrow, we may become friends in time, but trying to destroy my friends' reputations will not be the path. I bid you good day."

She saw the anger in his eyes she'd seen once before. A fury so complete it seemed to overtake him for a moment. He was a man who was losing control and who insisted on always having his way. She suspected his high-and-mighty world in Dallas had crumbled, and this was the last place where he could make a stand.

Nell made a promise to herself that she'd never be alone with Walter Farrow again. If he ever snapped, she wasn't sure how far he might go to get his way. He reminded her of a spoiled child hidden in a man's body. She wouldn't have been surprised if he'd stomped his foot.

Gypsy hurried out from the kitchen and opened the front door without taking her eyes off Farrow.

"We'll talk again," he said as he nodded once and passed through the open door.

Gypsy followed him out and stood on the porch until he was out of sight.

"What are you doing?" Nell asked as Gypsy stared down the road.

"I wanted to see if he hopped along when nobody was watching. I swear he's the biggest toad in Texas."

Nell smiled and rolled toward the kitchen door. "You can come out now!" she yelled. "I know you're in there."

Jacob, Harrison, and Marla all piled out like they'd been leaning on the door.

Before Jacob could do any explaining, Nell pointed to the dining table. "Everyone sit down, please." She glanced back at Gypsy. "You, too. I want to talk to everyone at once."

Jacob took a chair as he threatened Walter Farrow under his breath. Harrison pulled Marla's chair out for her and took the next one in line. Gypsy plopped on the last seat.

"I have one question." Nell stared at Jacob first. "Did you spend the night in a barmaid's room?"

"I can . . ."

"Just answer the question," Nell snapped.

"Yes," Jacob answered.

She raised her hand for silence before he could add more.

"Mr. Harrison, have you been in prison?"

"Yes," Harrison answered directly, offering no further explanation.

Nell didn't miss the fact that she seemed the only one at the table surprised by the revelation. She moved to Marla, and her voice softened. "Did you ever poison anyone?"

The cook shook her head.

"I didn't think so," Nell whispered. "At least he was wrong about one of my friends."

"What about me?" Gypsy resented not even being asked. "I heard what he said about me. He called me an old hooker."

"And were you?" Nell said, paying Gypsy her due.

"No," Gypsy shouted. "I was young when I made my living on my back."

Nell smiled. "It seems I have a wild gang here."

Jacob watched her closely. To his shock, she didn't seem angry about any of the news. "Aren't you going to ask a few questions?" He was ready to defend himself and Harrison at least. Gypsy and Marla's stories were nothing new.

"No." Nell rolled away from the table. "We've got far too much to do today. I understand why Harrison left prison off his letter of reference, and I'll murder you later. Right now, we've got to get you out of sight. It's going to be hard enough to hide Hank here without you hanging around."

Jacob followed her to the study. Strange, he was all ready to be mad at her for believing he'd slept with Pearlie. Either she didn't believe he'd really spent the night in the barmaid's room, or she didn't care. One frustrated him, the other confused him.

Nell broke into his thoughts. "If Farrow, or one of his spies, saw you this morning, then it won't be long until Kelly knows you're in town. And if he thinks you're in town, he'll reason that you will be here. Or at least come by on your way out."

Jacob nodded, taking his Colt from her lap, muddy rag and all.

Harrison followed them in and leaned over the map still spread out. "I have an idea." He pointed to a place on the map colored in red, meaning it belonged to Nell. "Here at the house won't be safe. Someone with a spyglass could see you from a mile away. But here, no one would find you."

Nell and Jacob looked at where he pointed.

"Stockard's old place?" Jacob asked.

"There's a cabin there on a hill. No one would sneak up on you. It would be all right for a few days until Kelly gets tired of looking and decides you must have taken the kid on to Fort Worth alone."

Jacob shook his head. He didn't want to leave Nell and the others. To his surprise, Nell agreed with Harrison.

"Jacob, he's right. You know you'd never be able to stay in this house for days. Someone could spot you even if you walked to the barn. But if you laid low until Hank was able to travel, no one would guess he'd be here. The best way to keep Hank safe is for you not to be near."

Jacob didn't like the plan. He'd never hid out from trouble in his life. But he couldn't take Hank anywhere in his condition. They were right, Jacob realized. He had to vanish.

"Kelly may be watching the roads, but I could bring supplies down to you when Nell takes her exercise in the river." Harrison planned out the details. "It's about halfway between here and the Stockard place. There's enough cottonwoods down by the water that no one would notice you riding in or me leaving supplies."

Nell added, "The place we stopped at yesterday was far enough away from the road not to be spied on. From the hill where the preacher sat, anyone could see for a mile or more. You could meet us there if you liked and not worry about being seen."

"How long?" Jacob asked knowing there was no answer.

"A week at the most," Nell guessed. "I'll tell Brother Aaron to go to town every day and follow Kelly around. Then we'll know when he leaves. Once he's gone, it should be safe for you to return. No one comes out but the sheriff, and he helped with the disappearance of Hank, so he won't tell anyone."

Harrison mumbled, "Having the preacher be Kelly's new best friend will probably encourage the head of the posse to book early on the next train."

Jacob ran his hand through his hair in frustration. "I'll leave when it's good and dark."

Every bone in his body told him not to leave Nell, but he saw no other way. Harrison was right; for once the best way to protect her might be for him to leave.

CHAPTER 31

THE REST OF THE DAY, JACOB FELT LIKE HE'D BEEN LOCKED IN prison. Sun shone through all the windows, but he was trapped inside. It wouldn't be safe for him even to sit on the porch. Besides Kelly, Walter Farrow might have lookouts watching for him to appear at Nell's place. If anyone knew he was at the house, they'd reason the boy would be there also. Jacob felt like he could handle Kelly or Farrow dropping by, but they might bring a mob of townsfolk with them, and then someone might get hurt.

He could almost see Walter standing in the saloon yelling that a killer was still in their town and it was up to the citizens to do something about him. He'd go into detail about how Hank was one of the men who'd pulled innocent people off the train and shot them.

Farrow, or Kelly, would probably buy everyone a few drinks before announcing his plan. Since he was a lawyer, he might reason that they could have a trial now and save time. Kelly would agree to take Hank's body back to Fort Worth.

And finally, when the crowd was ready, Farrow would lead them out to Nell's place to do what he'd decided had to be done. By the time they'd get to the house by the tracks, the crowd would have turned into an angry mob, and not even Farrow would have control.

Jacob couldn't risk that on Nell's property. He had a feeling if there was a fight, Nell would be right in the middle of it, even in her wheel-chair. So his only choice was to stay out of sight and wait for midnight.

By midafternoon, when Nell and the nurse left to go to the river for a swim, he was starting to bump into furniture like the top Harrison had bought the baby. He tried reading but couldn't settle enough to pay attention. He talked to Wednesday for a while, but to his surprise, the girl didn't seem all that interested in keeping him company. He cleaned and reloaded every weapon in the house, including his own Colt that had been packed in dried mud.

Jacob could only think of one other thing he could do with Nell to pass the time, and she was never alone. Even staying in the same room with her and not being free to touch her bothered him. So he paced and ate. Then, for a change, he ate and paced.

If the sun didn't set soon, they'd have to roll him out of the house.

Harrison seemed to be gone for hours with Nell and the nurse. Jacob was glad to see them return and frustrated when he couldn't go out front to carry her in. She looked tired even from twenty feet away.

Marla hurried out with more blankets and then stayed to help lift her off the wagon. Even Gypsy ran outside, leaving Jacob alone in the shadows.

When Harrison and Marla reached the entry, Jacob took Nell from them and carried her upstairs. Before he had time to say more than a few words to her, Mrs. O'Daniel ordered him out so they could give her a warm bath.

Jacob was banished back downstairs, where he pestered Harrison in the study until suppertime. Then, thankfully, Nell asked him to have dinner upstairs with her. She said she was tired, and he might be seen downstairs once the lights were lit.

Jacob didn't argue, and neither did anyone else in the house. In fact, Harrison and Gypsy almost pushed him up the stairs just before dark with a tray to take to Nell's room.

He shoved open her door and found her watching the evening shadows from her window. She was already in her gown and robe, with her hair combed down over her shoulders. The angels couldn't be more beautiful, he decided and was glad he'd finally have some time alone with her.

"I drove everyone nuts downstairs, and they sent me up here," he joked.

"I know," she answered. "Gypsy said you're harder to keep inside than a wild cat."

Jacob shrugged. "I don't care. This is where I'd rather be, anyway."

This time she smiled. "I know that, too."

He placed the tray on the tiny table between them and didn't bother to turn up the light. He pulled his chair close but out of view if anyone were watching the upstairs windows.

They ate the meat pies and sugared fruit Marla had cooked. To his surprise, Nell was quiet, only answering questions when he asked. He didn't care; it was good to be alone with her. She said she enjoyed the swim more each time, and Harrison had figured out how he could pull the wagon within a few feet of the bank, so she didn't have to walk much.

They fell silent as they nibbled on buttermilk pie. Jacob leaned back and reminded himself that no matter what, he wouldn't get angry tonight. This might be their last time together for a while, and he wanted to enjoy every minute.

Finally, he decided to bring up a subject he'd been careful to avoid talking about all day. He couldn't leave with something not clear between them. "I didn't sleep with Pearlie in town," he blurted out, telling himself he wasn't apologizing, only stating a fact.

She grinned. "I know. I never thought you did."

"But I was in her room all night. She and Dave carried me in when I was knocked out cold."

"Jacob, we're not married. I have no strings tied to you." She held her head high like she did when she knew she was saying something that was the right thing to say. "You're a free man."

He shoved his empty plate aside. "That's just it, Nell. I don't feel like a free man. Most of the time I feel like we're already married." He'd never thought a lot about it, but since she'd come home from school grown, he'd never looked at another woman. He'd told himself he was too busy, but it was more than that. He might not admit it to himself, but he wanted her. Not just in his bed, but in his life. When she'd run to him that first time, looking all grown, he'd known, deep down inside, that he really was her ranger for as long as she wanted him to be.

He studied her and finally said what he felt. "I don't want to leave you, Nell, not tonight, not ever. It doesn't matter whether I go to Stockard's place or halfway across the state, a part of me is always here with you."

She looked away. "I know, but we don't fit together. You'd hate staying here and running the ranges. I'd never be able to travel with you. There are so many things I'd never be able to do with you."

He stood and walked to the door. "When I come back from the Stockard place, I'll have to take Hank to Fort Worth and stay with him until the trial. I don't know how long it will be until I get back." Without saying a word, he closed the door and turned the lock. "One thing we *can* do, just for tonight. I'd like to hold you for a while before I have to leave. I'm not demanding you marry me or wait for me. I just don't want to go the rest of my life without this time alone with you."

Nell looked up at him, and even in the shadows of the room he could see her nod. "I'd like that, too."

He picked her up and carried her to the bed. Before he lowered her, he kissed her cheek lightly and rubbed his nose against her hair. "I love the way you smell."

"It's soap." She laughed as he lowered her atop the covers.

She watched him unbuckle his gun belt and pull off his boots. Her eyes were warm with need, but she didn't say a word.

When he knelt on the bed above her, he almost abandoned his plan. How could he hold her tonight and not make her his? He'd be in hell and heaven at the same time. The longing to be near her had pounded through him all day as steady as a heartbeat, and now, here she was, all soft and beautiful.

He slid beside her, letting his body touch hers from shoulder to leg. "Are you cold?" he asked.

"No." She cuddled closer.

He kissed her then as tenderly as he knew how. She felt so right in his arms, as if they'd both known forever that she'd find her way there eventually.

His hand moved over her gown, barely brushing her, but memorizing her curves. Her hair was still damp from being freshly washed, her skin soft from the water.

For the first time, he knew here was home. Not the house, or the town, or even Texas. His home was beside Nell.

Rolling toward her, he let his chest rest lightly atop her, pressing her breasts against him. She felt so good, so right beneath him. He swore he felt her heartbeat match his own.

The kiss deepened, and the warmth of her body set him on fire. He touched her throat, then gently moved his hand down the front of her gown, parting the robe as he moved. She was perfection beneath the thin cotton gown.

Her fingers dug into his hair, pulling him closer, demanding he please her.

With a slow pleasure, he spread his hand across her tummy and lower. Touching her where he knew no man had ever touched her. Loving the way she moaned and pulled him closer. Loving that she wanted him as dearly as he desired her.

He rolled above her, pressing her into the bed, needing to feel her body beneath him.

Then, through the passion, he felt her struggle and break the kiss. A moment later, she cried out in pain.

Jacob rolled from her, shaken to the core as he watched her fight for breath enough to scream.

He'd hurt her. Oh, God, he'd hurt her!

He climbed off the bed and ran for the door, hearing her behind him as she tried not to cry out.

Mrs. O'Daniel was at the door when he unlocked it. She pushed him aside and rushed to Nell.

Jacob stood helpless as Mrs. O'Daniel leaned her head close to Nell and whispered, "Relax, dear. Just relax. You've had these pains before. You know they will pass." As if Nell were a doll, Mrs. O'Daniel moved her, taking as much pressure off the small of Nell's back as possible.

Nell calmed, crying softly, silently, as Mrs. O'Daniel whispered, "Would you like some of your medicine?"

Jacob glanced at the tiny bottle of opium he'd seen before.

"No," Nell answered. "I can stand it."

He felt bad that he'd once warned her about getting dependent on the drug. Until this moment he had no idea how terrible her hell could be. But this time, he felt the pain with her.

The pain and a loss deep inside him.

He'd caused it, he realized as he swore he'd never cause her to suffer so again. Even now, pale and curled on the bed, she was so beautiful. His body, his soul ached for her, but he knew he'd never touch her again.

Jacob grabbed his boots and gun belt and closed the door silently. For the hundredth, maybe the thousandth time, he wished he could take the pain for her. He would die for her. He would love her until his last breath. But, he would never touch her again.

CHAPTER 32

NELL CRIED SOFTLY LONG AFTER MRS. O'DANIEL SAID GOOD night. The nurse asked her what happened, but Nell hadn't answered. She couldn't tell the nurse, or anyone. Mrs. O'Daniel finally decided the ranger must have turned Nell wrong when he'd tried to put her in bed. She offered to sit by Nell's bed for a while, but Nell needed to be alone.

She knew Jacob wouldn't be back. No tonight, maybe not ever. He'd blame himself for something they'd both started, both wanted. She wanted to tell him that the bullet left lodged along her spine had hurt her, not him, but he wouldn't listen. He wouldn't believe her.

She heard a horse outside her window and knew that somewhere in the darkness he was looking up, watching, longing for her. Then she heard him ride away into the night and knew he was gone. Her ranger had done the one thing he could never forgive himself for doing: he'd hurt her.

Tears fell silently, for Nell knew it was all her fault. If she'd kept her distance. If she'd have married another. If she'd told him from the first that she'd never accept his proposal. Then maybe he would have felt rejected, but he'd have gotten over it. He would have gone on with his life.

But now. Now he loved her and wanted her. She knew her memory would torture him the rest of his life. And the memory of how he touched her so gently would stay forever in the back of her mind. A promise of something she'd never have.

Wednesday slipped into her room. "Miss Nell, are you still awake?"

"I'm awake," Nell whispered. "Is the ranger gone?"

"He's gone," Wednesday said. "I just wanted to check on you. Mrs. O'Daniel said you got hurt again. Was it a bad fall?" The girl took Nell's hand.

"The worst yet," Nell whispered knowing she might never recover.

"I'm so sorry," Wednesday whispered. "Is there anything I can do to help?"

"No." Nell tried to smile but couldn't manage it. "I'll be better in the morning. Just help Mrs. O'Daniel out with Hank."

"I'll do that. And, Miss Nell, I want you to know that I love you."

"I love you, too, Wednesday."

The girl pulled the door as she backed out of the room, leaving Nell alone in the silence once more.

Nell closed her eyes, picturing Jacob riding through the night on his powerful horse. "I love you, too," she whispered wishing her words would carry on the wind to him but knowing that he wouldn't be listening.

CHAPTER 33

Jacob rode west into the night. When he reached the river, he followed the tree line, staying well into the shadows so no one could follow. He knew when the river turned, he'd have to leave the shadows along the bank and ride north onto old Stockard's land. Part of him wanted to keep heading west and go straight into the badlands where no one had bothered to settle and law rarely ventured. He'd get lost there, maybe change his name. Start over.

After all, what was he leaving behind? A few dollars in the bank. A few clothes and guns in a trunk at Ranger headquarters. A few memories that would rip his gut wide open if he thought about them too much.

The night felt warm, but a chill moved over his heart. He couldn't get Nell's brown eyes filled with tears out of his mind. He wasn't sure he ever would. When he'd realized he'd hurt her, his heart stopped.

Jacob tried to remember if he'd said he was sorry. No. He hadn't said a word. He'd just stood there and stared as Mrs. O'Daniel tried to comfort her. Then he'd disappeared like a coward. He wouldn't blame Nell for hating him. He hated himself.

The river bent south, and Jacob turned north across open country. Stars were out in full force, making the night bright, but he doubted anyone would see him riding so late. Though ranches bordered the Stockard place, none had homes that were close enough to see onto the property.

He avoided the rough road leading up to the house, knowing he'd leave far less sign in the buffalo grass and rocks he crossed. An hour later he reached the dugout where Stockard had lived.

Jacob walked around the boarded-up shack. It was bigger than most, and the sheriff had been right; Jacob could see a mile or more in every direction. He could understand why this would have been a good hide-out for outlaws back in years past. In fact, Jacob had a strange feeling their ghosts were still near, or at least something was. He swore someone was watching him.

Jacob moved into the blackness of the roofline and froze, staring out at the land, waiting for something to move. If he had been followed, they'd get restless and make a shift in position soon.

Nothing moved.

He crossed to the other side of the house. An old well and a few fallen-down buildings left eerie shadows. One looked like it might have been a barn, the other maybe a tack shed. The skeleton of a corral was visible, but nothing more.

Jacob took a long breath and unpacked his bedroll. Along with a sack of food and coffee, Marla had put in a small lantern. Jacob lit it and tried to find the door of the dugout. He didn't really think he wanted to sleep inside with the spiders and bugs, but he would like to look around before he turned in for the night.

The door was boarded up so that it looked more like one of the walls. It took him several tries and all his strength to pry enough boards loose to squeeze inside. The house was only one room. Most of the furniture seemed worthless or broken. A bed in one corner looked like it might have a village of insects living in it. There were tracks in the dirt floor.

Jacob bent down, holding the lantern low. Rabbit, possum, and skunk, he'd guess. And one more. Dog. The dog tracks were recent, not more than a few days old he'd guess. But, if there was a dog on the property, wouldn't the animal have barked when a stranger rode up? Maybe the four-legged trespasser was wild and had just been passing through. If the dog had belonged to Stockard, it would have had to survive out here alone for three, maybe four years. Jacob doubted, even with the cabin for shelter, that a lone animal would make it through one winter much less three or four.

He followed the prints and found a hole big enough for an animal to pass through in one corner of the dugout. He went back outside and picked up the trail. It was hard to tell with only the small lantern's light, but Jacob saw drops of what looked like dried blood mixed with the dog's prints. Maybe the dog had caught a rabbit inside the house and carried it out. That seemed unlikely, for dogs hunted like wolves, who usually ate their prey where they killed it.

He followed the paw prints into the rocks where they disappeared on the rough ground. Only now and then, he saw spots of blood. To his surprise, they led to a small cave with a waist-high opening well hidden by brush. Jacob was about to decide to come back after daylight and explore, when he heard a low whimper.

He pulled his gun and slowly crawled into the opening, shoving the lantern ahead of him. The cave opened up to be almost as large as the dugout, with a ceiling too low for Jacob to stand upright. Old crates littered the floor. Jacob guessed this must have been a hiding place for supplies back years ago. If old Stockard opened his home to outlaws, like everyone seemed to think, maybe he wasn't willing to share his store of food. With the cave so close to the house, he could easily get supplies when he needed them and still not share more then he wanted to.

The whimpering came again. Jacob moved to the far corner of the cave and pushed a box aside with his foot.

He found a thin border collie curled in a ball. The animal was too near dead to do more than whimper as Jacob wrapped a dusty rag he found around him and carried the dog out.

Once he was back to the dugout, Jacob made camp out by the well. There was no shortage of boards to use for a fire. Soon, Jacob had it blazing. He took care of his horse and set the food he'd brought on the well, hoping to keep it away from some of the critters nearby. Marla had packed several pieces of chicken along with bread and coffee.

Jacob put on the coffee to boil and eased down a few feet from the dog.

The animal had been watching his every move, and snarled like he might bite if Jacob made any advances.

"Easy now, old fellow." Jacob kept his voice low. "I didn't lug you out of that cave to kill you now."

Jacob didn't hurry; he gave the dog time. He had no idea what was wrong with the animal, but since the collie was or had been bleeding, Jacob figured it had to be an accident of some kind.

He moved a bite of chicken within the dog's reach.

The animal snapped it up.

Jacob placed another piece an inch closer.

The animal ate again.

The fourth time the dog took the bite of meat from the ranger's hand. "That a way to go, boy," Jacob said low and slow. "Might as well come to dinner."

By the time the chicken was gone, the dog let Jacob touch him. It took a few tries, for blood seemed to be everywhere, but Jacob finally figured out what was wrong.

The dog had been shot. Once in the leg, once in the neck. Both bullets had passed though, leaving both an entrance and exit wound. No bones were broken, but the neck wound still bled.

Jacob pulled some of the ointment from his pack that Mrs. O'Daniel had insisted he take to put on his knife wounds. "If this didn't kill me, it won't kill you."

By the light of the fire, Jacob smeared the salve on and bandaged the dog as best he could. Then Jacob drank his coffee and leaned back against his saddle. He fell asleep with the dog resting his chin on his leg.

At dawn, the fire had disappeared, but the dog was still there. His eyes were no longer wild as his gaze followed Jacob's movements.

"How about I see what we have for breakfast?" Jacob asked as he rummaged through the supplies. "Rolls for me and looks like a scrambled egg sandwich for you." He held out the sandwich, and the dog took it, bread and all. "Lucky thing you like it. I hate eggs, but I didn't have the heart to tell Marla."

He split the rest of his breakfast with the dog and poured water in his hand so the animal could drink. "I think I'll call you Fred. I never had a friend named Fred, and it always struck me as a good name."

The collie looked more sleepy than interested.

Jacob fed his horse, then began exploring the place again. With his skills in tracking, he could sometimes read what happened at a place the way other people read the paper.

There were boot prints of a man who walked mostly on his heels and rocked when he paused. Three shells were a few feet outside the hole where animals had come and gone from the dugout, which told Jacob whoever shot Fred had been standing less that five feet away. The dog must have run for the shelter and hid there until the heel-walker was gone.

Jacob knew Harrison and Farrow had both been to the land in the past week. One of them had shot the dog. Maybe out of fear. Maybe to keep him quiet.

"Well, whoever it was, Fred . . ." Jacob glanced back at the dog still lying by the fire. "He was a bad shot. Three shells. He was so close I don't see how he missed you completely once."

The ranger remembered Harrison saying he didn't much like guns. Which translated that he would probably be a bad shot. On the other hand, Farrow didn't strike him as being good at much of anything but talking.

Jacob continued his search. There were several places where someone had tried to get into the house, pulling a board or two loose. The bookkeeper wasn't strong enough to carry Nell, so he might not have the strength to pull the board free. Walter Farrow seemed to have spent his time lifting only a fork.

Jacob didn't like the idea of even considering Harrison in the same category as Farrow. If Harrison had shot the dog, he would have mentioned it when he made it back home. Nell wouldn't have liked it, but she'd understand.

He moved into the shack and began to search for anything that might make this old place valuable. Trash was everywhere. Stockard seemed to have the idea that stuff was easier to step over than burn. What few pots he had were scattered about. Plates were piled in a bucket along with a few forks. Old newspapers and letters were stuffed into cracks to keep out the wind.

Jacob picked up each piece of furniture, looking for something, anything that might be of interest. Maybe a key, or a map, or even money tucked away where no one would notice.

Fred limped in and watched Jacob for a while, then limped out again. The dog looked near death last night, but this morning it seemed like he might just make it.

Jacob pulled the newspapers out of the cracks in the wall. Most were from five or more years ago. A few crumbled in his fingers as he tried to unfold them. He found a couple of letters and envelopes. One had a return address of a prison down near Houston.

Jacob took the prison letter outside, but when he opened it, all he found was a blank piece of paper. Turning it over in his fingers, Jacob wondered if it had once borne ink marks but the rain and weather had soaked it too many times.

Jacob tossed the letters in the campfire. He searched for another hour but found nothing of value. Harrison's assessment had been accurate about the ranch. Whatever Farrow saw in the place was beyond Jacob.

Grabbing the last pile of letters, he moved to the fire. Just before he tossed them in, Jacob spotted one envelope with the return address still readable.

Zeb Whitaker.

Jacob's hand shook slightly as if he'd heard the voice of a dead man calling him. Zeb Whitaker had been the old buffalo hunter who'd claimed Nell's friends stole his saddlebags of gold. He'd been the man who ambushed Nell.

The ranger forced a smile. Zeb Whitaker was dead, had been for months. Even if this was his letter, he was beyond hurting anyone.

Jacob opened the envelope. Empty. He checked another. Nothing. Old Stockard had saved the envelopes to use for stuffing, but he must have burned the letters. Not that Jacob cared. Stockard and Zeb were both dead, and the letters had been written years ago.

He tossed the mail into the fire. Nell didn't need to be reminded of Whitaker or that he and Stockard even knew each other.

Climbing up by the cave, Jacob sat watching for a while, but saw nothing move but a few rabbits. By midafternoon, he knew he had to ride down to the bend in the river and see if Harrison had learned anything. If possible, he planned to talk to the bookkeeper while Nell was in the water.

If he and Harrison both agreed the place was worthless, maybe Nell would sell it. Jacob didn't know how to put it into words to Nell, but the place had a bad feeling about it. She'd be better off letting Walter Farrow have his uncle's place.

By the time the ranger reached the bend of the river, Nell and the nurse were already shoulder deep in the water. Jacob found Harrison standing on the far side of the wagon, watching the road from town.

"Afternoon," Jacob said.

From Harrison's smile, he guessed Nell hadn't told anyone how she got hurt. Otherwise, all her little army would hate him, too.

"How is it out at the Stockard place?" Harrison shoved his hat back.

"Lonely," Jacob answered.

"I figured that." Rand reached for the basket of food Marla had sent. "Marla said if you'll bring this back tomorrow, she'll keep you supplied."

"Beats jerky and beans." Jacob thanked him. "Any news?"

Harrison shook his head. "Got a telegram from the doctor who comes in to check on Nell. He said he'd be here in two or three days. Other than that, nothing."

Jacob leaned on the wagon guard. "Did you see a dog while you were out at the dugout?"

Rand shook his head. "Did you find one?"

Jacob nodded. "He was still alive, but he'd been shot."

They talked about all the possibilities for a while, then Mrs. O'Daniel yelled.

"I'll stand watch if you want to carry Nell out," Harrison offered. "It'll give you a chance to say hello."

Jacob hesitated, but he couldn't very well say no without everyone wondering why. Maybe Nell would let him carry her back to the wagon without screaming for him to never touch her again.

He tugged his boots and guns off and waded in. Mrs. O'Daniel greeted him warmly, but Nell didn't meet his gaze as he moved beside her and gently lifted her out of the water. It was a little late to say he was sorry, and Jacob hated having an audience to talk to Nell. But if he didn't say something, Harrison was bound to notice things weren't right between them.

"How's Hank?" Jacob asked, figuring it would be a safe subject.

"I think he's going to be all right," Nell answered. She trailed her hand in the water, making a tiny wave.

"How do you know?"

Mrs. O'Daniel seemed to feel the question was directed toward her. "I opened the door to the attic room this morning, and Wednesday was sitting beside his bed feeding her baby. The boy's eyes were open, and he was watching as if he were seeing the eighth wonder of the world." Mrs. O'Daniel hurried ahead of them now that they were in shallow water, but she raised her voice to make sure Jacob heard her story. "Wednesday looked up at Hank and smiled as though feeding her baby in front of him were the most natural thing in the world. And he smiled back like a boy does when he knows it's not long before he'll be a man and understand such things."

Jacob frowned, having no idea what the nurse was talking about. Maybe he'd yet to smile that smile. He looked at Harrison, but the bookkeeper showed no sign of understanding either.

"He knows he's not to leave the attic?" Jacob asked.

"He knows," Nell answered, but she didn't look up at him.

Nell gripped the seat as Jacob lifted her onto the wagon.

"An hour later," Mrs. O'Daniel continued as she climbed into the other side of the bench and wrapped Nell in a blanket, "Hank ate every last bit of his breakfast."

Jacob glanced up at Nell and smiled, but she wasn't looking in his direction. "Are you all right?" He couldn't stand her ignoring him much longer.

"I'm fine," she answered too quickly. "Marla said to tell you she'll leave the back door open if you want to go up the back stairs to the attic and check on Hank some night. That way you won't have to wake anyone in the house."

Jacob nodded, hearing every word she didn't say. He wasn't invited to visit her room.

He wanted to touch her hand when he said good-bye, but Nell had already pulled it beneath the covers.

"We'd better hurry back before she gets cold." Mrs. O'Daniel waved at him.

"See you tomorrow," Harrison said as he took the reins.

A few minutes later, Jacob was alone again. He rode back to his camp by the dugout and wished he were a hundred miles away in the middle of a range war.

After dark, he fed most of his supper to the dog and leaned back to watch the stars. He wondered if Nell was sitting by her window looking at the same sky and thinking of him.

Around midnight, he heard someone singing. Fred heard it, too, for the dog's ears shot up, and he growled.

Jacob reached for his rifle and moved beyond the fire's light. He listened as the voice grew nearer. *Gospel songs,* he thought and put the rifle back in its place beside the saddle.

A few minutes later, Brother Aaron showed up in his old buggy. He climbed down and handed Jacob a half-empty bottle of whiskey. "I thought I'd report in." He tried to salute. "And, since I was coming, I brought some of the devil's milk with me in case you were sleeping out in the cold. I hate the stuff myself, but I did test it to see that it was of some worth."

"Thanks." Jacob was too lonely to scold the man. "Join me by the fire."

They talked about the dog for a while, and Brother Aaron introduced himself to Fred as if the animal would answer back. The old man sat on one of the stools from the house and told Jacob all about what he'd learned in town.

"It seems that Walter Farrow got real friendly with the head of the posse, a man named Kelly. Everyone thought the sheriff in Fort Worth had sent them out, but turns out they were hired by the railroad."

Jacob wasn't surprised. He'd heard of that happening plenty of times. What surprised him was how fast the men must have hit the trail. They must have been loading their horses into railroad cars and leaving for the scene of the robbery within an hour after the news reached Fort Worth.

"One of Parker's deputies told me they weren't nothing but a bunch of hired guns. He said he heard one say he'd take any job as long as there was money involved." Brother Aaron coughed and asked if he might have a swallow from the bottle for medicinal purposes.

It must have worked, because he didn't cough again, and he kept the bottle.

Jacob enjoyed the company. When the reverend wasn't preaching, he could tell stories with the best of them. He also had a knack of summing up a man with only a few words. Jacob admired that about him.

"I don't trust that Farrow," he said after a short silence. "If he's such a high and mighty lawyer back in Dallas, why is he living in that tiny little house everyone said Stockard used to own in town? Some folks claim Stockard lost it in a poker game one night to an old drinking buddy who let him keep staying there. If that was true, the man died before filing the debt with the county. Since the house wasn't in Stockard's will but was still in his name, the sheriff says he guesses it goes to next of kin."

Jacob found the news interesting. Apparently, Farrow planned to settle down in town.

The preacher wandered off to have a talk with nature. When he returned, he held out a coin. "I saw this sparkling in the moonlight over by the well."

Jacob turned the coin over in his fingers and rubbed some of the dirt off. "It's a twenty dollar gold piece."

Brother Aaron moved closer. "You think it's part of that old buffalo hunter's stash that disappeared several years back?"

Jacob shook his head. Everyone in the state had heard the tale of Zeb Whitaker and his saddlebags of gold. He believed until the day he died that three young women robbed him of the treasure, and he almost killed them and Nell trying to get one of them to admit it. "I think more than likely, it fell out of old Stockard's pocket when he was too drunk to notice. Just because Whitaker and Stockard were friends doesn't mean the gold is around here. If it were, don't you think Stockard would have bettered himself with the money and not died begging food off Fat Alice?"

"Maybe. Maybe not. Who died first, Stockard or Whitaker?"

"Stockard's been dead a couple of years at least, I don't remember. But Whitaker died right after Nell was hurt last summer."

Brother Aaron scratched his beard. "Maybe Stockard was too

afraid to touch Whitaker's gold. Maybe he thought his friend would get out of prison and come after him."

Jacob shook his head. "Whitaker couldn't have put the gold here. He died not knowing where it was."

The preacher laughed. "Maybe only Stockard knew."

Jacob shrugged. "Maybe so. Someone had to have picked up the saddlebags the night Whitaker was knocked out. But, if it had been Stockard, the money had never done him any good."

The preacher looked over at the well. "You think Nell would mind if I rode back out here in the morning and took a look in that well?"

Jacob shook his head. "Right now I have no idea what she's thinking. You'll have to ask her."

Brother Aaron climbed in his buggy. "Until tomorrow," he yelled as he pulled away.

CHAPTER 34

Jacob made up his mind the next morning that he would
have to talk to Nell, and he needed to do it alone.

When the preacher hadn't shown up by noon, he began to worry.
What if something had happened to the old man on the way back home?
Or what if there was trouble at Nell's? Several things could have happened. She could have fallen again. Hank might have been discovered.
Walter Farrow could have even gone nuts and showed up at the ranch
with a gun. Jacob already figured the man to be about four hundred
pounds of crazy. He didn't seem the type of man who understood the
word no.

Jacob rode to the river and waited. He told himself he'd done so in
case they came early, but he knew that he simply could not stay put
any longer.

He walked the banks of the river and found a place where the water
circled around lazily in a small cove. There, the river looked as clear as
glass and probably measured about five feet deep.

When Nell and Harrison pulled up, Marla was with them and not
the nurse.

"What's wrong?" Jacob asked even before the bookkeeper touched
ground.

Harrison frowned. "It seems Brother Aaron had another wrestle
with the devil in the dark last night. He claims the devil shoved him

off the porch, but it looks like he may have simply fallen. We found him out cold in the flower bed this morning."

"Is he all right?"

Harrison nodded. "The preacher swears the devil stole a coin out of his pocket. He also says his leg is messed up, but he won't let Mrs. O'Daniel look at it. Plans to wait until Nell's doctor comes in from Cedar Point tomorrow. They were arguing when we left."

"So no swim?"

Harrison looked uneasy. "Nell insisted on coming. She said she'd go in with you holding onto her, if you're willing. If you don't feel comfortable, Marla says she'll try, but she's as afraid of the water as I am."

Jacob looked back at Nell, still in the buggy. "You agree to this, Two Bits? You'll let me take you in?"

She nodded.

"And Mrs. O'Daniel, she'll turn over her duties?"

"We agreed it would be best for her to stay with Brother Aaron."

"It doesn't make sense, but if you're willing, I'm here to help." He stripped down to the bottom of his long johns. He hadn't worn an undershirt because the morning was so warm, and he'd thought about taking a swim while Nell and Mrs. O'Daniel were in the water. Now, with Marla's cheeks reddening, he wished he'd worn more. He thought of wading in with his clothes on, but he didn't look forward to having to ride back to the Stockard place dripping wet.

He'd also forgotten how ugly the knife wound on his back must look. He was thankful when Nell asked for Marla's help and he could put some distance between the shy cook and his bare skin.

Harrison helped Nell out of the buggy, and Jacob carried her to the water. He stood waist deep before he let her legs into the water. "Just tell me what you want me to do," he said near her ear.

She laughed at the cold, then her feet touched bottom. She could stand when she didn't have to bear all her weight.

Jacob let her hold on to him for support, but he kept his hands close in case she missed a step. They half walked, half floated into deeper water.

He glanced back at the shore and noticed Marla and Harrison had climbed up an incline and looked to be spreading a picnic out on the blanket between them. He was too far away to hear what they were saying, but once, he heard Marla's laughter on the wind.

Nell circled around him, lightly keeping her balance with her hands touching his shoulders. Her touch was as easy and relaxed as it always had been.

He didn't know how to talk to her. Jacob couldn't bring himself to go back to two nights ago when he'd rolled atop her and hurt her. He could hardly look at her without wanting her so badly he feared his heart might stop in mid-beat. But touching her and talking about it were two different things.

"Why'd you agree to this?" he finally asked, guessing she felt as awkward as he did about coming face-to-face again after what had happened between them.

"I wanted to be alone with you." Her fingers brushed along his shoulder as she moved as Mrs. O'Daniel had taught her. "We can't go the rest of our lives without talking to one another."

He smiled. "I know." The girl . . . the woman . . . he knew was back. The girl that could never keep anything from him. The woman who liked to reason out problems as she talked to him, even when the problem this time seemed to be him. "I never meant to hurt you." He said the words before he thought.

She looked up at him then, her eyes wide and sad. "I know, Jacob. Don't you know that I would never think you'd hurt me on purpose?"

He felt one of the weights that had been around his heart disappear. At least she didn't blame him; that was something.

She leaned back and floated. "I love the water," she smiled into the sun. "Can we forget everything for a while and just enjoy being together?"

"All right," he said letting the gentle current relax him as well.

After a while he was afraid she might be getting too much sun, so he slowly backed up until they moved into the cove he'd discovered earlier. The sun blinked between leaves, making the water sparkle, and she drifted across it, gliding with only his slight touch between her shoulder blades.

They'd been silent for several minutes, and Jacob knew he might never have a chance to talk to her alone again. "Nell, I've been thinking." He tried to keep his voice easy as if they were just talking. "Harrison told me you said you wanted a marriage in name only. I didn't know that was part of your plan, but if that's what you want, I'd have no objection."

She stopped swimming. "But don't you want a wife, a real wife?"

"Well, yeah, but if you want to marry, I still think I'm the best man. We could just see one another like we do now. There wouldn't have to be anything physical between us." He had to make the lie convincing.

If he planned to protect her for the rest of her life, he'd have to make her believe that he could be happy with never touching her again. For the rest of his life he'd have to be willing to look at her, knowing that he could never touch her . . . not the way a man touches his woman.

"You mean you'd be satisfied with never making love to me?"

He took a deep breath. "My name would protect you."

"But we wouldn't sleep together."

"I'd come running whenever you needed me, just like I always have."

"But you wouldn't hold me."

He stared at her, hating the words he knew he had to voice. "I can never hurt you again like I did. I don't think I could take the blow."

She met his stare. "You'd take other lovers?"

"No." The resolution in his voice surprised even him. He knew without any doubt that if he couldn't have her, he'd spend his life alone.

She lowered her head. "I can't."

He held her gently with one arm. "You can't what? Marry me?"

"I can't be with you without touching you. I can't. I think you'd try, maybe even be able to never hold me again, but I'm not sure I could stay away from you."

Jacob closed his eyes. He felt the same, but he was willing to try. He thought he was being the strong one, but maybe she was being the honest one. "Then, what do we do?"

Nell moved her cheek against his shoulder, rubbing warm tears into his skin. "I don't know. I just know that I don't want to spend the rest of my life trying to keep you at arm's length."

"You could marry Harrison. He's a good man."

To his surprise, Nell laughed. "Great idea. We can't be satisfied making ourselves miserable, we have to hurt Mr. Harrison as well."

"But he wants to marry you," Jacob reminded her. "He agreed to the in-name-only part. He thinks a great deal of you, Nell, but he's said from the first that he would only be marrying to get half the land."

Nell stopped him. "Have you seen the way he looks at Marla?"

Jacob frowned, realizing he wasn't the only one who'd noticed. "Yes but . . ."

She slung her braid, splashing water against his chin. "So, now we're miserable, and so we include Harrison by my marrying him, and that makes Marla unhappy." She brushed the water from his chin. "We've made a fine mess of it, haven't we?"

He smiled but saw no way out.

"I've thought about it," she finally added. "I've decided to stay an old maid. Then, if you want to marry someday, you can. Harrison, if he wants it, will become my full-time bookkeeper and eventually figure out that he loves Marla."

"And we'll stay friends?"

"Friends?" she asked. "But before we agree, I'd like to kiss you one last time."

Before he could stop her, she moved into his arms, pressing her body against his.

He meant to kiss her gently, but she would have none of it. She wanted a real kiss. As they swayed with the gentle water, he felt her warm the length of him as her passion built inside of him.

Brushing kisses over her face, he whispered how soft she was before returning to her mouth. Then she did the same, laughing as his whiskers tickled.

The fact that he couldn't abandon himself fully made what he felt all the sweeter. He carefully moved his hands down her back and gently cupped her hips. He loved the way she dug her fingers into his hair and pulled his head to her, demanding, needing, and longing for what they both knew they'd never have fully.

This moment would have to last them forever, and he planned to make it a sweet dream for the rest of her life. He unbuttoned her camisole and spread the wet cotton aside. The water bushed against the peaks of her breasts, and he could do nothing but stare.

"You're perfect," he whispered as he leaned over and took one tip in his mouth.

She laughed in surprise.

He held her waist in an easy grip as he moved below the water, pushing material aside as he kissed downward.

Nell grabbed his hair and pulled him up. "You'll drown."

"I don't care," he answered and realized he meant it.

"Then, by all means continue."

Under the water he kissed all the way to her belly button. When he returned for air, she insisted he stay long enough for her to taste his mouth fully.

Widening his stance, he stood almost equal to her as she moved her hands over his chest. He knew what she was doing: memorizing.

Her touch grew bolder as she reached below his waist, wanting to feel all of him.

The shock of it startled him, but he didn't move. This was his Nell, the girl who'd never run from adventure, the woman who wanted, if only for a moment, to claim her man.

He grabbed their undergarments before they floated away and tossed them on a branch while she drifted around him, letting skin touch skin. Her breasts drove him mad as they slipped against his chest, and her long legs gently wrapped around him.

"If this is to be the last time we touch," she whispered, "I want to be able to remember the way you felt for the rest of my life."

He agreed. What they were doing was dangerous. Neither of them could trust themselves enough to always stop before it was too late. Jacob realized she wanted him as much as he wanted her. They couldn't play with fire again, but here in the water, her body could move without pain.

His hands slowly moved down. He closed his eyes, swearing he'd never forget a single line of her body.

She brushed her fingers over him, tracing the outlines of his scars and the way his muscles tightened to her touch.

"I'll make love to you every night in my dreams," he whispered. "Every night for the rest of my life."

Her arms circled his neck and held to him. "I know," she whispered. "I'm counting on it."

They stood together until the afternoon shadows stretched long and the water grew cold. He didn't want to turn loose of her. He wasn't sure his heart would still beat without hers beating beside it.

He loved her. He loved her enough never to touch her again after today.

And he knew she loved him, for she'd given him as much of herself as she could. She'd given him one afternoon that would stay with him for the rest of his life.

CHAPTER 35

NELL HELD ON TIGHTLY WHEN JACOB FINALLY CARRIED HER OUT of the water. She curled in the back of the buggy in the blankets and whispered a good-bye to her ranger.

With her eyes closed, she heard Jacob tell Harrison to drive carefully and Harrison say he'd go into town tonight and collect the news. The men agreed that if Harrison didn't stop by before midnight, there was nothing to report.

None of the conversation mattered, for Nell knew she was still lost in the arms of Jacob. She wondered how he could even begin to talk and make sense when the world had stopped turning only minutes before. As the wagon pulled away, Nell knew she'd left her heart with her ranger.

With Marla talking softly about the day, Nell drifted into sleep wishing she were still in Jacob's arms. The sun was setting by the time they pulled up to the house and her small army went to work. Mrs. O'Daniel helped her into a bath, and Wednesday brought her a cup of hot tea.

Everyone agreed to have a supper of cheese and apples. By nine, the house settled in for bed. Mrs. O'Daniel stopped in to make her report about the patients. "Brother Aaron is hobbling around swearing that he'll be right as rain in a few days." The nurse laughed. "He swears the devil took twenty dollars in gold from him last night. He says he was looking at it in the moonlight a moment before the devil knocked him off the porch."

Nell grinned. "The preacher probably never had twenty dollars in gold."

Mrs. O'Daniel continued, "Hank ate all his meals and stayed awake most of the day listening to Wednesday and playing with her baby. I think he'll be ready to travel in a few days if the ranger doesn't push him too hard."

Mrs. O'Daniel sat on the corner of Nell's bed. "How did it go with your ranger?"

Nell smiled. "You were right. We did need time to say good-bye as lovers if we are to be friends." She'd finally told Mrs. O'Daniel last night what had happened after the woman worried for an hour over what had hurt her so badly. To Nell's surprise, the nurse didn't blame Jacob.

The old nurse nodded. "I haven't always been old and stout. There was a time when I was young."

"It won't be easy seeing him and knowing that I can't marry him, but I know it would be torture if he married me and could never sleep beside me. I tried to tell myself that maybe after time my back wouldn't hurt so badly, but after days of exercise all that has changed is the level of pain I can endure. I don't want it to be like that when I'm with Jacob."

"The doctor may get in tomorrow." Mrs. O'Daniel tried to sound hopeful. "Maybe something has changed."

Nell shook her head. The bullet was still lodged near her spine. An operation might kill her. Nothing had changed.

The nurse tucked her in and left. Nell lay awake for hours reliving the dream she'd had that afternoon.

When she woke the next morning, another rainstorm had moved in across the plains. This was the rainiest spring that Nell could remember.

Everyone in the house stayed in and tried to think of ways to pass the time. Harrison seemed the only one happy. He worked in the study all morning, then cornered Nell about a few new ideas he had.

The next day mirrored the day before. Nell worried about Jacob, knowing he'd find shelter but hating to think of him out on the old ranch all alone. If she'd been able to, she would have ridden over to keep him company.

Sheriff Parker braved the weather to come to lunch. He complained about his aching bones and spent most of his time standing in front of the fireplace, even though the day wasn't particularly cold. He reported Walter Farrow had been drinking heavily since the posse left and complaining about how he'd been cheated out of his uncle's wealth. Except for a few traveling salesmen, who knew nothing of the past, no one paid any attention to his whining. He seemed to have a couple of troublemakers working for him, but Parker couldn't figure out what they were doing to earn their pay.

Parker waited to tell the bad news until everyone had finished eating. He stood and faced Nell. "I hate to relay this, but I got a telegram from Fort Worth. The posse delivered the three outlaws yesterday, and early this morning a judge decided to hold them in jail until Dalton delivers the boy. He wants to try them all together."

Harrison tossed his napkin on the table. "But the boy will hang if they're tried together."

Sheriff Parker winced as though the words hit him. "I know, but that's the law. He may only be fifteen, but a lot of outlaws have only been half grown when they killed someone."

Mrs. O'Daniel huffed. "Hank didn't kill anyone."

Everyone fell silent. They all knew nothing they could say would change anything. Hank had been one of the men who'd held up the train. If Mrs. O'Daniel could identify him, so could fifty others.

Finally, to everyone's surprise, Marla whispered, "Don't tell Wednesday until we have to. It'll break her heart. She and Hank have become friends."

Everyone at the table agreed.

"Maybe she'll feel some better knowing Jacob will stand with him," Nell said. "He has to take the boy in, but he promised he'd do everything he could to the end."

Nell wished she could add some hope that the judge might give the boy a lighter sentence, but she doubted it.

"Oh, one other thing," Parker pulled a telegram from his pocket. "The doc says he'll be in on the last train. I figured, with the rain, he might wait until tomorrow, but he's going to make it in tonight."

"I'll pick him up at the station."

"If it's not still raining," Marla added, "I'll ride along with you."

"Me, too, if you take the big buggy," Nell added. She didn't want to admit that the house was starting to feel like a prison again, even with all the company.

The weather cooperated. The rain stopped by midafternoon, and the sun even gave a weak appearance. The road might still be muddy, but at least it wouldn't be a river.

Just after dark, Nell and Marla climbed into the back of the buggy with plenty of blankets, and Mr. Harrison drove them. The preacher wanted to ride along, but his leg still bothered him. He finally said he'd help Gypsy keep guard while they were gone.

Nell couldn't hide her excitement. Dr. McClellan and his new wife Theda had become dear friends.

By the time they got to the train station, fog had moved in. Marla left Nell to help Harrison identify the doctor.

"I'll be right back," she called over her shoulder.

Nell laughed, "I'll be right here."

She closed her eyes and listened to the sounds of the train pulling in. The long, lonely whistle always made her feel like it was calling her.

The buggy suddenly shifted.

Nell opened her eyes, expecting to see Harrison and the others, but two young men dressed in black sat in front of her.

Her first thought was that they must have the wrong buggy. "You've . . ."

The buggy lunged forward as the man not driving turned to face her. "If you want to live, lady, you'd be wise to keep your mouth shut."

Nell held tight as the buggy rocked. She couldn't find enough breath to scream.

Fighting down the pain and fear, she managed to yell, "What do you want?"

The stranger turned around again as the buggy pounded down the road away from town. "We work for Mr. Farrow, lady, and he only wants what's his."

CHAPTER 36

Jacob watched the sun set, feeling even lonelier than usual. With the rain, he'd gone two days without seeing anyone. Nell hadn't come for her swims, and when he'd ridden over to the bend in the river, the basket of supplies was already there with only a note keeping him informed about Hank's recovery.

Two more days, he thought, maybe three, and the boy would be able to travel. Once they were on the road Jacob knew enough back trails that he wouldn't worry too much about them being followed. Right now was their dangerous time with Kelly still nosing around in town and Walter Farrow's men hanging about trying to learn what happened to both the ranger and Hank.

Jacob stretched. He didn't feel like turning in for the night, yet he had nothing to do. Dusty stomped, seeming as restless. "Want to go for a run?" Jacob mumbled to the horse.

He laughed when the horse nodded as if he'd understood.

Jacob patted the dog's head. "Stay here, Fred, and protect the camp." The old dog would be doing good to fight off a rabbit. "I think I'll ride close enough to watch the train come in."

As he saddled up and, out of habit erased all sign of his camp, Jacob wondered when he'd started talking to animals. He must be cracking up, but after days alone, it felt good to hear a voice, even if it was his own. The note Harrison had left with the supplies said Dr. McClel-

Ian would be coming in on the last train. Jacob admired the doctor. It would be good to see them, even if it was from a distance.

He pulled his hat low as he climbed onto the horse and rode off, enjoying the wind in his face.

When Jacob moved into the shadows beside the station, the train had just pulled in. He'd noticed Nell's buggy at the far end of the platform. Harrison must already be waiting to help the doctor and his wife with the luggage.

Suddenly, the horses harnessed to Nell's buggy bolted. He first thought he'd have to strangle Harrison for driving so carelessly, but then he realized something had to be wrong. The people hadn't had time to get off the train, and two men in black rain slickers sat on the driver's seat of the buggy.

As it galloped past him, Jacob caught a glimpse of someone on the back bench wrapped in blankets. Surely Harrison hadn't loaned the buggy out only minutes before the doctor arrived.

He rode closer to the platform, but the fog made the people standing around seem more like ghosts than real. Something was wrong; he could feel it.

Jacob was almost to where the buggy had been tied when he saw Harrison. The ranger moved closer and started to dismount, when he caught a glimpse of the terror in the bookkeeper's expression.

"What is it?" Jacob yelled. "Someone steal that rattletrap of a buggy?"

Harrison nodded once. "Nell was in it."

Jacob pulled his horse hard into a turn as fury galloped through his veins. "Get the sheriff and follow. I'll go after her."

He didn't know if Harrison heard him. Several others surrounded the bookkeeper, all talking at once. Jacob thought he saw the doctor and his wife, but he didn't take time to check. If Nell was in the buggy, he had to get to her fast.

The buggy headed out on the road he'd just come from, so Jacob had no problem following. They were away from the lights of town by the time he caught up with it.

"Stop!" he yelled from twenty feet behind.

Gunfire answered his demand.

Jacob pulled his horse and put some distance between them. With one man driving and one firing, it wouldn't be wise to get too close. The man riding shotgun would be firing back with Nell directly in the line of fire.

The ranger swung off the road. He might be able to get ahead of them and pick the two men off with a few shots, but then the buggy would be out of control and Nell would never be able to climb from the back to the front.

He couldn't risk exchanging any more gunfire. Not with Nell in the buggy. His only option was to follow and see where the men were going.

Within minutes their destination was obvious. The Stockard place.

When they turned off the main road, Jacob saw the buggy rock and knew Nell must be in great pain. Every time she rode in the buggy everyone around her took great care to protect her. These men had no idea they might be killing her.

Anger boiled in Jacob. He wanted to ride in and take both men on, but he had to pick his time for Nell's sake.

The trail up to the dugout was rough, so the men had to slow the buggy. Jacob waited, knowing there was no way he could follow without being an easy target. The fog offered him some cover, but not sufficient to get close enough for a clear shot.

"Wait," he mumbled to himself, pulling his years of training into play when all he wanted to do was storm forward. "Wait." One thing he'd learned was that in every standoff there came a window—a second—when he would have the advantage. One chance. His ability to take that chance had kept him alive.

Only this time Nell was in danger.

He moved as close as he could. They knew he was somewhere watching. They'd be prepared. And so would he. Waiting for the window.

CHAPTER 37

Nᴇʟʟ ꜰᴏᴜɢʜᴛ ᴛʜʀᴏᴜɢʜ ᴛʜᴇ ᴘᴀɪɴ ᴀɴᴅ ᴛʀɪᴇᴅ ᴛᴏ ꜰᴏᴄᴜꜱ. Tʜᴇ buggy had finally stopped. She hadn't died from the ride. She was surprised. The blankets had protected her some, but all she wanted to do was curl up and cry. Her back felt like it was on fire.

"Miss Nell," a voice shouted. "Nice of you to drop by."

She forced herself to open her eyes. Walter Farrow stood beside the buggy smelling heavily of whiskey. The two cowboys behind him couldn't be much older than twenty, but their faces looked distorted with pride in the wrong they'd done. "What do you want?" Nell managed to say.

Walter leaned close, flicking a match with his thumb before lighting the lantern latched to the side of the buggy. "The fellows just thought you'd want to come out here and have a little private talk." His words were smooth, but the light made his fat face look twisted and evil. "It's about time you came to me. Every time I come to you, there are always too many people around for us to get to know one another. In fact, I made a visit to your place tonight and was surprised to find you absent."

His smile made her skin crawl.

"When we saw you waiting in the wagon, you fell right into my plans for tonight."

Nell looked around. This had to be the Stockard place, but she saw no sign of Jacob. Knowing her ranger, he left little trace when he was staying somewhere. But where was he now?

She looked over to the north where the ground turned rocky and jagged. He'd be there. As close to her as he could get without being seen. She could feel him, and somehow his nearness gave her the strength she needed. "What do you want to talk about, Mr. Farrow, that can't wait until a proper time?" She saw no point in reminding him that his men had kidnapped her.

He swayed and smiled. "How about we stop playing games, Nell. I know why you've been stalling selling me this place."

"All right, why?" She watched the two young cowboys. They were standing a few feet away listening.

"You found a clue to Zeb Whitaker's gold. I had to find the one in the painting myself, but it's no good without others," Farrow hissed. "Hand your clue over. You know it should be mine."

"What!" Nell yelled. She'd been trying to guess why he'd brought her here, but Zeb Whitaker or his gold had never crossed her mind. "I have no gold, and I have no clue."

Farrow smiled and pulled a twenty dollar gold coin from his pocket. "That preacher who lives with you had this. So, you know something."

Nell finally understood. Farrow didn't want the ranch, or even to marry her; he wanted the gold. "I have nothing. The preacher only found a coin, nothing more."

He didn't look like he believed her.

"I don't know about any gold." She watched him frown and knew she'd better act fast.

"Maybe not," he shrugged. "But you know it's near. I thought the preacher might have some idea, but he didn't seem too willing to talk."

"I'll sell you the ranch." Nell sensed Walter's madness. Maybe if she promised him the ranch, he'd let her go.

He smiled. "No longer necessary. You see, I've become friends with the people in town. Your lawyer, for one. He told me an interesting fact. It seems you visited him after your accident and made out a will leaving most of your property to friends. Only . . ." He raised one fat finger. "You left this place to the town. So you see, Miss Nell, if you died, I could buy what I want without any trouble.

"I know the gold is here on this property somewhere, and with you gone, I'll have all the time in the world to look for it."

"You'd kill me in the hope of finding gold that's been lost for years?"

Walter Farrow laughed. "I'd kill you for far less. I'm not a man who allows people to insult me."

That was it, she realized. He might want the land and even Whitaker's gold, but what pushed the lawyer over the edge was simply the fact that a cripple had turned him down in marriage. She'd seen it in his eyes that day—a promise to get even—and tonight, he had his chance.

"But, my dear, I'm not going to kill you. The whole town talks about you. About how crazy you are. Poor little bastard crippled girl who takes in strays no one wants. Folks even know about how you try to swim in the river. Only, tonight you'll go beyond where you can touch bottom, and they'll find your body where the river bends."

"You'll never get away with it," she whispered.

Farrow reached in and tried to pat her cheek. "Oh, but my dear, we already have. Your friend the bookkeeper will never get here in time. I've already taken care of the misfits at your house, and then there is your ranger. I'm planning on him showing up to try to save you. But don't worry; no one will ever find his body. As far as they know, he's already been gone for days."

Walter Farrow glanced into the shadows by the dugout. Nell followed his gaze and saw them, a dozen or more men, waiting. "We'll be ready for him. If he steps out close enough to be seen, he's a dead man."

Nell could barely breathe. The lawyer had it all planned. He must have been waiting for days to pull this off. The rain had slowed him down.

"We're wasting time." Farrow pointed to one of the men. "Take her to the river."

"Alone?" the tall cowboy said.

"She's crippled, what's she going to do, jump out?" Farrow laughed again. "Just toss her in somewhere that the current is strong. You're not killing her; the river will do that." He nodded to the men in the shadows of the dugout. "You'll have plenty of company, but they'll be riding out of sight, waiting for the ranger to show up."

The tall man hesitated.

"I'll see your share is a hundred more when we find the gold."

The man nodded and climbed in the buggy.

"Make it fast down the hill. I don't want you running into the sheriff just in case that old dog was smart enough to follow."

Nell fought down panic as men saddled up around her and vanished into the fog.

. . .

A hundred yards away, Jacob rushed back to his horse. He hadn't been close enough to hear anything, but he could tell they were getting ready to move.

When he slid down the incline to where he'd left Dusty, he saw a man swing down from a mount. Jacob rolled and pulled his Colt as the shadow whispered, "Ranger, is that you?"

Jacob stood. "Hank?"

The boy nodded and moved out from between the horses. "I was hoping to find you. A few days ago the preacher told me where you were."

"Why didn't you ride up to the dugout?"

"I figured there were too many people up there, so I thought I'd hide out here. Then I spotted your horse." He patted Dusty's neck. "We got to be friends when I was packing you home."

"What's wrong?"

"Two men are holding Gypsy and Wednesday at the house. I heard Wednesday crying and snuck down to see what was up. The preacher was on the floor, maybe dead. I didn't know what was going on, but I figured I'd better come get you."

"You did right, kid." Jacob swung into the saddle. "I may need your help. You coming?"

The boy pulled onto his horse. "All the way," he answered.

Jacob stayed back until he heard the buggy pass at top speed. He had no idea where they were taking Nell this time, but he had a feeling it wouldn't be home. He followed, waiting for his chance.

"Stay in the shadows, Hank," he whispered, "Or you'll be a dead man."

Nell fought to hold on as they bounced over the rough road. She thought of the gun by her bed and the other in the main room of her house. Harrison and Jacob had given them to her for protection, and she'd left them both at home.

She had to do something fast. A sudden bump sent her to the floor of the buggy. Her hand reached out for something to hold onto, and she touched the leather belt Mrs. O'Daniel used to hold her up.

Nell grabbed the leather with one hand and gripped the seat in front of her with the other. Using all her strength, she stood and whirled the belt at the driver's head.

She heard a yelp, and felt the buggy shift as the cowboy tumbled out.

Nell fell backward, unable to stand a moment longer. Suddenly, she was in her nightmare. The horses were wild with fear, the road turned just ahead, and they were running toward it at full speed. She felt the pain in her back as the buggy ran out of control. Nell closed her eyes and cried for Jacob when the horses missed the turn and the buggy rolled.

Nell tumbled out, flying weightless through the air for a moment before slamming hard into the earth.

Jacob saw all of it from the edge of the tree line. The driver tumbling out, Nell falling back into the buggy too far away to reach the reins, then the buggy capsizing and her body hitting the earth.

Jacob jerked his rifle out. "Ride down to the main road and tell the sheriff where we are." He was surprised how normal his words sounded when he knew his heart was in his throat. "I'm going to Nell."

"But you'll be cut down." Hank's voice was high with panic. "She may already be dead."

"Then bury us side by side," Jacob yelled as he kicked his horse and thundered at full speed directly toward Nell.

He made it to within ten feet of her before a bullet stopped Dusty. Jacob rolled as the horse fell then was on his feet running. When he reached Nell's crumpled body, he had no time to see if she still breathed. He stood above her and fired at every shadow that moved.

They were all around him and still on horseback. The fog had cleared some but played tricks with the shadows.

Jacob felt a bullet hit his arm. Another bushed his ear, knocking his hat off, but he didn't stop firing. He'd fight until he fell and know one satisfaction. When he fell, he'd die next to Nell.

He emptied the rifle and reached for his Colts as another shot knifed through his side. In the distance he heard more gunfire. He prayed it was the sheriff and not men who were shooting at Hank.

Jacob stopped firing long enough to listen. The men who'd been shooting at him were gone. He could hear horses disappearing back up the hill while more rode in from the road.

"Dalton!" A rider yelled. "We're here."

Jacob lowered his guns as he recognized Harrison's voice. A moment later he crumpled like a shattered statue. As he passed out, he reached and took Nell's hand in his.

CHAPTER 38

BRIGHT SUNLIGHT BLINDED HIM AS JACOB TRIED TO OPEN HIS eyes. Maybe he was dead and this was heaven? No. He was in too much pain to be dead. He had to still be alive. He could see the tops of the bookshelves in Nell's study. He'd been here before.

Dr. McClellan leaned over him. "About time you woke, Ranger. I'm tired of digging bullets out of you. You got to find another line of work if we're going to stay friends."

"Nell?" Jacob mumbled. "Is Nell alive?" He didn't see how she could be after the fall she'd taken.

"She made it through the surgery fine, yesterday. Theda's with her now."

"Surgery?"

"How about we talk later?"

Jacob grabbed the doctor's arm. "How about we talk now."

McClellan laughed. "Dalton, it's a wonder to me how Nell could like you, much less love you, as bossy as you are."

Jacob didn't turn loose of the doctor.

"All right. The bullet in Nell's back moved when she took the fall. I took a big chance and operated, but I knew if it had moved a fraction of an inch in the other direction she'd be dead. We got it out, but I don't know how much damage I did to her back."

Jacob closed his eyes. She was still alive. That was all that mattered. He fell back into the blackness.

Two days later, he managed to sit up, but there was no change in Nell. A week of worry later, he left by train with Hank for Fort Worth without knowing if the operation worked.

He'd sat with her every day. She looked so peaceful, sleeping. So fragile he decided he'd never risk even touching her again.

Harrison took care of Nell's business as always. The sheriff rounded up the men who'd helped Walter Farrow. The fat lawyer hadn't been hard to find. He'd been at the doctor's in town suffering from a dog bite. He talked all the way to the sheriff's office, but Farrow couldn't manage to talk himself out of jail.

Jacob leaned back on one of the benches as the train rolled along and realized he didn't care about much of anything but Nell. He'd fight for Hank, and he'd see that Farrow was punished, but his thoughts were with her.

"You all right?" Hank asked.

"Stop mothering me," Jacob grumbled. "You're worse then Mrs. O'Daniel."

Hank smiled. "She told me if you got mean you'd be healing."

Jacob looked skyward. Not even the kid was afraid of him anymore.

"Ranger," Hank said.

"What?"

"When we get to Fort Worth, no matter what happens, I want you to know I appreciate what you did for me."

Jacob couldn't believe he was bringing in one of the train robbers without even putting handcuffs on the boy. Hell, Hank was taking care of him on the trip. But he had to be honest with the kid. "You may hang, you know."

"I know. I knew what I was doing was wrong when I did it, but I told myself I couldn't take one more beating from my pa."

Jacob leaned forward. "The judge may give you jail time. I'll stand with you."

"I'll take whatever he says. Wednesday said she'd learn how to write just so she could write to me."

Jacob didn't want to think about the kid growing up in jail. He hoped the letters he'd collected would help.

When they got to Fort Worth, Jacob turned the kid in and took a room in the nearest hotel. He planned to be sitting by the cell as many hours as possible until the trial. He wasn't taking any chances of something happening to the boy before the trial.

He kept Hank company, and at night, he thought about Nell. He wanted her next to him so badly, he ached inside. As the days passed his wounds healed, but he couldn't help thinking that if Nell died, he'd wish every day of his life that they'd died together.

The morning of the trial, Jacob walked in to find Sheriff Parker and Mrs. O'Daniel in the front row. He barely had time to ask about Nell when the judge took the bench.

The trial was short, but the judge took time to listen to everyone. Hank looked like he might cry a few times, but when questioned he stood straight and answered.

Around noon, they all went back to the jail and ate a lunch Marla had sent. Hank couldn't eat or talk. He was too frightened. Mrs. O'Daniel cried a few times. Jacob tried to get her mind off by asking questions about Nell, but Mrs. O'Daniel didn't have much to say.

Jacob felt hopeful when the judge asked to see the three other train robbers. It meant that he'd considered Hank's case separate.

When Hank's pa walked past his cell, he didn't even look at his son.

An hour later, the judge called for Hank.

They all stood behind the boy as the judge read Hank's sentence. Ten years.

Jacob took a deep breath as the judge gave his summary of why he was letting the boy off so easy.

When the judge left the courtroom, Jacob asked the guard if he could take charge of the prisoner for a few minutes. Suddenly, they were alone.

Mrs. O'Daniel cried and hugged Hank.

"You'll make it through this," the sheriff said. "Just keep your nose clean, boy, and the time will pass."

Hank tried to keep from shaking. "I know. I talked with Mr. Harrison before I left. He told me if I got hard time, he had a friend who can get me on a work crew where I'll keep busy."

The boy looked at Jacob. "Miss Nell said I'm always welcome at her place. I know by the time I get out, things will have changed, but I'd like to think that I had somewhere to go."

Mrs. O'Daniel pulled a note from her pocket. "I brought this. Wednesday wanted me to tell you she wrote it herself. Marla helped her trace the letters."

Hank opened the note.

"What's it say?" The sheriff asked the words that were on everyone's mind.

Hank smiled. "It says, 'I'll wait.' "

Then the boy who'd been brave through it all, cried.

CHAPTER 39

Jacob stayed with Hank until they moved him down to the Huntsville prison near Houston. Harrison's former boss sent a letter Jacob carried personally to the warden saying he'd like the boy put on a construction crew working on the capital. Hank would still be locked up at night and under guard during the day, but he'd be learning a trade and for the most part be away from most of the prison population.

When he hugged the boy good-bye, Jacob said, "I'll see you again, the day you walk out. I'll be there."

Hank nodded, fighting back tears as he turned away. "Thanks," he waved, not able to look back.

Jacob left the prison and caught the first train north. It had been almost two months since he'd seen Nell, and word from the doctor had been almost nothing. He'd written and asked about her, but all he ever got back said that she was still recovering.

He wanted to see her, but he wasn't sure how he'd stand it if he got home and found her in terrible shape. Last time she'd lost so much weight she'd been like a skeleton. What would she be now?

When he stepped off the train in Clarendon, he'd expected to see Harrison, or maybe the sheriff. After all, Jacob had sent a telegram. But no one met him.

He walked over to the livery and rented a horse. He thought about buying one, but none came near matching the power of Dusty.

Taking his time riding out to Nell's house, he noticed spring was in full bloom. Nell would be happy to see all the wildflowers. With the rain, they were everywhere. When he saw the house, he almost didn't recognize it. Flowerpots covered the porch.

He thought of yelling, *Hello the house,* but the way his luck was running this morning, no one would be home. He opened the gate and walked the last few feet to where the path started up to the porch.

He'd taken one step up the path when he heard the door open.

Nell walked out, looking like a fine lady. She was a little thinner, but she balanced on her own two feet.

Jacob couldn't move. He just stared as she slowly walked down the path toward him. Her steps were as easy as if she'd been floating. When she reached him, she smiled, "I'll run to you soon, when I'm a little steadier on my feet."

He reached out to hug her.

She closed her arms around his neck and leaned into him. "You can hug me, Jacob, I won't break."

He held her as tight as he dared. Over the months he'd thought of all the things that he'd tell her, of how he'd offer to carry her the rest of her life if the operation hadn't helped. But never, not once, had he dreamed she might come to him.

"I'd like that ride to the windmill. You promised." She poked at his chest. "Maybe we'll be alone there."

Jacob looked up. Her little army, all of them, were watching from the windows.

"I'd like that," he said as he gently lifted her onto the saddle and swung up behind her. "Are you sure you're all right?"

"I'm fine," she whispered as she leaned against him. "I'm growing stronger every day, and there is no more pain."

"None?" Jacob smiled down at her.

"None," she answered. "But that doesn't mean we can't go swimming again sometime."

He nudged the horse into a walk. "You wouldn't lie to me, would you, Two Bits?"

She laughed. "It's going to cost you a lot more than a quarter, Ranger, to ever be rid of me."

"I kind of figured that it might." He rubbed his jaw against her hair. "Don't suppose you found Whitaker's gold?"

"No. Why?"

"Because . . ." He pulled a ring from his vest pocket. "I didn't figure you would, so I thought I'd offer you this so you could say you had some gold."

She stared at the ring and lifted it from his hand.

"If you take that band, Nell, you have to take my name with it."

She smiled and twisted in the saddle. "Oh, I want a lot more than just your name, Jacob."

He swung from the saddle and lifted her down in the center of a blanket of wildflowers growing around the old windmill. When she wrapped her arms around him and kissed him, he lost all fear of holding her . . . of loving her.

EPILOGUE

Jacob Dalton knew he could have reached home faster if he'd taken the train, but he wanted to ride across Texas one last time as a ranger. He needed to feel the wind and watch the sun cross the sky from dawn to dusk. The smell of sagebrush and open range welcomed him as he moved toward Clarendon. The lead rope, tied to his saddle horn, pulled a young colt, the grandson of his favorite horse, Dusty. The colt had Dusty's markings and, Jacob hoped, his grandfather's heart. Jacob looked forward to watching the young horse grow.

Times were changing for Jacob and for the state. When he reached home this time, he'd be turning in his Ranger badge to Sheriff Parker, the man who'd pinned it on his chest almost fifteen years ago.

He'd been alone for three days and, much as he loved riding, he missed Nell more. They'd been married for almost six months, and the only thing that made it possible for him to leave her to do his job was the knowledge that she'd be waiting for him when he came home.

Closing his eyes, Jacob could almost see her running down the steps and jumping into his arms. Each month she'd grown stronger and more beautiful to him. They'd developed a ritual with his homecomings. He'd wait for her at the end of the walk, loving seeing her move so easily on her long legs. Then they'd ride to the windmill and hold one another without anyone watching.

They'd married a week after he'd returned home last spring from helping Hank. It had been a simple ceremony in the big room of Nell's house, with wildflowers everywhere. Rand Harrison had stood as his best man, Gypsy and Marla had been Nell's bridesmaids. Dalton swore everyone in town tried to cram into the house. Once folks decided to accept Nell, they couldn't wait to see the inside of her place.

Jacob smiled as he rode, remembering how he'd had to threaten Brother Aaron to make sure the preacher kept the service short so Nell wouldn't get too tired. Because she was still recovering, everyone in the house except the bride and groom had disappeared after supper, leaving Jacob and Nell alone for their wedding night.

The ranger had been brave all his life, but that first night, he'd been afraid to touch his wife. Nell sensed the problem and talked him into taking her for a swim. They'd made love in the water, that night and almost every night for a month. He'd kidded her that their children would all be born as tadpoles.

Jacob saw the town before him and realized he was finally home for good. He kicked his mount lightly and headed straight for the sheriff's office. He wanted to get business over with before he saw Nell, for he didn't plan to leave her side until he'd grown used to the feel of her next to him once more.

Parker met him on the steps. "I was wondering when you'd make it in, Dalton." The old sheriff smiled. "About time. Nell said you'd be in today or tomorrow. She and Marla have been cooking all week."

Jacob swung down and tied his horse. He patted the colt, pushing him out of the way so he could step up beside Parker. "You think it's time?"

"I've been ready for years, just waiting for you to make up your mind." Parker turned into his office. "I sent the deputy for the judge. I'd like to get the official part over with tonight. There will be time for celebrating tomorrow."

Jacob understood. The old man hated a fuss. By the time Parker poured him a cup of coffee, the judge arrived with a warm greeting. He stood before the two lawmen. "You want to hand me that ranger badge, son?" the old judge said.

Dalton pulled the circle star from his vest. "I do." He pressed the metal against the palm of his hand one last time before passing it to the judge. It had been a symbol not just of what he did but of what he was.

The judge took the badge and glanced at Parker. "You ready?"

Parker winked. "That I am." The sheriff pulled his star from his shirt and handed it to Jacob. "It's all yours now, Sheriff Dalton. Take care of my town."

"My town." Jacob smiled as he laid his hand on the judge's Bible and took the oath.

They all shook hands, and within minutes Jacob was riding toward the house out by the railroad tracks.

The sun was low in the sky when he neared what once had been Fat Alice's brothel. Jacob slowed, marveling at how grand the old place seemed. Another month, and the flowers would be gone and the leaves from all the trees Nell had babied over the summer would disappear, but this would always be his home.

He could see Harrison's buggy tied up out front. The bookkeeper had done wonders with the ranches in the past six months. He and Marla were taking their time courting, but everyone knew they'd be married before Christmas. Nell had offered him a house on one of the ranches, but Harrison had turned it down and bought his own place in town. Jacob had teased him more than once about why the bookkeeper needed his own place. He was usually drinking coffee in Marla's kitchen by dawn and never left until after supper.

Jacob reached the gate. He could just make out the preacher sleeping in his favorite chair on the porch. Nell had given Brother Aaron the Stockard place, but the old man still rode over for dinner every night.

Just as Jacob clanked the gate closed, he heard the front door open and Nell ran toward him. If he lived to be a hundred, his heart would always pick up a beat at the sight of her. His Nell. His Two Bits. He'd always loved her. He'd love her with his last breath.

"You're home," she cried as if it had been weeks and not just days since she'd seen him. "It's about time."

And then she was in his arms, and he could breathe again. It didn't matter if fall and winter came, he had his wildflower in his arms.

After he kissed her soundly, he whispered, "Want to ride with me up to the windmill?"

"No," she whispered. "I'd like to go for a swim."

"Now?"

"Now." She laughed. "I need to talk to you about tadpoles."

THE DALTON LINE

Jacob and Nell Dalton were married for fifty-three years. They had three girls Nell named after her three friends who accepted her when she'd been a wild child. The oldest was Lacy, the second, Bailee, and the baby, Sarah. They also had one son who grew up to be a Texas Supreme Court judge. They named him Jacob Randolph.

Brother Aaron retired from preaching and, though he never farmed or ranched on the Stockard land, made a living charging people to hunt for Zeb Whitaker's lost gold. Every few years another clue would turn up along with men willing to pay to search. As of this date, the two saddlebags of gold have never been found.

Hank and Wednesday were married three weeks after Hank was released from prison. He became one of the finest builders in Texas, and several small town courthouses still remain as tribute to his fine work.

Randolph Harrison used his skill to enlarge Nell's property until she owned the seventh largest ranch in the state, and he became the best-paid bookkeeper between Dallas and Denver. Marla and Rand's only child, a daughter named Hope, married Nell and Jacob's only son. Hope Dalton is credited for founding one of the nation's largest teachers' colleges while raising six sons.

Jacob Dalton didn't stay home as he'd planned. Five years after taking over as sheriff, he ran for the Texas State Senate and became a powerful force in moving his beloved state into the twentieth century. The townsfolk often turned out to watch him return home from Austin. Some said they wanted to see a great man, but most admitted they just wanted to see a man in love swing his wife into his arms.